MERCURIAL

Naomi Hughes

FOR BRITTON,
without whom both I and this story
would be incalculably lesser.

The Unforged God looked out upon the emptiness of the universe and was displeased. Desiring a new creation, he tore himself into pieces: copper, silver, gold, iron, platinum, and all the other metals. With these pieces, the world was created. Into some of the men and women who rose up were planted the seeds of divinity: metal flowing through their blood, lending them one of the divine magics and a special connection to the Unforged God. These people, God named Smiths.

—HALLOWED REVELATIONS OF SAINT YVETTA, THIRD REFRAIN

PROLOGUE

ONCE, THERE WAS A BOY WHO BELIEVED.

He'd been having visions for a year. They showed him doing exactly what he was doing right now: walking up the docks toward the most dangerous girl in the Alloyed Empire, preparing to offer her his oath of service.

In the visions, his hands hadn't been trembling. In the visions, he hadn't seen the look on the girl's face: gracefully curious brows, starlight-silver eyes, a predatory curve of lips. It was the face of a murderer. But he believed in his visions, believed what his god had promised through them, so he kept walking.

The gleaming Alloyed Palace rose before him in the moonlight. Made of plated scales, it looked like the skin of some monstrous, colorful snake perched above the tumbling river. The boy could feel the shimmer of the palace's magic from here. He could pick out the scales that hummed in sync with the forbidden silver that ran through his own blood. Though he couldn't sense any of the other metals, his keen eye picked out plates of copper, iron, nickel, tin, gold. All of them were enchanted, their natural magics Smithed by the metallurgists of the high courts to protect against invaders.

The boy stopped at the intersection of the docks and the palace's great porch and looked again at the girl above him. At this distance, in this angle of moonlight, her smile no longer looked quite so predatory. It seemed tired instead, even strained, but those bright silver eyes were still locked on him like he was either her prey or her salvation. She was young, too. Maybe sixteen—his own age. He hadn't expected that. In the whispered warnings, she was ageless.

He gripped his hands behind his back, standing at a loose attention the way he'd been taught. The dual short swords that were sheathed at the curve of his spine pressed against his forearms. Before he could lose his mettle, he spoke the words he'd heard a hundred times in his dreams. "I've come to swear my oath of protection to the Destroyer."

His voice shook. That hadn't happened in the visions either. He worried over what else his god might not have shown him about this moment.

The Destroyer looked down at him. She had been walking when he'd first started up from the royal docks. She had paused to watch him approach. Two imperial guards were at her back now, watching him just as closely.

"You're frightened," she observed, her voice low and lovely.

Terror gripped him, a noose around his throat. Why had the Unforged God asked this of him? *Are you certain?* he prayed silently. *I will do anything for you, but are you certain?*

His god didn't answer. The boy summoned his faith, reminded himself of what the visions had promised. He would save the Destroyer. He would save the Alloyed Empire through her. He wasn't sure how this moment could possibly lead to that one, but he believed anyway.

"Of course I am," he answered her. This time, his voice didn't shake.

They were silent for a long moment. The banners of the palace rippled around them: cobalt blue and rust red. The breeze lifted above the churning river and blew its fine mist over them, over the whole of the royal docks and the palace's great porch where they stood, until everything was sparkling with it. Dewdrops hung suspended in the girl's dark, curly hair and glistened on her black crown. She made no sound, giving him long moments to reconsider.

He didn't.

"I have the whole imperial guard to protect me," she noted. Her voice was even, but he thought there might've been a note of curiosity in it.

He inhaled. He could taste the river on his tongue. The Entengre flowed underground through a copper mine in the mountains, and carried the acrid taste of old coins downstream. "They aren't sworn to you, my lady. And technically they serve your sister the empress," he forced himself to say the next phrase, "long may she live. You have no one who serves you alone."

The girl didn't move. She was so still that her mercurial eyes seemed to flicker like flames in the shadows. "And you want to swear to me directly?"

"I want to swear to you on metal," he clarified.

That graceful brow rose higher. Behind her, the two imperial guards shifted and murmured. Swearing on metal was a rarity; that sort of oath could only be given willingly, and it could only be undone by either death or the fulfillment of its terms. Anyone who gave a metal oath could be trusted to deliver on whatever it was they had promised, because there was no other option.

"And what do you want in return?" the Destroyer asked.

The impossible, he thought, but he answered, "Nothing."

She barked a short laugh, a sound so sudden and violent that it made him flinch. "Everyone wants something," she said, her tone bitter like the old-coin taste of the river. "You want fame? Infamy, rather? Do you want your family excused from paying taxes?"

"I have no family," he said. It was only partly true. His parents had been killed in the Silver Coup, but he had a sister. One who was probably cursing his name right now as she read the note he'd left behind for her. His heart twisted at the thought.

"Then why do you want to swear to me?" the Destroyer demanded. Suspicion flickered in her voice like live embers. White-hot sparks began to dance around her fingers, snapping into existence so brightly they burned afterimages into his vision. She could flay him to ash with a gesture if he answered wrong.

Carefully, he phrased his reply. This conversation was outside the bounds of what his visions had shown him. He was in uncharted territory now. But he knew one thing, and that was that no one dared lie to the Destroyer, Lady of Mercury, leveler of cities, and the most volatile weapon the empress possessed. So he answered with complete honesty: "I believe the Unforged God wants me to protect you."

He'd been bewildered when the visions had first started. He couldn't understand why his god would ask him to defend one of the people who'd been oppressing the empire for generations—one of the people who would execute him instantly if she learned that the element of silver, which gave him a gift of truth-seeing and foresight and thus was forbidden, flowed through his blood. But he trusted that somehow, eventually, it would make sense.

The Destroyer blinked in surprise, then again in amusement. The sparks dancing around her fingers fizzled away. "Ah. You're religious."

The old religion had mostly died out in the last few centuries. Few kept it now beyond the zealot rebels, the men and women with no rank or chain of command who lived in the honeycomb of the old mountain mines. Their rebellion had brought together people from all over the continent: nomads from the desert ward, colonists from the southern valleys, northerners from the great glaciers at the rim of the world. The most committed of the zealots had lately taken to snorting metal powders in the hope that it might bring them closer to the Unforged God. The only thing it had brought them closer to was death, though, as only those born with a Smithing affinity—like the boy, like the girl before him—could withstand the toxic effects of metal in their bloodstream.

"I'm not a Saint," the boy replied. "But yes."

"And you have training in protection?"

"I've trained with soldiers since I was twelve. I'm one of the best fighters in the mountain ward." He'd had to be. He couldn't risk letting his opponents see his blood.

The girl regarded him for a moment longer. "Very well," she said suddenly, and took off her crown. It was a dainty thing, slender and feminine but made of sharp, twisted edges. It suited her. "Swear on this, then," she said, holding it out to him.

He looked down at the crown. He struggled for breath. The crown was made of wrought iron. Not the Destroyer's metal, but that of her elder sister, the empress. The boy couldn't feel the magic that stirred within it. He didn't need to. Once he gave this metal his oath, the magic that lived within it—that lived within all metals—would take his promise into itself and compel him to keep it.

Feeling as if he were floating somewhere far away, he reached out a hand and gripped the crown. Its twisted edges dug into his palm. "I swear," he said, forcing the words out, "to protect you, and to not allow harm to come to you—"

"And to never harm me yourself," she cut in sharply.

He swallowed. "And to never harm you myself," he added, his voice sounding choked. He tried to think of what else he should add. A term of some sort? Conditions? His thoughts were a muddle, tangled like a snarl of yarn. Then the girl stepped back and it was too late. The oath had been sworn.

They looked down at the crown in her hands. The boy panicked for a second, thinking that he might've gripped it too tightly and drawn his own blood, but no telltale silver dripped down the twisted black edges.

The Destroyer put the crown back on her head. Then she waved at one of the guards behind her and told the man, "Attack me."

The imperial guards were trained to instantly obey an order from any lord or lady, and from the empress's family most of all, but this one could only stare back at the Destroyer for a long moment as if struck mute. "My lady?" he said at last.

White flames flickered around her head and shoulders like a halo as her gaze snapped to the man. "Do as I've ordered," she said, anger banked low in her voice.

The boy was backpedaling, confused and afraid, when the guard drew his iron sword—Smithed metal, its edge impossibly sharp—and slashed it out toward the Destroyer.

That was the first time the boy felt the pain of disobeying his oath.

It hit him like a derailed train. Unready for it, he gasped and bent double beneath its weight. Every vein, every muscle, singed as if on fire. He was a red-hot iron in a Smith's forge and the pain was the anvil and the hammer both: pummeling him, shaping him into what he had promised to be.

In a spasm, his hands gripped his dual short swords. He drew them. In a quick one-two move taught to him by the soldiers, he raised his left sword to block the guard's weapon inches before it would have speared through the Destroyer's shoulder, and drove his right sword into the guard's chest.

The boy's pain vanished as if it had never existed. He and the guard stood stock-still, staring at each other from opposite ends of the blade. The guard cupped his hands around his wound. Red spilled between his fingers, across his knuckles. The boy pulled the sword out and it glistened with blood and river mist. When the guard staggered backwards and crumbled to the polished wooden boards of the great porch, the boy began to realize, with dawning horror, what had just happened.

The Destroyer had been threatened. And his oath had compelled him to defend her.

The Destroyer stepped forward. Something was bright in her eyes, and the boy couldn't tell if it was madness or hope. "What's your name?" she asked, ignoring the wet, rattling breathing of the dying guard.

The boy's swords hung now at his sides, dead weight. He wanted to drop them. He couldn't. "Tal," he managed after a moment. "Tal Melaine."

The Destroyer nodded, accepting his name as if she were taking possession of it. Then she turned, glancing at the downed guard and the other one, who was still standing frozen at his post. "Take him to the physicians," she ordered the unhurt guard. "He may survive. Far be it from me to waste my sister's resources when they may yet be of use."

The standing guard's gaze was emotionless. "I cannot leave you unguarded, my lady," he replied.

She smiled. Predatory. Tired. Hopeful. "I am not unguarded," she said.

And finally, with the moon bright above, with the Alloyed Palace gleaming like a monster, and with his god utterly silent, the boy began to understand exactly what his belief would require of him.

CHAPTER ONE

2 years later

The Destroyer was having a nightmare.

Her suite—which took up an entire train car—was lit only by a thin slice of ashy moonlight that had managed to slip around the heavy velvet curtains. It was just enough to illuminate the sudden tension in the Destroyer's frame, the way her mouth curved silently around a cry, the way her fingers curled in the sheets. She sucked in a hoarse rasp of a breath and held it.

Tal, standing impassively beside the bed, looked down at her. He'd been sleeping in his cot by the door a moment ago, having his own, quieter nightmares. He'd have liked to let the Destroyer stay in hers, but he couldn't risk her wrath if he let her suffer through the dream without waking her. Carefully, he lay a light hand on her shoulder.

She came instantly awake. He stood still, knowing from past experience that she was likely to lash out in the seconds before she came to full alertness. After a moment, those gray eyes sharpened and focused on him. "Tal," she said, her voice rough.

He didn't respond. She was identifying him, not speaking to him.

She swept the covers aside with a single graceful movement and climbed out of her bed. She was wearing an elegant nightdress. She opened the small closet, withdrew an even more elegant robe embroidered in blue and rusty reds, and shrugged it on. Then she slid the door of her bedroom compartment open and stepped into the train's cramped main corridor.

Tal lifted his sword belt from the end of his cot and followed. When the Destroyer stopped in front of the doors that led to the raised platform outside, a servant appeared, bowing obsequiously over a cup of steaming tea. "My lady," he said, "your sister the empress, long may she live, sends her deepest regrets, but asks you to stay inside. The imperial guard has reported that the risk of assassins is high today. After...the events of yesterday."

The Destroyer snorted indelicately as she pushed the door open. Chilly night air and the claustrophobic tang of smoke crept in, along with the watered-down light of pre-dawn. "When is the risk of assassins ever low?"

"If my lady will please just stay inside and perhaps enjoy a cup of soothing tea—" the servant begged, but she gave him a sharp look and he fell silent, bowing his way backwards, nearly tripping over his feet as he went. The cup spilled scalding tea over his fingers and made dark spots on the luxurious cream-colored rug. The servant froze, going rigid with fear.

The Destroyer ignored him and exited the train. She paced to the corner of the cobblestone platform outside, brushing away the ash that had settled on the railing so she could rest her hands there. Tal followed, a silent shadow, pulling the door closed behind him. The latch was gilded with gold and veined in spiderwebs of frost that made the metal stick to his fingers where he touched it. He pulled his hand free and paced after his charge.

Halfway between the exit and the Destroyer, he stopped to scan the landscape for potential enemies. He doubted he would find any. His oath would have compelled him by now if she was in immediate danger. But still, he could avoid a great deal of pain if he was proactive about stopping any assassination attempts before they got that close.

There was nowhere he could see where an enemy might be able to hide. Most of the buildings in this small, once-prosperous mining town were now no more than ash and rubble. A few walls still stood, and here and there a blackened chimney jutted out from the remnants of a house, but almost everything else had been leveled.

The building before them was still burning, though. Its orange light flickered over the Destroyer, casting her expression anew with every passing second, making her seem by turns malevolent or tired or grave. When she turned to glance over her shoulder, her face fell into shadow and her expression was hidden. "You should be sleeping," she called to someone behind her.

Tal twisted around to look. The train was a hulking bronze monstrosity behind him, the magic in its metal humming quietly as it waited to be activated for its return journey. A woman was descending its steps onto the platform. Her dress shimmered in the moonlight. Its flourishes were sewn with shimmering metallic thread, which made it beautiful, and also allowed it to be Smithed to protect its wearer as well as any suit of armor. Atop her head rested the Iron Crown.

The woman, who was the empress Sarai, shook her head at her younger sister. "As if I could rest, knowing you were out here risking your life just to get a breath of fresh air."

The Destroyer shrugged one shoulder, then lifted a hand, summoning a foot-tall flame with no visible effort. The light of it glinted off Sarai's silvery crown and was swallowed up by the Destroyer's black one. "It's not as if I can't protect myself."

Sarai clucked her tongue chidingly and raised her palm toward the flame, using her own magic—the ability to manipulate air—to create a vacuum that smothered it. The Destroyer dropped her hand and let the last few sparks die. The darkness washed over her expression again.

"If you truly think you can protect yourself so well," Sarai said, strolling over to join her sister at the railing, "then will you finally get rid of that one?"

That one. She meant Tal. He didn't look, instead continuing to scan the remnants of the city for potential enemies. He couldn't quite tamp down the hope that stirred within him, though.

"No. He's mine," the Destroyer said, a note of finality in her voice. Tal's hope died. He clenched his jaw, being sure to keep his face turned away from the pair.

He shouldn't have hoped. He should have known better by now. Even if the Destroyer was willing to dismiss him, his oath couldn't be so easily lifted. Some of the more malleable metals, in the hands of a skilled Smith, could be convinced to give up the promises they held within themselves. Gold or even copper could sometimes be reasoned with. But never iron. It would force him to stay close to the Destroyer and protect her for the rest of his life.

In any case, he was sure that the empress hadn't been suggesting he be freed from his oath anyway. When she suggested "getting rid" of him, she'd been alluding to a more permanent solution. He and the Destroyer didn't spend much time in the empress's company, but she never had liked Tal. And bad things usually happened to anyone Sarai didn't like.

A shadow moved in the darkness between train cars. Tal's hands went to the hilts of his dual blades. He strained his eyes but couldn't make out any further movement. Likely it was just a feral cat. Or, less likely but still possible, a villager who had survived the city's punishment. He hoped it wasn't the latter. Survivors were to be hauled back to the Alloyed Palace to face a mockery of a trial for whatever offenses their city had committed–in this case, supporting the rebel Saints–which would almost certainly end in a far worse death than being instantly incinerated, as most of the townspeople here had been yesterday.

"As you wish," the empress said, good-natured puzzlement in her tone as she conceded to Tal's survival. She leaned against the railing and reached out to brush a stray curl away from her sister's cheek. "You had another nightmare?" she asked.

The Destroyer turned her face away, gazing over the rubble of the city. The dawn was breaking in full now, the murky light sharpening, defining the shadows in unforgiving lines and angles. "I'm fine," she told her sister.

Sarai pursed her lips in concern. "I'll send for the Lord of Copper. He can do your next treatment on our way home today."

The Destroyer's answering smile was thin. "Another injection? There's no need for me to worry about assassins after all, when you're the one constantly poking holes in me."

The darkness between the train cars shifted again. This time, in the growing bluish light, Tal was able to make out a human form–and the flash of a bronze mask.

Heart suddenly pounding, he drew his weapons. A bronze mask meant a Saint, one of the zealots trying to overthrow the ruling class. Their assassins had been growing bolder than ever lately. Last month, one of them had succeeded in killing a lesser lady of the Platinum family. Maybe, just maybe, this one might be better than Tal. Maybe this one might be able to kill the Destroyer.

He tried to tamp down the hope. As ever, he didn't succeed.

The Saint was closer to the Destroyer than he was. By the time Tal started running, the assassin—a girl, or perhaps a young woman by the way she moved, with brown skin and dozens of long black braids—was already a step ahead of him. A gleam of metal was in her hand, flashing orange with the light of sunrise. She was completely silent and as quick as a mooncat.

He tried to slow his steps. Just a touch, barely enough to matter. It didn't work. His oath demanded his best effort, shoved him forward as surely as a battering ram between his shoulder blades. He reached the Destroyer first, just as she turned to see what the commotion was.

The Saint pulled her dagger back for the final lunge. She lifted off on her left foot and stabbed forward. The Destroyer inhaled sharply, the empress behind her just now looking to see what was the matter, as Tal flung himself between his charge and the assassin. He sliced one of his blades upward and the other one out.

His left sword clanged against the lifted dagger. The small weapon spun away from the girl's grip, flying uselessly into the ash of the city below. His right sword cut through the Saint's shoulder, meeting bone. She gave a muffled cry of pain—which made Tal pause for half a second, trying to understand why the girl's voice had sounded faintly familiar. But the girl didn't slow, instead pivoting her momentum into a sideways tumble that took her between the bars of the railing. She landed nimbly on the street below. A charred piece of wood, which might have been a door, crunched beneath her.

The Destroyer's expression darkened in anger. She lifted a hand toward the Saint, who had found a nearby well and was now hauling herself over its edge, likely in an attempt to escape through the underground aqueduct that fed it.

She wouldn't escape. The Destroyer would stop her. And then she would kill her, slowly and painfully, her normal businesslike ruthlessness made outright cruel by the attempt on her life. Tal would hear the assassin's oddly familiar voice—perhaps she was someone from his home village in the mountain ward—scream again and again.

Rational thought left him, replaced momentarily by an instinct he couldn't deny any more than he could deny his metal-sworn oath. He dropped his swords. He leapt forward. He grabbed the Destroyer's uplifted hand in both of his. The flame was just starting to erupt from her palm, and instead of lashing out at the Saint across the street, it cracked into his own palm like a barbed whip. Agony arced through him. He gasped beneath the twisting weight of it and then locked his jaw, trying desperately not to scream.

The Destroyer's head snapped toward him, her eyes wide with shock. He hadn't tried to step between her and her victims since those first few excruciating weeks. Her startlement took her focus away from maintaining the fire in her hand and the flame snuffed out. The two of them stood there for a second longer, staring at each other over their interlocked hands, until the empress stepped around her sister and slapped Tal hard across the face.

His head snapped sideways with the force of the blow, making him lose his grip on the Destroyer. He staggered to one knee. The empress, like most Smiths, was much stronger than she looked.

"You should've made him swear to respect you as well as protect you," Sarai said, disapproval sharp in her tone. "How dare he touch you without your permission?"

Tal stayed on the ground for a moment. He looked at the back of his left hand, the one that he'd used to snuff out the flame. No silvery blood dripped from it. The injury must've been instantly cauterized. He could hardly fathom what he'd done, what a massive risk he'd taken, unless he thought that perhaps deep down he'd *wanted* to finally be discovered as a silver Smith and executed. That, at least, would be one way out of his oath.

He turned his hand over, but he couldn't bear to look at his palm and averted his eyes at the last moment. When he looked away, though, his gaze landed on the Destroyer instead.

She was staring at him. Her hand was still raised as it had been a moment ago, her long, delicate fingers curved slightly, like a pianist who'd been about to play a familiar melody. It was several long heartbeats before she lowered her arm. He couldn't tell what emotion was flickering in her eyes. Usually he was good at reading her—he had to be—but now her expression was like a candle guttering in the wind, shifting too quickly between rage, shock, and something strange and wild that he couldn't quite name.

Grasping the railing with his good hand, he climbed

slowly to his feet. He cradled his burned hand against his body. He could feel his oath winding through him, tugging him toward the well, toward the threat against the Destroyer. He'd kept the Saint from being tortured to death, but now he would have to hunt her down and kill her himself.

He swallowed and finally managed to pull his gaze away from the Destroyer's. As if that connection had been the one thing keeping his pain at bay, the agony rushed in all at once, and he bowed over his hand with a long, hissing exhale.

He would not scream. Not in front of these two.

"You will go kill the assassin yourself," the Destroyer said at last, her voice as unreadable as her expression. Her words were half a question, half a flat order.

Unable to speak without crying out, he nodded.

A rustle of fabric. A shimmer of something coppery and gleaming, stopped up in a small bottle. Tal lifted his head to see the Destroyer holding out both her hands toward him. One held the bottle, and the other was empty, waiting.

Sarai clucked her tongue. "You're going to use your personal healing tincture on *him*? You're going soft."

The Destroyer quirked one eyebrow. "No one has ever accused me of softness."

Sarai shrugged her shoulders, as if to say, *true enough.*

The Destroyer inclined her head at Tal, still waiting. He eyed the vial in her hand. It was a general-use healing tincture, which every Smith carried so they could heal their injuries quickly enough to avoid the risk of the rust phage, an infection that could kill those with metal in their blood. He didn't know why she would offer it to him. He'd been injured in her service before, and had never merited such treatment in the past.

But there didn't seem to be a good enough reason to turn the medicine away, so he forced himself to hold his injured hand out. It shook when he laid it in hers. She pulled his fingers open—he couldn't stop a short cry of pain then—and poured half of the little bottle over the injury on his palm. The pain instantly abated, his charred flesh flaking away, new pink skin growing rapidly beneath it.

The Destroyer re-stoppered the bottle. "I can get more from Albinus," she said to her sister, using the name of the Lord of Copper, who was also their cousin. "Meanwhile, Tal can't hunt down an assassin with only one hand."

"You'll come inside, then?" Sarai asked. "To your treatment?"

The Destroyer tucked the bottle away in the pocket of her dress. "After a proper breakfast, yes." Without looking at Tal again, she turned and gracefully climbed the stairs back into the train. Within the bronze monstrosity, which was Smithed for protection as well as movement along the magicked rails, she would be safe from any further attempts on her life.

Tal looked down at his hand. The tincture she'd used on him had flakes of Smithed copper—the metal of healing—in it. When he brushed away the bits of metal and charred skin, his palm looked good as new.

He can't hunt down an assassin with only one hand.

Briefly, he allowed his eyes to slide shut in despair. He tilted his head to the sky. He didn't pray, because he hadn't prayed in over a year and refused to start up the useless practice again now, but he did allow himself a few heartbeats of peace. Of stillness, before he had to go kill another of the Destroyer's enemies.

He could barely remember what it had been like for him before the oath. He couldn't quite grasp the depths of his own naivety in swearing it. It felt as if an entirely separate person had presented himself on the palace's great porch that day. The boy he'd been had trusted—impossibly, unfathomably—in a god who had promised to use him as an instrument of salvation for the whole empire. Instead, Tal had become an instrument of death to his own people, and to his own soul. He would never forgive his god. He would never forgive himself.

Tiny flakes of ash dusted onto his eyelashes like snow. The warmth of the still-burning train station brushed across one side of his face, while the cool of dawn feathered over the other. He inhaled. Exhaled.

And then he picked up his swords, leapt over the railing, and followed the Saint.

CHAPTER TWO

TAL MOVED THROUGH THE BRICKED-OVER AQUEDUCTS WITH a grim sense of purpose. He focused on where he put his feet—avoiding the puddles of stinking water, avoiding the loose rubble that might shift beneath his boots—so that his journey through this silent underworld wouldn't be tracked by his prey. He'd been on the assassin's trail for nearly half an hour now, a quiet chase that had led him through a maze of tunnels and sewers and half a dozen seeming dead ends. The Saint was good. But she wasn't quite as good as Tal.

The spots of blood Tal had been following led through a shallow spot where brackish water pooled atop the bricks. Tal stepped around it, then knelt to examine a smudged print at its far edge. It was wet, less than a few minutes old, but it was smaller than the prints of the assassin. Which meant someone else was down here. Slowly, he turned his head.

Speckles of sunlight speared through the dark from the places in the tunnel's ceiling where bricks were missing. The light was hazy and gray, filtered through the still-settling rubble of the city above, but it was enough to illuminate the shapes of the several dozen townspeople who were huddled in a side tunnel. Their clothing was smeared with soot, their faces gaunt with fear. They stood motionless like rabbits before a wolf.

The group stared at Tal. He stared back. A part of him, bone-deep and hidden, wanted to shrink away from the looks in their eyes. The only concession he could make to that part of himself was to glance back down at the puddle, bowing his head for the space of an exhale. It was meant to be a respite. Instead, he was faced with his own reflection.

A tumble of dark hair. Impassive green eyes. Lean muscles, dark clothes. A thin slant of lips—an expression that reminded him too much of the lady he defended. He looked away.

Then he stood and faced the group. He put a finger over his lips, signaling them to silence. Disbelieving hope flickered in their eyes. Not a single one of them moved or even breathed as he stepped further into the main tunnel, and further from them.

The Destroyer had ordered that any survivors be arrested. But he'd only sworn to protect her, two years and a lifetime ago—not to obey her.

A shadow rustled ahead of him. A gleam of steel flickered in one of the beams of ashy light, the only warning of an expertly-thrown dagger that was now spinning toward Tal's chest. In an instant, Tal's dual blades were in his hands, and he angled one outward even as he dove to the side. *Clang.* Metal struck on metal. The hilt of Tal's left sword jerked painfully against his hand with the impact, but the dagger clattered harmlessly to the ground rather than spearing through his ribs. Picking it up and tucking it into his belt—because he knew better than to offer an opponent the chance to re-arm herself—Tal moved cautiously toward the shadow on the far side of the aqueduct.

"Damn," said a weak female voice, again faintly familiar though he still couldn't quite place it. "That was...my second favorite blade."

Tal didn't slow. He stepped over a smear of blood. It shone dully against the bricks and all over the assassin's arm, which the girl was now cradling against her chest. The red-brown shade matched the blood that had begun to dry on the edge of one of Tal's swords.

The girl shoved herself backwards, muffling a curse when the movement jostled her injury. He couldn't see much more of her than her clothes, her skin—a few shades browner than Tal's own—and her tightly-curled, dark hair. Her face was hidden beneath her mask of rough, unworked bronze. He didn't ask who she was. It would only make this worse.

The assassin was panting now, trying to shove herself to her feet. "They said you were unstoppable," she admitted. "I have to say, I didn't believe it till now."

"I'll make it quick," was all Tal said in response. It was the only thing he could offer her. His tone sounded empty, betraying not even a shred of the bitterness that ate away at him. Every time he had to hunt down another of the Destroyer's enemies, every time he had to kill someone he would rather help, it ripped out another little piece of his soul. Someday, he reasoned, he would run out of pieces, and then it wouldn't hurt anymore.

He raised a sword. He spared a brief, regretful thought for the townspeople hidden in the tunnel at his back, hating to have so many witnesses see him this way. Then he swept the sword toward the girl's neck in a quick, fatal arc.

The girl ripped off her mask and thrust it forward like a shield. As she did, she shouted something. The clash of the sword hitting the mask obscured most of the word. Sparks erupted where the unforged metal met the steel of Tal's blade, blinding him for a moment, and he jerked back to a defensive pose as he blinked the spots away. The girl wasn't attacking, though. The force of the blow had knocked the mask out of her hands, and it now lay face-up in the puddle, brackish water seeping through one eyehole.

It was then that Tal's mind began to register what it was the girl had said when she'd lifted her mask. *Tal.* His name.

He peered into the shadows before him, a strange tincture of dread and hope trickling through his veins. It had been a long time since anyone but the Destroyer had called him by name. Many nights, he'd lie awake fantasizing about what it would feel like to see a friendly face, to hear his name on the lips of someone he didn't hate with every fiber of his being. But if the girl before him knew Tal in more than just the vaguely familiar way he'd expected, it would only make this infinitely harder and more painful than it would have been otherwise. Because the assassin had attacked the Destroyer, and Tal could even now feel his oath ghosting through the hollow spots between bone and muscle, ready to take hold and compel him to end the girl's life if he refused to do it of his own volition.

Still, a terrible, morbid curiosity nudged him forward. He edged closer to the shadows. "Who are you?" he said, regretting the words even as he spoke them.

A strangled laugh. Her voice was sounding less flippant and more pained with every passing moment. "I know it's been two years, little brother, but I thought you'd recognize my blade if not my face."

Tal froze. The dread rose up, drowned his hope in horror, and swallowed him wholly after. He fumbled at his belt. His movements were clumsy, and the dagger he'd tucked there fell onto the ground with an ungraceful clank. The handle was etched silver. Scratches marred the blade. He'd put most of them there himself, when she'd been training him.

"No," he breathed, trying with all his strength to stop the next word from slipping out, trying to stop it from being true, but he was helpless against it: "Nyx."

His older sister. The one he'd left behind that day two years ago, when he'd gone to fulfill his visions against her will. His gaze shot back to her. She'd grown into herself while he was gone. Her lanky limbs were now lean with muscle, her face sharp with angles and intelligence. A multitude of small scars crisscrossed over her arms. Training injuries. She could afford them as he could not, because she had no affinity, no unsanctioned metal in her blood to connect her to the Unforged God and provide her with a special magic. Not that she'd ever wanted to be a Smith anyway. She'd raged against his visions, raged against the god who would have him fulfill them.

And yet here she was in a Saint's mask.

It was an unimportant mystery compared to the urgency of the moment. Tal could feel the oath sinking its tendrils into him now, like a vine strangling a tree. He had seconds to figure out how to save his sister. His mind jolted from possibility to plan to wild idea and back again. In the last two years, he'd tried everything to get out of his oath. Throwing his weapons down only meant he had to kill with his bare hands. Holding the oath back through sheer force of will sapped his strength quickly and only bought seconds. He'd even tried destroying the crown that held his oath—an act that he knew would kill him along with it—once last year, when his bitterness had finally grown beyond the reach of his faith. It hadn't worked. The magic of his promise had taken over and moved him like a puppet to safety.

But he hadn't been truly desperate then, not like he was now, with his sister—the only family he had left—standing before him. "Nyx," he ground out, "run."

But she shook her head and pushed away from the wall, moving toward him. He flung himself backwards. His hands were clenched so tightly that his swords shook and his knuckles ached. *"Run,"* he ordered again as the tendrils of his oath sank deeper. He had seconds. *She* had seconds.

His god was cruel, or perhaps just uncaring. Tal had realized that long ago. This, though, this was beyond cruelty, and far beyond indifference. The boy he used to be urged him to pray, to repent of whatever he'd done wrong to earn this horrific fate, but he shoved the urge away with as much violence as he could muster.

"I want to be taken to the Destroyer," Nyx said, stopping in front of him. She wavered on her feet. He'd cut her shoulder deeply, and she'd lost a lot of blood.

He registered her words. His eyes widened. "No. Nyx, no, that's *worse.*" Whatever the Destroyer might do to a failed assassin would be far, far more painful than the quick death she'd sent Tal to deal out.

"It's my right," Nyx insisted. Her words were still labored, her familiar voice made alien by pain. "I have…a right to a trial."

It was true. The oath eased away, gave Tal full control of his limbs again, but he could only stare at his sister. His mind was still working frantically but he could think of no solution. Either he killed her now, or he took her to the Destroyer to be killed later. Both options were unfathomable. He squeezed his eyes shut.

A gentle hand, sticky with blood, touched his face. "Tal. It will be well. Trust me."

He swallowed. Shook his head. It was his last effort at denial, though, and just as useless as all the attempts before. He opened his eyes. "I don't have a choice," he admitted roughly.

Nyx's lips curved. She patted him on the cheek. "I'll need your help to walk."

"I'll carry you."

"I'd rather look heroic and noble...limping my way off the field of battle like one of the old legends."

"You mean you'd rather die of blood loss before you even reach the train," he snapped back, and then flinched–both because he remembered he'd been the one to injure her so gravely, and because a comparatively peaceful death by blood loss might be preferable to what she was about to face.

She heaved a sigh. "Always so serious," she muttered. "Fine. Carry me. But set me down when we get to the surface. I'll at least look noble...when anyone else can see."

He looked away. "The Destroyer is not impressed by nobility."

Nyx leaned into him, and he wrapped his arms around her, lifting her carefully off the ground. They passed the side tunnel where the townspeople were still hidden. The group stared out at the pair, eyes even wider than before.

Nyx lifted her head off her brother's shoulder to address the survivors. "If you get away, go to the mountain ward. The township closest to the pass," she told them in a low tone. "Ask for Helenia of the Saints and tell her I sent you. She'll see you resettled."

The townspeople were silent for a moment, then a rustle went through them like trees rattling their branches in a winter breeze. One man at the front slowly lifted his hand. It formed a fist with his thumb turned toward himself, as if he were holding a hammer, about to drive it downward onto red-hot metal fresh from a forge fire. It was a salute. One by one, the other townspeople copied it.

Nyx returned the sign, though her fist shook with the effort. Tal turned his gaze forward again as an ache clenched deep in his chest. The survivors were honoring his sister. They knew where he was taking her.

He walked in silence after that. When they'd reached the surface and were staring at the train before them, he picked up Nyx's dagger—which had been left where it had landed in the street—and tried to give it back to her, so she would at least have some small measure of self-defense. His oath wouldn't allow it, though, and locked over his muscles to make him throw the weapon further into the ashes of the city. He stared after it, hopelessness and hatred twisting around his chest like a bone viper.

"What's this?" came a low, dangerous voice from behind him.

He turned around. The Destroyer was framed by the train's doorway. Petite as she was, her anger filled up the space like another presence, like a storm about to break. Her mercurial eyes snapped and crackled with fury as she stared at Nyx—who was, despite her orders, still alive.

Tal, despairing, fought back the urge to throw himself in front of his sister. The Destroyer couldn't know that they were connected. She would use it against both of them. She wouldn't be able to tell simply by looking at the pair that they were siblings—they'd had different mothers, and looked almost nothing alike—but any attempt by Tal to defend Nyx would only make things far worse than they already were.

He gritted his teeth. "The Saint demanded her right to a trial," he managed. "I have brought her back to you."

Against his will. Against everything he'd ever hoped for or believed.

He wanted to squeeze his eyes shut again. He wanted to scream. He wanted to—he wanted to pray. He teetered on the urge like a man on a cliff before desperation finally tipped him over its edge. *Please,* he begged his god silently. *Please. I've given you so much. Don't take her too.*

Nyx was leaning heavily against Tal's side, staring at the Destroyer, her expression mingling insolence and disgust as only a big sister could. "Take me back to the Alloyed Palace with you," she commanded, as if she were the lady and the Destroyer her prisoner.

The Destroyer bared her teeth. She held up a hand that glowed red with heat, giving Nyx a long moment to understand what she would do with it, and then reached out and clamped her fingers around Nyx's injured arm. An awful sizzling filled the air. A thin trail of smoke rose up, curling its way through the ash that drifted down around them. The tendons in Nyx's neck went taut as she tried, and then failed, to hold back a shout of pain. Every muscle in Tal's body tightened in response.

...and to never harm you myself. He'd never regretted more that the Destroyer had made him add that clause to his oath. He wanted to run her through with his blades. Wanted to

incinerate her, the way she'd incinerated so many towns-people yesterday. He wanted her to feel the way he did now: helpless, afraid, alone.

"You wish to face your trial? Very well," the Destroyer said, her anger vanished like mist, leaving no trace besides a distant, satisfied iciness in her voice as she shouted for the guards. "Take her to the cells," she ordered when they arrived, thrusting Nyx at them. "And give the order to set off, if it pleases my sister. I am past done with this place." Then she turned on her heel and strode away.

Tal was left with nothing to do but follow. The light fabric of the Destroyer's robe wafted around her as she walked ahead of him, revealing dots of Nyx's blood spangled across its hem in a violent constellation.

His hands clenched and unclenched. His breathing was jagged with rage. He wanted to smash something. Wanted to throw things, break things. He couldn't; nothing on this train belonged to him, and he would join the prisoners in the cells if he intentionally broke something that belonged to the lords and ladies.

And, he realized suddenly as an eerie, otherworldly calm slid over him, he couldn't risk ending up in the cells. Because there was something he needed to do while he was free.

The train shuddered, a great beast waking from hibernation as the Destroyer's order was relayed. Magic hummed through the intricate patterns inlaid on the cars' metal wheels. The ash-swathed town outside the windows slowly gave way to a wintry landscape: stark gray trees draped in a delicate lace of freshly fallen snow, the polished-black eyes of a wary fox gleaming in the shadows, the looming Sky-teeth mountains whose icy peaks shone with glaciers. Tal ignored it all.

His footsteps were muffled on the thick, luxurious rug as they made their way to the Destroyer's room, which held the cot where he spent so much time suppressing his nightly visions until they morphed into regular nightmares. Today, when the Destroyer allowed him to rest, he wasn't going to suppress them.

Today, he would *make* his god give him the answers he needed.

He was going to find a way out of his oath. He was going to free his sister. And then, he was going to kill the Destroyer.

CHAPTER THREE

Once, there was a girl who was afraid.

It was not an unreasonable sentiment. She'd lived through more than a dozen assassination attempts in the last year alone, after all—at least one of which had been strategized by a member of her own family. Under such circumstances, a healthy dose of paranoia was mere self-preservation. But every once in a while, when she allowed herself to feel around the jagged edges of her corroded soul, she wondered whether she would have so much cause to fear if her blood flowed crimson rather than quicksilver.

These were the thoughts that came to the Destroyer as she strode down the corridors of her sister's train, cloaked in a nightgown and in her own icy, billowing dread.

Her gait was commanding, her expression as gracefully cruel as ever as she stepped from one car to the next, but inside, she writhed. That assassin—that *girl,* barely older than the Destroyer herself—had gotten far too close. She remembered what it was like to taste the wind from the assassin's blade, remembered the sound of steel meeting steel like temple bells pealing through the town where no bells should have ever rung again. Most of all, she remembered the awful, seething vulnerability that had caught in her chest, in the exact spot where the girl's blade would have struck.

She planted a hand on the door to her chambers and pushed it open, leaving a slender handprint charred into the lacquered wood. It sizzled and smoked but it couldn't satisfy her. Her heart rapped out a rhythm so strong it was almost painful, and she burned with the need to pace, to scream out her anger, to punish someone so she could prove that she was not and would never be the vulnerable one. She really did need to go to Albinus for her treatment as soon as she could. His medicine was the only thing that could help her at times like this, the only thing that could make her feel in control again, untouchable, encased in the shield of her power.

She envied her sister. Sarai wore the Iron Crown, a relic of the ancient emperors. It housed one of the strongest enchantments in existence, one that had taken the power of dozens of great Smiths to forge. It was the secret to the power of the entire metallurgic class; wearing it, Sarai must never feel vulnerable.

Footsteps sounded behind her, paced so precisely they could be set to music. The sound paused as someone closed the chamber door behind them. Tal. She didn't look at him, but the harsh rhythm of her heart abated ever so slightly at the reminder of his presence.

He was with her. He could be trusted to protect her, as no one else could.

She pulled open the door to her wardrobe and selected an outfit without looking, then slid out of her nightgown and robe. Glacial mountain air crept around the edges of the car's velvet curtains and exhaled over her bare skin, raising goosebumps. She didn't look at Tal and he paid no attention to her. No man in his right senses, especially not one bound to her by a metal vow, would look at her with a gaze of desire rather than one of fear. And that was fine with her; desire protected no one, while fear was the most useful tool in her arsenal.

She pulled her chosen outfit on. It turned out to be a blouse woven from fine, soft, wine-red wool, with a sweeping cape dangling from one epauleted shoulder. She pulled on the black trousers that went with it and then laced up her sturdy heeled boots. She began to close the wardrobe door, but paused as she caught a glimpse of her reflection.

Her black hair tumbled wildly around her shoulders, still unkempt from the night of lost sleep. She'd been having a nightmare. Bits of the dream drifted back to the surface of her mind: a shadowed, towering bear of a man looming over her, and her own weak, warbling attempt at a scream as her mouth filled with blood. Not a nightmare, then, but a memory.

Her eyes tightened. She looked away from her reflection, and spotted Tal's. He stood at a loose attention behind her. His brown hair was unkempt, too. It fell over his face in strands, cutting his expression into slivers. Tight jaw, a dark slash of brows etched above stormy green eyes. He was angry with her. That was normal. Angry enough that he couldn't hide it, though—that was new. It hadn't happened for over a year. Not since he'd finally accepted that she was a force he would never evade.

Her gaze fell to his hands. They were curled into fists, but she could see an edge of pink skin where she'd healed him. Her own hands curled, her fingers brushing lightly over the spot where she could still feel his touch on her palm, feel the incandescent flame that had smothered between them. He hadn't screamed then. Not until he was on his knees.

Sarai had liked that. Satisfaction had settled over her like the ash on today's wind, clear to see for anyone who knew her. The Destroyer hadn't liked it, though. The sound of his anguish had unsettled something deep within her, a feeling like bones grating against each other. The feeling hadn't stopped until she'd healed him.

You're going soft, her sister had scoffed. In the mirror, the Destroyer tore her gaze away from her guard and set her jaw. She was fire, she was mercury, she was death. She was a weapon in the hand of her empress. She was not and could never be soft.

She snapped the wardrobe's door shut hard enough to rattle the mirror as it swung out of view. "My crown," she said flatly. It wasn't often that she gave Tal orders—he wasn't a servant—but she needed to see her crown in his hands, needed to reassure herself that the oath it kept still held.

Without comment, Tal stepped to her bed, where her discarded crown hung on a cant off a bedpost. He picked it up with both hands. It was a barbed, twisted thing, reminiscent of brambles and rose thorns, and she always looked suitably elegant and terrifying when she was wearing it. She didn't like the way he gripped it now, though—like it was a thing he could break.

Her heartbeat finally settled then, going slow and cold like a viper's. Her thoughts cleared. Her worries crystallized into ice: frozen and still, clear facets open to her study.

She leveled her gaze on Tal, coolly watching his approach. When he reached her, she held out a hand, the same one that had burned him earlier. He flinched. She raised one eyebrow and waited. After a moment his grip on the crown eased and he dropped it into her hands, lowering his eyes.

He turned to pace back to his corner. She let out a quiet breath. He was still hers, then. Still unable to harm her no matter how he might wish to.

Something was wrong with him, though. Something was different about today. Or perhaps...perhaps something was different with today's assassin. The Destroyer paused, her hands half-raised with lifting the crown to her brow, casting her mind back to when the assassin had stood before her. The girl's sharp, high cheekbones and strong facial features marked her as having ancestry from one of the Skyteeth mountain tribes. Perhaps she was from the same ward as Tal, then, maybe even someone he knew from his life before. An ex-lover? A childhood friend, maybe? Or simply a face that brought back memories of his past?

Whatever it was, there was something off about that girl. The Destroyer would have to endeavor to find out what.

She set the crown on her head and stepped toward the door. She would interrogate the prisoner now. She would not wait until her trial and inevitable sentencing, could not afford to sit back and do nothing during the time it would take for the leisurely return journey to the Alloyed Palace. If Tal was somehow connected to the assassin, she needed to know about it.

As she reached for the knob, a timid knock sounded from the other side of the door. A servant stood in the hall-way, half-bent already in an obeisance, tugging at the fingers of his white gloves in agitation. One finger was stained a watered-down brown.

"What?" she demanded, faintly irritated. "Have you brought more tea to douse me with?"

His head jerked upward like a startled doe's, and his gaze skimmed over her outfit. His eyes widened when he noticed she was wearing new clothes. "My—my lady," he stammered. "I was unaware that the tea spilled on you and not only the carpet, I offer my sincerest—"

She stepped past him into the corridor, cutting off his apology with a hand wave. He flinched, because a hand wave from her was not usually the forgiving gesture it often was from anyone else, but she didn't spark her powers, only strode onward without comment. This servant was a misfire, if she remembered correctly, one of the unlucky souls who'd been born to a Smith lineage but held no magic of his own. Such outcasts were sloughed from the ranks of the nobles and given roles as palace servants or army officers. He was right to fear her, as she could easily fire him—either in the job-related sense, or in the burning-to-ash sense—but fortunately for him she had more important matters to attend to at the moment. And she never had found pleasure in unnecessary violence anyway. It was the fear of others that she craved, and that was accomplished neatly enough through the bloody assignments her sister doled out.

The man scuttled along behind her, trying to find the words for whatever message he was supposed to be relaying to her.

She saved him the trouble. "My sister requires that I attend Lord Albinus immediately."

His features sagged in relief as she slid open the door to the dining car and stepped through. The air was cooler here than the rest of the train, curling over her shoulders in eddies that whispered of mountain blizzards as the train climbed toward the cloud-capped peaks of the Skyteeth. This car was walled with windows from floor to ceiling. It was meant to give the effect of openness to the beautiful scenery as they passed, and it did, but it also made for unbearably chilly meals when they were in the mountains. It also meant this car was the most vulnerable place on the train, as there was far less Smithed metal here to be enchanted with protective magic. It was one of the reasons she never ate in the dining car while on journeys, preferring to take her meals in the safety of her room. An added benefit of that arrangement was the lessened opportunities to interact with any other members of the metallurgy class.

The servant noticed she'd drawn ahead and hurried forward until he was standing at her side. He bowed again, a short, jerky bend from the waist that nearly upset a nearby cake trolley. The delicate confections resting atop it wobbled.

He cleared his throat. "The Empress Sarai, long may she live, begs you to—"

"My sister does not *beg*." She continued moving forward through the compartment, heedless of how he had to scurry out of her way, bumping into the trolley again as he did so. Several chocolate curls and a shred of gold leaf drifted to the floor. He grimaced and glared imperiously at the trolley's attendant, as if she were at fault. The lower-ranking girl flushed and quickly bent to clean up the mess.

The Destroyer continued onward, weaving between the tables laden with sausages, braided bread, and truffle omelets. The rich smell of food did nothing to tempt her from her course. Neither did the handful of cousins and twice-removed aunts and uncles who waved her toward their tables. She didn't deign to acknowledge their invitations; they were vipers, every one of them, and if they wished to talk to her it was only in order to glean secrets about her elder sister. Half of them were perpetually involved in some stage or another of a usurpation attempt.

The messenger servant turned away from the trolley and hastily caught up with the Destroyer. "Your presence is indeed requested in the chamber of the Lord of Copper, my lady. When may I tell the empress to expect your arrival there?"

To everyone but Sarai and Albinus—and possibly Tal, who likely knew an uncomfortable number of her secrets—the Destroyer's regular visits to the Lord of Copper were nothing but luxurious skin and hair treatments. Though this servant didn't understand the vitality of the message he carried, the Destroyer could read between the lines to see that her sister worried she was allowing too much time to lapse between her previous treatment and this one. That may have been true, but the Destroyer could think of nothing else at the moment beyond discovering the secrets of today's assassin. A spiky, apprehensive sense of betrayal was already fomenting in her chest at the thought of Tal being somehow compromised.

"You may tell her I have other important business to attend to, and will present myself in Albinus's chambers this evening." That should be enough time to interrogate the assassin. Though, she realized, it might also be beneficial to interrogate Tal as well. Or perhaps interrogate the assassin in front of Tal or vice versa; if they were acquainted, a threat to one of them might force the other to tell the truth.

She glanced over her shoulder. Tal was walking three steps behind her and slightly to the side as always, his gaze calm and alert, his expression blank—but she could still see that stain of new, pink skin on his hand, could still hear the echoes of his cry and sense the uneasy tension it had wrought in her.

She would not include him in the interrogation. Not yet, anyway. She would likely have no trouble wrenching the truth out of the assassin on her own—and if not, well, that was when she could reconsider Tal's inclusion in the process.

Soft, whispered Sarai's voice in her mind.

"Strategic," the Destroyer bit out aloud. Several nearby breakfasters glanced up in surprise, then carefully looked away and went back to their conversations—albeit rather stiltedly—when they saw it was her who was talking to herself.

The Destroyer's shoulders squared, and she wrenched open the next door so hard it cracked loudly against the interior wall. Perhaps she ought to visit Albinus sooner. He'd invented her medical treatment—a specialized transfusion process—to counter a childhood poisoning that still wreaked havoc on her mind and body when she went too long between doses. Her growing unsteadiness today could mean she was risking losing consciousness or even going into a fugue state, the way she had in a few prior instances when she'd let her treatments lapse too long.

But still, the prison car pulled her forward like a lodestone. Her medicine could wait a few more hours. She swept a glance back over her shoulder, taking in Tal and the servant. "I will go on alone from here," she told them both.

Tal froze mid-step, his gaze snapping to hers. She tried to read the emotion framed in his expression, to see if he'd guessed she was headed to the prison car, if he worried for the girl she was about to question. But Tal had become skilled at hiding from her; she couldn't guess what he was feeling.

"Yes, my lady," was all he said. He pivoted and strode back toward her chambers, his steps a clipped, staccato drumbeat. The servant followed.

She stepped through the doorway and pulled the door closed behind her. Two cars later, the cool air turned downright frigid, draping itself heavily over her as soon as she moved into the prison. She banished the chill with a snap of her fingers, cloaking herself instead in a flickering shawl of sparks. The warmth of her magic licked eagerly at her and brightened the dim interior of the prison with pops of dazzling white and orange.

Behind bars of unyielding iron, prisoners winced and huddled, curling into themselves at the sight of her and shielding their eyes from her magic. Several of them moaned and whimpered, and a few began openly sobbing. The coppery tang of blood sank cold tendrils down her throat with each inhale. She ignored all of it. She had already burned their town, her sole duty for this journey. She had no further business with these folk.

She stepped forward, her boots cracking like cannon shots against the sheet-metal floor as she surveyed the prisoners, searching for the girl from this morning. She found her easily. The assassin was the only one not cowering in her single-occupant cell, sitting instead with her legs crossed, wearing a haughty expression that spoke nothing of the pain she must be in. The blood on her shoulder glistened black in the bursts of light.

"My guard has impeccable aim," the Destroyer said

conversationally, tilting her head as she stopped outside the cell. "You never stood a chance, you know."

The assassin bared her teeth in a smile. "Lovely to see you again. Why don't you come in? I'd be happy to stain more of your clothes with my blood. Or your blood." She delivered the words in a careless tone, but was panting with the effort of it by the end.

"Such bravado for one so young," the Destroyer murmured.

"Please, I'm two years your elder. It's only all the murder that makes you feel so old."

The Destroyer reached toward the bars and skimmed one with a finger. The magic within the metal recognized her touch and the door to the cell swung open on silent hinges. She stepped onto the threshold. It was time to begin the interrogation proper. She held out one hand and allowed her magic to seep through her skin, curling to life as a surly red flame in her palm. "What are you called?" she asked.

The girl remained seated, her smile widening. "Your doom."

Irritation and something else—a faint nudge of admiration, quickly smothered—stirred. "When you fled after your ill-fated attempt at some murder of your own, my guard reacted as if he recognized you. What do you know of him?"

The girl shrugged her uninjured shoulder. "Never seen him before in my life. What do *you* know of him?"

"I know that he is mine, and I will suffer no threat to him."

An honest expression flicked across the girl's face at last. She mastered it quickly, but she wasn't nearly as practiced at concealing her emotions as Tal, and the Destroyer had more than long enough to recognize the fury and anguish that tightened the girl's eyes and twisted her smile into a brief snarl. "He is not yours," the girl said in a low tone void of her earlier bravado, "and it is not *me* who poses a threat to him."

The Destroyer's anxiety deepened a touch. Such strong emotion spoke of a close bond. It was as she'd feared, then— Tal did indeed have some sort of personal connection to the assassin.

A sudden anger cracked to life, swallowing up her anxiety. How dare this girl presume a claim to Tal, to the sole person the Destroyer could trust with her safety in a palace full of pretenders?

She stepped closer to the assassin and knelt down gracefully, her cape pooling behind her on the damp floor of the cell. Staining more of her clothes, indeed, she noted ruefully. "It wouldn't do to have you bleed out before you get to your trial. That wound ought to be cauterized," she said, and kept her eyes on the girl as she held out the hand with the flame and pressed it hard against the girl's shoulder.

The girl screamed and jerked. To her credit, she managed to turn the flail into an attack, driving her head forward into the Destroyer's chest. The Destroyer twisted smoothly away before the blow could do more than graze her ribs.

The coppery tang of blood turned acrid and smoky as the Destroyer pulled her hand away from the assassin's wound and brushed off her palms, giving the girl a few seconds of respite to consider her situation. "Perhaps you wish to give me your name now," she suggested.

The girl was on her hands and knees, fingers splayed against the floor. She took a shaky breath. "Thank you for that," she said. "I've been demanding they bring a doctor in here to see to my wound before I bleed out...but it seems I no longer need to worry about it."

The Destroyer considered the girl for a long moment. The earlier nudge of admiration crept back in and this time would not be smothered. She struggled with it briefly, but her fortitude was already weakened by having gone too long without her medical treatment, and after only a few seconds she gave in.

She leaned forward and inclined her head. "My name is Elodie," she told the girl quietly. "And now you may thank me in truth, because unlike torture, my name is a gift I have given no assassin before."

Few people remembered the Destroyer's true name. It was a secret long kept hidden, not because public knowledge of it represented any sort of threat, but because she needed her sister's empire to see her as a weapon—merciless, unbendable—and not a person.

Sometimes, though, she missed the syllables of her real name spoken aloud. Such an unpresuming name it was that her parents had given her. If they hadn't been long dead, she might have asked them what they were thinking, to give a deadly princess such an incongruously sweet name.

The admission caught the assassin off guard. She eyed her as she pushed herself weakly to a sitting position.

"What...what do I care about your name?" She panted. "You are nothing but the Destroyer to me and to everyone I care about...and that's the only name you'll ever hear from my lips."

The words should have meant nothing. The Destroyer had heard far worse from the lips of far more powerful people. But somehow, in her weakened state, the declaration sank its roots into her soul and bloomed black with thorns.

She shoved to her feet, snagging her cape on a bolt in the floor in the process. It tore off a frayed shred of wine-colored fabric. The Destroyer barely noticed. Her magic crackled and grew, lashing itself into a whirlwind that threw violent orange light against the bars of the cell. "Then perhaps," she hissed, her words blending with the snapping of flames, "I should bring Tal in for my next visit to your cell, and we might see what it takes to convince *him* to give me your name."

The girl's gaze found hers and all traces of bravado fell from her expression. Defeat took its place—hooding her eyes, carving shadows into her features as she bowed her head. "Nyx." The word shuddered and cracked.

Elodie accepted the name: the first true thing this girl had told her. Her fire, sated, died down to sparks. She crossed her arms—to hide how her hands trembled, though she wasn't sure why—and let her lips thin into a satisfied smile.

"Nyx," she repeated. "Good. Now, we can talk."

CHAPTER FOUR

Nyx believed in exactly one thing, and that was her brother Tal.

He was why she had trekked to that doomed mining town yesterday. He was why she was here now, kneeling on the floor of a mobile cell made filthy with blood and magic. And he was why she allowed the Destroyer—a murderess framed by intractable iron bars, wearing a twisted crown and a cloak of fiery power—to believe that she, and not Nyx, had the upper hand.

Her mouth tasted of copper and salt and agony. She spat onto the floor but a veneer of blood still coated her teeth, so she put it to good use and smiled at the girl in front of her. "Sure," she said, forcing the word out between labored breaths. "I can probably free up...a few minutes from my schedule to ignore more of your questions."

The Destroyer's thin smile didn't waver. Her hands were shaking, though. She probably thought she was hiding it, but Nyx had always been accomplished at reading people. Nyx was getting to her—which only meant more pain for Nyx, of course, but that suited her purposes just fine.

"Do you care so for Tal, that you would defend him at the cost of your name?" the Destroyer asked.

Nyx shrugged, albeit carefully, since her whole body stung with the echoes of fire as if sparks were clogging her veins. Her tongue and throat stung particularly, though that wasn't because of the Destroyer's torture; rather, it was the aftereffects of the foul potion she'd downed last night that still lingered and burned. "My name's not worth much," she replied.

One of the Destroyer's delicate eyebrows arched. "And yet you required torture to give it to me."

"You're not worth much either."

The Destroyer snorted. The sound caught Nyx off guard. It didn't match, just like the Destroyer's name didn't match. The sister of the Iron Empress should have a name that brought to mind vipers and nightshade: something elegant, graceful, deadly. She shouldn't have a kind name, and she shouldn't snort like some amused commoner. And she shouldn't look so small, either—even when she'd gripped Nyx's arm with a burning hand earlier, Nyx had been struck by how petite and even breakable she looked. She was beginning to worry that the ordeal she had prepared herself for bore little resemblance to the girl who actually stood before her.

Nyx shook herself. Neither the Destroyer's name nor her habits had any bearing on the situation. Nyx was here to kill the Lady of Mercury and free her brother, and she could do neither if she couldn't focus. She turned her attention inward, wrapping herself around the core of hate that had been hardening for two years now—ever since she read that goddamned letter Tal left for her the day he pledged himself to a monster. Nyx's old rage simmered easily back to the surface, and her focus sharpened.

There. That was better.

The Destroyer was watching her. "You have strong feelings toward me," she observed.

Internally, Nyx cursed. Apparently she wasn't the only one good at reading people. "You're not my type," she retorted. That was certainly true enough. The Destroyer's cruel, cold beauty couldn't hold a candle to Helenia: the kind-hearted, no-nonsense girl back in the mountain ward who'd tearfully promised to wait for Nyx in the case of her potential—though unlikely—survival.

"Why did you try to assassinate me?" the Destroyer mused, as if to herself. "To avenge Tal? To free him? That is impossible without my death, which, fortunately for me, you have already proven yourself incapable to achieve."

Nyx said nothing.

The Destroyer held out her hand, the one with a flame curling just above it. Its fire flickered dull orange. Nyx wondered what the color meant, whether it had to do with her mood or with how much energy or magic she had left. There was so much the Saints didn't know about the metallurgic class, and about the Destroyer in particular. The handful of non-noble Smiths born each year usually had pitifully small amounts of metal in their blood, far too little to allow for accurate studies, and no prior mercury Smith in any class had ever survived early childhood due to the volatility of incendiary magic. The few brave Saint spies who'd managed to infiltrate the palace had been able to smuggle back a little more intelligence, but not nearly enough to deconstruct the lethal puzzle that was the Destroyer.

The Destroyer allowed the flame to grow until it was a bonfire in miniature, hissing and snarling like a wild animal in her palm. "What exactly is Tal to you?"

Nyx couldn't help baring her teeth. "What is he to *you*? Just another guard dog, just another toy for you to break and discard? How dare you call him yours? No person can own another, and you are nowhere near worthy of him in any case."

The Destroyer's expression cracked then, straining along fault lines, allowing an incandescent fury to shine through from beneath. Nyx saw it and flinched.

The Destroyer steadied herself. The fury vanished. "He sought me out and pledged his service of his own will," she said coolly. "I haven't made him do anything he did not freely swear to do, and I have certainly not broken him."

"He has new scars," Nyx countered. Anger lashed through her at the memory of the white lines creeping over Tal's shoulder and curling around his collar bone. Had she had him beaten? Did she torture him too, in her free time?

The Destroyer's shoulders drew back and she lifted her chin. "I do not torture people without a purpose, and I have never put him to the question. I don't have to. He is loyal. He is *mine*. His scars are from my would-be assassins and from accidents, nothing more."

"Accidents that wouldn't happen if he guarded anyone but you," Nyx said, but she relaxed incrementally. This was something she'd had nightmares about, what the Destroyer might do to Tal when he was under her power. But if she was telling the truth–and the Destroyer seemed raw enough right now that Nyx believed her, at least on this–then Tal suffered only because he killed for her, and not because she actively tormented him. Not that that was truly better. Tal's soul had always been so much more fragile than his body, and Nyx feared what his work must be doing to him.

"You've not answered my question yet," the Destroyer said, her tone darkening. "I will ask it once more, and not again–"

"Do you promise?" Nyx interrupted.

The Destroyer ignored her. "How do you know Tal? You will answer me, or regret the consequences."

From a few cells away, a strangled cry broke out. "Just– just do it," a woman's voice sobbed hoarsely. "You must do it. Make her stop."

Up until now, the townsfolk in the car had kept silent, nothing but clumps of huddled, horror-tense bodies in the shadows of their cells, hiding like mice from a serpent. But apparently they couldn't bear their fear any longer; the woman's words whipped through the prisoners like an icy wind, leaving them shuddering and moaning.

Nyx took them in—the whites of their eyes gleaming, the stench of burnt clothing and skin, the bitter, flaky taste of ash that lingered even here. The hatred at her core grew a few more layers, and she used them to strengthen herself for what was to come.

She turned back to the Destroyer. "Torture me all you want," she said, and the words within her burned like the fire before her. "I have said all I care to say."

The Destroyer's expression grew cruel. She stepped forward, and the flame in her palm coiled into itself like a spring, tension winding through every spark and flicker as the color changed from dull orange to white-hot.

The Destroyer held out her hand. And then the pain began.

The day before, Nyx had been drinking her daily dose of poison when her mother burst into the Saints outpost.

"We have the location," the older woman announced. Her voice was triumphant. Cold. So were her eyes, and they only warmed a little when they landed on the vial in Nyx's hand.

Nyx swallowed, licking the last traces of bitter liquid from her lips. The concoction always tasted like blood. Which was fitting, she supposed. "Where?" she demanded. "Will we have enough time to reach it?"

Time was always their enemy, almost as much as the metallurgy class was. Twice before in the last six months had the Saints been tipped off to the location of a town the Destroyer was set to punish, only to fail because it was too far from any of their hidden outposts. Both times, they'd arrived too late. Both times, they'd failed to either save any villagers, or to kill the Destroyer.

Or to rescue Tal. To everyone else, he was no more than a potentially valuable source of intelligence; he'd lived in the Alloyed Palace for years, and once freed, he could assist the rebellion in a way no one else could. But to her, he was the sole reason for the mission. For him, she drank poison every day.

For him, she would doom herself.

"The spies were right. It's in the Copperreach, praise be to the Unforged God," her mother said, icy ferocity coating her words and burning in her eyes. "We will make it if we leave now. Are you ready?" She paused for a moment, her gaze darting from the flask to Nyx's face. Nyx wondered what expression she wore, to put that concerned look on her mother's face. "It has to be you, you know," her mother said, putting an end to Nyx's speculation. Of course. She was worried Nyx might second-guess the mission.

Nyx lifted the flask to her lips and drank deeply, far more than her usual daily sip. The liquid swirled sourly in her stomach and stung her lips. She set the flask on the table before her, and it made a hollow thunk: the sound of emptiness.

"I know."

When the worst of the pain was over, Nyx returned to herself. The Destroyer was withdrawing her hand. Nyx didn't know if her expression was still cruel, because she couldn't see anything but the afterimages of fire, couldn't smell anything but char, couldn't feel anything but anguish. Her cheek was pressed to the floor. One of her hands was spasming weakly, scrabbling against the sheet metal like a dying spider. Her skin looked uninjured but she could still feel the burning in her bones.

She couldn't do this anymore. She couldn't. She couldn't.

For Tal, she thought fiercely, and forced her head up.

The Destroyer's back was to her. The graceful arch of her spine, the gentle angles of her shoulders, the aristocratic tilt of her chin—all of it said that this business affected her not one bit. Nyx wondered if that was all torture was to her: business.

Then a shudder, light but unmistakable, quivered over the Destroyer's shoulders. Her cloak of sparks flickered out for barely a second and then flared to life more strongly.

One of the prisoners—the woman who had cried out a moment ago—inhaled sharply. The sound was quiet but unmistakable.

Nyx squeezed her eyes shut. She gave herself three heartbeats to gather her courage, to burrow as deep as she could into her hatred. And then she levered herself back up to her knees.

"You are a fool," the Destroyer said, not bothering to turn around.

"And you..." replied Nyx, carefully placing one foot on

the ground, her voice coarse and splintered, "are a bitch."

The Destroyer glanced over her shoulder. The whites of her eyes gleamed like glacier ice, buried so long in the heart of the mountain that it remembered no sunlight. "'Bitch' is what people call women whose power they fear."

Nyx swallowed convulsively. She leaned her good shoulder–"good" being very relative–against the wall and pushed herself far enough up to put her other foot on the ground, so that she was no longer kneeling. "It's also...what they call serial murderesses. So I stand by it." She was gasping for air by the end of the declaration, and nearly ready to reconsider her commitment to goading her way to her own death.

The Destroyer turned fully around now. She looked Nyx up and down, reconsidering her. "Why do you fight so hard?" she said softly. "Only loss lies down this path. Whatever you want, it is as far from your reach as the moon." There was an odd wistfulness to her voice, something childlike, there and gone almost before Nyx could notice it.

"What do you know of loss?" Nyx snarled.

The Destroyer quirked an eyebrow, and one corner of her mouth curved up humorlessly. "Nothing. You can't lose what you've never had."

"You've had *everything*," Nyx spat. "You grew up with *everything*. I had one thing, one precious person, and then you took him too just because you could." She inhaled painfully. "Mark my words: one day soon, you will face a reckoning."

The Destroyer tilted her head. A calculating light came into her expression. "What is your name?"

"I told you. Nyx."

"No. Your family name."

Nyx took a breath. There it was. The Lady of Mercury had guessed her secret. If she was certain enough of her relation to Tal, she would kill Nyx; she seemed obsessed with ensuring no one else had a claim to him. Nyx knew that she was dying, but she couldn't give in to it just yet. She had to last at least a little longer. Just long enough for her plan to work.

So she took a strangled breath and met the Destroyer's eyes. Then she spat on her boots. Red splattered across the finely dyed leather. "Go to hell," Nyx said, and hated that the words were half a sob.

The Destroyer stepped forward again.

The night before, tremors had wracked Nyx's body as she hurried through the aqueducts. She'd built up enough of a tolerance to the poison that it wouldn't kill her—the Destroyer would be the one to do that—but it was still havoc on her nerves. She cursed under her breath. She needed to be strong. By the light of the coming dawn, she would be attacking the Destroyer, and if Nyx wasn't at her prime she could be killed first thing rather than being pursued and captured as she needed to be.

Ahead of her, a child cried out. Nyx was shepherding one of the last loads of townsfolk through the aqueducts to safety, and just in time too. Above them, an ominous rumble shook dust from *the ceiling and made the bricks tremble. Flakes of mortar crumbled away and drifted down like snow.*

"It's the train," the child whimpered. "She's here. We won't make it!"

One of the other Saints on the mission, a pale-skinned man with hair so red it was nearly orange, scooped the child up to comfort her. When the girl's face was turned away, he sent a significant look at Nyx. She nodded at his silent message and then quickly helped him herd them into a side tunnel where they would be better protected from the fire that was about to rain down on the city—and on the hundred-odd soon-to-be-martyred Saints who had volunteered to take the townspeople's place in their homes tonight. The Destroyer would know if the city she burned was empty, but she'd be none the wiser to incinerating the wrong people.

Some of the Saints would survive, though. It was all part of the plan. All Nyx had to do was her bit, and allow the toxin flowing through her veins to do its own part.

The poison had been formulated by her mother working in conjunction with a copper Smith, and was made by dissolving hemlock oil in an enchanted copper suspension. It was created to be absorbed by the body of the one who drank it—and then transmitted to anyone who channeled magic into the drinker.

Nyx was immune.

The Destroyer wasn't.

This time, Nyx didn't return to herself.

She couldn't bear it any longer. Not the agony, not the smell of burning hair and skin blistering from the inside, not the contradictory planes and angles of her captor's expression. She floated instead, drifting just below the surface of the pain, peering into the dim, distorted light of the prison in the way a swimmer sees the sun from deep underwater.

"No!" cried a voice, cutting through the haze. The word rang across the iron bars and bounced painfully inside Nyx's skull. Distantly, she thought that it sounded like her mother.

An errant tear, or perhaps a bead of blood, slid across Nyx's nose. Against her will she resurfaced. The distorted light turned into flickering sparks. The Destroyer was walking away, frowning down at her hands, where colorful flames wheeled about like a kaleidoscope. She must have realized something was wrong, that something was affecting her magic. If she walked away now, that was all it would do: drain her magic, weaken her until her body recovered. It wouldn't kill her.

Nyx's gaze slid sideways. Like metal meeting a magnet, she found the eyes of the woman in the next cell, one of the "captured townsfolk"–the one who'd cried out earlier, and again just now. The woman's skin was a darker brown than Nyx's own but their cheekbones were the same. Their eyes were the same too, had always been lit with the same ferocity. Nyx's hair was long where the woman's was cropped short, but the memory of the woman's fingers still lingered in Nyx's braids.

Mom. Nyx's mouth formed the word, though no sound escaped.

Her mother swallowed. Nyx could barely make out the bob of her throat through the gloom and the flickering sparks as the Destroyer opened the cell door.

Her mother's jaw tightened and her gaze grew urgent. *You must do it,* she'd called out earlier. To the Destroyer, it would have sounded like she was begging Nyx to give up so the torture would end. But Nyx knew she'd meant the opposite.

Nyx shook her head, a pitiful motion, barely a tremor as her cheek pressed deeper into the floor. She couldn't do this. Not any longer.

But the Destroyer was halfway out the door already, and if she left, it meant Nyx had failed. It meant Tal would be forever lost. And, Nyx reasoned despairingly, she herself was already likely going to die anyway. At this point there really was no hope of winning back her life, only of eking out a little more time. If she traded away that time, she could free her brother. She could make it all mean something. She could win.

She could still win. She could still make it worth it.

There was one thing that could make the Destroyer stop, could make her turn around, could make her come back to finish the job she'd started. *Your family name,* the Destroyer had demanded a moment ago.

Nyx forced in a breath. "Melaine," she whispered.

And the Destroyer turned around.

CHAPTER FIVE

BESIDE TAL'S COT, AN EMBOSSED CLAY CUP ROLLED BACK and forth with the motion of the train. The dregs of his tea dribbled out with each pass, turning the carpet soggy and fragrant with the scent of gold-infused sleeping draught. He'd requested triple his usual dose from the kitchens, but it had still taken nearly twenty minutes for the medicinal herbs and golden sleep magic to force Tal into an uneasy rest.

To a silver Smith, sleep was like being buried at the heart of the earth: encased in granite, enveloped in an immense, directionless pressure. This was what he feared. This was what he faced every night, what he fought every time he dared to sleep. He was surrounded by the vast, gentle, inescapable weight of his god, and he could not take another instant of it.

Tal tried to breathe. There was no breath to be had in this silent nowhere, though, and no body here for him to breathe with. This was the in-between place, the almost-dreaming place. If he concentrated, he could move past it, step beyond the disorienting pressure and into his normal nightmares. But that wasn't why he was here.

He was distantly aware of the tautness of his muscles, of the coarse linen sheets that were crumpled in his grip. The tea had drawn sleep over his mind but did nothing to relax his body, which would have betrayed his terror and rage to anyone who could see. Wasn't it fortunate, then, he thought bitterly to himself, that the Destroyer wasn't here to notice?

The pressure—the *presence*—that surrounded Tal's sleeping mind began to lighten. A rushing sensation built in his gut, making him dizzy. And then all at once everything simply released: no pressure, no weight, nothing tethering him to the world or to himself. It was as if gravity had suddenly reversed, and he was plummeting headlong into the great emptiness between the stars.

The vision was about to start.

My sister, he said, throwing the words into the empty blackness. *Show me how I save my sister.*

He briefly considered what else he should add. He used to worship in this time. Used to fall bodiless through the midst of his god and pray, so very certain of his belonging. Then, later, this was the time he begged and wept, clinging desperately to his fraying belief that his god had brought him low for a reason—that somehow, his pain would serve a purpose. But there had been no answer to any of it. Tal had wished then that he could be like one of the unbelievers, that he could imagine the Unforged God was an ancient myth, nothing but a fascinating story that had never been true. He hated that he knew otherwise. Hated that he could sense the god who had betrayed him in every dream, in every beat of his heart, in every ounce of his silver blood.

Maybe if he begged again. Maybe if he pleaded. If it was his suffering that sated his god, Tal could give it, to save Nyx. But when he tried to form the words of a plea, something within him rebelled, unwilling to be so vulnerable again in front of the one he used to trust.

You owe me, he said instead at last, blasphemy though it was. *You owe me this much.*

The vision slammed into place around him. The dizziness stopped abruptly. His stomach surged, and in his bed, his body curled in on itself as he tried desperately to not be sick. The vision was of a dilapidated cabin that smelled of copper and hemlock, and housed a woman and a girl. The woman he recognized as Saasha—his father's on-again off-again first wife, who was Nyx's mother. She'd cut her hair since he'd seen her last. It hugged her scalp now in a short black halo, but beneath it, her eyes burned with the same fanatical devotion Tal had always recognized.

It has to be you, you know, she said. Her mouth moved with no sound. The meaning of the words simply slid into Tal's consciousness, in the way of dreams.

Nyx lifted a flask—the source of the hemlock smell, which Tal would recognize anywhere, because Saasha was an apothecist. Their house had smelled of nightshade and gingko and lavender and flax ever since he was seven years old and newly orphaned.

Nyx tipped the flask and drained the contents. Alarm spiked through Tal's veins as he registered what she'd done, what she'd drank. With the strength of his emotion, the vision distorted, going milky and grainy.

I know, whispered Nyx from somewhere in the murk.

She'd drank poison. Why would she do that? He tried to swim forward through the gloom, strained to pick out clues that might ascertain whether it was the past or the future that he saw, but his emotion strangled the vision until he could barely make out the shape of his sister. He struggled to calm himself.

The dream wavered for a moment and then crystallized into a new scene. The Destroyer, wearing a diaphanous cloak woven from sparks and smoke. At her back: iron bars and a sheet-metal floor. At her feet: Nyx.

Clothing charred in spots. Long hair burnt to nearly shoulder length. Spots of melted, steaming brass clinging to her tunic here and there: the beads that had once decorated her braids.

Something formless and horrible roared through Tal. *Hate,* he named it, and turned on the Destroyer. His phantom hands reached for nonexistent blades, only to grip the nothingness that he was here. He was as helpless to stop her as he had ever been.

He tried to tear himself from the fabric of the dream, thinking only of running to the prison car before this vision came true, if it hadn't already—but a great stillness suddenly wrapped around him and held him in place.

Wait, came a whisper.

Tal froze. The voice rippled through him with unbearable gentleness, tugging at his blood like a lodestone. He had never heard it before, but every ounce of metal in him was singing with it, basking in it. He trembled before it—no, he trembled before *himself*. Before the wild, desperate hope that had instantly awoken, though he'd sworn it was long dead and buried deeper than he could ever reach again. He trembled before the knowledge of just how much power his god still held over him.

Before him, in the vision, the Destroyer knelt in front of Nyx. Her expression was alight with a mad sort of fury that Tal had only seen a handful of times. *So you are his sister, then,* she said in a tone that spoke death. She reached out a hand. In it was a white-hot flame. This was it; she had unmasked Nyx, and now she would kill her.

Stop, he tried to shout. The words echoed only inside his own skull. But still, despite himself, he clung to hope. His god had spoken. After two years, after a lifetime, he'd made himself known. Maybe it meant something. Maybe Tal hadn't been abandoned, not forever.

The Destroyer paused then. Her head tilted as she gazed at the flame in her hand. Tal followed her line of vision. The fire was flickering in and out of existence, one moment miniscule and the next leaping so high it nearly burned the Destroyer's own face. Her cloak of sparks was flickering too.

She looked down at herself and back at Nyx, her forehead wrinkling, and then in a swift movement pushed herself away and stood. *What have you done to me?* she demanded. She staggered then, falling sideways into the cell door. It swung open under her touch.

It was then that, beneath the acrid scent of burnt flesh and charred hair, Tal smelled the faintest trace of hemlock and copper.

The stillness surrounding him lifted. Dizziness lurched into him like a train slamming through a snowbank, and he sat up in bed and was immediately sick over the side of his cot.

He gasped for air. Disoriented once again, he shoved himself off the other side of his bed, falling to one knee in the process. He grabbed for the bedpost to steady himself and with the other hand covered his eyes. He was shaking.

Nyx had poisoned the Destroyer. That was why she'd drunk the flask, which had smelled of hemlock and copper—a poison which could apparently be transmitted from Nyx to the Destroyer in the course of her torture. That was why she'd come here. To kill the Lady of Mercury, and to free Tal.

He covered his mouth. A sob wrenched out anyway. His sister was assassinating the Destroyer, probably right this very moment, for his sake—and because he had seen this vision, he would have to stop her. *Again*.

He scooped up the clay mug and hurled it against the window. It shattered, spraying tea dregs across the pristine landscape of snow and mountains. It was all he had time to do before his oath ghosted through his veins, wound like roots around his bones, and yanked him upright. It reached out with his hands and buckled on his sword belt. It forced him toward the door.

His god. His god had done this. If Tal had left the vision when he'd tried to, he wouldn't have been compelled to save the Destroyer now, because he wouldn't have known she was in danger. He wanted to cry, wanted to rail—at both the Unforged God and at himself, because for that one moment, he had nearly allowed himself to believe again. Having his hope crushed a second time was even more agonizing than the first, because it was *his fault.* He had known better, and still, he had hoped.

He yanked the door open. In the hallway, he tried again to fight the oath, but it propelled him forward mercilessly, taking over his muscles, jerking him down the corridor. A servant was in his way. He shoved them aside, and a tray of cranberry tarts splattered against the carpet like blood. He wrenched open the door to the dining car. The empress was there. She stopped midsentence, a bite of truffle omelet lifted halfway to her mouth as she took him in. The glass walls beyond her framed the serrated peaks of the Skyteeth looming on every side: his home, so near and forevermore out of his reach. He barreled past it all, not pausing to answer the empress's shouted demand or even register what it was she said. The next door rebounded off the wall to slam back into his shoulder, and when it closed behind him, it made a splintering noise that probably meant it would be difficult to open again.

The door to the prison car was next. He pulled it open. A rectangle of light stretched out before him, feeble and blue against the shadows that seethed through the car's interior. Then the door shut behind him and the light was gone.

He breathed in the darkness. Let it coat his lungs, his mind, his soul. And then he turned and searched for the Destroyer.

She was on the ground. Struggling to raise herself up on her elbows, to drag herself further into the hallway and out of the cell. Flames burned madly all around her, a whirlwind of fire that tightened, loosened, dissipated and formed again. Her magic was unstable. He had only seen this sort of thing happen to her twice before, though then it hadn't been poison but exhaustion that had spurred it on. The first time, the empress had hurried her to the Lord of Copper—who was also their cousin and the royal physician—before her condition worsened. The second time, she'd burned down a wing of the Alloyed Palace before losing consciousness. That was how he'd gotten the scar on his collarbone.

His oath took control again, commandeering his body to make him kneel at the Destroyer's side as her fire blinked out. His hands curled on her shoulders, just barely gently enough to not be considered "harming," and flipped her onto her back so that he could pick her up.

She inhaled sharply at the touch—she hadn't seen him enter—and jerked away. Her eyes snapped up, wild and...

Afraid?

The sight hypnotized him. Fear paled her cheeks and drew her jaw in all sharp angles, shrank her pupils until the mercurial silver of her irises seemed to swallow them. Her breath came in short gasps. A sadistic pinprick of satisfaction lanced through Tal's wildly beating heart; he had wished to see her afraid, and here it was, painted before him in clear shades of terror. But as soon as the satisfaction came, shame slipped in to dilute it. A person was cowering before him, and he was *glad.* That was not how he was built.

He shoved both the shame and the satisfaction away in disgust, and scooped up the Destroyer.

She cried out and flung a hand instinctively at the sudden movement. Tal turned his face away and braced for fire, but nothing came.

He looked back at her. She was blinking, her pupils adjusting. "Tal," she said, and the word quavered with a profound and wholly unfamiliar relief.

A shuffling noise sounded from the cell behind them. Tal braced himself once again, tore his gaze from the Destroyer's, and then, finally, turned to look at his sister. Emotion crept through him, a slurry of horror and guilt and a terrible, terrible fear. He had avoided looking for Nyx until now because he was afraid the oath would make him kill her. He had waited until the Destroyer was in his arms, hoping that his oath would then prioritize getting her to the healer over killing her would-be assassin.

He'd already seen Nyx in his vision, he knew what to expect, but he was still unprepared for the sight of her so damaged. Her skin was only burned in a few places. The Destroyer knew how to do that—how to turn her fire inward through an entry point, to bring pain without doing untoward outward damage. But it was the uncharacteristic despair in her expression, and the ominous rattling of her breaths, that nearly brought Tal to his knees.

They stared at each other for a moment. "I'll...I'll come back for you. I'll save you," Tal promised, though he knew he had no business swearing any such thing. He would swear it on metal, though, if it could ensure it came true.

Nyx exhaled a garbled laugh. "Supposed to be...me saving you, little brother." She reached for him then, as if she was helpless to do anything else. Her fingers grazed the hem of his pants. In the gesture, he saw the ghost of the girl she'd once been: a snarling terror on the sparring grounds at eleven years old, gripping the dagger he'd gifted her in those same hands.

Before she could touch him, Tal took a step away. He ground his teeth. "You shouldn't have come, Nyx. Not for me. I'm lost already." The oath jerked him another step toward the door.

Nyx stared back at him, then her gaze fell, and her eyes met the Destroyer's. Something passed between the two girls in that instant, and a change came over Nyx: some alchemy of ferocity and fatalism that scored away her despair, leaving only hardness in its wake. She curled both hands around the iron bars of her cell. "Destroyer," she said, low and brutal and certain, "I swear on this metal that I will see your empire fall, and your reign ended, and you dead. Do you hear me, *Elodie*?"

"*NO!*" Tal shouted, but he was too late. He saw the moment the metal accepted his sister's oath. She shuddered as it sank in.

"Nyx–" Tal said urgently, but before he could get out more than that the Destroyer sagged in his arms, her eyes rolling back. Her whole body jerked. Fire lashed out in tendrils all over her. He was moving toward the exit before he registered taking a step. He tried to turn back around to get one last glimpse of Nyx, but he was too late again; the Destroyer's fire blocked everything behind him out. It charred the edges of the doorframe as they passed through it and snapped like whips against the floor, but somehow, none of it burned him. The flames arced around him instead as if he were encased in an invisible barrier.

He kicked open the door to the dining car. It took three tries, because this was the door that had been stuck shut. When the hinges finally broke and sent the door cracking open, it knocked back three servants who'd been clustered around the other side, and another one leapt aside barely in time to avoid a broken nose. Everyone shouted at once when they saw who Tal was holding and the condition she was in. Several nobles—the wise ones—fled, heading for the open hallway at the other end of the car. Others pushed through toward Tal, their eyes alight with curiosity or, in several cases, a predatory glee. Chairs clattered as they were kicked aside. Bits of breakfast splattered on the floor as one woman shoved a table out of the way, a carnage of jam and butter smearing across the thick cream carpets. Tal barreled through it all, intent on getting through the horde of people and to Albinus, who could mend the Destroyer. And then maybe, while she was recovering, Tal would have time to think of some way to get Nyx free of both her oath and her prison.

The fire whirling around the Destroyer tightened. It went white-hot, roiling with barely-leashed energy. When Tal pushed past a table, it caught fire instantly, and the flames quickly spread to the dress of the lady standing next to it. Screams erupted as the nobles and servants surrounding them all tried to scatter at once, finally realizing the danger.

Someone stepped in front of Tal. He made to shove past them when he registered that it was the empress, and stopped. She took in the scene in a single, sweeping glance, the nobles around her falling back in a wave as her gaze scythed through them. She held out a hand and let it hover over her sister. Then she stepped back. "I can't put out the fire," she stated. Her posture was calm, but her words snapped with tension. She turned, grabbing an older noblewoman—a distant aunt of hers, who had bronze communication magic— by the arm. The woman squawked in outrage but went pale and silent at a look from Sarai. "Send a mental message to the conductor immediately," the empress ordered. "He is to enact the emergency transportation magics. If we aren't at the Alloyed Palace in less than thirty seconds, I shall have both him and you garroted and your families' bodies hung from the city walls for the crows."

The older woman shrank back in shock. A younger man, one who had the same hooked nose as the older bronze Smith, put his arm protectively around her shoulders. He was the Head of Transport, Tal recalled.

"You can't enact the teleportation protocols!" the man protested, turning to the empress, raising his voice to be heard above the shouting. "It will ruin all the enchantments on the train, it'll take me weeks to repair, we wouldn't be able to use it at all in the meantime—"

Suddenly he stopped speaking. His mouth continued opening and closing but not a sound passed his lips. He blinked in surprise at first and put both hands to his throat, as if to feel for whatever was keeping his words penned up. Then his surprise rippled into a dawning horror, and his mouth opened wide, gaping.

He was suffocating.

Sarai watched him impassively, one hand lifted to control the flow of air around the man. "Albinus cannot treat my sister for this on the train," she said. "He will need his office at the palace. And if she is not treated quickly enough, her magics will explode with a force no one here would wish to see. Hence my transport order."

The man nodded frantically.

Sarai arched a brow. "I take that to mean you will no longer quibble about how long repairs may take?"

He nodded harder.

"Neither," said the empress coldly, "will the new Head of Transport."

The man reached out for her, his eyes glassy with tears, his grasping fingers gone knobby and white with panic. The empress swept one foot back as if she were dancing in the palace ballroom and the man overbalanced, falling to his knees and then onto his face. His shoulders shuddered and went still.

"One less for the crows," Sarai murmured, then looked back at the older woman. "You've ten seconds remaining, and three more family members present on this train. That's rather more math than I'd planned on doing so early in the morning. Send the message now and save us both the trouble, won't you?"

The woman's face had gone hard, her expression marble-carved as she gazed down at the young man at their feet. She raised her eyes. "Yes, Highness," she said flatly. "I am sending it now."

In Tal's arms, the Destroyer spasmed again. She inhaled once, a sharp, shallow sound that Tal was surprised to have heard over the commotion. He looked down at her: wreathed in destruction and trembling with it, flames lapping angrily over the whole of her body. The smell of burning fabric wafted up. Both her clothing and his were beginning to singe as whatever invisible barrier that protected them began to corrode. She had never been burned by her own magic before. Tal knew, to his bones, that this could only mean she was about to lose control entirely. From what Sarai had said, that would be fatal for anyone nearby. For him, certainly... and potentially also for the Destroyer, if she could no longer protect herself from her own power.

Those who live by the rule of fear shall die by it as well, thought Tal, and immediately hated that his last thought would be a scripture.

The Destroyer's eyes snapped open then, unfocused and unseeing. She inhaled again. This time when she exhaled, it was on a scream. Her back arched so violently that Tal had to scramble to keep his hold on her.

Around them, the contours of the train suddenly blurred. All of the metal went bluish and gleaming. The train juddered, its components humming in a low metallic choir as the emergency teleportation magics began to take hold.

Looking down at the Destroyer screaming in his arms, Tal knew it would be too late.

Her eyes suddenly focused. Her gaze snapped to his. He closed his eyes, because she had owned his life for two years; she would not own his death, too.

He thought of Nyx.

He thought of home.

And then the Destroyer's magics exploded out of her, and Tal thought of nothing at all.

CHAPTER SIX

WHEN THE GIRL WOKE, A GRAY SNOW WAS FALLING, AND the world was silent in the way it only ever was in the aftermath of a great cataclysm.

She lay on her back for a long moment, enfolded in an empty sort of peace. The sky above her was an even darker charcoal than the snow. The clouds grew ponderous while she watched, lumbering in and out of her field of vision, their fat dark bellies scraping against the saw-toothed mountains that surrounded her. A blizzard was imminent—but for now, the strange and lovely snowflakes were drifting on the merest of breezes, and she had the sudden impulse to stick out her tongue and taste one. So she did.

It didn't dissolve the way she'd expected but was instead uncomfortably hot and horribly bitter. In a fit of shock, she thrust herself onto her side and up on her elbows and spat into the snow. Not a snowflake at all; it was ash. And she was covered in it.

She jolted to her feet, shaking out her hair and her clothing—which was charred and burned through in spots, and definitely not warm enough—with an unfamiliar sort of desperation. She didn't want to be covered in ash.

Her gaze caught on a twisted piece of blackened wood that might have been part of a column. She paused. She raised her head and, for the first time since waking, looked at her surroundings.

She stood in the middle of a pit. Tall snow walls curved around her, pocked here and there with smoking, twisted debris that was slowly melting its way to the frozen earth. Lying half a dozen feet away was a chunk of something that looked like it might once have been a train wheel. The ground beneath her feet sparkled coldly, not with frost but with glass, shattered to dust and shards.

A great cataclysm, she'd thought earlier, but she realized now she had no idea what it had been.

She frowned. She reached for the memory, but only emptiness greeted her. Her brow wrinkled and her concentration turned inward as she dug deeper, rummaging for a memory that might spark more recollection, but nothing came at all, not even her own name. After a moment she shook her head. It would return to her eventually, in the way that memories did, when she wasn't trying so hard to search for it. In the meantime, there were more urgent things she needed to be doing. It was freezing, and a blizzard seemed to be looming on the horizon, and she was, as far as she could tell, alone. She needed to—what? Build some sort of shelter? Calculate her location based on the stars, or the alignment of the mountain peaks, or...something?

She suddenly realized she was not well-versed in matters of wilderness survival.

She huffed an irritated breath, which clouded the air for a moment before dissipating. Her apparent lack of specific knowledge aside, she did possess a basic grasp of logic, and that was all she needed to be able to address her most pressing concerns. Shelter would be important, as would warmth and food. She should attempt to ascertain her location too, though the stars would be of little help there, both because they were hidden behind the heavy clouds and because she had no idea what their arrangements meant with regard to her position. First things first, though, she needed to climb out of this pit so she could get a better look at her surroundings. Perhaps something up there might give her a clue to what had happened to her, or jog her memories.

She turned in a circle, glass crunching beneath her boots, eyeing the walls of snow as she considered the best path by which to reach the top. There was one slope that seemed both slightly shallower and pocked with fewer bits of debris that might have melted and caused instability in the wall, so she strode to that section and began her climb. She learned quickly that she had to punch her hands and the toes of her boots hard into the snow, as it wasn't snow at all but permafrost, compacted tightly and slick as ice in some places. Her arms began to tremble after only a few seconds of being off the ground, and by the time she was halfway up, her breath was coming as hard as if she'd been sprinting.

She gritted her teeth. She would not be defeated by *snow*. She gathered her strength and punched her hand harder than usual into the frost for her next handhold—and yelped aloud when her fist sank straight through a patch of mostly-melted snow and into something sharp. She yanked her hand back out with a wince and inspected it. Her knuckles were raw already from punching through the permafrost, but now there was a jagged wound in the side of her palm just above her wrist. Dark red blood leaked from it, trickling down the lines in her hand like tiny rivers.

She stared at the blood. Something in her mind lurched at the sight. *Wrong,* it whispered. She squinted harder at her palm, trying to lure that little voice out further, but it vanished. She growled in frustration. What was wrong about her blood? Was she worried about infection? Did she have some sort of hemorrhaging disorder that made bleeding deadly? Did it simply make her squeamish?

Not the last one, she decided. Somehow, she didn't think she was a squeamish person at all.

As she'd been examining her injury, she'd had to support most of her weight on her other arm, and now suddenly its strength gave out. She tumbled three feet to the ground and twisted her ankle in the process. She lurched back to standing with a snarl and marched to the base of the wall, hands curled into fists—which reminded her with a bolt of pain that she was injured.

There was a length of torn fabric dangling from one of her shoulders, the remnants of some sort of cape or cloak. She tore a strip of it off and wrapped it clumsily around her injured hand, tying it as securely as she could and then wondering whether the binding ought to be kept loose instead. Apparently her medical expertise was as limited as her wilderness survival skills. She left the makeshift bandage tight and then sat down in the glass dust to take off her boots. They had tall, elegantly curving heels that made them objects of beauty, and would now also make them objects of great use. She turned them around and drove them heel-first into the wall before her. They carved handholds about as well as punching the permafrost had, and saved her any further injury. She was breathing harder than ever now, and her entire body was trembling with effort, but she pushed herself onward remorselessly and soon reached the spot where she'd fallen before.

She paused to peer at the melted hole where she'd been injured. A bit of debris was in there, gleaming silver. Curious, she secured her current footholds more deeply—doing her best to ignore the freezing-cold snow melting into her socks—and then carefully freed one hand to reach into the hole.

She drew out a twisted black crown.

It was a beautiful thing, delicately wrought, made for someone with a petite brow. The design brought to mind brambles and thorns—which was why, she thought dryly, it had gouged a hole in her hand. It didn't look familiar but it did look valuable, which meant that she might be able to either fetch a reward for returning it to its owner or perhaps sell it if—*when*—she extracted herself from whatever situation she was currently in and returned to civilization. In any case, it was light enough to cause her no trouble to carry. Moving carefully so as not to upset her footing, she tore the rest of the cape off her shoulder and tied the crown to her belt with it before continuing upward.

When at last she hauled herself—slowly, painfully, powered by sheer grit of will—over the top of the snowy wall, she flopped onto her back and did not move for several long minutes. Snow melted beneath her and seeped through her tunic. Her breaths came in long shudders and her muscles burned in a way that said her regrets would run deep tomorrow. But today, she had accomplished the first of the tasks set before her, and she was, for a brief but fierce moment, proud of herself.

The feeling was alien. She prodded at the edges of it cautiously.

A light scratching sound, like tiny claws on ice, pulled her from her thoughts. She raised her head and looked around.

She was surrounded by debris, a stain of catastrophe on the otherwise pristine landscape. Shards of half-melted metal thrusted up from the frost like twisted trees. Unrecognizable bits of char littered the ground. The trail of destruction led upward to a mountain slope some distance above, where she could make out train tracks. The beams and rails had been laid into a wide notch carved into the mountainside.

The craftsmanship of it was exquisite, she noted, or at least it must have been before whatever had happened. The tracks were utterly ruined now; a good fifty feet of them were simply gone, a crater pocking the side of the mountain where that section had been. Still, though, those tracks had to lead *somewhere*. She could follow them and be assured of eventually reaching whatever destination she had originally been travelling to, or from. It was very good news indeed.

The scratching sounded again. She glanced around in search of it, and that was when she saw the bodies. There were perhaps a dozen of them. Many had been burned to unrecognizability, but some seemed to have died not from whatever explosion or fire had caused the...train wreck, she guessed it must have been...but had instead been impaled by debris or killed upon impact with the ground. The snow steamed red all around her.

Some of the bodies, she noted, still wore clothing that could be salvaged. And hers was soaked through and highly impractical in any case, made of formerly fine fabric that aimed for beauty rather than warmth. Her boots, in particular, would need to be replaced. They weren't practical at all for walking on snow. If she was very lucky she might even find a pair of warmer socks.

Keeping an eye out for the source of the scratching, she moved toward a body whose clothing seemed mostly intact. It had been a woman, a kitchen servant from the looks of her uniform. Her feet looked to be about the right size, and her tunic was warm and sensible, though her trousers were too shredded to be of use. Quickly, Elodie stripped the body down and changed, trying to minimize the time her bare skin spent exposed to the frigid air. The boots were a touch too big but spread her weight much more evenly atop the frost. The tunic smelled like smoke but she supposed that was the least of her worries.

The scratching sounded again. She followed the noise quickly enough this time to be able to spot its source: a stoat, its fur a gorgeous ermine white, its little claws skittering against the crusted ground as it made off with the mangled body of a snow hare. The hare was singed, one leg missing, and it was nearly decapitated with its head dangling from just a few strips of flesh—another casualty of the wreck, likely killed by debris.

Food had been on her list of immediate needs. The hare would do nicely; she already knew she would make a miserable hunter and might succumb to starvation if she was forced to rely on her own skills, but here was a meal ready-made. All she had to do was retrieve it from the stoat. Or perhaps kill the stoat, if she could manage it. Then she would have two meals. Perhaps she could find some way to use the fur too. A pair of mitts, maybe. Her hands were freezing.

She scanned the wreckage for anything that might serve as a weapon. She settled on a shard of metal about as long as her forearm. Its edges were sharp enough to cut her hand as well as the stoat, so she tore off the sleeve of her discarded tunic and made a wrapped hilt from it. All the time, she kept her gaze locked on the stoat, who stared fearlessly back. It twitched its nose, likely trying to scent her. Was she down-wind? She had no idea.

It didn't matter. She was far bigger and stronger than the tiny creature, and more importantly, she was desperate.

She crept slowly forward, clutching her clumsy weapon in her good hand. The stoat flicked its whiskers at her and scampered away, dragging the bloodied hare–which was several times larger than the stoat itself–behind. She followed the track it was taking and spotted a neatly-dug hole in the snow not far ahead. Its den, likely. If it made it into that tunnel there was no way she'd be able to catch it. The stoat apparently came to the same conclusion as her, because its lurching movements hastened as it bounded across the snow toward the den.

She cursed. Throwing stealth to the wind, she sprinted after it and then dove the last few feet. The stoat had made it to the tunnel and was tugging the hare in after it.

"No you don't!" she shouted, grabbing onto the rear half of the rabbit and yanking. The stoat growled at her from within its den. She growled back, pulling harder. A wet tearing noise sounded and she flopped suddenly backwards, the rabbit still in her hands. Well–most of the rabbit. It was now completely headless. The stoat popped its nose back out of the tunnel, hissed at her, and then vanished, snatching up the fallen rabbit head on its way.

She stood, holding her trophy aloft and grinning in triumph. She'd won half a rabbit and one more day of survival. If, of course, she could find some way to prepare her meal. She would eat it raw if she had to but she much preferred it roasted, and she would soon need a fire—and a shelter—for warmth in any case. The sky had darkened further and the wind was beginning to pick up, fat white snowflakes mixing with the still-falling ash now. She also still needed to find some thicker trousers to replace her thin, snow-soaked ones. The rabbit dangling from one hand, she set off on her new mission.

The first two bodies she passed were too mangled and bloody for their clothing to be of any use. One of them, though, did have a beautifully tooled dagger still sheathed at his waist. The thing was obviously ornamental and had never seen any actual use, but it was far better than her metal shard weapon, and she might be able to sell it along with the crown later too. She shoved the large body over to unbuckle the belt and then drew it around her own waist, having to tie an awkward knot to secure it, as she was far smaller than the dead man.

Her gaze caught on another body, and she straightened, casting an assessing eye over it as she approached. This one was a younger man, perhaps even around her own age. His clothing—and most importantly, his trousers—were singed through in spots but still plenty useable, of quite high quality and thick enough to give her more protection from the coming blizzard. Even better, he had two short swords sheathed at the small of his back. She didn't want to weigh herself down too much, but she also would feel far less vulnerable if she had proper weapons, even if she had little idea of how to actually wield them.

She knelt next to the body. He didn't seem to have been as badly injured as most of the others. The only sign of trauma was his left leg, which was twisted beneath him at an angle that could only mean a broken bone. The boy's face was unmarred–and, she mused, beautiful in a tragic sort of way. Strands of dark hair splayed over his forehead and hid his eyes. A sudden impulse surged through her: she wondered what color those eyes had been. Curious, she reached out and brushed his hair to the side.

His eyes snapped open. They were green, she noted in a moment of shock before his hand jerked upward and latched onto her wrist, locking her in place.

CHAPTER SEVEN

A JOLT OF UTTER PANIC SHOT THROUGH HER. SHE WAS defenseless. He'd moved quicker than thought, and the muscles cording along his forearm meant he was far stronger than her. She couldn't reach her stolen dagger when she was bent over like this—the attempt to do so would likely topple her, putting her even more at a disadvantage against this boy. She shouted in wordless panic and lifted a hand to strike him, hoping to surprise him enough to loosen his grip so she could get away.

Those sharp green eyes jerked from her face to her raised hand. He reacted as quickly as he had a moment ago, releasing her wrist instantly and turning his face away, closing his eyes and bracing his shoulders as if anticipating a blow from someone much stronger than her.

Hand still raised, she paused. He looked...painfully defenseless. The way she'd felt a moment ago.

She dropped her hand and scrambled backwards, putting enough space between them that he wouldn't be able to get to her without standing, which he wouldn't be able to do very quickly on that leg. Then she stopped and stared down at the boy.

He took a shuddering breath, eyes still squeezed shut. The hand that had gripped her wrist a moment ago was now splayed white-knuckled on the snow, as if he was still bracing himself for a blow.

"Are you well?" she asked before she could stop herself, and winced at how ridiculous her question sounded. Of course he wasn't well. He was in obvious pain. No wonder, if he'd survived the train wreck. It was a miracle that she herself had somehow escaped it unscathed. With the exception of her memory, obviously.

The boy didn't open his eyes. "My leg is broken," he said flatly, his voice hoarse and cracking.

"Oh. Of course," she replied, feeling foolish again. She cleared her throat. What was she supposed to do now? Snow was whipping all around her, beginning to fall more thickly. She needed to find or build a shelter as soon as possible. Trying to help this boy would only slow her down. Still, she didn't move. As far as she could tell they were the only two survivors of the wreck. That meant they were in this together. And more importantly, she realized suddenly, she didn't *want* to leave him. She didn't want him to die, which he certainly would, alone with a broken leg in a mountain blizzard. But helping him would be hard to manage too, and not only because of her lack of skills. Their first introduction a moment ago had been a bit of a disaster, and now she was simply standing and gawking at him while he kept his eyes tightly shut, bracing himself against the pain he was obviously in.

She hesitated a moment, uncertain of how to improve matters. Perhaps lightening the mood might help? She held up her amateurishly bandaged hand, then motioned to his broken leg and tried for a smile. "I'm afraid I'm not much use with medical treatments, but I could probably manage a mercy killing if you'd prefer."

His eyes opened. He turned his head and looked at her, though his face was expressionless. "What do you *want*?" he asked roughly, his tone raw.

Unsettled by the unexpected emotion in his voice, she took a step back. "I just wanted your pants," she said before she could think better of it.

The boy stared. A bit of an expression–incredulity, confusion–leaked into his features. Then, suddenly, his gaze sharpened. "Your eyes," he said. "They're brown."

She pursed her lips, glancing from him to the ominous sky. "And yours are green. Now that we are finished stating obvious facts, we need to find some shelter and quickly, unless you prefer that mercy killing after all."

He was still staring at her. The mercy-killing witticism had apparently not landed as planned. Perhaps an introduction might help move matters along, so he would stop gaping at her and lend a hand, or at least some expertise. Of course, she couldn't actually remember her own identity, but maybe trying to introduce herself might jar it back to mind.

"My name is..." she started, and then jerked in surprise when the memory of a voice whispered, *Do you hear me,* Elodie?

She blinked. The words were a memory—a recent one, from the strength of it. A surge of triumph mingled with unease low in her stomach. She had finally recovered something of herself, but whoever had spoken those words in that shred of memory sounded furious. Furious at *her,* and broken with it.

What had happened on that train?

"Elodie," she finished, forcing her mind back to the moment at hand. "I think, anyway. What's yours?"

The boy frowned. His brow crinkled when he did that. "Tal," he said slowly.

Finally, they were making progress. "Well, Tal," she said, "I possess an ornamental dagger, a crown, and half a rabbit. What can you contribute to our shared survival?"

He eased himself up onto his elbow, his movements and expression still cautious and confused. Perhaps his memories had been jarred in the course of the wreck too. "Why... do you have half a rabbit?" he asked, eyeing the corpse dangling from her hand. She lifted it up, still proud of her victory.

"I got in a tug-war with a stoat," she said. "I won. Mostly." She looked back at Tal, assessing his bearing, his muscles, his soldier-like clothing. "You look like a young man who knows how to start a fire. And perhaps hunt?" she added hopefully.

"We'll need both, if we're going to make our triumphant return to civilization." Transport would be a concern too, especially with his leg, but that was a concern for after the blizzard passed.

Tal's brow crinkled more deeply. "You need me. To start a fire?"

She narrowed her eyes. Was he mocking her? Or perhaps he didn't know how to start a fire either. "Never mind," she said shortly. "I'm certain I can figure it out." She tossed the rabbit onto his lap, where it landed with a squelching sound. "While I do that—and find a passable place for us to weather the blizzard without freezing to death—you can put those blades to use and skin this."

Without waiting for an answer, she turned and marched away. The silence at her back lay heavy on her shoulders, which was how she knew he was staring after her. A thought struck her and she turned back. "Do you...you don't know me, do you? Did we interact at all on the train? Or before that?" Perhaps that was why he was acting so standoffish. She tried to strangle the hope that bloomed in her chest—if he was acting standoffish because he knew her, and not because he *didn't* know her, that hardly boded well—but hope was a weed hard to kill. She wanted to remember herself, even if it also meant remembering why this boy seemed to dislike her so much.

But: "No," Tal said, finality ringing in his voice. "We don't know each other at all."

It turned out disappointment made a fine weed killer. "Of course." She hesitated. "Do you remember where the train was going? Where it came from?" Maybe that could give her some hints, at least.

He shifted, gritting his teeth at the pain the movement caused as his broken leg bent further beneath him.

"You shouldn't be moving around," she interjected.

"I'm fine," he snapped.

She crossed her arms and made ready to fire back a retort, but before she could, he held up the hare by its back legs. "I can't skin a rabbit with a sword," he said in a level, utterly emotionless tone that told her he must be feeling quite a lot of emotions indeed. "Give me your dagger."

Fear feathered along her spine. Her fingers curled, nails digging into her palms. "I'm not giving you my only weapon. How do I know you won't turn on me while I'm defenseless—"

"*Defenseless?*" he scoffed, incredulity breaking through his emotionless mask for a scant instant.

She uncrossed her arms with a violent movement, true anger finally snapping to life within her. "Listen," she hissed, stalking forward a step so she loomed over him, "I have been nothing but considerate to you. I could have left you here to die, and come back to steal your trousers when you were a frozen block in the bloody snow. Instead I offer you a portion of *my* hare, and a spot by the fire that *I* will figure out how to start, and am willing to build a shelter *by myself* that you may share, and you offer nothing in return except surliness and threats."

He dropped the hare back onto the snow. "I have never threatened you," he said flatly.

She snorted. "You threaten with your every glance. Your every word. You think I can't see it in your eyes, hear it in the evenness of your voice? You are bitter. A rage stalks you that has nothing to do with me. So yes, of course, I suspect that you might stab me while I am defenseless and take for your own all of the things I have already freely offered to share."

He looked away and took a steadying breath. Then he gazed back at her, those green dark eyes a nameless accusation. "I will protect you, and not allow harm to come to you, and never harm you myself. Is that good enough for you?" Bitterness leeched every word drought-dry, revealing the bare bones of truth beneath. He didn't like what he said, but he wasn't lying.

"I don't know how you expect to 'protect me' in your condition," she said, mollified slightly, "but I appreciate the sentiment." She drew her dagger from its sheath and tossed it at him. Alarmed, he jerked sideways just in time to avoid being impaled by it. It made a crunching sound when it sank into the snow two inches from his neck. She tried to look regal and slightly intimidating, as if that had been exactly what she'd meant to do rather than an unthinking and nearly disastrous accident, and once again turned her back on him.

Shelter. She needed to focus on finding a shelter.

She scanned the landscape before her, focusing now not on the bodies but on the debris. There was one mostly-flat sheet of blackened metal not too far off that she could perhaps...lean up against another piece of metal? She shook her head, displeased with that idea. Even if she found a convenient coil of rope and more useable sheet metal, there was no way she would be able to build a passable lean-to in time. They needed something secure, and insulated if at all possible. Wind bit cold on her face already, flushing her skin, building to a low howl in the distance. Time was growing short.

The mountainside sloped sharply downward not far away. She slogged her way through the snow, boots breaking through the crust every few steps, to get a better look at what lay below. Perhaps extra debris, or the rest of the train and more helpful survivors, might be down there. But when she reached the edge of the slope, what she saw was even better: a distant dark hole in the craggy mountainside that could only be a cave.

Excellent. A cave would be both secure and insulated. But now that she'd solved one problem, another became more urgent. How was she to get Tal all the way down there? The slope was treacherously steep. If he tried to walk down, even with her helping, he was likely to injure himself even worse. And that was if they could make it in time without getting lost once the blizzard began in earnest.

Maybe a crutch might make his descent safer. She turned in a slow circle, peering again at the debris field, searching this time for a rod or long piece of wood. Then her eyes fell once again to the mostly-flat sheet of metal she'd already collected. She tilted her head and narrowed her eyes, then walked up to it and gave it a light push. It moved easily across the snow. She grinned, and then began gathering wood.

By the time she returned to Tal, she was proudly dragging the metal over the snow with a rope made of clumsily tied-together—and bloodstained—clothing. Atop her homemade sled was a stack of wood fragments she'd gathered from the debris: a bit of door panel here, a mostly-intact floorboard there. From the size of the pile she guessed it would hopefully last at least a few hours as firewood.

She dropped the clothing-rope and gazed down at Tal. He'd been busy while she was gone. The rabbit had been not only skinned but carved apart, bones dropped in a pile and meat wrapped up in a bundle of fur. It was an impressive job—not that she was about to inform him of that—but also a messy one. The hare's blood had gotten everywhere, including all over his trousers. Though of course she couldn't be sure how much of that blood was the hare's and how much was his.

He hadn't looked up yet from where he sat cleaning her dagger, though she had to assume he'd heard her approach.

"I've found shelter," she announced, raising her voice to be heard over the growing wind. "And transport. *And* firewood."

Tal looked at the sled. His eyes fell to the rope made of clothing and his lips tightened. "So you're a corpse robber now."

"That's what you're worried about? How about the fact that *we* are about to become corpses if we don't get moving?"

He was still looking at the clothing. His gaze was intense, as if he were trying to pick out details in the bloodstained fabric. He hesitated then, looked at her and then away. "Is there…" He cleared his throat. "How many bodies?" he asked, sounding brisk and businesslike, which didn't fool her at all.

"Around a dozen, perhaps more," she answered cautiously. "Surely you're not squeamish? I thought you were a soldier, from the looks of you. You have to have seen dead bodies before. But if you like, you can close your eyes while I help you onto the sled."

"I am a bodyguard," he said quietly, "and I have seen many dead bodies."

She turned around and gazed across the snow. She couldn't see all of the bodies now, as the snow was falling more thickly, but she had a good eye for detail and had given each at least a cursory glance. She had begun to understand what Tal meant to ask, and decided to help him along. "You're looking for someone. If you describe them to me, I can tell you whether they were among the bodies I searched."

He gritted his teeth. His jaw worked. He was trying very hard to say something difficult, or perhaps working to not say something. At last, he spoke. "She's two years older than me. Brown skin. Long hair—" Here he stopped abruptly and took a deep breath before continuing, his hands curling into fists in the snow. "—short hair," he corrected. "Dark brown eyes."

Elodie quickly shook her head. "No one like that was among the bodies."

Tal's whole body sagged. He raised a hand as if to cover his eyes, but then saw how bloodied it was and dropped it back to his lap. "Then she may have made it back," he said roughly, but his voice was still nearly as tense as before.

Elodie finally asked the question that had been nagging at her. "Tal, what happened on that train?"

He picked up the bundle of rabbit fur and meat and tucked it into his shirt. He rose up on his good knee, balancing with one hand on the ground and wincing as he tried to leverage himself up. "There was an explosion," he said shortly. "It destroyed the dining car."

Elodie ducked down to help him, pulling his arm over her shoulders so she could support some of his weight. He went stiff but didn't protest. "Do you know what caused it?"

"No."

His answer was sharp in a way that told Elodie he didn't want to talk about it further. She supposed he couldn't be blamed for that. She helped him get to his feet, hunching her shoulders against the wind as she did so. When he tried to take a step, he let out a sharp breath and went alarmingly pale. He squeezed his eyes shut. Beneath her arm, he shuddered in pain.

She tightened her hold on him, feeling strangely helpless once again. If only she had any medical knowledge at all, or even, she was willing to admit, a more keenly-tuned sense of empathy, she would be better at helping him. But no, she had to throw knives at him and accuse him of squeamishness.

She could distract him from the pain, at least. "You said you were a bodyguard. So whose body did you guard?" She helped him take a hobbling step onto the sled, where he quickly sank down, resting his back against the wood pile. He didn't answer her question; something else he didn't want to discuss, apparently. She dropped the subject and gave up on her attempt at distraction. Instead, she grabbed a few pieces of less-bloody clothing that hadn't been woven into the rope and dropped them on top of him like a blanket. He gave her a strange look.

Feeling self-conscious, she shrugged. "The slope we're going down is steep, and the wind is strong. You should stay warm."

He didn't answer, but he did tug the clothing more snugly around himself.

She grabbed the rope with her uninjured hand and started forward. The sled was heavier now with Tal on it, but she refused to be stymied, and threw all of her weight into dragging it toward the slope. By the time they reached it, the wind was nearly gale-force, and the snow blinded her to anything further than a few yards away.

She pulled the sled to the very edge of the slope, tossed the rope onto the metal, then sat down in front of Tal. Then she waited. She hadn't told Tal her plan yet, mostly because her plan involved travelling at inadvisably high speeds down a dangerously steep slope with no safety belts or braking mechanisms. Any moment now, he was going to question her wisdom. She readied her retort.

Tal squinted past her. He exhaled, and he was close enough now that his warm breath brushed over her cheek before the wind snatched it away. "Where are we going?" he asked, raising his voice to be heard.

"There's a cave at the base of the slope."

He raised one eyebrow, still looking past her. "The very steep slope? That you are no doubt planning for us to career down, on a slab of decrepit metal, in the midst of a blinding blizzard?"

She drew herself up to sit straighter and raised her own voice above the wind. "I know exactly where the cave is, if you are insinuating that I'm going to get us lost. And it's not the 'midst' of the blizzard. It hasn't even truly gotten started yet."

"But you have no answer to the 'decrepit metal' or 'career down' accusations."

Her lips thinned out, and she inhaled to begin her prepared arguments. But before she could, he brusquely shook his head and leaned back against the wood. "It's not as if I'll dissuade you," he said.

She smiled. "Quite true."

His gaze lingered on her expression for a long moment before he looked away, that expressionless mask of his firmly back in place.

She stuck out one leg and pushed to move the sled forward until they were teetering on the edge of the slope. The world lay before her, veiled thickly in snow. An unfamiliar exhilaration juddered through her bones as the sled slowly tipped beneath her. The world seemed to hold its breath; everything was frozen and glittering and full of possibility. And then they tilted all the way forward, and flew.

The wind was a roaring beast, flinging snow like grit against her skin, frosting her lips and cheeks. The landscape was a cacophony of gray and white and speed. She squinted through the ice that had begun to coat her eyelashes, trying to keep her gaze—and the sled—trained on the spot where the cave was bored into the mountainside. Behind her, the wood rattled in its pile, and a few pieces slipped out before Tal threw out an arm to secure the rest.

The exhilaration strengthened. She felt odd up here–deliciously powerful and utterly out of control at the same time. The feeling was alien but amazing. A wild laugh rioted its way out of her, and then she gave in wholly and whooped a shouted cheer.

The sled began to twist sideways. Behind her, Tal growled a curse and thrust one arm down into the snow to try to slow them and right their angle of descent. But they were moving too fast, and the effort nearly tore him from his seat.

Elodie risked taking her eyes off their path to throw a glance back to her passenger. "Stop that!" she shouted. "You'll hurt yourself!"

"I am aware," he called through gritted teeth, and did not withdraw his hand.

He began to slip sideways. Elodie quickly calculated their trajectory and speed. They were quite close to the cave now, and although they'd slowed somewhat, if Tal fell off he was certain to further worsen his injuries. With her own shouted curse, she made a decision.

Letting go of the rope that she'd been clutching, she lunged backwards, wrapping her arms around Tal. The movement sent the sled into a wild spin that flung them both off–but she twisted around so that she hit the snow first, with him landing atop her, cushioned from the worst of the blow.

They skidded down the slope, with Elodie just barely managing to avoid a head-over-heels tumble that would surely harm Tal. He was rigid in her arms, so much that she worried the crash had already jarred him into further injury. She dug the heels of her boots into the snow to slow them down until they finally came to a halt. The mountainside loomed only a few yards away, a slab of slate gray through the sheet of blowing snow. The cave was a dark, gaping maw in its side.

"What," said Tal, in a low and dangerous voice, "are you doing?"

She eased him off of her and stood up, brushing the snow from her clothes before it could melt through. "Saving your life," she snapped, exasperated. "Again. Though I suspect I'd be a fool to expect gratitude."

"Stop *touching* me."

"Of course, I will respect your wishes," she bit out, raising her voice to be heard above the wind. "Enjoy walking the rest of the way to the cave by yourself on a broken leg."

She glanced around for the sled. It was coming to a stop not too far away, but all of their precious firewood was now scattered across the lower third of the slope. She'd have to hurry in order to gather it back up before the weather buried it or made navigation impossible. Then she squinted, pausing in her assessment. A smear of red was moving across the snow. A fox—rusty-crimson, with patches of white winter fur coming in—was darting away. The bundle of hare meat dangled from its mouth.

"No!" Elodie shouted, charging through the snow at the creature. She waved her arms madly, hoping to scare it away. "Drop that this instant!" The recalcitrant fox did not obey, instead breaking into a faster lope, and within moments vanished within the veil of the oncoming blizzard.

Elodie stormed back to where Tal was attempting to ease himself to standing. He didn't look up at her, only asked, "Am I correct in assuming that fox just made off with our entire store of food?"

"Yes. I despise wildlife."

He nodded and continued trying to push himself off the snow. His face was grim and beaded with sweat. She wasn't sure what that indicated, but knew enough to understand that sweating in a snowstorm couldn't possibly be a good sign. Frustrated with his obstinance, she thought quickly, trying to come up with some way to convince him to allow her to help. Earlier he had sworn to protect her, to allow no harm to come to her. She had no real reason to trust that he'd meant what he said—people were untrustworthy in general, and as prone to betrayal as that thieving fox—but somehow, she had a suspicion this boy put a high value on duty. Which was sheer foolishness, in her opinion, but she could use it to both their advantage now.

"You vowed to protect me," she said, crossing her arms. "You can hardly accomplish that if you insist on dragging yourself through the snow without assistance, likely worsening your injury even further. You need to be in as good a shape as possible to defend my person."

He paused. His jaw tensed and his hands curled into fists, as if he were fighting something internal. Then he let out a long breath and slumped. "It seems I have no choice."

She swooped in and tucked her arm around him again, bracing him until he staggered up to standing at her side. His body was rigid and tense wherever she touched him. No matter. He didn't have to relax, only survive. Together, they hobbled slowly toward the cave. The wind cut out as soon as they entered, and although it was still freezing and also smelled far worse than it had outside, Elodie breathed a sigh of sheer relief. Safety, at last.

She carefully lowered Tal to sit against one of the slightly-damp walls. The air here was caustic with the bite of mildew, rotting vegetation, and decaying...something. Perhaps a wild animal or two had sheltered here during the last snowstorm and then perished. It wasn't the most encouraging thought. "Maybe it will smell better in here once we start the fire," she murmured.

The cave was laden with gloom and her eyes were still adjusting, but she spotted a gleam of silver and heard the rasp when Tal unsheathed one of his swords. She stilled for a moment, feeling like that hare must have when the deadly debris was hurtling toward it. She keenly felt the absence of the dagger's weight at her waist and recalled, too late, that Tal had never returned it to her. Had she misjudged him after all, and he was as prone to betrayal as she ought to have suspected? Was this the moment he would turn against her? Surely he knew how foolish that was. Surely his need for her outweighed his obvious distaste for her company.

Tal exhaled a breath that turned to mist and hung in the air between them. "I'll keep watch," he explained, eyes on the cave's entrance. "It smells bad in here because something carnivorous has been using this as a den. Hopefully it won't return before the blizzard is over."

Elodie's dread evaporated. It left behind a vast tiredness that weighted her marrow and made her want to curl up and sleep right where she stood. Fear, she reflected, was exhausting. She much preferred the weightless exhilaration of her sled ride.

"Of course," she replied, managing to sound mostly normal and not as if she'd momentarily been planning how she might kill him before he could waylay her.

She fled back into the blizzard. Three steps out of the cave, she stumbled on one of the bits of bloodied clothing that Tal had used as a blanket before their crash, and she stopped to wrap it around her head like a macabre scarf. Then she went in search of the wood. She forged through the growing blank whiteness of the storm for as long as she dared, periodically returning to the cave with her armfuls of kindling and occasionally another piece of the lost clothing, before Tal stopped her.

"The blizzard has grown too much," he said. "Stay inside now."

Irritation prickled. She filed that away under the category of things she'd learned about herself: she didn't like being ordered about. But he was right, so she stomped the snow off her boots and dropped her current load of firewood atop the rest.

Time to start the fire. Purposefully not looking at Tal, and trying to seem as decisive as possible, she unhesitatingly grabbed a chunk of wooden floor tiling about the size of her arm. She sat down on the freezing rock and placed the wood in front of her, then reviewed what facts she could infer about fire-starting. Ideally, she'd have some sort of magical mechanism that could provide a spark, or a piece of...what was it? Some sort of stone that could be struck to make a flame? Flint, that was what it was called. But she had nothing like that, so it would have to be friction that would start her fire. The question now was how to create enough friction to actually make a spark.

She dared to quickly glance at Tal. His attention was fixated on the cave's entry in a way that told her the whole of his attention belonged to her current activities. Her skin prickled in embarrassment and she snatched up another piece of wood at random—a long piece of door framing—and rubbed it as fast and hard as she could against the side of the floor tile.

A smothered choking sound alarmed her. She glanced up, and in the dim gray light saw that Tal was *laughing* at her. From his shocked expression, the laughter had caught him by surprise as much as it had her, and she had only a moment to marvel at how completely humor had transformed his features before his gaze went hard again.

On the heels of her surprise flashed a jolt of anger—how dare he mock her efforts to save them both?—before that too quickly fizzled out under the weight of her tiredness and worry and shame. She dropped the wood, turned her face away from him, and cried.

She did it without making a sound. It was easy, as if she had practiced it often. Her tears did nothing to ease the turmoil of feelings twining around her chest, and the tracks of wetness on her cheeks only chilled her further. Crying was foolish. She should stop immediately.

She couldn't.

A long moment passed. "Are you giving up?" Tal asked, his tone a challenge. "I hadn't thought you the type."

"Be silent," she snapped, but her voice was too strangled to make the command as sharp as she wanted it to be.

There was a long quiet. In it, Elodie felt Tal realize that she was crying, and debate what, if anything, he ought to do about it. Her shame curled its roots deeper. She was not some defenseless maiden who needed to guilt a boy into saving her. Except, apparently, she was. She had proven utterly useless; she had failed to rescue their only food from a mere fox, failed to start a fire, failed to even remember more about herself than her first name. They would both die here and it would be her fault.

"You're starting too big," Tal said.

She took a deep, shaky breath, trying again to force her tears to cease through sheer willpower. "What?"

"The wood. The pieces you're trying to start a fire with, they're too big. You need to break one up into kindling—much smaller pieces, about the size of twigs."

If she listened very carefully to his voice, she could almost hear a kernel of kindness in it. She didn't want to need his kindness but it warmed her nevertheless, which irritated her further. But at least it also managed to stop her crying. "Oh, now you have useful advice," she muttered, but did as he said. The wood had already been cracked and splintered by the explosion and broke apart easily, and the bits from the inside of it were dry, untouched by the snow. Soon a pile of wood slivers sat before her.

"Fire needs oxygen," Tal told her next. "Arrange the kindling so that air can circulate through it."

She leaned the pieces up against each other, building a small, flattened cone-line structure. She sat back. "Now w-what?" she asked, her teeth clattering together as she shivered. The temperature was beginning to drop sharply.

"Take one of the longer sticks and put it between your hands—no, flatten your hands out—there. Now rub your hands back and forth to make the stick spin."

She followed his instructions, her brow crinkling as she concentrated. She put the stick against a slightly larger piece of wood, which was in turn placed next to the pile of kindling. Then she repeated the rubbing motion. By the time the wood started to smoke, her palms were full of splinters and her already-injured hand was bleeding once again, but she only hunched her shoulders and bore down harder. She had not been defeated by snow, and she would not be defeated by wood. She would start a fire or die trying.

Then, miraculously, a tiny flame leapt up from the shallow

hole she'd drilled in the wood. "Quickly," Tal told her. "Use one of the twig-sized pieces to move the flame over to the kindling."

Not daring to breathe, she snatched up a splinter and touched it to the flame. The little fire withered down to a barely-visible blue core as she watched, but then caught to the splinter just before it went out. Moving slowly, she slid the now-burning bit of kindling beneath the stack she'd built—and the fire began to spread.

She raised both hands in the air and shouted in victory. She was *not* useless. She had proven it.

A sharp intake of breath sounded from across the cave. "Your hand," Tal said. His voice sounded strange, faraway. Elodie looked up with a frown.

"What?" She glanced at her hands and winced. She'd have plenty of splinters to pick out, and she really ought to rebandage her injury too. Blood was streaked across her palms and down her wrist and had already soaked through one sleeve.

"You're...you're bleeding," Tal said, staring at her hands as if he'd never seen blood before. Perhaps he was squeamish after all. This time, she determined, she wouldn't make fun of him for it. He had just helped her learn how to build a fire, and as she saw it, that could be the start of a fragile truce between them. She was loath to ruin that.

"I am, but not nearly as badly as you were," she said, motioning at his crimson-stained trousers. He didn't respond. He was staring at her bloody hands, shock paling his features, one hand clenched tight around the hilt of his sword as if it was his anchor. "Tal?" she inquired, finally lowering her hands. "Are you well?"

His gaze jerked back to hers and he shook himself. The shock fell away, his features schooled into blankness. "Fine," he said abruptly. "You should rest. I'll keep watch and build the fire up."

"You need to rest too."

"I wouldn't be able to sleep right now," he said, his tone tight.

She shrugged. She was very tired—still recovering from whatever had happened on the train, she supposed, and the trauma of losing her memories—and unwilling to argue further. She curled up on the rocky ground and slept.

CHAPTER EIGHT

THE DESTROYER WAS HAVING A NIGHTMARE. THIS TIME, TAL let her stay in it.

Instead of waking her, he occupied himself with carefully unwinding the bandage wrapped around his broken leg. It was too tight and crusted with the dried hare's blood he'd smeared it with; he'd been in a hurry to hide the silver bloodstains before the Destroyer saw them. But over the last hour or so—while he stared motionlessly at the sleeping "Elodie" over the fire that he had taught her how to build—the injury beneath the makeshift bandage had begun to take on a new and foreboding type of ache. It felt like grains of sand were caught just beneath his skin, gritting against one another every time he moved. He'd known what it had to mean but had delayed checking because he wasn't sure whether he wanted his suspicions to be confirmed, or to be found unmerited.

The bandage peeled away. His injury wasn't overly dramatic, merely a gash the length of his hand. Viscous silver blood leaked slowly from the torn flesh and muscle. The broken bone wasn't visible. But what was visible was far worse: tiny dark-orange flakes peppered throughout the wound, each one producing a lacy, crystalline vein structure that dusted his skin like snowflakes.

Rust phage.

Grimly, he rewrapped the bandage. Such was his luck. Nearly eighteen years of successfully avoiding injuries that would expose his blood to either infection or the metallurgy class, all to be ruined in a single morning.

His choices were few now. He would not heal naturally from this. It was fatal to anyone with metal in their blood in a matter of days. He would grow weaker, and then feverish, and then lose consciousness and ultimately die. A copper Smith would be able to heal him at this early stage, of course, but revealing his illness to any member of the noble class meant revealing his silver magic. And *that* meant death. It had been so for ten years now, ever since a group of silver Smiths failed in their attempt to lead a coup. With the significant advantage of being able to see bits of the future, the rebel faction—which had included both of Tal's parents—had hoped they might finally succeed in overthrowing the nobles. Instead their attempt ended in the empire-sanctioned slaughter of anyone who had silver in their blood. If Tal's secret was revealed, not only would he be executed, but his entire home ward would be punished for illegally sheltering him.

All of this he considered with a remote sort of calm. He felt far away from himself, disconnected from the world as he had understood it. Too many impossible things had happened in too short a time. He could not maintain his shock any longer. He needed to move forward. He needed a plan. But, of course, there was a massive complication to any plan he might come up with, and she was sleeping directly across the fire from him.

The Destroyer. *Elodie.*

An eddy of wind slithered into the cavern, making the fire leap momentarily higher. Sparks hissed into the frosty air. They wreathed Elodie's features, dancing in the space between him and her, framing the tension in her petite jawline and the way her lips twisted in a quiet cry. Hearing the soft, familiar sound made him remember how different she had sounded a few hours ago, when she'd laughed wildly as they careened down the slope. And before that, the unrepentant triumph in her voice when she held that headless hare aloft. *I got in a tug-war with a stoat,* she'd proclaimed. *I won. Mostly.*

His hands curled into fists against the cold stone ground. How dare she be funny? How dare she expect his gratitude? How dare she smile, and banter, and *laugh*, as if she hadn't murdered hundreds of people only the night before and listened without remorse to their screams?

He hadn't thought anything could be worse than protecting the Destroyer, but this was so much worse. Elodie was everything he despised hidden away inside the shell of a girl he might otherwise have admired.

He wanted to be sick as soon as the thought came into his mind. Earlier, once or twice, he'd caught himself talking to her unguardedly as if she really were someone else. He had told himself at the time that it was to keep her from suspecting him and remembering her past, but the truth was, she was treacherously easy to talk to. Her cruel air had been replaced with an oddly innocent ferocity. She spoke differently too—less formal, less measured, unweighted by her own past. He wondered if this was who she might have become, had she not been born the Lady of Mercury.

He shook himself. Her blood might be red now and her eyes brown, but she was yet who she had always been. The fact that his oath still compelled him to protect her proved as much. The question now was, how could she possibly have been so changed?

It had to be a side effect of the poison. Or perhaps this was what the poison had been intended to do—make her forget, render her powerless and weak. He wondered how long it would last. He wanted to hope that it would last as long as possible, but couldn't deny there was a part of him that would rather the Destroyer return soon. If things were far more difficult with her at his side, at least she was easier to hate.

But in the meantime...maybe this situation could prove beneficial.

The idea came together slowly. His oath required that he deliver the Destroyer to safety, which in this case could only mean the Alloyed Palace. But between them and it lay the mountain ward—the Skyteeth, the peaks and alpine valleys he'd once called home. The Saints had an outpost near his old township there. If Tal could tweak his route back to the palace so that he and the Destroyer travelled through his home...then perhaps the Saints would find them, and be enabled to finish their assassination attempt after all.

The Destroyer would be too wary to be led into such a trap and her powers would make springing it too dangerous. Elodie, though, was a different story. She seemed to have no access to her magic. And more, she seemed to have a drive to help him, some sort of warped sense of care for him. He could use that. He could win her trust—and then lead her straight to the Saints. She wouldn't be able to fight back. He would still be bound to try to protect her, but this time the assassins would have an advantage. It might just be enough.

Across the fire, Elodie curled in on herself and shivered violently. The crown she'd tied to her waist rattled on the rocks. Her dark hair slid over her shoulders and splayed in long curls over the stone, exposing her neck to the night air and to him. His hand tightened on the sword at his side. He looked away.

Was it righteous, what he was planning to do? It would be a betrayal akin to murder. He had killed before, so very many times, but this was different. This wasn't something he was being compelled to do; he'd be earning Elodie's trust and then leading her into a trap, and doing everything he could to give the Saints the chance to spring it.

But Elodie—the Destroyer—deserved death. Her soul was crusted black with the blood of good men and women.

The count of her victims might even include Nyx by now. Tal flinched from the thought but forced himself to think it anyway, because it steeled him to the task he'd set before himself.

Helping the Saints kill Elodie might not be righteous. But it was *right*.

And, he recalled suddenly, the Saints would likely have access to a copper Smith who could heal the rust phage, too. The poison Nyx had drank, the toxin that she had then transferred to the Destroyer during her torture, had smelled of hemlock and copper. It had to have been a magical tincture, which could only have been sourced from one of the few copper Smiths who were not members of the metallurgy class. Which meant if Tal went home, the Saints there might be able to save his life in more ways than one.

Decision made, he lay his head back. He didn't sleep, though. He had to stay awake at least until he'd built the fire up enough to last the night, and also, he did not want to face the possibility of another vision. Two years ago, his god had betrayed him to the Destroyer with a promise that he would be the one to save her, and save the kingdom through her. Tal's new plan to have her killed instead would likely not meet with the Unforged God's approval.

He didn't care, he told himself. His god had betrayed him. Perhaps this was the way to make him sorry for it.

He closed his eyes and rested.

Weight. Quiet. A silent darkness dazzling with possibility, with the presence of something unfathomable–like being cradled in the womb of the earth.

Or like being entombed.

Despite his efforts, Tal had fallen asleep, and now a vision was coming. He could feel it humming at the corners of his consciousness. It felt oddly urgent, trembling in its desire to be birthed. He caught glimpses of it: tall trees, crimson moss draped across branches, a starlit night.

Like lightning from nowhere, the numb, distant shock he'd been feeling flashed to fury. The last time he had allowed a vision in, it had led to him rescuing the Destroyer instead of his own sister. And now his god wanted in again. To do what–to enforce Tal's oath, to make him cease his plan for justice against her?

No. *No.* "NO," he bellowed into the darkness, with his voice that was not a voice here in this dreaming place. He wasn't sure if his god could hear him–there had never before been any real indication to that effect–but Tal suddenly, fiercely hoped he could. "I will not listen to you any longer," he said, his silent voice rebounding throughout his sleeping self. The words built quickly in him, roiling like a tsunami headed for a disastrous landfall, one that he could not and, he found, did not wish to stop. "I will not be manipulated by your purpose any longer. I am not the naïve boy I used to be, to still believe that you are good. How could you be after what you have done to me? Is it only the Destroyer who you care for? Am I but a tool to you, too?"

The emotion rending through him was no longer fury, but a dark and sudden pain. It had been trapped beneath the layers of his soul for two years and would be denied no longer. Like an old, badly-healed wound, it had broken open under new strain, and now he was bleeding out.

A sob tore from him. It startled him, and he realized that the tsunami of his pain was indeed making landfall but not in the way he'd thought it would. His ghostly dreaming self didn't move, but faintly he felt his real body double over, his head knocking against the stone as another sob wrenched through him and then another, until he was weeping without relent.

The weight surrounding him tightened slightly but it did not feel like a reprimand. It felt like being held. That was worse. Tal tried to shove it away, but moving beyond this place and avoiding the waiting vision would take more concentrated effort and he was too emotionally compromised to summon it.

Then, from outside of his dream, he felt a hand land on his arm. The touch was familiar in a way that thrust him immediately into consciousness. He opened his eyes.

The Destroyer stared down at him, those impossible brown eyes framed by the loose dark curls that fell across her shoulders as she knelt over him. They looked at each other silently for a long moment while Tal registered the tracks of wetness on his cheeks and the way his body shuddered with the aftereffects of weeping.

He'd been sobbing here as well as in his dream. Had he been shouting here, too? Quickly, he retraced his words, trying to recall if he'd said anything that might have alerted the

Destroyer to her true identity or to his purposes for her.

Her hand was still on his arm, warmth slowly seeping from it into him. "You were having a nightmare," she said unnecessarily. "I hope I didn't offend in waking you from it. I...I was having a nightmare myself earlier and I know that I would have wanted to be woken."

There was no censure in the words, only an awkward sympathy. She pulled her hand back quickly as if she'd just remembered she was still touching him, and that he had asked not to be touched.

Humiliated to have been found in such a condition–especially after years of successfully hiding the majority of his tears–he opened his mouth to snap at her. Was there no part of his life that she wouldn't insinuate herself into? Could he have no privacy even in his own emotions?

Then suddenly his plan returned to his mind, and he closed his mouth. He was supposed to win her trust. There was a wary set to her mouth already, her weight balanced so she could stand back swiftly in case he shouted at her. Which he had indeed been about to do.

He needed to change her opinion of him if he was going to put her off guard, if he was going to give himself and the Saints the best chance of success. So he tried to make his expression and his voice mild and said, "Thank you."

She tilted her head and raised a sardonic brow. "I might almost believe you mean that."

"I do mean it." He tried to soften his voice further, but even he could hear how false it sounded. He barely held back a wince. Although he'd hidden much of himself from the Destroyer over the last two years, he had rarely been openly untruthful with her, preferring instead to stay silent and distance himself. He had little practice with falsehoods.

Elodie snorted and stood up. "You are far too honest to make a good liar, Tal." She found a long stick—the last of their firewood—and poked at the smoldering embers with it. "Who was he?" she asked abruptly, her back turned to him.

Tal blinked blearily and dragged a hand across his face, trying to wake up more fully so he could focus. He had never had so much trouble concentrating after sleep before; it had to be an effect of the phage. His deterioration had begun already. "Who do you mean?"

"The Destroyer."

Tal froze.

Elodie kept her back to him, poking the stick into the remnants of their fire, making it hiss and sizzle. She said nothing. He realized belatedly that her silence, her turned back, was an offering. She was giving him the space to think about his answer and whether he wanted to make one. She was not insinuating herself into his privacy, but offering herself as a confidant. And he had no idea what to do with that.

Use it. He should use it. She must have heard him crying out in the midst of his would-be vision, and now she wanted to know what—who—it was that tormented him. She had assumed the Destroyer was a man. Perhaps he ought to let her believe that, mislead her so she wouldn't accidentally stumble onto her own identity.

You are far too honest to make a good liar, she'd said earlier. Which meant he had to risk the truth.

"The Destroyer is...the Lady I guard," he answered gruffly.

Elodie's stick didn't pause in its scraping through the stones and coals. Outside, the wind whistled, though it wasn't as wild as it had been a few hours ago. "And you were having nightmares about her?" she asked.

"All my nightmares are of her."

"Is she the body you asked me to look for earlier?"

Tal was confused for a moment until he recalled describing Nyx to her, asking her if any bodies matched his sister. "No. That was...someone else. Someone I love. Someone who is alive," he added fiercely, as if he could make it be true.

"Oh," Elodie said in surprise, turning around. The end of her stick glowed red and traced afterimages through his vision as she gestured with it. "So this 'someone else,' she's your lover, then?"

"No," Tal said shortly.

Elodie tilted her head again and squinted. Tal waited, and now he was the wary one. The Destroyer had a foxlike mind, canny and calculating, and had always been quick to spot patterns that might remain hidden from others. If she guessed too much of the truth, his plan would be over before it had begun.

"A sister, then. Or perhaps a close friend. She's the one you hope lives." Elodie glanced back at Tal and apparently his expression was confirmation enough, because she nodded in satisfaction and dropped her stick on the fire. "But you didn't ask if I'd seen the Destroyer's body earlier, which means either you know she's dead, or you hope she is. Unless she wasn't on the train with you at all…but you're her body-guard, so you won't have left her side. Which means she *was* on the train. So which is it: dead, or hopefully dead?"

Tal ground his teeth, searching for an answer that wouldn't sound dishonest. He eased himself up further to sit braced against the wall and ignored the responding burst of pain from his leg. "She was injured in the wreck," he said at last. "She will not survive long."

The angles of Elodie's expression sharpened. For a moment, the ghost of her old malice settled over her like a veil. "If she was cruel enough to cause you nightmares, then I am glad for her death, and I hope that it hurts."

Tal had no response to that.

Elodie blinked and one corner of her mouth curved up, rueful. The trace of the Destroyer in her features vanished. "My apologies. I suppose I could have found a kinder way to say that, but, as it turns out, I don't seem to be a kind person."

Tal felt wrong-footed, off balance. The Destroyer had just apologized to him: one more impossibility in a day full of them. It didn't help that he was still recovering from his almost-vision. The urgency of it lingered in his mind, tainting his emotions, making him unsteady. He tried to keep his focus on the conversation before him—it was like a chess match against a master, trying to anticipate what she might ask and how she might corner him, or how he might inadvertently corner himself—but he was distracted by the worry that the vision might have been warning of something dire.

He tried to push the nagging uncertainty from his mind. The Unforged God's warnings came with strings attached, and Tal was done with trusting him. "We've discussed my nightmare. What of yours?" he said to Elodie, trying to put her on the defensive. "You said you'd had one too."

Her rueful half-smile fell and she bit her lip, an expression that made her seem strangely young. "I'm not sure if mine was a dream or a memory," she admitted. "There was a man standing over me and my mouth was full of blood and I was screaming." She lifted one shoulder, clearly uncomfortable.

Tal shifted. He'd never known what her nightmares were about, as she'd never talked about them to anyone, and certainly never to him. Knowing even this bare sketch of their content now made him as uncomfortable as it did her. He had no wish to be her confidant.

"I should check the perimeter," he said, starting to gingerly push himself up to standing, leaning on the wall for support.

"Oh, I can do that," Elodie said, stepping toward the cave's entrance. The oath latched onto him painfully, about to thrust him toward her like a puppet.

"No!" he said quickly. "No, let me. There could be...something dangerous out there." The urgency of the vision rose in his mind again, and this time he couldn't shake it off. Perhaps it wouldn't hurt to be more cautious than usual until he could ascertain if there was indeed a threat.

Elodie scoffed but paused. "And if there is, what, you're going to fight it off? Let me help you."

He stooped carefully to sweep up his sword from where it had been lying at his side and re-sheathed it. "I can fight it off well enough if I need to."

"Give me my dagger back and I can help," she insisted.

"No." It wasn't so much that he was worried she would hurt him if he armed her—he'd seen the amateurish way she'd held the dagger earlier—but more that it was viciously satisfying to see her defenseless. To see her fearful, even if it was him she was fearful for.

He shook his head, disgusted with both her and himself, and hobbled to the cave's entrance.

The snow had stopped falling. It was a deep, quiet hour of the night, and stars glimmered icily through the gaps in the thinning clouds. Shafts of viscous moonlight dappled a landscape made new: snowbanks heaped in unfamiliar patterns, carved and reshaped by the blizzard's gales. As Tal was observing this, the gusting wind wailed one last time and then died, and all was calm and still and picturesque.

"The snow will have buried the bodies," Elodie said from behind him, sounding regretful.

Tal didn't turn. "You wished to have done it yourself?" His words were biting but he couldn't help it. There had been innocent servants among the dead, people like him who had no choice but to serve those who oppressed them. It angered him to hear her treat their loss so casually—and unlike any time before in his service to her, he could now speak his true feelings aloud without fear of reprisal. It felt like lancing a wound: painful, but carrying with it an unexpected relief.

"Of course not," Elodie answered. "I only wish there'd been more time to search them for anything useful first."

Tal wasn't sure what expression he made then, but it must have shown in the tension of his shoulders and back, because Elodie sighed deeply and said, "What? You wish I would mourn them? Weep and gnash my teeth and perhaps sing some poetry over their poor sad corpses, bury them with my own two hands six feet deep in the permafrost? We have already established that the girl you care about is not among those bodies, and I neither remember nor grieve any of them. If they were alive right now, I'm sure you would convince me to rescue them too, but they are not, and we are, and I will do what it takes to keep us that way."

Tal spotted the mostly-buried edge of the sled just outside the entrance to the cave. He leaned down to grab the rope and pulled, careful not to upset his injury further in the process. "You were right before," he said.

"About what?"

"You are not a kind person."

Elodie didn't respond, but there was a scuff of stone. She had taken a step back. "Not kind, no," she said softly, almost to herself. "But I can only be what I am."

"That is true," Tal bit out.

Elodie stepped forward and snatched the rope from his hands, yanking it with all her strength—which wasn't a lot, as the Destroyer had rarely done physical work of any kind. But she was still more capable than him in his current condition and also very determined, and after a few moments, the sled slid free.

"Lucky for you," Elodie panted, dropping the rope and sweeping her hair up into a loose knot that she tied with a shred of fabric, "what I am, is willing to drag you back to civilization on this sled. Get on. The storm is over, and we need to leave before whatever predator that lives here returns."

Tal drew a breath to argue but then released it without speaking. She was right. He was in no condition to go traipsing across the mountain range. He'd barely been able to make it to the front of the cave, and he had had a wall to brace himself on then. And they did need to leave the den as quickly as possible. Time was running out, and not only because a predator might be on its way back. "Very well."

Elodie smiled. "At last, you see sense." She kicked at the snow atop the sled until its surface was mostly clean, then she went to fetch the bundle of clothing that comprised all of their supplies for survival.

"We are going to need food," Tal said, easing himself down to sit on the sled.

Elodie dumped the stained clothing atop him. "Maybe I can wrestle another stoat."

To Tal's surprise, a quick chuckle slid through his guard. Elodie grinned in unabashed triumph at the sign of his humor. The expression was dazzling, and so unlike the Destroyer that for a moment Tal felt like he was seeing double. So disorienting was it that he smiled in response. Before he could return to himself and wipe the expression from his face, Elodie had turned her back and moved to the front of the sled.

He bowed his head, confused and ashamed. He shouldn't be smiling with her. How could she rouse any emotion but hatred in him? But at least it might have had the effect of softening her further toward him, which, he reminded himself, was the goal he was supposed to be working toward.

She picked up the rope and dragged the sled away from the cave. Tal lifted his head, scanning for potential threats, but all seemed peaceful. "Do you know where to go?" he asked, trying to sound normal.

She gestured at the steep mountainside that loomed above them. "I assumed we would follow the train tracks. They have to lead somewhere."

"A good plan," Tal allowed, because that much was true. "But those tracks are carved into the sides of mountains and go across bridges that would be inaccessible by foot. Or sled, for that matter. It would be better for us to use the pass just east of here. There is a township that should be about two days' journey beyond it."

Elodie stopped and turned all the way around, pinning him with her stare. "You know how to get to a nearby township," she said, enunciating each word slowly, "and you are only now deigning to inform me?"

Her anger was familiar, and though it was toothless without her fire to enforce it, it could still mean the ruination of Tal's plan if he didn't allay it quickly. This was it: the first test. "We wouldn't have been able to make it anywhere until the blizzard was over in any case," he told her, trying to sound apologetic.

She pursed her lips. Her anger passed. "True enough. But if you have any more key information that can boost our chances of survival, please tell me *immediately*." She paused. "How do you know about the pass and the township, exactly?"

"I grew up in the mountain ward. Here, in the Skyteeth," he explained. "I don't have all the geography memorized, but I know enough to have a general sense of direction."

"The Skyteeth," she mused, picking the rope back up, her gaze faraway. "That's right. I couldn't remember the range's name before."

Tal's senses went on high alert. "Do you remember anything else?" he asked cautiously.

She frowned. "No. Or...maybe? I'm not certain. I have these flashes of familiarity, of recognition, but nothing specific. I keep waiting for things to snap back into place but it hasn't happened yet. I thought yesterday that it was merely the trauma of the crash, some sort of shock state, but if it was it would have passed by now, right?"

Tal hid his relief. "I can't be sure. I have little medical knowledge."

She smiled over her shoulder at him. "That is one way we are the same, then, at least." She trudged through the snow and moonlight in silence for a few more minutes, then said suddenly, "There are a few guesses I can make about who I am. Or at least, what I'm like. I know that I've rarely felt proud of myself before. I know I have few survival skills—few practical skills of any kind, really—which indicates I led a privileged life. Or perhaps simply a sheltered one. Maybe I was a nun," she mused. "I could have led a life of silence and prayer, cocooned by the walls of an isolated monastery."

"I can see you neither praying nor being silent," Tal contended.

"Keep your opinions to yourself, unbeliever," she said playfully.

That struck a bit too close to home, and Tal looked away. She caught his hesitation.

"Oh," she said, realization dawning. "*Oh*. But you're not an unbeliever, are you? You're the religious type. Ah, it makes so much sense now. The dutiful nature, the care for the dead—"

"That is a normal quality of decent humans," Tal interjected.

"Yes, yes, we have established that I am not a decent human," she said impatiently. "But we are discussing you right now. So tell me: is it true? You believe in the Unforged God?"

"Yes," Tal said stiffly.

"But it is a sore topic," she mused, shrewd as ever.

"Yes. So can we talk about something else?"

"Certainly. There are many other topics of interest which we can discuss at length. Maybe you could teach me other survival skills beyond building a fire while we travel."

"Or we could be silent and rest."

She gave an exasperated sigh. "Come now. I'm hauling you across a mountain range. The least you can do is teach me something useful, or else entertain me with your story while I labor."

"My story is not entertaining."

"Is it a tragedy then?" she teased. "I happen to find tragedies entertaining. Try me."

"*Elodie,*" he grated out.

She dropped the teasing tone. "Tal. We have seen each other cry—though if you tell anyone I cried, I swear I will find a way to visit some terrible retribution upon you which I reserve the right to define later—and we have been through a great trauma together. Whether you prefer my company or not, we are stuck with each other until we either reach that township, or die in the attempt. It might be good to try to be friends in the meantime, to keep our spirits up. Right?"

Friends. She wanted to be friends. He took a deep breath. He could do this; he had done much worse. "You are right. I'm...sorry."

"You don't have to share all the sordid details of your past if you don't want to. But I'm afraid I don't have much in the way of my own stories to regale you with. Also, it's not exactly easy to talk while pulling this thing." Her arms were trembling already with the strain, but she didn't slow down, only kept floundering through the deep, newly-fallen snow.

He turned his gaze to the landscape because it was easier than looking at her. The snowbanks glittered with the cold blue light of the coming dawn, making the world look pristine and promising. He took a breath to speak, and allowed himself—only briefly—to believe that the person pulling the sled was indeed a girl named Elodie who had no shared past with him, who had saved his life because she cared rather than because it was in her own self-interest. Maybe he could even allow himself to believe this Elodie was a girl he could have been friends with, in another life.

"I grew up believing in the Unforged God," he told her, still watching the landscape. "Both my father and my mother—and my stepmother for that matter—were believers, and I was proud to follow their lead. But for me it was more than just believing he existed. I...I thought he loved me. I thought he was watching over me, guiding me into some grand destiny. I thought he'd chosen me. I thought I was *important*, because I was important to him." The words were ashes in his mouth: a cloying, bitter truth. "But instead of leading me to my destiny, he led me to the Destroyer."

Elodie was quiet for a moment. "Ah," she said at last. "That is a tragedy, then, and not even an entertaining one. Maybe we could travel in silence after all."

He let out an exhale. "Thank you," he said, and this time he almost meant it.

She hesitated, then peered back over her shoulder. "I know you aren't one to enjoy my company—or perhaps human company in general, it's hard to tell—but I want you to know I'm glad I found you in the wreckage. It would have been...hard for me, had I been out here on my own."

"I'm sure you would have managed." He couldn't picture the Destroyer being anything but indestructible, even as he strove to prove that image false.

"No, that's not what I mean. I would have survived. In fact," she said, her voice taking on a teasing tone once again, "I probably would have moved a lot faster without the need to drag your carcass behind me."

"I shall endeavor to lose some weight to ease your labors," he replied dryly.

"We could always amputate that leg. That would displace perhaps a good fifth of your weight. More if you lose a lot of blood in the process."

"But the blood might attract predators," he pointed out.

"That is a consideration." She nodded decisively. "We shall save that option for a last resort, then."

"That's good to hear," he said, weaving together every bit of control he possessed to reinforce the illusion of the new and unknown girl before him.

There was a moment of silence. "In any case," she said, her voice stiff and awkward now, "what I meant was—I'm glad I saved you. Not because I wouldn't survive this alone, but because it…it makes me more hopeful, to survive it with you. I'm not sure I would feel that way with anyone else."

Tal fumbled for a response. "Oh."

"Now that's said, we should be quiet, as you suggested," she said hastily, walking a bit faster as if she might be able to outrun the embarrassment he could clearly hear in her voice. "We don't want to scare off any wildlife that we could turn into a meal."

"Yes," he said, at a loss for how else to reply.

Silence fell thick around them like a new snow. After a

few minutes, it softened the edges of his unease, and he managed to turn his mind to other matters. Or rather, one key matter, the one that he'd been avoiding for an entire day but could avoid no longer.

The prison car had been three lengths away from the dining car. Judging by the debris he'd seen, the explosion had destroyed perhaps two cars, three at the very most. Which meant Nyx may have survived.

Except the door to her cell had been open. She'd been badly injured, but if she was anything she was determined, and she might have tried to go after him. If she had gotten to the next car over before the explosion, her chances would have been reduced. But, he reminded himself, with the feeling of treading a rut worn deep in his mind, her body hadn't been among the dead. That made it more probable that she had survived.

Although of course, if she *had* survived the explosion, she would almost certainly not survive what came next.

Tal turned his face away, despairing. The empress had spoken of emergency transport magics. Tal didn't have authorization to know all the details of the royal train's enchantments, but he knew enough to put the pieces together with what he'd overheard from the now-dead Head of Transport. The train had a special, last-resort magic Smithed into it that could return it almost instantly to the Alloyed Palace in case of an emergency. Such an enchantment would take a massive amount of power and wreck all of the train's other Smithings, including the ones that ran its engines—although it unfortunately would not affect any oaths that had been sworn to the metal there. It meant the train couldn't return to check for survivors, not for weeks. It also meant that if Nyx was alive, then she was likely now at the palace, utterly helpless.

The other prisoners would tell the metallurgists what had happened. Nyx was already slated for a mockery of a trial for her attempt to assassinate the Destroyer; what worse punishment would they mete out for the one whose machinations had killed many nobles, potentially including the empress herself and, as far as they would know, the Destroyer too?

Tal closed his eyes. In his chest, something hitched, like a frayed bowstring pulled too tight to last.

"Nyx," he whispered, too quiet to be heard over the shush of metal on snow, "please be safe."

CHAPTER NINE

THE SKY WAS A PRETENDER. SWEPT CLEAN OF CLOUDS, IT shone a delicate gauzy blue hung with the low diadem of the dawning sun, as if there had never been such a thing as a storm. But Nyx had seen too many lying dawns to believe the sky today, just as she had seen too many Skyteeth blizzards to underestimate the one that had greeted her last night, when she had awoken half-buried in a snowbank.

The sky hadn't been pretending then. It had fomented openly, chunks of slate-gray scraping through the maw of the Skyteeth, breaking open to rain snow and death onto the peaks. Nyx had been so sure it would kill her. She could still taste the despair and fury at the back of her throat, could still remember her vow to curse the Destroyer with her dying breath.

"I know that look," came a wry voice from behind her. "You're thinking violent and poetic thoughts again, aren't you?"

An involuntary smile crept over Nyx's mouth. She twisted in her nest of blankets to look up at Helenia, who stood at her back on the runners of the dogsled. The other girl was swaddled in furs—nearly as many as she'd piled atop Nyx—leaving only her bright, kind brown eyes showing above her thick foxtail scarf. Her dark brown skin was spangled with freckles, and her hair was tucked neatly into her hood. Nyx wished it was warm enough for her to let it down. She loved the way Helenia's hair looked when it was loose: a gorgeous, bouncy cascade of tight black ringlets.

Nyx answered her question. "I'm always thinking violent and poetic thoughts."

Helenia quirked a brow. "Except when you're thinking about me."

Nyx battled her smile, and lost. "Only poetic, then," she agreed, and laid her head against the rail where Helenia's hands gripped the wood.

It felt like a miracle that she was here. Here, with the girl she loved, covered by warm blankets that smelled of home while she recovered from her injuries. Helenia had found her last night, had dug her nearly-frozen body out of the snow with the pocked aluminum shovel she'd brought along just in case it might come in handy. It might have been more romantic if she'd clawed Nyx from the snow with her bare hands, perhaps weeping over her prone body in the process, but Helenia was far too practical for such things. Nyx had found that trait exasperating in the past. Now, though, she was pathetically grateful—especially because Helenia had also thought to steal a small vat of the Saints' carefully-guarded healing tincture supply. She had probably charmed it right out of the guards' hands, with her shimmering, tearful gaze and her quavering voice full of faith and hope and goodness. Nyx had fallen under its sway herself too many times to count.

The most admirable–if somewhat insulting–part of Helenia's singlehanded rescue mission, though, was that it had been preemptive. To have reached Nyx as quickly as she did, Helenia would have had to already be following her. Which meant their tearful goodbye in the township had been a sham, since she must have already had her own sled packed and her hauler dogs primed to go. Nyx was both annoyed by and more attracted than ever to her scheming girlfriend.

Only one part of the rescue had bothered Nyx: Helenia had used every last drop of the stolen healing tincture on her, saving none for Tal or any other survivors they might yet find.

You are here, Helenia had said last night, *and they are not, and you are my beloved, and they are not, and so you are going to drink every last ounce of this medicine and if you complain I will bash you over the head with the carafe and* then *you will drink it.*

It was an unwise person who said no to Helenia. Nyx was not unwise, and so she had meekly obeyed. And now she was recovered, and heading home to recoup and report the Saints' losses before they set out to find any more rebels who had survived the explosion.

Well. The other Saints would be searching for rebels. Nyx would be looking for her mother and for Tal and them alone.

Tal, she knew, had to be alive, because the Destroyer was alive. Nyx felt the latter truth deep in the hidden recesses of her soul, thanks to the oath she'd sworn on the iron bars of her cell. No part of her oath was yet fulfilled; no part of it had yet released her. The Destroyer had not perished in the explosion.

Nyx fingered her dagger—her own silver dagger, the one that had been a gift from her brother. Helenia had happened upon it in the burned mining town and recovered it for her. Nyx was glad, because whenever she'd dreamed of driving a blade into the Destroyer's heart over the last two years, it was always this particular blade that she'd pictured.

A yelp from ahead broke Nyx from her contemplations. The lead dog, a bushy blue-gray hauler named Kenna, was limping. Red flecks of blood gleamed on the snow, and on the edge of a twisted piece of metal that stabbed up from it.

"Ease!" Helenia called, shifting her weight to brake the sled. The five-dog team slowed reluctantly, pink tongues lolling from grinning mouths. Kenna, who sat down and held her hurt paw in the air, looked apologetic as Helenia approached to check her over.

While Helenia crooned to her hauler, Nyx leaned over to peer at the metal poking out of the snow. A charred wooden plank was attached to one side of it with a thick bolt. It was a piece of a train track—one that had been snapped off and warped by some unimaginable force.

A feeling like electricity swept over Nyx. She threw off her furs and stood. She whirled in a circle, searching, and found what she'd been looking for. The peak across from them sported a crater, freshly-fallen snow gathering in the bottom of it, with train tracks running along either side.

"This is where it happened," she whispered.

She had only dim recollections of the explosion. Her mind had been drenched in too much pain to fully hold the moment. She remembered Tal leaving, carrying the Destroyer, and then some sort of odd bluish enchantment had begun rattling the whole of the train. Then came the fire. It had bellowed like a wounded animal, carving a gaping hole through the front half of the prison car and knocking Nyx unconscious in the process. At some point she must have been thrown through the hole and onto the mountainside some distance further down the tracks from where the explosion itself had happened.

Had her mother survived? Saasha had been in the rear half of the car, so the explosion wouldn't have gotten her... but neither would she have been able to escape through the hole as Nyx unintentionally had.

Tal, though—Tal would have been right in the epicenter.

Helenia glanced up from Kenna's paw. "What did you say?"

Nyx bent down, shoved the furs on the sled aside and yanked the snow shovel out without answering. She thrust it into the frost and immediately hit something hard that had a slight give to it. When she pulled the shovel out, its edge glittered with red-brown crystals. Frozen blood.

It couldn't be Tal. His blood was not this color.

She still had to be sure.

She tossed the shovel aside and dropped to the ground, scooping handfuls of snow out with her bare hands, revealing the body beneath the frost like a sculptor carving away stone to expose the art hidden inside. But this was a grisly art indeed: a man in servant's clothing, his open mouth packed with ice, one of his hands still clutching an empty, heat-warped tray like a shield.

Nyx didn't spare a prayer on him. She had never been the praying type, and anyway, though it might make her a heathen, she cared little for this dead but anonymous servant. Once she had uncovered enough of his corpse to be certain he wasn't her brother, she left him and snatched up the shovel again to dig in another spot.

A hand on her arm, made thick by a knitted green mitten, restrained her. Nyx whirled. "Don't—" she started, but Helenia wrapped her in a hug that smothered the rest of her sentence, which she probably would have regretted saying anyway.

"Be still a moment and let me help," Helenia murmured, releasing her. Though it made Nyx's skin crawl to stand in one place while her brother's body might lay buried in the snow nearby, she trusted Helenia and waited.

The other girl waded through the snow back to the row of dogs. Most of them were lying down now, taking the opportunity to rest and save their strength as they had been trained, but one was straining at his harness and whining. It was Maluk, a grizzled old veteran with gray-peppered fur and eyes that had begun to go bluish. Despite his age, Helenia had kept him on the team because he was canny, with an innate sense of where the ice was too thin to bear the sled's weight and where to find the wily mountain goats whose meat fed their township during long winters. Now, he had caught a scent that made him lay his ears back and stare at the approaching Helenia with begging eyes, and once she unclipped his harness from the lead, he leapt over the snow like a cannon shot and began digging.

Maluk had been raised by Tal, Nyx remembered. She hadn't seen the old dog this intent on anything since he'd left.

Breathless, she followed Maluk. Every other footstep broke through the thin, new crust of frost to sink deep into the fresh snow beneath, but she gave no care to the bite of cold on her shins. By the time Nyx had reached the dog's side, the hole was as deep as he was. She stood back a bit and waited, arms folded so she wouldn't be tempted to shove him aside and finish the hole herself. Helenia caught up and wrapped an arm–and a fur she'd grabbed from the sled–around Nyx's shoulders. Together they held a tense, silent vigil until Maluk leapt out of the hole and went to his owner with a low whine. His muzzle shone oddly. It was, Nyx realized, crusted with silvery crystals.

She lunged forward. She dropped to her knees at the edge of the hole. She peered in. Her breath stuttered, a haze of steam that she wished would cloud her vision entirely. Her shadow fell long and blue-black over a grim scene: a patch of snow stained silver.

"His body isn't here," Helenia said. Her voice was loud and clear enough to cut through Nyx's paralysis. "If it was, Maluk would've dug it up. It's only blood."

Only blood. Only blood.

"He was here," Nyx said, her words choked as she carefully scooped out the snow around the blood, widening the hole to search for more evidence of what had happened. "He was injured." *Because of me. Because I failed him.*

Her questing fingers caught on a tuft of fabric. She pulled on it and it unfurled into the snow, smooth as butter: a twist of burgundy silk. It was ragged, torn, barely a scrap—but oh, Nyx remembered what it had looked like when it was whole.

A wine-red cape pooled on a filthy floor. A torn corner where it snagged on a nail. *My name is Elodie. And now you may thank me in truth, because unlike torture, my name is a gift I have given no assassin before.*

Nyx didn't realize she was shaking until Helenia dropped another, heavier fur over her shoulders. Nyx tugged the warmth closer around her and managed a strangled laugh; her girlfriend, only nineteen and already a mother hen.

"What is it? What does it mean?" Helenia asked, picking up the silky slip of fabric.

Nyx's lips felt numb. Her skull echoed with memories, too crowded to admit the present moment. After a moment she managed to force out, "It was hers."

Helenia dropped the silk like it was something rotten, something that might infect her. "She was here, then, with Tal. She is alive."

"I already know she is alive."

Helenia frowned. "How do you know? I thought you said the last you saw of her, she was in a bad way."

"I know she is alive because my oath tells me so."

Helenia was deadly silent for a long, long moment. "Your *what* tells you so?" she asked, calm in a way that meant she was envisioning murder. Probably because Nyx hadn't yet been brave enough to tell her all the details of her torture and the events immediately following it.

Nyx didn't answer her girlfriend. She'd heard a scuffing sound behind her and turned to follow it, and saw Maluk a few dozen yards away. The land beneath him sloped downward sharply and he was pacing at the edge of it, his gaze fixed on something at the bottom. Nyx scrambled after him and followed his line of sight.

At the bottom of the slope was a dark hole in the side of the mountain. A thin, watery trail of smoke led upward from it, a gray etching against the sky. Inside the cave, something orange and red flickered in the darkness: embers, or sparks.

Nyx's dagger was in her hand. She was crashing heedlessly down the slope, tripping, nearly falling, righting herself and lunging onward. Helenia didn't shout after her—she'd spotted the cave too, and didn't want to alert anyone who might be inside. Nyx barely heard her or saw the blur of gray at her side that was Maluk. All of her focus was on the red of the embers, which matched the color of the flames that had pinwheeled in the Destroyer's palm when she had finished torturing Nyx. All her attention was on the hilt of the dagger in her hand, the way it warmed to her touch and seemed to mold itself to her grip, as if it thrummed with the same eager fury that tore through Nyx's veins. Her oath sang within her, and her very soul joined in its chorus.

I will see your empire fall.

She reached the cave. The darkness smelled like old death. She plunged into it without waiting for her eyes to adjust.

And your reign ended.

She drew back her dagger to throw it. This time she wouldn't miss.

And you dead.

Do you hear me, Elodie?

But there was no target for her aim. Even before her eyes had fully adjusted, she could tell the cave was empty. She held her breath anyway, tried to silence her thundering heartbeat, and took in the details of the cave in a long, sweeping glance.

Campfire in the middle. Clumsily built, burned down to bare embers, with the evidence of a full night's burning in the ash piled beneath it. To the left, a strip of abandoned fabric and a space that had been cleared of dust and pebbles, just the right size for a single body to sleep. To the right: a piece of stained cloth, wadded up and half-hidden beneath a rock, and a shallow white line where a blade had scraped against the ground.

They were not here. But they had been.

Something was raging through Nyx. An emotion, or an emptiness—something that she had never felt before and could not harness now. She drew her arm back and hurled her dagger with all her might. It clattered loudly against the cave's wall and fell. She would be lucky if it wasn't chipped. She would be lucky if it wasn't broken. Trauma like that could do things to a blade that couldn't be repaired. It would never be like it had been before.

Nyx didn't realize she had sunk to the ground until she felt Helenia ease down next to her. She didn't realize she was sobbing until Maluk licked her tears from her cheek.

"She has stolen him again," Nyx choked out.

"We will find them."

Nyx tangled a hand in Maluk's thick fur. The contact calmed her a bit, enough to be able to speak almost normally. "We waited two years for this chance. Mother said the opportunity was sent from God. I drank poison every day, Helenia."

"I know." Helenia's voice had a hint of hardness to it now, but Nyx barely heard it.

"I promised her I was ready." Nyx squeezed her eyes shut. "I failed."

She could still see her mother's steadfast eyes, watching from the darkness of her cell.

"You didn't fail," Helenia replied.

"She said—"

Helenia stood up in a sudden and uncharacteristically violent movement. "I don't care what Saasha said," she bit out, her eyes shining. "What kind of a mother sends a daughter to be tortured?"

The argument was old, frayed around the edges, ready to shred open anew with a single rough word. "It was my plan," Nyx reminded her girlfriend. "My choice."

"Encouraged by her. Nyx, she *formulated the poison*. She somehow tracked down a copper Smith willing to sell her the ingredients. She lobbied the Saints' leadership to enact your plan."

Nyx set her teeth. She didn't want to argue. She wanted to find her family. She stood up, swiped an arm across her face, and strode to the edge of the cave. From there, she could see what she had been too focused to spot on her run down the slope: a mess of tracks, leading away from the cave toward the east. She knelt down to examine them. If the fire that the Destroyer and Tal had started last night was still burning, it had to mean they'd left recently. Nyx could still catch up. The oath curled around her bones, whispering its agreement.

Behind her, Helenia's boots shuffled as she stepped across the cave. "This silk fabric matches the piece we found above," she said. The shuffling paused. "But it's bloody." She sounded puzzled.

"Good," Nyx bit out. "If she's injured, it'll be easier to kill her."

"No, it's—Nyx, it's *red* blood."

Nyx lifted her head and glanced back. "What?"

"Red. Not mercurial. And there are wood splinters all through the fabric too, like whoever had it on was working, trying to start the fire maybe. Not something the Destroyer would be likely to do." Helenia held the silky fabric aloft.

"So...it's not the Destroyer who's with Tal?" Hope and disappointment twined together in Nyx's chest. Hope because the Destroyer's absence could mean an easier rescue for Tal; disappointment because Nyx needed very badly to kill her, and now might have lost her only lead.

"I'm not sure," Helenia mused, tugging her foxtail scarf down so she could examine the ground better. "I'll look around a bit more and see what clues I can find."

Nyx turned her attention back to the tracks. The snow was kicked around near the entrance to the cave, and it was hard to make much out, but when she moved further out into the shadow of the peak the trail became clearer. Some sort of makeshift sled had been dragged through here. It nearly obscured the footprints of the person who'd been pulling it. Those footprints weren't big enough to be Tal's, but they didn't match the prints that the Destroyer's heeled boots would have made, either. Nyx was still frowning over them when she heard Maluk's warning growl.

Nyx jerked her gaze up. Maluk was a few yards further down the trail. His hackles were up and his body was rigid. Another low growl rippled from him.

Helenia exited the cave, a wad of balled-up fabric in her hand, a grave expression on her face, but whatever she'd been about to say was cut off when she spotted her dog. "Maluk, what is it?"

Nyx was already at Maluk's side. Her body went numb with fear as she stared down at the new tracks he'd found: pawprints the size of dinner plates, with imprints of wicked claws pricking the snow above each toepad.

Mooncat.

Too late, Nyx recalled the scent of old death that had permeated the cave, and realized what it meant. This cave was the den of a mooncat. It had returned after the blizzard, probably made hungry by the winter that had turned harsh unseasonably early, only to find its lair had been invaded. And now it was hunting down the invaders.

Tal was injured. Whoever was with him was injured. The scent of their blood would have left a trail, one invisible to the eyes of humans but clear as day to a predator. Mooncats were at the very top of the Skyteeth food chain, as large as the great white bears of the north and twice as territorial. Every year, a handful of mountain ward hunters fell prey to them—and those hunters had weapons, crossbows and daggers and ferocious hunting hounds. Tal was a superior fighter, but if he was injured, what chance would he have against a predator that outweighed him by a thousand pounds?

"We can't go after them like this," Helenia called, because of course Nyx was already hurrying down the path of trodden-down snow.

"I can and I will."

Helenia hurried after her and grabbed her arm to stop her. Nyx meant to pause to explain herself, but instead saw her hand lash out, knocking her girlfriend back into the snow. Helenia yelped and winced when she landed. Nyx jolted. She hadn't meant to do that. It had been as though her hand had been controlled by some outside force.

No. By some *inner* force. Her oath was reeling her across the valley like she was a fish on a line. She thought there was a decent chance the Destroyer was with Tal, and she knew Tal was at the end of these tracks; therefore, she had to follow them, because she had sworn to see the Destroyer dead.

Nyx's lip curled in shocked abhorrence. Was this what the metal oath had been like for Tal? Like someone else controlled your body, like you were an arrow aimed at a target by some unseen hand? "Helenia, I'm sorry," she said, but was unable to force her feet to stop moving. "I've got to go after them."

Helenia sprang to her feet. "No, you don't! You can't take on the Destroyer *and* a mooncat on your own! Come with me—we'll go back to the township, gather reinforcements first."

"No," Nyx grated out, "I mean, I *can't stop.*" Quickly, as Helenia trotted to keep up, Nyx explained the oath she had made and why it was drawing her forward now. When she was done, Helenia stared at her for a long moment, then lifted her chin.

"So. You have no choice but to follow. But *I* have a choice. I'll take the sled and get to the township and bring every man and woman who can carry a sword back with me. You take Maluk with you."

"Maluk can't help me take down the Destroyer and a mooncat."

"No," snapped Helenia. "But this way you'll be forced to think about his safety before you do anything idiotic, if you won't consider your own. If you get him killed I'll never forgive you. There; now you have no choice but to keep the both of you safe."

Nyx hunched her shoulders. Helenia was being sensible. It was far worse than when she yelled, because now Nyx couldn't even argue or accuse her of overreacting.

"Okay," Nyx said meekly.

Helenia swallowed, hesitated, and then spoke again more softly. "Nyx. How could you?"

Nyx wanted to shrivel and vanish beneath the broken accusation in Helenia's voice. She knew that tone; it had been Nyx's own tone for the last two years. How could Tal have left her? How could he have been so selfish as to gamble away his own life without a thought for what it would do to her? A metal oath was unbreakable, except by death or the fulfillment of its terms. It was stronger than blood, stronger than family. He'd chosen it over her. And now she'd chosen it over Helenia.

"I'm sorry," was all Nyx could say. She meant it with every fiber of her being. But sorry as she was, she would still do it again, to save Tal. They both knew that truth, and so there was nothing left to say.

But then Helenia lifted the wad of bloodied fabric she was still holding. "There's something you should know. This sleeve was used as a bandage. It has Tal's silver blood on it." She hesitated again. "Nyx–there's also evidence of rust phage."

At that, Nyx's horror eclipsed all else, and her feet stumbled to a brief stop. "*What*?"

Helenia shook the torn-off sleeve out. One side was coated in red-brown blood, with bits of white fur–rabbit fur?–stuck to it. The other side was crusted silver with flecks of orangish crystals reminiscent of tiny snowflakes.

The Destroyer. A mooncat. Rust phage. How could Nyx protect her brother from so much? What sort of sadistic god would demand such a test of faith from him?

Nyx's feet began to move again. Her voice shook. "I will save him," she said quietly. *Even if you will not.* It was a silent and unholy challenge, and Nyx regretted it not one whit.

Helenia shrugged off her coat and thrust it onto Nyx. "I love you," she said fiercely. "Go and find your brother."

"I love you too," Nyx replied, trying to put her whole heart into the words, afraid she might not get the chance to say it again. "And I will. I swear it."

CHAPTER TEN

THE SUNGILL HAD EVADED ELODIE FOR NEARLY AN HOUR, but she refused to admit defeat.

She sat unbowed before the jagged hole in the ice, through which she'd dangled a thin, reedy vine. A beetle and a sharply whittled twig were tied to its end. The little fish—whose shadow she could see flitting about in the alpine lake below the cap of ice—had not yet taken the bait, but it was only a matter of time.

"I told you, we don't have the right bait for sungills," Tal noted unhelpfully from his spot by the shore a few yards away. Behind him rose a crown of peaks haloed by creamy, whipped clouds, which the late-morning sunlight painted in delicate shades of champagne and coral. Such a beautiful rendering of such a lethal landscape. Idly, Elodie wondered if the morning sky was trying to trick them or trying to redeem itself. Or, perhaps, if it simply was what it was: both transcendent and merciless.

She jiggled the fishing lure. "And I told you, this is the only bait we have. Also, I don't recall asking for commentary."

"It's been an hour. If the fish is still evading you, we should move on."

Elodie set her jaw. "You need food. You're looking even paler today than yesterday. If you're going to recover, you need a proper meal."

Tal looked away. His hair—which was unkempt, flecked with snow and rabbit blood—spilled over his face and hid his eyes, but not the tense line of his jaw. For a disorienting moment, an image flickered in the recesses of her memory.

A boy with hair splayed over his face, cutting his expression into slivers. Tight jaw. A dark slash of brows etched above stormy green eyes. A mirror snapping shut: *my crown,* said a voice, so clear and cold that it hurt, like swallowing a chunk of ice whole. Beyond it, she faintly heard Tal's voice saying something to her.

Elodie reeled sideways. She caught herself on one hand, and blinked. "What—what did you say?" she asked Tal, shaken by whatever had just happened. A vision? A memory? Some odd trick of her mind, a result of lingering shock?

"I said I can eat when we get closer to the township," Tal repeated, his voice tight, his face turned away from her. "I can go a day without food. And you shouldn't be out on the ice anyway. It's not thick enough."

"It's held me so far."

"And while it's held you, it has been slowly melting from your body heat. It could crack at any moment, and then I'd have to jump in and save you, and then we shall both die of exposure."

"I will not be cowed by a bit of melting ice. And I have faith that if I do fall in, you would find a way to save us both."

Tal rubbed a hand through his hair, a quick, frustrated motion. He muttered something under his breath.

"See," Elodie said, turning her attention back to the fishing hole, "your hunger makes you irritable. Further proof that stopping to resupply now is the best course of action."

"It is not my hunger making me irritable."

Elodie only continued gazing serenely at the hole. A thin crust of ice had begun to grow back over it, and she leaned forward to knock it loose with a stick. The noise sent the sungill darting away, its shadow blending back into the murk at the bottom of the alpine lake. Elodie glared at it, then sighed. Maybe there was other, more attainable game nearby that she could hunt instead, or warrens or dens beneath the snow that she could pillage. She would be happy to wring the neck of a fox or a dusk mouse or even one of those stringy-looking burrowing owls she'd spotted a few times. She was starving. More than that, though, she was growing genuinely concerned for Tal.

She snuck a glance over her shoulder at her travelling companion. He sat with his back against a scraggly lone pine tree, his eyes unnaturally bright and half-lidded as if the sun was too much for him. He'd barely moved since they'd stopped and a light sheen of sweat shone on his brow. She worried he was getting some sort of wound fever, and she had no idea how to cure it or how to help him at all, really, other than getting some food in him. Disgusted yet again at her own helplessness, she vowed that if she lived through this, she would immediately apprentice herself to a physician or a wilderness explorer or both so that she would not find herself in such a situation again.

A flash of movement caught her eye. Jiggling the vine in an attempt to lure the sungill out of hiding one last time, she scanned the shoreline. She was expecting to see potential prey, a goat or perhaps another hare—so it took her three long seconds to recognize that the creature creeping up behind Tal was a mooncat.

Sinuous shoulders draped with a wide ruff of ivory fur. Canny moon-yellow eyes. Deceptively soft, broad paws that extended gently across the snow, distributing the great cat's weight so that it seemed to float atop the thin crust of frost. The crescent fore-fangs that scissored down on either side of its jaw were the white of bones picked clean. Huge as it was, it had managed to steal up behind Tal without making a sound, and was now near enough that if it exhaled, its breath would ruffle his hair.

Elodie scrambled to her feet, a movement made slow and ungainly by horror. She flung out her hands as if she could stop the massive predator through nothing but the force of her will alone. She screamed, *"Tal!"*

Tal reacted at once. His eyes snapped to hers, registering the direction of her gaze. He reached for the small of his back, tucked one shoulder down into a roll, and came up kneeling several feet from where he had been with a short sword in each hand.

He lifted his head and looked at the mooncat. The cat gazed back, assessing. All was silent, Elodie's scream hanging shattered in the air, serene peaks looming above, icy lake stretching below. She saw the thoughts of Tal and the thoughts of the mooncat.

Tal was injured. Couldn't stand, couldn't walk. He would go down fighting—but he would go down.

The mooncat lunged.

Rather than rolling away again, Tal dove forward. He twisted agilely in midair and drove a sword upward. The blade came away wet. Blood steamed on the snow and glowed in the cat's fur, garnets on ivory. The creature roared. The mountains seemed to shake with it.

Elodie was racing across the ice, heedless of the way it crackled and snapped under her sharp footfalls. A desperate hope thrilled in her chest. Tal had injured the cat. He was a skilled fighter. He stood a chance.

But he'd overextended himself with his lunge and was now panting, struggling to shove himself up on his elbows, one sword trapped beneath him. The cat leapt—powerful back legs taut as springs, front claws extended, teeth bared. Tal stopped struggling and looked up. He regarded his coming death, head thrown back, neck bared, eyes bright. Elodie saw the moment a dark sort of peace settled over him.

He would die. He could not escape it. He would no longer try.

The cat landed with its paws in the snow on either side of Tal's chest. It leaned down. Its teeth shone cruelly in the sunlight as its jaws snapped shut around Tal's legs.

Tal's hands spasmed. He dropped both swords. His back arched and his palms drove downward into the snow as if to brace himself, and then he screamed.

The sound pried hot fingers into Elodie's chest. It cracked her open. And what spilled out was a memory.

She had heard this scream before. No—she had *imagined* this scream before. She had imagined what it would do to her. What it was doing to her now. It was why she had never put Tal to the question. It was why she had never willfully hurt him, except in the way it always hurt him to be with her.

The thought snapped into place like a broken bone being set. She cried out with it, tripped and fell hard on her knees. Her palms scraped over a sharp ridge of cracked ice. She lifted trembling hands and looked at them. Blood, red and slow, dripped from her fingers.

Wrong, repeated an instinct in her, and this time she could almost remember why.

Tal screamed again, his voice raw and breaking, as if the sound had been hooked on a line and dragged out of him. Elodie's head jerked up. The mooncat was stalking away across the snow, dragging Tal with it. Tal's eyes were shut, his brittle peace shattered, his face twisted in a rictus of pain.

Elodie launched herself after them. Tal's fallen swords lay akimbo on the bloody snow ahead of her. She swept one up. She pushed herself into a sprint, every ounce of her strength focused on thrusting her sword into the mooncat's skull. She wanted to see more of its blood on the snow, all of it, a new lake to baptize the wilderness.

The mooncat spotted her and growled a low warning, and she screamed back at it, not realizing that her cry contained words until she heard them echoing in her own ears:

"He is not yours! *He is mine!*"

If you truly think you can protect yourself so well, whispered another memory as it locked painfully into place, *then will you finally get rid of that one?*

No, she'd answered, a prickly, possessive fear flitting over her, though she hadn't allowed it to show in her expression then. *He's mine.*

She leapt. She was a weapon aimed true; the mooncat was reluctant to let go of Tal to defend itself against such a small attacker, and her blade sliced a gash through its brow and into its left eye. It shrieked in pain and anger, dropping Tal and jumping backwards to paw at its face. The force of the blow drove the hilt into the heel of Elodie's hand and she reflexively pulled her fingers away, dropping the short sword.

Tal was laid out in the snow at her feet. She knelt at his side, sweeping her arms under him, about to...try to carry him somewhere, maybe the sled, she wasn't sure yet–and then he opened his eyes and saw her. And it wasn't relief that came into his eyes. It was something broken and bitter, something grown too far from the sun.

Voice rough with pain, he said, "You will never let me go, will you?"

She didn't understand the words, but she was afraid that she would soon if her memories kept surfacing, and she discovered that she didn't want to. "Shut up and let me save you," she snapped, trying to heave him up without jostling him too much. He closed his eyes and turned his face away, his breath coming in shallow gasps, his skin pale and stained silver with blood.

She froze.

Tal didn't have silver blood. He couldn't. So why was the color seeping over him, smearing across the snow, dripping in rivulets down her arms where she held him?

She pulled one of her hands out from underneath him. He sagged back to the snow. Her fingers crept to his legs, to the new wounds that the cat had rent in his skin. His trousers were torn, flayed, as was the flesh beneath. Disbelieving, she dipped a finger into one of the tears, barely feeling him shudder beneath her touch. When she withdrew her hand, her finger was stained with forbidden silver blood.

Tal was a silver Smith. Tal was a silver Smith, and he had hidden it from her for the last two years, because the color of his blood was a death sentence.

Two years, she thought again. Not a day. She had known Tal for two years.

She lifted her gaze. Tal's eyes were open again and he was looking at her. Hopelessness and an odd, mercurial relief tightened the corners of his mouth. He expected her to...what? She could almost feel the thought, the supposition, the memory of what her old self might have done.

Behind her, the mooncat roared. It ceased scraping at its ruined eye and turned its head fully around so it could locate her.

Hurriedly, Elodie shoved her hands under Tal's shoulders and yanked him backwards, pulling him across the snow. There would be time to figure out her memories and the mystery of Tal's blood later. First, she had to save both him and herself.

The cat was wary now, its good eye trained on her as its bad eye wept blood and fluids. Its tail lashed against its back legs. It stalked forward, teeth bared, intent. It would no longer underestimate her.

Ice groaned beneath Elodie's boots. She had reached the frozen lake again. An idea blinked into being, the only way they might stand a chance at survival. She swallowed hard and then stopped, setting Tal down and bracing herself. Then she took a slow, careful step away from him.

The mooncat's gaze followed her. Good.

"Elodie," Tal coughed, rolling on his side to watch her. The sound of her name from his lips, thoughtlessly spoken without bitterness, made her mad heartbeat slow a fraction. "What—what are you..."

"You were right," she said in a low tone, not taking her eyes off the cat. "I will not let you go."

She took another step. A piece of ice snapped beneath her heel and splashed into the water; she'd reached her little fishing hole. The place where her body warmth had been slowly melting the ice, weakening it.

She stopped.

The cat paused. It paced around her in a half-circle, keeping its good eye toward her, cautious of her now—but she had no weapon, no natural strength. She was an easy kill. She flung her arms out and bared her own teeth. "Come and get me," she shouted. The ice caught her words and flung them out into the peaks, into the sky, into the champagne-and-coral clouds: transcendent, merciless. The echo rattled another memory loose within her.

I swear to protect you, and to not allow harm to come to you, and never to harm you myself. A younger voice, one full of emotion that he'd not yet learned to hide.

The mooncat snarled and pounced. Elodie did not close her eyes. She was many things, but a coward was not one of them.

No one has ever accused me of being soft, whispered her own voice, corrosive as it settled back into her heart.

The mooncat struck. It jaws latched onto her shoulder. Its front feet landed next, driving her downward, but even its big, broad paws could not distribute such a blow evenly over the weakened ice.

I am not unguarded. Old words: a precious safety net, the only thing she could trust.

Elodie's breath was a stuttered gasp. There was no room to register her past as it burrowed back into her bones. The pain had come now, and it was a wave of fire burying fangs in her shoulder, and two rows of claws piercing her back.

She would scream. She owed Tal that much.

The thought was true, but she couldn't yet recall why. Still, she inhaled a jagged breath and let it out in a wail—just as the ice beneath her cracked and gave way.

The cat's weight drove them both instantly into the freezing deep. Her cry cut off. The water was cold enough to feel like an inferno on her skin. The shock of it made her inhale. She choked on a lungful of water.

It was dark, but there was a dim light above her—sunlight through ice. It was mostly blocked by a writhing ivory mass. The cat was lashing out, snapping off more plates of ice as it desperately tried to free itself, widening the hole in the process. One of its back legs smashed into her with enough force to break a rib and force all the remaining breath from her body. She went reeling away into the murk.

Air. She needed air. She needed air *now.*

She curled in the water, found the dim sunlight, and twisted toward it. She reached not the hole, not the air, but the cap of unbroken ice. There was a shadow on the other side of it. She could almost make out a face. She could almost make out the sound of her name. She tried to call Tal's.

What is he to you? Just another guard dog, just another toy for you to break and discard? How dare you call him yours?

She pounded on the ice. The water slowed her blows, rendered them ineffective. There was nothing she could do. Nowhere for her to go but to her death.

She could make out the shouting now. It was Tal. He wasn't calling her name; he was crying out in pain.

Because of his oath. It was trying to force him to save

her, and he was trying to fight it. It would hurt him. But not for long.

Instead of leading me to my destiny, he led me to the Destroyer.

She flattened her palms against the ice. Her memories were slipping back in, one by one, and she still didn't have enough to wholly make sense of the puzzle that was her. But oh, she remembered why her blood was wrong, and she remembered what color it *should* be, and she knew what she could do now to save herself.

She called up her fire, concentrating on the palms of her hands. She didn't need much magic. Only a little bit. Enough to melt the ice. And, if she was lucky, enough to warm herself before she died of exposure.

Nothing happened.

Tendrils of watery red snaked away from her injured palms into the icy water. Her power was gone. It had been gone ever since the explosion—the explosion caused by her poisoning—and without it, she was doomed.

It should be impossible. Magic lived in the metallic blood of its bearers. Even if the poison had weakened her, stolen her strength, it could not have changed her so wholly. But changed she was, and she could no longer fathom how she might save herself.

Tal's shadow was still above her. She fixed her eyes on it. At least she wasn't alone. She had been alone all her life. She didn't want to die alone, too.

The need for air finally became too great. It pried her mouth open and forced her to inhale. Water shoved itself down her throat, a cruel and painful invasion, a leaden weight in her lungs. Her body jerked violently. She began to drown.

You are nothing but the Destroyer to me and to everyone I care about.

Elodie discovered, to her chagrin, that she was a coward after all. She was alone and freezing and dying and scared, scared, scared. Darkness like ink bled over her vision, stealing even Tal's shadow from her. Her sodden lungs forced her to inhale again, and her body jerked and burned with it.

What little strength she'd had evaporated. Her body stilled. Her hands floated away from the icy surface. She began to sink. Her flesh would bloat and rot and then her bones would drift down to the lakebed, food for the sungills that had evaded her.

Mark my words: one day soon, you will face a reckoning.

The Destroyer remembered everything.

And then she died.

CHAPTER ELEVEN

Tal's swords were too far away. He could not break the ice with his bare hands. He had lost too much blood already, was shivering uncontrollably with the shock and the cold, was battered by the memory of Elodie's fingers glazed in his silver blood and her possessive cry as she'd launched herself at his attacker. He could not save her. And yet his oath drove him to do the impossible anyway.

His hands curled into fists against the ice as he cried out. The pain was a blur, a lace of agony laid over his whole body until he could not tell the pain of his wounds from the pain of the oath. Between his fists, through the ice, the Destroyer was a blur of light on dark. Her palms were pale smudges laid flat. He couldn't see her expression.

The oath bore down on him. Helpless against it, he drove a fist into the ice. It didn't even crack beneath the blow, but the oath forced him to do it again, and again, until his knuckles were another point in the map of pain that was his body. Somewhere nearby, the mooncat howled and splashed as it finally latched onto a solid piece of ice and hauled itself out of the lake. Its fur was a double-coat, insulated enough to trap warm air in its layers and keep its hide dry; it would not freeze to death. The creature shook itself and water droplets arced through the air, a thousand rainbows. It snarled one last time and then loped away down the valley, giving up its meal as too costly.

Tal paused in his blows, shuddering, every breath a gasp that cost him far too much effort. That was when he remembered the knife in his boot: the ornamental dagger that Elodie had taken from a corpse, which she had given him to skin the rabbit, and which he'd never given back because he wanted to see her helpless. A feeling crashed over him now at the realization that he still had it, something akin to relief, but there was no time to register it. He snatched the little weapon from his boot, lifted it high, and brought it down hard on the ice.

It was a thoughtless blow, one that could have ended with him being dumped into the freezing water along with Elodie, but he was too used to saving her without thought for his own safety. It was sheer luck that the ice cracked away from him, toward the hole a dozen yards away where its structure had already been weakened. He stabbed downward again, then swung himself sideways to kick through the spider-webbed ice, crying out at how the movement jarred his old and new injuries.

The ice broke into shards. The hole was just wide enough for him to reach through. He managed to pause long enough to peel his coat and shirt off–if he got them wet, he would surely die of exposure even before his injuries or the rust phage had the chance to do the trick–and then laid flat on his stomach atop the ice and reached into the water to find the Destroyer.

She was sinking. Her form was a blur, her hair blocking her face. One of her hands trailed upward, thin red blood leaking from it, mingling with Tal's as he grabbed her forearm and pulled her upward with all his strength. She came in a wash of icy water, limp and yielding, her waist and legs still in the hole. The ice crackled ominously at its edge. He wrapped his arms around her torso–soft, freezing, drenched–and braced himself, then pulled one more time with all the strength he had left.

It wasn't until she was lying prone on the ice, head in his lap, hair soaked with red and silver blood and glacier-clear water, that he realized she was already dead.

Time seemed to crystallize. It spread out from them, webbing the sky, the lake, the ice, the peaks, until everything was veined white with impossibility.

Earlier, he had thought that his pain was so great and so muddled that he could not tell which part of it sprung from his injuries and which from his oath. Now, too late, he realized that none of it sprang from his oath at all. He was sitting immobile, staring down at the body of the girl he'd sworn to protect, and his oath was not grinding down on his bones or driving him to action. It was…gone.

It was gone, and he was free.

And it felt *wrong*.

The wrongness spread itself within him. Its wings opened, feathers whispering over his soul. This was not how it was supposed to go. This was not what his god had promised him. And he thought he had no longer wanted what his god had promised—for him to save the Destroyer, and save the empire through her—but he realized with a terrible suddenness that he did, *he did*, and it was too late.

He closed his eyes. Tipped his face to the sky, and despaired. The moment he'd fantasized about for two years had finally come to pass, and all he could think about was the way she'd cried without making a sound when she had failed to build a fire. The fierce, innocent triumph in her smile when she'd held up the rabbit she'd won from the stoat. The defiance in her cry as she'd launched herself at the mooncat for his sake.

He had done this. He had led the Destroyer into the wilderness in the hopes that this, or something like it, would occur, and even as he had, he hadn't quite believed it truly could happen. Even as he'd struggled to break through the ice and save her a moment ago, he'd imagined her saving herself: a column of fire and steam geysering against the mountains as she rose from the lake like an avenging goddess. But instead, the way she'd died had been wholly human. More like the way he'd thought *he* would die—saving someone else, with no care taken for his own life.

He tilted his head down and looked at the Destroyer. At Elodie. She was splayed brokenly over his lap, her lips blue, frost creeping over them already. She was gone. Her heart-beat had ceased and his obligation to her had died along with it. Whatever wrongness he felt now, he could do nothing about it. It was over.

Except it wasn't. He had grown up in the Skyteeth, in the harsh winters full of alpine blizzards and homemade ice skates and fishing holes carved into frozen ponds. He had been taught from his childhood how to rescue someone who fell through the ice. Even minutes after death, his stepmother had taught him, a person could be saved. She had demonstrated how to breathe air into someone else's lungs. Had warned him that wet clothes had to be immediately removed lest they steal all the remaining body heat. She'd told him that even if these efforts succeeded, the rescued person would likely need further attentions immediately—a warm fire, blankets or furs, potential medical treatment for frostbite or hypothermia—or they could perish again in very little time.

There were no further attentions to be had. He was far too weak to build a fire and they'd used all their firewood in the cave anyway. The sled with the scavenged clothing was too far away for him to drag both himself and her. He was bleeding out, and even if he survived that, he was still dying of rust phage. He could not take care of both himself and Elo-die. If he revived her, she would surely only die again without the attention she needed, and he would swiftly follow.

But it was the right thing to do, and Tal was as helpless as he had ever been against that—so in one final act of faith, he lowered his mouth to the Destroyer's.

He pressed his lips to hers and exhaled. His breath feathered across her lips, melting the frost. He felt her chest rise against his with the inflow of air.

He lifted his head and gasped an inhale. Pain curled its grip tighter on him, unbalancing him, dragging him toward unconsciousness. He resisted. He had chosen to do this and he would see it done. "Help me," he rasped. The prayer was coated with bitterness and the expectation of answering silence, but a prayer it was nonetheless. The Unforged God didn't answer, but Tal found himself able to bend down and breathe into Elodie's mouth again, and again, found the strength to lay her flat on the ice and push his palms hard against her breastbone the way his stepmother had shown him. He pressed down once, twice. Again.

The wrongness within him eased. A slow, gentle warmth replaced it: his god's support. He couldn't find it in himself to push it away.

Beneath his hands, Elodie's chest suddenly contracted. She jerked onto her side and violently vomited up the water that had drowned her. Spasms shook her and she made a soft, reedy sound that was nothing like the Destroyer. He found himself reaching for her. Pulling her hair back–her loose, wild curls crunched in his hands, already frozen–so he could see her expression. Her eyes were open but glazed, unfocused. She looked as if she were half in a dream. She turned her face to his and lifted a trembling hand to touch his bare shoulder, the white line on his collarbone.

"So...so many scars," she murmured, with the hoarse,

drowsy tone of someone who wasn't awake at all. "Who gave them to you?"

"You did," he answered, his voice wretched.

Her hand fell away. Her eyes drifted shut again. She was breathing, but now she was shivering hard enough to crack her head on the ice.

He reached for the shirt and coat he'd thrown aside. There was no oath driving him to defend her, no outside force left to puppeteer his actions, but nevertheless he moved quickly to strip off her wet and freezing clothing. He had seen her naked before, but never vulnerable, and the difference now seemed immeasurable. It was the Destroyer lying with her head in his lap, her body bare and bleeding against the ice, but it was also a girl. Someone helpless, and God help him, someone he *wanted* to protect.

He cradled her head as he pulled his own shirt over her, and then his coat over that. Both were large on her petite frame. She pulled up her knees, curling herself into the new warmth. He drew her onto his lap and she curled into him too, ducking her head tightly against his breastbone, her panting breaths warm on his chest, her shivering wracking his own body. Her weight drove sharp points of pain into his injured legs but he didn't have the strength to shift her, and he doubted there was any way he could hold her that wouldn't hurt him.

There was nothing else he could do. He was still losing blood, and she was still half-frozen and unable to maintain consciousness. Death was coming for them both. He held the Destroyer and waited for it.

Minutes ran and blurred like a painting in the rain. The sun crept higher in the sky. Its light felt liquid, but not in a pleasant way. It poured too brightly over the ice, thick and cold and biting like liquor gone bad. A thin glaze of ice began to form back over the hole in the lake. Tal wasn't sure how long had passed before he realized, with a dangerous sort of slowness, that he no longer felt the cold.

Elodie's frozen hair was plastered against his chest. Her whole self was tucked into him as if he were the only safe place in the world. Her breathing had slowed and her own shivering had stopped; a bad sign. Just an hour ago he would have considered it a good one. He no longer knew what he wanted. He no longer understood how he felt. His god had betrayed him, which had been devastating, but now he had betrayed himself and he was still doing it—sitting here cradling a murderess as if she were a thing that could be broken, a thing that could be loved.

Except she wasn't a thing. She was a person. He hadn't thought that of her for years and had expected never to think it again, and yet here she was: Elodie, murderess and Destroyer, person. Deadly and then dead, and now, somehow, neither.

His thoughts spun slowly into one another, putting down roots, spreading web-like branches that stretched one into another until he couldn't make sense of any of them. He bowed slowly forward, head dipping toward the ice, vision blurring.

His last thought was of Nyx. She dropped to her knees before him, grasped his face in her hands, leaned her forehead against his. Her sobs shook him. He laid his head on her shoulder and let himself close his eyes. Hers was a good face to carry with him into the darkness.

Nyx slapped him. "Stop dying *immediately*, Tal, or I swear I will kill you myself."

His head snapped back with the force of the blow and his eyes opened. He blinked. His vision went from dream-blurry to painfully sharp. Nyx still knelt before him but now he registered the details of her: short braids with burnt ends, expression set in furious lines wet with her tears, a heavy fur coat draped over her shoulders. Her clothing still had spots of melted metal on it from her hair beads.

"Nyx?" Tal dared to ask. His voice came out as a croak. The sound of it made Nyx's expression twist. She swept the coat off her shoulders and wrapped it around his. Something furry and gray and vaguely familiar wiggled underneath it with him, panting against his side. Pinpricks of warmth began to spread over him.

He was not dead. He was not hallucinating. His sister was here. Alive. And recovered, somehow, from her torture.

Her torture at the hands of the Destroyer.

Involuntarily, Tal's gaze fell to the girl in his arms, his breath hitching as he registered the new danger of this situation. Nyx followed his gaze. He saw the moment she recognized who he was holding. Her expression turned to something flat and hard and utterly emotionless. He realized, with a jolt, that it was the same expression he himself had worn so often over the last two years. The grief of seeing it now, here, on the face of his sister, was enough to pull him fully from his shock just in time to clap a hand over the Destroyer's neck, where Nyx's dagger was already slicing toward skin.

The blade that had been meant to open Elodie's throat slid over his knuckles instead. The pain was dull compared to everything else. He scrambled for the right words, the words to make Nyx stop, to make her understand something that even he couldn't yet understand.

His sister made a choked sound when she saw her dagger wet with silver, but she barely paused before she grabbed a handful of Elodie's hair and wrenched her head backwards to expose more of her neck. Her movements were quick, vicious, fluid, the way she had taught Tal. He knew her thoughts. She believed him to be acting under his oath to protect the Destroyer. She thought if she moved quickly enough, she could kill her before he could stop her, and then he would be free.

He couldn't tell her he was already free. He couldn't tell her—if she didn't already know—that part of her own metal oath no longer bound her, either. If he explained that the Destroyer had already died, he would have to explain why she was alive now, and that was something he was not at all prepared to do.

So he lied.

"Stop," he said, blocking Nyx's blow, latching his hand over her wrist. The fur slid half off his shoulder and the furry gray thing beneath it—was that Maluk?—whined. "Nyx, stop.

My...my oath, it's the only thing keeping me alive. So that I can protect her. If you kill her it'll kill me too."

Nyx didn't move the dagger, which was hovering not far from the Destroyer's now-exposed neck. Elodie's shoulders shuddered lightly. A frown creased her mouth as she tried to curl back into Tal, and Nyx snarled to see it. "I'll save you," she promised. "Helenia is coming. She's bringing help. And she's almost certainly stolen more healing tincture, too. You will live."

"Not unless you let the Destroyer live." He had to say the words through gritted teeth, but still, he said them.

Nyx's blank mask shifted to frustrated rage, and Tal shook with relief. He did not want his sister to need that mask the way he'd needed it. Nyx said, "If I let her live, she'll kill me. She was about to kill me on the train."

The memory of that moment rose in Tal's mind. He flinched from it. "She doesn't have her powers," he replied, straining to get the words out, fighting the tug of his over-whelming pain and of unconsciousness. "Her blood is red. She has no fire. I had to save her from the ice, she couldn't even use her magic to save herself." It took too much effort to say so much and his hand dropped from Nyx's, numb and useless. The dagger hovered where it was for a moment longer, trembling with Nyx's need to drive it home.

"Fine," she snapped at last, sheathing the dagger with an angry motion. "I'll kill her after help arrives."

She could do it, and easily. Even if Tal had still been under the sway of his oath, he couldn't have stopped her, not with his swords so far away, not weakened nearly to the point of death by the cold and his injuries. He dragged in a shaky breath and tried to force his mind to think. "A trial," he said. "She should face a trial. The Saints should pass her judgment."

Once a jury ruled her worthy of execution, he would surely be able to accept her death. It would be out of his hands, no matter what he felt or how little he understood those feelings.

Nyx hissed an exhale, still hesitating. Her eyes tightened in consideration. "They could have her staked," she said slowly. "They could have her flayed. They could open one vein for each of her victims. They could burn her."

Tal looked down at Elodie. He did not want Nyx to see his face when he thought of those verdicts, any of which a Saints jury could surely pass down. He didn't want her to see the way the thoughts twisted into him with both discomfort and a terrible, hungry keenness. He was ashamed anew at how he felt: hopeful that they would hurt the Destroyer, and ashamed of that hope, and hopeful that the Destroyer might live, and ashamed of that hope as well. But more than anything else, he abhorred the dark satisfaction in Nyx's voice when she spoke of torture and death. She had changed while he'd been gone.

She had changed *because* he'd been gone.

"Nyx," he said brokenly, because he did not know what else he could say.

Nyx sheathed her dagger. "A jury, then," she said, and together, they waited for the Saints.

Chapter Twelve

The sound of screams, as familiar as a chorus to an orchestral conductor, dragged Elodie slowly from the emptiness of her dreams. At first, she thought she was moving from the blackness of deep sleep into her old familiar nightmare; it happened often enough that she was sometimes able to jar herself to waking at this point and avoid the nightmare entirely. She pulled herself, hand over hand, toward consciousness. She said the name of the person who was always there to wake her: "Tal."

The word was barely a murmur but it did the trick to drive her closer to wakefulness. The arms that were wrapped around her shifted slightly, which was when she realized she was being held. The movement also shifted her legs and allowed frigid air to slither further beneath her shirt, which was when she realized she was mostly naked.

She stopped moving. With crystalline clarity, she recalled exactly what had happened.

The mooncat. Tal's scream wrenching at something within her, something she hadn't known she possessed.

The fall through the ice.

The freezing water pushing itself into her lungs.

The *memories*.

She squeezed her eyes shut more tightly, but her breathing sped up, betraying her wakefulness. She felt the person holding her go suddenly very still.

One of her hands was tucked against the warm skin of a collarbone. Carefully, slowly, she splayed her fingers over it. Her thumb grazed the narrow, puckered line of a scar. With that, she ascertained who it was that held her.

So many scars, she faintly recalled murmuring. *Who gave them to you?*

You did.

This scar was from the fire at the palace. She'd lost control. Burned down nearly an entire wing. He'd saved her. Not before she'd blasted him with a beam of bright white flame, though, one that had carved deeply enough to notch bone.

Her hand was shaking now. From the cold, she tried to tell herself.

Her fingers crept sideways. The notch below his neck. This one was ragged, messy. An assassin's crossbow bolt meant for her. He'd been left behind as the guards hustled her to safety, and had treated the injury himself before returning to the palace. Now she knew why; he couldn't risk anyone seeing his blood.

Lower. Fourth rib from the bottom. He'd woken her from a nightmare. Startled and still under the influence of its blind terror, she'd lashed out at him with a hand full of sparks.

Now, Tal's chest trembled beneath her palm. "Please," he said, strained in a ragged, broken way she'd never heard before. "Stop."

Returning to herself and the present moment, she was thoroughly horrified. He was under an oath. That was why he'd been helping her, why he'd promised to protect her yesterday, why he'd rescued her from the frozen lake today. He was bound to her, and here she was, running her fingers over his chest like a lover. It was a violation. She had no right.

She had never, she realized with the same quick and lurid clarity as a moment ago, had any right to Tal at all.

She snatched her hand back, her body going as rigid as his. "Tal, put me down," she said. Her voice was hoarse and her throat ached like fire. Near-drowning did that to a person, apparently.

He disobeyed, as he always did whenever he could. His hands tightened around her. Despite herself, she felt immediately safer. Or at least, she did until he said in a low tone, "If I put you down, they'll kill you."

She could keep her eyes closed no longer. She opened them, and saw who had been screaming.

The Saints had found her.

She was curled on Tal's lap on the ice of the frozen-over lake. He had no shirt or coat because she was wearing both.

Her own clothing lay in a sodden heap a few steps away. A gray dog was curled up against her and Tal, bushy tail covering its nose, calm bluish eyes tilted up to regard her. Draped over all three of them was a fur the size of a cloak. Beyond the cloak, the Saints screamed for the Destroyer's head.

There were perhaps a dozen of them, and they mostly seemed to be directing their screaming toward each other or toward the figure of a girl who stood between them and Tal, arms crossed, chin lifted. Many of the people Elodie could make out wore the Saints' traditional mask, a mostly-flat plate of metal with only the barest contours of a nose and cheeks, and empty holes for eyes. Several of the Saints were still hurriedly tying the masks on; they didn't want the Destroyer to be able to identify them, she realized.

Here, her thoughts stuttered. *The Destroyer,* she'd thought, as if she were a different person. But it was *her* head they were shouting for, it was *she* who they feared might identify them and then find and punish their families in vengeance.

She retreated into herself. She couldn't face this. Not yet. She would sink back into the darkness of sleep and perhaps, when she woke, she would better understand what it was she was supposed to do now. And who it was she was supposed to be.

She gave herself over to unconsciousness. It stretched up and swallowed her—but just before it did, one last recollection slid into her mind.

Blood. Silver blood on the snow, on the mooncat's jaws, on her hands as she dragged Tal to safety. He was injured.

Worse than he ever had been before in her service. And here they were—with him shirtless and bleeding out on the ice to save her.

She tried to fight her way back to consciousness. Tried to push off the heavy mantle of sleep she'd already started to pull around herself, so she could help him, so she could make him put her down and save himself. But it was too late. Sleep, and her old nightmare, had already claimed her.

The dream started as it always did: with her sister.

They were young. They were in the woods outside the palace. Scorch trees, unfathomably tall, dripped their name-sake red moss toward the forest floor. Elodie wanted to stop and weave a fairy dress from it, but Sarai was gripping her hand hard enough to grind her knuckles together, hauling her through the maze of trees at a near-run. It was dark. Elodie tripped.

Sarai turned back and hauled her to her feet, her fingers leaving imprints on Elodie's skin. Sarai was twelve, older and stronger than Elodie's six years, and her grip hurt. Elodie didn't complain, because she knew something was wrong. She could smell it in the dense, humid silence of the air, the way it crowded close around Sarai, as if to protect her.

Something heavy, something inescapable, was crashing through the brush behind them. The moss quivered with it.

Sarai stopped. "We can't run," she said, and then she bent

down to look Elodie in the eye. "You shouldn't have to run. You shall never have to run again, I swear it."

Terror rose up through the nightmare then, coloring everything with its touch, turning the dreamscape surreal and disjointed. The sky was a web of crimson moss on black night, the stars pinpricks too far away to shed any light at all. Elodie was lying on her chest. Something had knocked her to the ground. Something had stabbed her in the back. Her blood was thick in her mouth. She was drowning in it. Wind raged all around her, a keening scream that made her want to cover her ears. A man stood above her. She couldn't make out his face—but he was more than the blank, looming shadow of her usual nightmares. In fact, she thought distantly, all of this dream was far clearer than it normally was. Then her lucidity faded, and she was wholly her dying child-self again.

She managed to turn her head. Spit out the blood. It speckled bright on the crunchy brown leaves. She tried to scream but it was barely a weak warble of a cry.

All at once, the wind died down. Sarai knelt at her side, picked her up like she used to do when Elodie was a toddler. "It's okay," she whispered, carrying her back toward the palace. "No one will know."

Elodie broke the surface of her dream and came gasping into the real world. The filaments of her nightmare drifted invisibly around her, a spider's web she had been caught in for over a decade now—because it was not only a dream, but a memory. That day, the night before her seventh birthday, had been the night of the Silver Coup. She had been pursued into the forest by assassins and shot with a poisoned arrow. Sarai had been the one to save her, to kill the assassins and carry her afterwards to their cousin and physician Albinus, who managed to concoct an antitoxin in time to save her. But the poison, much like the memory itself, had lingered—had sunk itself into her and claimed her, biding its time to do its deadly work. It necessitated a monthly administration of the antitoxin to stave off its effects, a regimen that she would be forced to adhere to for the rest of her life. And her father, he hadn't even been that fortunate. His body had been found later, dead in his rooms, throat opened by an assassin's dagger.

She was breathing too fast. Her eyes were open but her mind could not yet absorb her surroundings. Too much of her was still entrenched in the nightmare. It sank ghostly talons into her shoulders, knifed coldly through the gap between her ribs, surrounded her with the smell of dead leaves and wet scorch-moss. The dream, the memory, it had been so powerful this time. Details had surfaced that she hadn't remembered before. She didn't want to remember them. She had no idea where she was now, but wherever it was, she would far rather be there than sunk in the quicksand of her own mind.

Her mouth moved. "Hello?" she whispered. No one answered, but something shifted beneath her hand, and she realized that her fingers were tightly curled in something warm and furry. It breathed, its ribs moving gently up and down beneath her palm like a ship rocking at sea, and after a moment her own breathing began to slow to match it.

She looked down. Bluish-white eyes met hers. It was the dog, the gray one that had been with her and Tal on the ice.

Her breath stopped. *Tal*. He had been injured, close to death. She shot to her feet—a mistake, as she was quickly unbalanced and toppled over, smacking her cheekbone hard against the stone-tile ground. The fall only slowed her for a moment. She sat up and braced herself against the wall, about to use it to climb to her feet once again, when she heard the rattle of a chain and felt something cool and unyielding clamped around her wrist.

She froze. It was a manacle. There was one on each hand. She was chained to a cedar-planked wall. Imprisoned. Trapped. But no longer half-naked, she realized, looking down at herself. She wore unfamiliar, roughspun trousers along with Tal's shirt and jacket. And the points of pain on her back and sides where the mooncat had bitten her were gone. Movements made clunky by the chain, she pulled the shirt up and twisted around to try to see the injuries. Had they given her healing tincture? Surely if they had, they would also have healed Tal. Unless…unless the Saints knew nothing about him except that he was her guard. Unless they considered him no better than her, and more expendable, in which case they might have executed him already.

The thought sent starbursts of panic flickering over her skin. She yanked hard at the chains holding her, tried to call up her fire to melt them, but nothing happened.

From one of the dark corners of her little room, a female voice spoke. "Well. That's reassuring."

Elodie jerked around. The panic intensified to hot, fizzing trails of sparks. If only she could will them into existence, could wield them to defend herself, to free herself—but no matter how fiercely she concentrated, the sparks tormented only her.

"Who are you?" she demanded, squinting to find whoever had spoken, tugging her shirt back down while she did.

The person stepped forward. Guileless light brown eyes, curly black hair and freckled brown skin, a mouth that looked made for smiling. She was shorter even than Elodie and perhaps a year or two older, with more generous curves and a sturdy frame. Every inch of her proclaimed kindness and naivety. "I am Helenia," she said. She moved closer, just out of reach of Elodie's chains, and held out something. A loaf of bread.

Elodie stared at it. They were feeding her? What did this mean?

Helenia's mouth curved slightly. "It's only rye bread. I was going to bring you a bowl of soup, but the others worried you might use the bowl as a weapon. You're far less likely to bash me in the head with a loaf of rye, although I will admit it's probably stale enough to do at least a little damage if you care to try."

Elodie's stare moved from the bread to the girl. Her mind worked furiously. She had many, many questions, but the person asking the questions usually held the least amount of sway in any given conversation, so she stayed silent a moment while she debated what to do. Her priority was to find out about Tal. But if she was going to regain at least a shred of control, she couldn't reveal that she cared about him or he might be used against her.

She blinked. She cared about Tal—and not only because he had been the only person she could trust to protect her in the cesspit of the palace. The thought was a revelation that only added to her panic. She was more vulnerable now than she had been half-naked on the ice, and she couldn't let this girl or any of her other captors know that or they would surely tear her to shreds.

They had to know she was the Destroyer. They wouldn't have taken so many precautions with her otherwise. If they thought her dangerous, she would conform to their expectations, and in so doing gain back some leverage.

She pulled the memory of her old self over her like a coat of Smithed armor. The Destroyer settled into the lines of her expression, the cant of her shoulders, the cruel and ready grace of her stillness. "Where," she said, her voice steady and slow and deadly, "is my guard?"

"With his sister," Helenia answered, "preparing for your transportation to the Saints headquarters, where your trial will be held."

In a single sentence, Helenia stripped away all of Elodie's imagined control, and she did it without ever letting her smile fall. Elodie began to realize that she had underestimated this girl. Helenia's face still radiated warmth and naivety, but Elodie began to see now how she might use that as a weapon.

Elodie's mind raced through the information that Helenia had revealed. Tal was alive. He was with Nyx. He was well enough to travel to her trial, an event which would certainly not end well for Elodie.

Helenia lifted the bread. "Go on, take it. You must be starved."

Elodie was indeed starving after more than a full day of eating nothing, but if she accepted this kindness it would only weaken her. She lifted her chin.

The other girl sighed. "It's not poisoned. Though I suppose I would be the type to kill with hospitality, if I were planning to do a murder."

"But my murder you shall leave to the jury of Saints," Elodie said, threat weaving through her voice like a bone viper slipping through the grass. "Who will be the witnesses during this trial? Tal and Nyx and a horde of Saints, of my victims' kin? That hardly seems fair. Will I even be permitted to make an appearance to defend myself?"

Helenia's smile dropped like a light flicking off. "So you do know her name. How long did you torture her before she gave that up?"

The memory of it dropped back into Elodie's head, and it felt like falling through the ice all over again.

You are a bitch.

What do you know of loss?

One day soon, you will face a reckoning.

Her scream. The smell of burnt hair. Nyx's blustering bravado, the way it broke, the way she kept going anyway.

Elodie had tortured her because she'd feared Nyx held sway over Tal, and she wanted no one in that position except herself. She had nearly killed someone precious to Tal *because* she was precious to Tal.

An emotion rose thick in her throat. She could hardly breathe past it. It was alien, sour, unbearable. It demanded action but there was nothing she could do.

What was happening to her? She felt like her past was half a dream, like her memories were no longer quite part of the equation that was her. She did not know herself. It was as frightening a sensation as she had ever felt. She longed for her power, longed for the tongues of fire that would cloak and conceal her, and just as strongly wanted to be sick at the thought of wielding her magic again—as if it would swallow her up as wholly as it had all her many victims.

Helenia was watching her, gaze sharp and assessing as if she were picking thoughts out of Elodie's head and examining them one by one. "Interesting," she murmured.

"What?" Elodie snapped, realizing too late that she sounded nothing like the Destroyer.

"You regret torturing Nyx."

Elodie said nothing. There was nothing she could say. If she agreed, it would be taken as false posturing in the hope that the jury might be merciful and grant her a quick execution. Even so, she couldn't bring herself to deny it, either. "What do you want?" she demanded instead, giving up on her useless attempt to gain control of the conversation. "Why did you come in here?"

"I came to bring you bread. And to see, with my own eyes, the one who tortured the girl I love."

Elodie inhaled. The panic that had been sparking over her skin liquefied and congealed, coating her whole body like a plaster. She didn't move, lest it crack.

Helenia tilted her head, observing, seeing too much. "Regret is not absolution."

No. Of course it wasn't.

After another long moment of silence, Helenia shrugged one shoulder, tore a chunk of bread from the loaf, and tossed it into the air. Elodie flinched before she realized the other girl was feeding the dog, who was still lying placidly at Elodie's feet. He lifted his head to snatch the food from the air and swallowed it in one gulp, then settled back down as if nothing of any import was going on.

Elodie nudged him with a toe. He grunted his annoyance but didn't move. It was foolish of the Saints, she reflected, to leave this animal in here with her. If he was supposed to be a guard dog, he was a poor one. Still, she said nothing about it, because she was afraid if she did Helenia might take him away and then she would be even more alone than she already was.

"I want to see Tal," she said. She tried to make her voice imperious and cold again, but it wavered on his name.

Helenia snorted. "Certainly not."

Elodie flinched. "Is he—is he well?"

Helenia's eyes narrowed. "Exactly how much do you remember?"

"Of the accident on the ice? Enough to recall he must have been near death when you found us." She said nothing of Tal's silver blood, which was probably what Helenia was truly asking. She couldn't imagine they hadn't already figured out he was a Smith, but if they didn't know, she wasn't about to betray him to them.

"No," Helenia said. "Of your past."

She wanted to know if Elodie remembered being the Destroyer. Which meant Tal must have told them how she had forgotten, how the poison must have made her forget, how it had stripped away her powers and her very self. If they knew that, then she had nothing left to threaten them with and no vestige of control over her situation. She was at their mercy, and they were unlikely to show her any at all.

She had heard of Saints trials. Sometimes they sent the bodies back afterwards. The Cobalt Baroness had been torn apart by wolves. When Albinus had performed the autopsy, he found she'd been half-eaten before finally dying. One of the lesser ladies of the platinum court had been assassinated more recently, poisoned with a toxin that had rotted her from the inside out. Her screaming had wracked the palace for days before Sarai finally gave the order to end her suffering.

Elodie looked at a point in the distance over Helenia's shoulder. "I remember enough to know that my sister will raze you all to the ground if you kill me."

That was true enough. Elodie didn't necessarily trust Sarai—she and her sister loved each other fiercely, but Elodie was her weapon as much as she was her family—but she knew without a doubt that Sarai would bring the entire empire crashing down around the Saints in retribution for Elodie's death.

Helenia tore off another hunk of bread and tossed it to the dog. "She already suspects you're dead. Any retribution she has planned is likely in motion against us as we speak."

Elodie's gaze snapped to Helenia's. If the Saints were already facing the empire's full wrath, perhaps they might ransom her back to stave it off. But before she could demand more information or ask how long it would take to travel to the Saints facility, Helenia tossed the rest of the loaf of bread toward her. It landed with a hollow clunk on the tiles at her feet. The dog lifted his head and looked at it, licking his lips.

"You'd better eat that before Maluk does," Helenia said, and then turned on her heel and left without another word.

"Wait," Elodie called after her involuntarily, straining to the end of her chains. They clanked dully against the wall and against the delicate bones of her wrists. Her heartbeat was a mad, flailing thing, a rabbit trapped in its own burrow. "Please, let me see Tal." She hated begging, hated the film it left on her tongue, but she needed to see him. She couldn't fully believe he was alive and well otherwise.

Helenia stepped outside the threshold of the door, which had been kept ajar this whole time, and into the shadows on the other side. "Do you really think we would let your protector in here, so that he could die defending you from his own kin?"

"No, that's not—that's not what I want," Elodie said, but was at a loss for what she *did* want.

Helenia paused for a moment, the faintest hint of pity in her kind smile. "I do not believe you will see Tal again."

She closed the door, leaving Elodie in darkness.

CHAPTER THIRTEEN

THE RUSTY SHEARS RASPED AS THEY SCISSORED THROUGH Nyx's curls. The sound was gratifyingly violent, the strands of burnt hair landing at her feet even more so. With each twist of her wrist, she sawed off more memories. When she was finished, she would sweep the hair into a pile and burn it the rest of the way. She would never have to look at it again.

She raised her head to check her progress, eyeing her reflection in the polished tin plate that served as a mirror. It reflected her well enough: muscled shoulders, strong, straight nose, brown skin, brown eyes that simmered appealingly with anger. She wasn't sure if she liked her hair this length, though. Her curls haloed close around her scalp in a way that made her look too much like her mother.

What kind of a mother sends a daughter to be tortured?

Nyx set her jaw and tossed her shears into the hand-washing bowl, where they splashed loudly into the dirty water. Saasha hadn't "sent" Nyx to be tortured. She had gone with her. She had risked her own life to ensure the success of Nyx's mission, to make sure Nyx didn't waver. She'd had to *watch* Nyx be tortured. Surely that was just as hard, if not harder, than what Nyx had gone through.

But still: *what kind of a mother,* whispered the words in the back of Nyx's mind, and it no longer quite sounded like Helenia's voice. It sounded like Nyx's own.

Nyx snatched up a straight razor and bent toward the mirror. She placed the blade at the back of her scalp, planning to shave herself bald.

"That," said a ragged male voice from her back, "looks like a terrible idea."

The razor clattered to the floor and went spinning. Nyx cursed and leapt back just in time to avoid getting a toe sliced off. A hand, paler than her own, dipped down to grab the razor's handle mid-spin.

Nyx's gaze jerked up as Tal straightened to standing before her. He had grown in the last two years. She had known that, of course she had known that, but it was easier to take in the details of his transformation now that he was neither trying to kill her nor attempting to bleed out on a frozen lake against her express orders. His hair was longer than when he'd left home, his cheekbones sharper, and the shadows beneath his eyes looked permanently carved there. But it was the way he held himself that was the most different.

He'd always had the strait-laced posture of a soldier, but now it looked fragile, as if he held himself together only by force of will.

When he held the razor out to Nyx, the echo of another moment drifted between them: him standing above her with his blades drawn, anguish and horror bleeding over his expression when he recognized her. Now, though, he only looked haggard and a little bit lost. She accepted the razor from his hands and then lunged forward, throwing her arms around him in a hug.

He was stiff at first, shocked for a few beats too long, as if he'd forgotten what an embrace felt like. After a moment, he softened slightly and his arms went around her. "I love you very much, Nyx," he said, a tiny trace of his old humor in his voice once again, "but it is perhaps not the best idea to throw yourself at people while holding a razor."

She sniffled loudly and withdrew, blinking her tears back. "You woke up," she said unnecessarily. "How are you?"

Tal glanced around, rubbing his head with the manner of a person still half-befuddled with sleep. "I am well enough, I suppose. What happened? Where are we?"

"At a Saints outpost. We're a few days' journey from the main facility, where we'll be headed once you're ready."

He looked down at himself, examining his clothing—a worn sweater and borrowed pants—and the room, which was a tiny area with barely enough space for the bed, a single dresser, and the washstand. Then, finally, he glanced down at his left wrist, which was connected via manacle and chain to a bedpost. He looked bewildered for a moment and then inhaled sharply, his eyes snapping up to find the sheathed twin swords that Nyx had retrieved and then placed across the room, out of his reach.

"Nyx," he said urgently, turning back to her, "where is—the Destroyer?" He fumbled her name but recovered quickly. "What did they—"

Nyx bared her teeth. "Don't worry, little brother, she's alive and well enough to face her trial. Your oath is satisfied for now. Helenia even insisted on giving her what little of the healing potion supply they didn't use on you. Personally, I think we should've let her bleed all the way to the base."

Tal reached out to steady himself against the bed and then sank down on it. He covered his face with his hands. The manacle's chain clanked against the wood. He took in a shuddering breath. "I fear," he said, his voice muffled, "that I have done something foolish."

Nyx hesitated, gazing down at him. She considered, not for the first time, the ways in which the past two years might have changed him beyond just the way he looked. She spotted the edge of a scar at the neckline of his shirt, and remembered the Destroyer running a hand over it on the icy lake. A black rage rose up and Nyx waited until it passed before easing down on the bed beside her brother.

"You can tell me anything. I won't judge you," she said as gently as she could, trying to channel sweet Helenia. She hesitated again, not sure how to phrase what she needed to ask. "Back on the ice...you'd given her your shirt. She was mostly naked. And she—" Her throat closed up, thick with anger. In her mind, she ran through a few different methods in which she could kill the Destroyer, until at last she felt calm enough to go on. "She acted...familiar...with you. Tal, has she ever used you in any way other than as a guard?"

Tal lifted his head, looking genuinely confused for a moment until his eyes cleared and he huffed a dry, startled-sounding laugh. "Nyx, no. It's never been like that. I don't think she's ever been with anyone that way, in fact. And I would be the one to know. I was at her side every moment of the day and night."

"I saw her face," Nyx insisted. "I saw the way she was looking at you."

His mouth twisted. "That was Elodie. Not...her."

He'd managed to tell them the barest details of what had happened after the train wreck before succumbing to unconsciousness as they'd packed him on the sled. He'd explained how the Destroyer had forgotten her identity, how her powers had seemingly evaporated, how she'd dared to call herself by a name other than the only one that suited her. Nyx's face twisted and she desperately wished she could spit on the floor—but Helenia was staying in this room too, and her girlfriend would first kill her and then put her on eternal mopping duty if she dared transgress against its cleanliness. She settled for hissing, "Elodie *is* the Destroyer. That's her birth name. She told it to me, when she was *torturing* me."

He recoiled, and Nyx immediately felt terrible for reminding him of what she'd been through.

His hands fisted in the sheets. "I had a vision of what you did," he said quietly. "The poison. Nyx, how could you? How could you do such a thing for me?"

She wanted to shake him. "I did it for you because I love you, dolt. And I would do it again." Then her mind caught up with his words. "Wait, you had another vision?"

He nodded, looking miserable. "The only one for the last two years. I wanted the Unforged God to show me how to save you. Instead he showed me how to save her."

Now Nyx did spit on the floor—right in time for the door to creak open and admit Helenia, who immediately slanted an arch look at her girlfriend.

Nyx put up her hands. "We were discussing the bitch. I can't be blamed."

"You can and will be blamed," Helenia said with a smile, "and also, why are you holding a razor?"

From behind Helenia, one of the other rebels leaned past the doorway, probably hoping to get a glimpse of Tal. This outpost was tiny, only big enough to house the dozen rebels stationed here if they all piled together like a heap of kittens on the floor of the common room, and every one of them had either been fascinated with or repulsed by her silver Smith, oath-bound brother. "Off with you," Nyx snapped at this one, and the man glared at her but turned away.

Nyx allowed herself a moment to worry about how the rest of the Saints would react when they learned of Tal's magic. Only a handful of people had known his secret before, but there had been no way to hide it today, not with him leaking silver blood everywhere. Now that the Saints knew what he was, they would surely want to use his foresight to help leverage the rebellion in their favor. They didn't understand, or care about, the complicated relationship he seemed to have with his abilities now. Nyx wasn't sure if it would make the situation better or worse that the Saints had no formal ranks or leadership, no single person who could wield the power of the rebellion as a whole to enforce their will on Tal. It might just mean more factions would develop amongst them, which could only lead to further complications.

She pushed the thoughts away. One worry at a time, she told herself.

Tal was smiling at Helenia. A fleeting joy lightened his features. "Hel," he greeted her, using her nickname. The two of them were old friends, having been raised in the same township, both holding aspirations of being priests until they grew out of it. Though Helenia, Nyx supposed, had never truly grown away from her devotion to the holy texts. Lately she had taken to debating various translations of scripture with Saasha, conversations that sometimes went too long and grew too charged for Nyx's comfort. The two women tended to have wildly different interpretations of what the Unforged God asked of his followers.

"Tal," Helenia responded. "It is very, very good to see you. How are you feeling?"

"Not poorly, all things considered. Thank you for the timely rescue."

"Ah. You have your sister to thank for that. I must admit I tried to dissuade her, though I'm grateful now that I failed in that respect." Her tone was light enough, but something complicated and unhappy flickered beneath it. Nyx winced. She had a lot to make up to her girlfriend, but she was grateful that Helenia was apparently willing to save that difficult conversation for later, when they didn't have an audience.

Helenia closed the door behind her and swept across the floor, carefully stepping over the wet spot. Wanting to distract her from her worries, Nyx held out the razor. "Tal thinks it's a bad idea for me to shave my own head," she explained. "Would you care to do the honors?"

Helenia grinned, looking delighted. Nyx immediately felt warmer and somehow softer, a better version of herself, as she often did when Helenia was near. "I've always thought you would look gorgeous bald. Yes, of course. Come sit at this end of the bed and I'll get started."

Neither of them mentioned that Tal would also be capable of shaving her head. They had talked, in low and careful voices while he was asleep, about what measures would be best to ensure that his oath could not force him to free the Destroyer or hurt anyone who might threaten her. Keeping potential weapons out of his reach was one of the measures they'd agreed on. Although, judging from how easily he'd handed the razor back to her a moment ago, it might be an unnecessary one. Odd, that—she'd thought his oath, which he'd had to fight tooth and nail in the aqueducts in order to keep from killing his own sister, would have now forced him to be more active to protect the Destroyer. She wasn't about to bring it up, though, in case the mention of his vow might somehow jar it back into effect. She had little experience with metal oaths, and having a newly-formed one herself didn't make her any more knowledgeable of their vagaries.

Helenia bent down to drop a kiss on the top of Nyx's head, and then placed the razor at the bottom of her scalp. Slow and smooth, she stroked it upward. Nyx's curls scattered to the floor.

"I've just been to see the Destroyer," Helenia said then.

Nyx went rigid. Only the sensation of the sharp razor skating above her ear kept her from whirling around and yelling at Helenia—which was probably the very reason Helenia had waited until this moment to tell them. The thought of the girl she loved alone with that monster...it made her want to yank the razor back from Helenia, march down the length of the short hallway, and use the tool to open the Destroyer's throat as she should have on the lake.

Tal stood in a sharp, jerky movement, all of his attention suddenly fixed on Helenia. "What? She's awake? You should not have spoken to her alone, she could have—"

Helenia pursed her lips. "Could have what? Slain me with merely the force of her glare? Destroyer or not, the girl is harmless as she is now."

"She is not," Tal bit out, "harmless."

The razor went still on Nyx's scalp. "Forgive me, Tal," Helenia said quietly. "Of course not."

The razor began to move again. Helenia continued,

"She did some posturing about how her sister would bring the empire's hounds down on our heads if we executed her, which is fairly valid as far as threats go. In fact, the Saints who are stationed here informed me that they intercepted a messenger hawk just a few hours ago who carried a warning that the Iron Empress is throwing her armies and spies at every suspected safehouse in the country already."

A muscle in Tal's jaw tightened. "So Elodie—the Destroyer—she remembers who she is, to have made such a threat against you."

"I can't be certain exactly how much she remembers, but yes, she knows who she is."

Tal took a breath. His expression was carefully neutral, giving away none of his thoughts. "The Iron Empress is hunting us, you said. Sarai survived the explosion as well, then?"

Mentally, Nyx added the empress's name back to her list of people who needed murdering.

"Yes, I'm afraid she did," Helenia replied. "And she's mobilizing her troops with frightening speed, committing vast resources to avenging the Destroyer. Her sister must be very dear to her."

"Dear, yes," Tal said tightly. "And useful."

Helenia made a thoughtful humming sound. "Not so useful in her current condition, though. Even if they find out she's alive and manage to retrieve her, she will not be able to turn her fire on us. Speaking of which, do we have any idea of how she came to be in that condition?"

Nyx frowned. "I have no idea. It should be impossible to strip a Smith of their powers. Right? The poison was meant to weaken her, to make her magic unstable and drain it away so she could be killed, but her powers still should have recharged before long and her blood certainly shouldn't have turned red. It can't have been the poison that did that." But even as she spoke, she hoped she was wrong. The idea of having such an effective weapon to use against the noble class, one that could level the field between the metallurgists and Saints, was a heady thing.

"But that poison had never before been tested," Helenia interjected. "We can't properly know for certain how it would typically act, and whether the way it affected the Destroyer is different from that."

Tal frowned. "Her treatments," he said slowly. "She goes to Albinus every month for them, and she was overdue for her appointment on the train. She and Sarai try to pass the treatments off as a mere beauty regimen, but I believe it might be something more vital. Perhaps that process, or the fact that it was delayed too long, may have exacerbated the poison from Nyx or interacted with it somehow to strip her of her powers."

"Unfortunately, we lack the information to make more than a guess," Helenia replied.

Tal sighed and leaned back against the bedpost. "I fear you're right. Did the Destroyer say anything else when you spoke to her?"

Helenia glanced at him. "She asked to see you. She was quite keen on it, actually."

At this, Nyx couldn't hold in a snarl. "Of course she wants to see him. He's her human shield. I hope you told her the next time she sees him will be right before her head rolls, and that's *if* she's lucky."

Tal stiffened. "The jury will decide her fate."

"As if they'll show her any mercy," Nyx scoffed. "Half the Saints at the main base have lost a loved one to her. I hope she dies slowly. I hope it hurts."

Tal's gaze went distant. "She said that too," he murmured, a strange look passing over his expression.

Nyx brushed his comment off, not certain who he meant and too focused on her own anger to care. "I hope they let me do it myself," she went on.

Tal's gaze went to her then. He reached out, gently, and touched her cheek. "I'm sorry," he said, sounding helpless.

She blinked, startled out of her tirade. "For what?"

But he only turned away and let his hand fall.

She remembered what he had said earlier, that he had done something foolish. She realized now that he never had told her what it was. She didn't want to push him, though, not now that she'd just gotten him back. He probably only needed time to adjust; once the Destroyer was dead, it would be easier for him to heal, and easier for him to make whatever confession was weighing on his soul. Changing the subject, she asked Helenia, "Did you speak to the physician yet about Tal's prognosis?"

The razor paused in its movements across Nyx's scalp. Helenia sighed. "There's no physician stationed here, only an assistant with some medical training, but I'm afraid he didn't have good news. The potion we had on hand was enough to heal the broken bones and most of Tal's other injuries, but to cure the rust phage will require a more concentrated tincture than we can make."

Nyx and Tal looked at each other for a long moment. He didn't seem to react beyond that, but something inside Nyx coiled in fear at the pronouncement, cinching tight around her ribs. "More concentrated than we can make *here*, you mean, right?" she asked, hating how high-pitched her voice sounded. "We can get some at the base when we arrive?"

Helenia's answer was soft, nearly too kind to be borne. "No. None of our copper Smiths are powerful enough to make what we need. Only the palace Smiths are—it might even be that only Albinus himself could cure him, if that. The rust phage has been absorbed into his blood already, and it seems to be a virulent strain."

When Helenia drew the razor back for another pass, Nyx slammed the side of her palm into the nearly bedpost, making the bed shake. "Then the physician's assistant has to be wrong. He only has a little medical training, you said. He's unlikely to have ever even seen rust phage before, much less treated it enough to gain any real knowledge of it. The copper Smiths at the main Saints facility will be able to do better. I'm sure of it." But her voice cracked, betraying her fear.

Helenia only squeezed Nyx's shoulder, turning a sympathetic look on Tal, who still hadn't reacted other than looking a bit grimmer than before. "I'm sorry."

Nyx swallowed. "We'll... we'll stage a theft at the palace, then, to get more potions. We need to plan a rescue anyway, if Mother and the other Saints who were imprisoned on the train are being held there."

"You know the Saints will have to vote on that. They may not want to commit so many resources to a rescue."

Helenia made one final sweep of the razor. A cascade of short black curls rained down across Nyx's forehead and into her lap and she swept them onto the floor in one violent motion. "I don't care what they say. I'll go alone if I have to."

Tal's hand was suddenly tight around her wrist. "No, you won't," he said, his gaze intense. "Not for me. Never again for me."

She wrenched her arm away. "You do not get to decide who can and can't risk their life for the people they love. I swear I will see you alive and well and free of your oath if it's the last thing I do." He had nothing to say to that, but only stared at her, his eyes pleading. She crossed her arms. "Put away that sad, stoic look," she told him. "It doesn't work on me."

Helenia set the razor down atop the dresser and pulled a broom from the corner. "If you two are ready, we really should get going. That is, if you're feeling well enough to travel, Tal?"

He was still looking at Nyx. "Just promise me you won't do anything until after the trial, at least," he said. "Please."

She thawed, but only slightly. That sad, stoic look might have worked on her a *little*. "Very well. As long as you promise not to die in the meantime."

His smile was a small, rare thing, and it filled her up like light after a long winter's evening. "I do so swear," he pledged, nudging her with a shoulder.

Nyx rolled her eyes and looked to Helenia. "How are we planning to transport the Destroyer without her discovering the location of the base? She ought to be drugged before we bundle her into a sled."

"Already taken care of," Helenia said serenely as she swept the hair into a pile. "I dosed her bread with laudanum powder."

Both Tal and Nyx turned fully to stare at her. "You did what?" Tal said.

"Not to worry, it was a safe dose. She'll fall asleep within a few minutes and then we'll be able to keep her dosed and unconscious as we travel, until we get to the base. Although Maluk will have to ride on a sled for the first leg of the run. I'm afraid I had to feed him a bit of the bread to ease the Destroyer's suspicions. He's likely snoring away next to her as we speak."

Nyx laughed out loud and stood up to sling her arms around her beautiful, devious girlfriend's neck, planting a kiss on her cheek. "Hel, I admire you more every day." Then she frowned and stepped back. "Wait, why was Maluk in the room with you?"

Tal stirred, looking uneasy. "I...I told him to stay with her. When you were putting us on the sled to bring us here, before I passed out."

Helenia swept the hair into an empty night pot and set the broom aside. "She had a ferocious grip on his fur and wouldn't let go, even when she was unconscious herself. I didn't want to pull out Maluk's fur in getting him away, and he seemed happy enough to stay with her anyway, so I left him."

Nyx shook her head. "She could have hurt him, or threatened him to try to get something from us. You should have taken more care. Tal raised him from a pup, he's part of the family."

Helenia took the polished-tin mirror off its stand and handed it to Nyx. "I felt she wouldn't hurt him. The girl is many things, but I don't think she's cruel." Nyx inhaled sharply at that outrageous statement and started to respond, but Helenia raised a hand to forestall her. "I apologize, I misspoke. What she did to both of you was unspeakably cruel. I only meant...I'm not sure. I feel as though something is disjointed, or perhaps new, in her. She doesn't quite match what I expected, given the descriptions of her that I've heard. In any case, I'm sure it'll all come out in the trial, but first we have to get her there."

Nyx held up the mirror to examine herself. Helenia had done an excellent job. Her head was smooth now, her face sharper and more angular without the softening effect of her braids. Her eyes looked darker than she remembered, her mouth less kind—though it had never been overly kind to begin with—and slanted with a new hardness. She felt, suddenly and unexpectedly, like herself.

She set down the mirror and stood up. "I'm ready," she told her girlfriend. "Let's go."

CHAPTER FOURTEEN

Tal did not watch when they retrieved Elodie from her cell. When the huddle of silent, on-edge rebels carried her prone body past his room, they kept her head wrapped up in a wolf skin. He didn't see her face.

One of her hands fell, though. The rebels jostled her as they maneuvered down the tiny hallway and nearly dropped her. They caught her in time, shifted their grip and eyed each other with an apprehension so loud it was nearly audible, but none of them folded her arm back where it had been. It slid along the floorboards, her evenly-trimmed fingernails whispering against the doorframe, her slender pianist's fingers curled slightly toward her palms.

Nyx rose from the bed and kicked the door shut.

Tal exhaled. Nyx slung an arm around him, a gesture that seemed comforting and sisterly, but the lean muscles in her shoulder were tight. She was ready to restrain him in case he leapt up to defend Elodie. He could tell her she wouldn't need to, but then he would have to tell her why, and he would have to give the reasoning behind what he had done—and that he couldn't do, because so much of it remained unfathomable even to himself. There were too many things he couldn't explain. He couldn't tell them that it was his fault Elodie was alive again. He couldn't tell them why the thought of her death at the hands of the Saints jury made him feel both desperately afraid and darkly, ravenously hopeful. He couldn't tell them that in his head, she was no longer *the Destroyer,* but *Elodie*.

He couldn't tell them what he'd dreamt about while he was asleep: Elodie's hands light on his chest, and him shivering beneath her touch. He couldn't tell them that he'd asked her to stop not because he couldn't stand the feel of her skin against his, but because he had *liked* it, because it had made all of him lean in to her like she was the sun he orbited around— and *that,* he couldn't stand.

He was finally free of her, and yet more of him belonged to her now than ever before.

They waited in silence while the sleds were readied and Elodie's limp form secured upon one. Then Nyx produced the key to his manacle and walked with him to the outside of the small building. There were four sleds all in a row, nearly two dozen dogs barking and tugging, excited for what they sensed would be a long run. Their anticipation was a sharp contrast to the uneasy countenance of the rebels, the way the mushers shifted their weight on the foot boards, the way their eyes went from Tal to the unmoving, body-shaped bundle on the last sled in the line. Tal ignored them all as Nyx clamped the other end of the manacle to the first sled's handle. She touched his shoulder when she was done, a gentle gesture entirely at odds with the scathing look she then turned on her comrades. They shifted and murmured and turned away, finding other things to be busy with as the caravan prepared to leave.

And then they were off. The dogs galloped cheerfully through the mountain pass, the serrated peaks jutting to either side as the sled runners hissed cleanly against the packed snow. That night they camped in a creaky, ramshackle waystation, a small cabin whose doors were left unlocked for travelers. There wasn't nearly enough room for all of them, but Nyx and Helenia both insisted that he be among the ones who slept inside near the little fire.

He didn't dream of Elodie's hands on him. He didn't wonder whether anyone was giving her water or waking her from her nightmares. What he did know was that she would be well-guarded, and that was all he would allow himself to be concerned with.

Maluk woke from his laudanum-induced sleep the next morning. When the door of the cabin creaked open before first light, the old dog bounded in and buried Tal beneath his furry body, jaw lolling in a canine grin. Tal smiled and sat up. When he ran a hand down the dog's back, he felt the spot of crinkled fur where Elodie had gripped and refused to let go.

"You too, old boy?" Tal murmured, and then got up with a sigh to make ready for the day.

His leg ached as he dressed himself. The broken bone had healed, the open wound vanished into a thin pink scar, but spots of rust phage still speckled his shin and sank tendrils into his blood. He was dying, probably: something else he didn't allow himself to think about.

The caravan ran hard all through the day. By lunchtime, the early mountain winter had retreated like a tide, leaving behind pools of spring: a reedy ash tree straining valiantly toward the sun, a clump of blue-green clover waiting in vain for the arrival of bees, stubborn white snowdrop flowers watered by glacial melt. When the ground beneath the sleds' runners changed from packed snow to mud and bumpy rocks, they stopped briefly to retrofit wheels to the sleds and then pushed on. But it was far harder for the dogs to pull in such conditions, and they were already tired from the long run the day before—so when the caravan reached the ruins of an old temple at the foot of the Skyteeth, the Saints agreed to stop for an early dinner and to make camp so the dogs and mushers could rest.

The wide clearing that housed the temple was a natural cathedral of its own. Towering sycamores and mote trees bowed over it, and the light that filtered through their leaves was still and green and holy. Buoyant bits of fluff—mote tree seeds—skimmed and drifted through the air, falling gently on the dogs and Saints like a benediction. From beyond the clearing came the thoughtful rippling of moving water: a tributary of the Entengre flowing toward one of the lakes at the bottom of the mountain range.

Tal looked at it all, and hated it.

He hated the peace of it, the invitation to reflect, the gentleness that contrasted so sharply with what his god had required of him. He hated the unassuming temple that seemed to meld with the forest, half-in and half-out of the clearing, its blocks run through with veins of copper and nickel and zinc; he hated how it was similar to the smaller and newer chapel in his old township, the one that he'd prayed at so fervently when he hadn't understood what lay in store for him. But most of all he hated the presence he could sense here. His god was waiting for him, had perhaps been waiting for him for a long time, and Tal could no longer put off the confrontation that had been two years in the making.

Helenia, who was standing beside him as she supervised the unpacking of the food stores, noticed the direction of his gaze. She looked to the temple and was still for a long moment, a sad sort of peace sliding over her expression, before she touched Tal's hand. "I feel the need to pray. Would you like to come with me?" she said kindly, because of course he would not be allowed to go anywhere without his manacles, without a guard.

Nyx overheard from the sled behind them. She straightened with a frown. "Hel," she said uneasily, looking from her brother to her girlfriend.

"Not to worry," Tal said with an attempt at a smile. "I think it will be fine. Elodie is perfectly safe and asleep, I have no urge to leap to her defense at the moment."

He caught his mistake too late. Helenia and Nyx traded a glance heavy with some silent conversation. "Elodie?" Nyx replied.

"The Destroyer," he amended.

Helenia squeezed his shoulder and unlocked the manacle that had been on the sled's handrail, clamping it instead around his free wrist. "I'm not worried. It's just a bit of prayer, and you've no weapons and a dozen Saints between you and your oath."

Nyx watched them go, worry creeping over her features, her gaze fixed on Helenia. Tal wondered when her childhood crush on Hel had deepened to such an obvious love, and regretted that he might be a complication between them now. But there was little else he could say to reassure her, so he simply tried to seem as docile as possible while Helenia led him toward the temple. He didn't look at all at the last sled in the caravan, where four Saints were gathered watchfully around Elodie's sleeping form.

They walked through the temple's shadowed entryway. The outside world grew muffled and more distant than it quite should've, as if this building could offer a refuge beyond merely the stones that made up its four walls. It smelled of earth and metal and the white-flowering vines that grew here even in the darkness. The floor was cool, packed dirt, a rich loam that bore no footprints. Hewn pews stretched to either side of them as if they'd risen straight from the bedrock. Directly ahead was the bowl of a low altar. It was empty, except it wasn't, because what the Unforged God required was not coins and trinkets but souls. It was Tal's whole self lying in that shallow clay bowl in front of the pews: his past, his imagined future, his relationships, all sacrificed in the name of faith. He'd given everything to his god. All of himself. And what had he received in return, except pain and confusion and cruelty, and now an impending death?

"Do you ever hate him?" he asked Helenia in a low voice.

She snorted. "Oh, of course."

He blinked, surprise pulling him from his thoughts as he turned to look at her. Her gaze was soft and fixed on the altar, a rueful smile curling at the edge of her mouth. "When Nyx first told me how she planned to free you, I cursed his name. I railed at him for a good few months, actually. Stopped attending prayer services, stopped bothering to argue with Saasha about scripture interpretations...stopped everything, really."

"I thought you were a true believer." *As I used to be,* he thought.

She nudged him with a shoulder. "I don't know about 'true,' but I do consider myself a believer."

"Even when you cursed his name?"

"I still curse his name every once in a while. I doubt I'll be over it anytime soon. But anger is not the absence of belief."

Tal said nothing for a while. He did not sit on the pew, nor did he go to the altar. His god was waiting for him there. "He lied to me," he said at last, softly.

Helenia tilted her head. "About what?"

For the first time in two years, Tal quoted scripture: "'I shall say 'go,' and you will go, and none shall stand against my victory fulfilled in you. I am the great Smith and you are the tool of my forge, and the purpose to which I will bend you is to mend that which is broken.'"

It was the text he had come back to, again and again, during the months he'd had the repeated vision of pledging himself to the Destroyer. He had seen the scripture everywhere he looked. He'd eventually taken it as a sign from the Unforged God, a personal promise penned in an ancient text just for him. How naïve he'd been, how full of faith and arrogance. And oh, how he'd paid for it.

"That's Saint Yvetta's translation," Helenia remarked. "Did you know the word she translated as 'victory' is actually the same word she translated as 'purpose' in the next sentence? From my studies of the original language, I believe both iterations should be translated as 'purpose.'" She glanced over at him and grimaced. "Not, I suppose, that it would make you feel any better. I'm sorry. Sometimes I get carried away when I'm talking about the holy texts. You should hear me and Saasha get into it, we sound like a shed full of cats yowling at each other."

Tal glanced at her, willing to be distracted. "What do you yowl at each other about?"

For the first time, Helenia's voice took on an uncharacteristically bitter tone. "Oh, I natter on about historical context and underlying themes and the biases of the authors, and she howls about 'scripture being plain as day' and 'the inerrancy of the holy texts.' She thinks I am a corrupting influence on your sister."

"Nyx is fully capable of corrupting herself."

"Truer words were never spoken." Helenia sighed, her head dipping. "I do worry for Nyx. She can be so single-minded, and Saasha raised her on those gruesome texts of the ancient Saints' martyrdoms, on vengeance and victory as the scriptures' ultimate aim. Saasha completely glosses over the deeper message of how violence is a self-perpetuating cycle. She willfully misses the beautiful core of redemption that the whole of all the texts are rooted in. Nyx doesn't take any of it very seriously, of course—she doesn't really consider herself a believer—but her mother's influence has seeped in. I fear it has affirmed, and even deepened, her..." Helenia searched for the words.

"Natural inclination to violence?" Tal supplied.

"Yes. That. When Nyx does read the texts, she always gravitates to the tales of retribution, of victory coming only through terrible sacrifice. It's as if she's only willing to see the things that support what she already believes and wants, rather than—"

"—considering the historical context and underlying themes and biases of the authors," Tal finished for her.

Helenia made a rueful face and turned away. "I'm sorry. I tend to get worked up when I talk about these things. Please, ignore me. You wanted to come here for your own purposes, not to listen to me preach about scriptural interpretation."

"Please don't denigrate yourself. I have always enjoyed listening to you preach," Tal said. "And I am concerned about Nyx as well." He hesitated. "Did you...are you aware that she..."

"Swore a metal oath?" Helenia closed her eyes, her face settling into lines of pain. "Yes. She told me."

Tal was helpless, as he had been helpless against his own oath—only this was worse, because this was his *sister*, and she had sworn it for his sake. Just as she had poisoned herself for his sake, had undergone torture for his sake, had nearly allowed herself to be murdered by the Destroyer for his sake.

And then, when he'd begged her at the frozen lake, she'd agreed to spare the Destroyer's life. Once again, for him. And in return he had lied to her, betrayed her, and betrayed himself.

Elodie's cool fingers against his chest, counting his scars. Him shivering under her touch. Dreaming about it afterwards. It was *wrong,* and he had never been more ashamed. How dare he protect Elodie—*the Destroyer,* he reminded himself fiercely—over the only kin he had left? He could not pretend he had no choice now, because for the first time in years he did have a choice. And now he needed to make it.

He inhaled. Steeled himself. Then, looking straight ahead at the altar, he said, "One part of her oath is already fulfilled."

He felt the whole of Helenia's attention swivel to him. "What do you mean? Which part? She swore—"

Tal had to be the one to say it. He was the one who deserved to hear the words coming from his own mouth, to bear the hurt of them. "To see the Empire fall, the Destroyer's reign ended, and her dead." All of him quaked. All of him feared. His god moved within him and the weight of a new vision began to pull at his consciousness, but Tal thrust the feeling away with all the strength he had.

"She was dead," he told Helenia. "The Destroyer was dead. She lured the mooncat away from me and onto the ice, and it drove her into the lake with it. She drowned. She was gone by the time I pulled her out. And then..." His face was wet; he was crying. "And then I saved her. I brought her back."

Helenia stared at him. She shook her head, frowning in puzzlement. "Your oath must have compelled you."

"No. My oath was gone. It is gone. I am no longer sworn to protect her, but God help me, Helenia, I still *want* to. Elodie was like nothing I ever expected. She's...she's *funny.* She cried in front of me, Hel, and she hid it, she didn't make a sound, and I could tell it was something she'd done many times before. She's ferocious in this...this terrible, innocent way. I don't know what to do with her. I don't know what to do with myself. I don't understand what I have done or how I feel, except to think that I might be able to love her, and I cannot, I *cannot,* let that be the reason why I have saved the Destroyer."

He had finally spoken the truth that had been growing within him, eating through his soul like acid for the last two days. He cared for Elodie. For a murderess. He had watched her burn thousands at her sister's command. The Destroyer had looked on as Tal had stymied and slain assassin after assassin, as his hands grew red with the blood of his fellow believers–of anyone who dared to rise up against the Empress's favorite weapon. And now, all he could think about was the dread he felt at the thought of her trial and execution, and how he no longer hoped for her death at all.

The wrenching shame, the drowning horror of it, overwhelmed him then. It drove him to move, lest he fall to his knees and disintegrate beneath its weight. He strode toward the altar. It was reddish brown and slightly misshapen, obviously very old. When he was near enough to see into its bowl, he realized it was not empty after all; a bone viper was curled there in a nest of leaves and dried white flowers.

These snakes were lethally venomous. They were also vulnerable. They had no scales and skin so thin it was nearly see-through, and so had taken to protecting themselves by using a special secretion to glue the bones of their victims to their backs. A living thing, clad in an armor of death until no one could see what was beneath.

Rage and pain and guilt rose in Tal, a tide that had been held back for too many moons. He lashed out, kicking at the altar with all his weight. It shuddered and cracked.

"Tal," Helenia said from behind him, her voice choked, but he didn't answer. The bone viper hissed and slithered in a bolt of ivory over the far side of the altar.

Tal fisted his manacled hands together and drove them down like a hammer on the clay's edge. This time it cracked, fault lines snaking through its side. He hit it again. Kicked it again. A starburst of pain flared in his shin, above the spot where his leg had been broken, right where the rust phage was even now festering and spreading. One more kick and the altar broke in half. It was not a clean break. Red-brown clay shards smashed against the ground and shattered. The dead leaves and wilted flowers tumbled out of the broken bowl around Tal's feet. At the sight of them, ruined, used as fodder to line a viper's nest, he finally fell to his knees and opened his mind to his god.

The dreaming space pulled him in immediately. Pressure grew around him, folding him into itself. The vision—one with the same urgent feeling as the one he'd avoided when he'd slept in the cave with Elodie—waited just beyond. It didn't swallow him up, though, didn't pull him in. It waited for him to say what he needed to say.

My God, he whispered into the darkness, *I don't know who I am any longer. I don't know who you are.*

The silence seemed to diminish around him, to soften, though no sound disturbed it.

I hate you, Tal said, feeling his distant real body shudder with the truth of it. Then, shuddering with another truth equally strong: *I love you. I cannot make myself stop loving you. I am helpless against it, as I am helpless against her. Please tell me what you want from me.*

The vision wrapped warmth around him. It beckoned him forward. Utterly spent, utterly without the strength to resist, he allowed it to draw him into itself.

CHAPTER FIFTEEN

THE VISION BLOOMED AROUND TAL UNTIL HE WAS AWARE OF nothing else, not even himself.

A girl, perhaps six years old, lay in a luxurious bed. Silken scarlet sheets and a puffy chenille blanket seemed to swallow her whole. Only her eyes, brown and mouse-quiet, looked out of place amidst the extravagance.

There were footsteps in the hall, and she was afraid.

Two men came in. The door didn't creak; it was too well-oiled. The girl quickly shut her eyes and feigned sleep, but her little rabbit heart tripped in her chest.

The men stood over her bed. If she opened her eyes, she knew who she would see: her father and the royal physician, Albinus, who was also one of her cousins. She knew why they had come. She did not want to hear what they would say. She wished she was well and truly asleep.

"Has there been any change?" asked the oil-slick voice of Albinus.

"No," answered her father–the Emperor–gruffly. "Her blood runs red as the day she was born. I can cut her, and you can see for yourself."

The girl quaked, quaked. Already she had a line of scars and scabs marching up her forearm like army ants. She didn't want him to hurt her any more.

Albinus sighed heavily. "I have researched your questions until my eyes bleed, uncle. A few metallurgists have historically been born with common blood, but even in those cases they usually quicken by toddlerhood, and always before seven years old. I'm afraid it's confirmed: she's a misfire. My condolences. At least you have the other one."

The emperor was a bear of a man. The girl could feel the weight of his shadow on her chest, making it hard for her to breathe. Or perhaps that was simply his magic. He was an iron Smith, after all, like her sister and their late mother. Like all of the members of her family going back for generations–except her.

"How well this has worked out for you, Albinus," her father said softly. "With my youngest daughter a misfire, you take her place as second in line for the throne."

Albinus was wise enough to stay silent.

The emperor's shadow seemed to lighten, shifting like a phase of the moon as his voice changed tone and became more business-like. "Not to worry–my eldest is surely able enough to keep you in line. As for this one, there are already too many rumors that the

Iron Crown's magic is weakening. I cannot let it be known that its power has allowed a misfire even in the royal family."

"Shall I fetch a poison? I have some that are quite quick and untraceable."

"No," said the Iron Emperor. "I will do it myself. It is a father's duty. Come, have a drink with me first."

Their footsteps receded. The girl lay in her bed, rabbit-heart thrumming, mouse-eyes welling up, and wondered what she might do to convince her father not to kill her.

On the other side of the room, a shadow shifted. Another bed was there, one as well-appointed as hers. A figure sat up in it: her sister, twelve years old and ferally beautiful with eyes that burned in the darkness. "Elodie," she said, not bothering to whisper, her voice a low and certain alto that Elodie had always envied, "I will not let him kill you."

"How will you stop him?" Elodie whispered.

"You could stop him. You don't have to be helpless. You shouldn't be helpless."

"My blood won't quicken. They've tried everything." The misery of it, the terrible vulnerability, welled up in her like water through the cracks of the earth.

"You don't turn seven for a few hours," her sister insisted. "It is not yet midnight."

"Sarai," Elodie whispered, almost soundlessly. "I am a misfire."

Sarai threw her covers off. "Then I will save you myself," she hissed, and crossed the room to tug Elodie out of bed.

Sarai flung the window open and threw herself out of it as if she were a thing with wings, a thing that had never known fear.

Elodie crept out behind her. They fled through the gardens, blanketed in the heady scent of jasmine. When they slipped through the secret side gate, petals from the wisteria vines rained down and cloaked Elodie's shoulders in shades of mauve and amethyst. Heather grass brushed at her ankles, making her itch, a welcome distraction.

It wasn't until they entered the scorch-tree woodland that they heard the sounds of pursuit.

Sarai wound her fingers tightly through Elodie's. They ran. Leaves crunched beneath them, moss draping the trees with crimson as bright as commoner's blood—as bright as Elodie's blood.

And then: a root, twisting from the ground at just the wrong angle. A sharp pain in her ankle. Hitting earth that was padded with dead things, leaves and rotted mushrooms and fallen moss.

The twang of an arrow being released. A pain like fire in her back. She screamed and tried to turn her head. Her cry turned to a gurgle as her mouth fill with blood. A shadow slid over her, a man standing at her back with his greatbow slung over his shoulder. Her father. He sneered in disgust. "You will die as you lived, I suppose: a mess."

"Don't touch her!" came Sarai's furious cry. She was kneeling over Elodie, hands wet with red.

The Emperor pursed his lips and lifted his palms. "I don't need to touch her, small one."

All the air in Elodie's lungs vanished. She gasped like a stranded fish but no matter how her lungs worked, no air would come. Her father was killing her not with a quick and merciful poison, but with his own magic.

She looked at her sister. Sarai was strong, the iron in her blood giving her the same powers as their father. Even so, she was not yet skilled enough to best him.

But Sarai had never needed magic to prove herself strong.

The older girl tore the arrow from Elodie's back and, while their father was distracted with working his magic, drove it into his throat.

Air flooded into Elodie again. She gasped it in, watching in wordless horror as their father dropped to his knees and then fell on his stomach, his warm iron blood splattering the dead moss. He tilted his head against the leaves to look at Sarai, and the last emotion in his eyes was admiration. He had always taught his daughters to be ruthless; it was their heritage. He had not expected his eldest to take so well to the lesson.

Sarai wrapped her arms around Elodie and picked her up like she was a mother and not merely a sister. "It's okay," she whispered as Elodie's vision began to dim. "No one will know."

Sarai bore her unconscious sister to the royal physician's office. The Alloyed Palace rang with shouts and the occasional blast of cannon fire. The rebels must have mustered for yet another attempt at a coup. It was providing enough chaos for Sarai to perhaps be able to slip through the palace halls unseen.

She didn't want to be unseen. She bore her sister with a straight back, her chin lifted, a dark dare in her eyes to meet the gaze of any noble or servant that might glance in her direction.

They all parted before her like a sea of reeds. They were her subjects now. A part of them knew it already.

Sarai snapped at a servant to open the door to Albinus's office and then kicked it closed behind her. She was surrounded by cots, but she marched straight to her cousin's desk–where he was sitting, pale eyes wide, frame rigid with shock–and laid Elodie atop it. Her sister promptly bled all over Albinus's important papers, which Sarai found satisfying.

"Heal her," she snapped.

A calculating sort of hardness slid over his expression then. He stood, carefully pulling his robes far enough away from the desk to avoid the rivulets of blood. "My dear young cousin," he started, "I think we should fetch your father–"

"Then you may fetch him," Sarai interrupted. "I will tell you exactly where to find him: lying in the scorch-tree woodlands with his throat cut open, watering the forest with royal blood."

She watched him begin to understand. Fear replaced his calculated look, and another thrill of satisfaction uncurled down Sarai's spine.

"I killed him because he was going to kill her," Sarai went on. "I shall do the same to anyone who threatens my sister. Are you among that number?"

Albinus swallowed, licked his lips. His eyes flitted from his bloodied desk and the unconscious girl atop it back to Sarai. Then he ducked his head and stepped away from his desk, coming around its side. He bowed in a full obeisance, forehead brushing Sarai's slippers, palms flat against the floor, lips dusty from brushing the ground. It was the bow made of a penitent subject to their liege.

"My Empress," he said, voice tight. *"Order me."*

"Heal her," Sarai commanded again. As he rose and began to grab bottles and tools off the shelves nearby, she tilted her head, listening to the distant booms of cannon fire and the shouts from the hallway and the gardens. *"I take it that the palace is under attack?"*

"From the intelligence gathered before your...arrival, it seems to be a force of Saints led by silver Smiths." He opened Elodie's mouth and poured a tincture down her throat. Immediately the pain that had been twisted her sleeping features eased, and her breaths came more clearly. The flow of blood from her mouth ceased.

Sarai's lips twisted. *"Then the silver Smiths have foreseen the events of tonight, and attempt to take advantage of the uncertainty that will be caused by a royal patricide."*

"I suspect so, Highness."

"Then there will be no patricide," Sarai decided. *"Call for two guards—unimportant ones who won't be missed. Promise them a year's wages and swear them to silence, then have them go and retrieve my father's body from the forest. They are to clean up any evidence of his death there and transport him to his own bed, where he will be found with a rebel's arrow in his throat. As soon as they are finished, arrange to have them killed in the Saints attack as well."*

Albinus scooped Elodie off his desk and laid her on a cot, sending a tight look at all the documents that were now drenched red. *"Yes, Empress,"* he replied, and tugged a nearby cord to summon a servant.

"After that," Sarai said, *"I want you to give my sister magic."*

Albinus, who had been gingerly cutting off Elodie's shirt, paused. "What?" he said, forgetting in his incredulity to address her properly. She stared at him until he amended, "My Empress."

"Give her magic," Sarai repeated.

"I'm...I'm sure you have to know, Your Majesty, that is impossible. The quickening cannot be induced. If the element that will make someone a Smith is present, they will become one, and if it isn't, they never will."

"You are the royal physician. You were granted this position because you are brilliant above and beyond the rest of the House of Copper. I am taking all limits off your funding and ordering you to find a way to put metal and magic in my sister's blood."

Slowly, Albinus finished cutting Elodie's shirt off. "I...have often wanted to experiment with something in that direction," he admitted. "I will try. Likely she would make the ideal subject, since her blood will probably already have the right receptors, thanks to her genetics. What metal shall I attempt to work with?"

Sarai turned, scanning the shelves around her. The natural answer to Albinus's question would be iron, but Sarai didn't want Elodie to be an iron Smith. She didn't want her to be what was expected, what was known. She wanted Elodie to be a force to be reckoned with; something new and fierce, a girl who would never be helpless again.

Her eyes landed on a vial of gleaming silvery liquid. She picked it up, held it to the light. "This one," she said decisively.

"Mercury?" asked Albinus, startled. "But mercury Smiths never live past childhood. The incendiary magic is too destructive to be controlled. I only keep that vial as a poison. Mercury is

known to induce madness and paranoia, violence, even."

"Violence is exactly what I'm looking for. Find a way," she ordered. "And keep her asleep until you do. Give her a memory tonic. I want her to remember as little of tonight as possible. She has suffered enough."

Albinus bowed his head and went back to his work. Sarai stood by and watched as he gave her orders to the servant and then the two guards he called for. She pretended to be only a concerned, dutiful sister. She and Elodie had been attacked in their beds, she told anyone who asked. Saints had gotten in through the window and managed to kidnap Elodie, who had been injured before Sarai rescued her from the rebels' clutches. No one doubted the story.

Sarai was still awake when they found her father's body in bed an hour later. The royal priest, a dour, useless old man, came to fetch her. He put on her head the Iron Crown, freshly scrubbed clean of her father's blood.

Her first order was the immediate execution of all known and suspected silver Smiths. Their foresight and ability to peer into the past was too dangerous, she said. They had killed their own emperor; it was not to be borne.

In truth, she could not suffer to live anyone who might see the truth of what had happened this night.

The fully grown Iron Empress stood on the deck of a war zeppelin. The great balloon above her hummed with magic, a

Smithed aluminum skeleton overlaid with sturdy blue-and-rust canvas. Sarai's golden hair streamed in gentle waves around her as if she was underwater: the wind's normal bluster, tamed by her own magic. If she had worn a gown, its fabric would have streamed around her too. She would have looked beautiful.

Today was not a day for beauty. Today, she wore plate armor. It shone brilliant beneath the moon, light reflecting keenly from its edges as if her whole self were a blade. At her waist hung a sword, entirely unnecessary. She waited at the prow of the zeppelin's under-deck, loaded cannons to either side of her, rows of soldiers at her back, great balloon rising above, and searched for the rebels who had so foolishly stolen her sister.

Ahead, a low mountain rose. It was pocked with holes like a stone anthill, old tunnels bored into the rock by generations of copper miners. The Entengre river surged from its deep aquifer source here, borne upward by the force of ancient volcanic geysers until it exploded out of the many tunnels in a cloud of steam and waterfalls that wreathed the mountain in an eternal sea of mist. Moonlit rainbows shone off it now, shifting and shimmering as the balloon approached. It made for a stunning sight. It also made for an excellent place to hide a rebellion.

She raised one eyebrow, cool and slightly amused. The Saints had been admittedly clever to hide here, in plain sight of the Alloyed Palace that was no more than a day's walk to the west. They could spy on their enemies from hidden waterways and recruit rebels from her own capitol, all with little fear of being discovered; the volcanic gasses and heat interfered with her zeppelins' ability to fly over this area. She was expending a great deal of her magic to get even this close without sending the great war balloon into a deadly tailspin.

But the Saints had underestimated just how badly she needed to find, or avenge, her sister.

She turned to the soldiers. "Go," she said simply. She strode toward the dismounting dock and they ran past her, throwing themselves off the dock and into the air. They spread their arms and legs wide as they dropped and the thin membranes sewn into their suits stretched to catch the air and slow their falls. They glided silently toward the tunnels, controlling their direction by small movements that changed the way air flowed over their clothing's special webbing–which had been woven only this morning for this very occasion. When they were a few yards from the peak, she lifted a hand and sent a cushion of air to catch them and lower them the rest of the way to the ground. Then she stepped off the bottom of the dock's stairs and fell to the earth behind them like a bolt of bright lightning.

They surged through the tunnels and killed everything in their path–everything except the one person Sarai had come here to save.

Time passed; not long. A pair of hands held the Iron Crown over a girl's head and then, slowly, lowered it. Beneath the heavy crown, the girl lifted her head, and her silver eyes shone like mercury.

CHAPTER SIXTEEN

TAL WRENCHED HIMSELF AWAY FROM THE DREAMING PLACE. He was still on his hands and knees in the temple. His hands were coated in clay dust. Helenia's hand was on his shoulder. Dead leaves and flowers from the viper's nest brushed against his legs. He stayed there, gasping in air like a drowning man, as he tried to process what he'd seen.

That last vision. The empress had found the Saints base. She had found it, and she had killed everyone inside, and she had rescued her sister. And then the Destroyer had been crowned.

"Tal? Are you all right?" Helenia asked. She was kneeling next to him now, a hand on each of his shoulders, trying to pull him upright so she could see his face.

He laughed, a bit wildly, and shook his head. "No," he said. "No, not at all."

And those two earlier visions, the ones that had shown Elodie and Sarai as children. If they were to be believed, it meant—

He shook his head and lurched to his feet. He could not think of those now, could not take the time to understand what they implied. Could not allow the sight of Elodie as a child to change the truth of Elodie as the Destroyer—of Elodie the soon-to-be Empress, if his final vision was correct.

He spun around, found the temple's entrance. Not much time had passed since he'd come in here. It was sunset now, the air outside the entrance stained purple and red, still peaceful. "The moon," he said aloud, and sprinted for the clearing.

Helenia hurried after him. "Tal! What in the name of the Unforged—"

He was already outside. He spun around, scanning the sky, ignoring the floating mote seeds and the quiet, distant shushing of the streams. He found the moon. It was waxed nearly full, only a sliver of a crescent missing. "Two nights," he said aloud. "The moon was full in the vision, bright enough to create rainbows in the mist. She will attack in two nights."

Helenia was at his side. Her hand clamped onto his shoulder, surprisingly strong. It anchored him—he had not realized until this moment that he felt like one of those mote seeds, spun about by the wind until no one could know where he might land.

"You had a vision?" Helenia asked.

He raised a hand to rake it through his hair, then remembered that his wrists were still bound together by the manacle.

"Yes. Of the empress, attacking the Saints base."

The lines of Helenia's body went taut all at once, and her expression turned fearsome. "Then we must tell Nyx and the others immediately."

Yes. Of course. That was what they needed to do. His mind wouldn't clear, wouldn't quite process the present moment. It kept curving back to six-year-old Elodie in bed, mouse eyes and rabbit heart, a line of scabs marching up her forearm like army ants. The fear and helplessness she'd felt when she'd realized her father would kill her. The weight of his shadow on her back as her mouth filled with blood. *Red* blood. The blood she had been born with, the blood that hadn't changed to mercury until her sister and cousin had injected it into her veins without her knowledge or consent.

Helenia was pulling him toward the campfire. The Saints stood around it, empty bowls in their hands, waiting impatiently as the pot of stew began to simmer above the flames. Someone had dragged Elodie off her sled and dumped her next to the fire to keep her warm, but they had placed her too close—her forehead wrinkled in her sleep and the muscles in her neck twitched as she tried to turn her face away. The brown glass bottle of laudanum sat next to her, unstoppered. They must have just dosed her, or perhaps been about to dose her when it was announced that dinner was nearly ready.

He wondered what she would say if she were awake. Did she know what had been done to her? No, he realized, Sarai had given her a memory tonic. Which meant as far as Elodie knew, her blood had at last quickened naturally on the eve of her seventh birthday, perhaps due to the adrenaline of her attempted murder.

But the girl she had been, Tal reminded himself, hurrying his steps toward the Saints, did not excuse the young woman she had become. The memory tonic had not forced her to burn villages, to incinerate the families of suspected seditionists, to torture Tal's own sister.

But...but the mercury. Poison, Albinus had called it. It induced madness. Paranoia. Acts of violence. Only a Smith could withstand the toxic effects of metal in their blood and Elodie, as it turned out, was no Smith. She would not have become what she had become, would not have done the terrible things she had done, without the imbalance created by that toxicity.

Sarai had not simply given mercury to the Destroyer. Mercury had *made* the Destroyer.

Helenia had tugged him into the circle of Saints who were waiting with their bowls. The group had begun to line up now, jostling and laughing, completely unaware that they were slated to die in two days' time when they reached the Saints base.

"Nyx, everyone. Tal has had a vision," Helenia said loudly, cutting through the chatter. The man who'd been stirring the stew dropped the ladle in surprise and one of the nearby dogs whined, trying to sneak close enough lick the bit of spilled soup. Nyx, who had been sitting on a downed log and staring unrelentingly at the Destroyer from across the fire, jerked her head up.

"What?" said his sister, rising. "Another one?"

He swallowed, uncomfortable beneath their sudden scrutiny, uncomfortable in his own mind. Every bit of him could sense the presence of Elodie at his back, the outline of her clear as if it were carved on his own skin. She was still too close to the fire. Someone should move her before she burned. He caught that thought, held it immobile and looked at it and laughed aloud at it, the sound harsh and biting as if it had been scraped from his throat. A mere week ago, he would have wished nothing more fondly than for her to burn. Did he not still? He didn't know what he wanted. He only knew that he had seen her young and small and vulnerable and wished he could protect her, and he had seen her grown and vulnerable then, too, and it was all too much for him to quite fathom.

"Yes," he said, facing the Saints, forcing his attention away from Elodie. "It was of the Empress. She will attack the Saints base in two nights' time."

He explained his last vision in full–or at least, almost in full. He left out the part about Elodie being crowned, because he knew if he told them that there was no way they wouldn't immediately kill her and he at least needed to explain everything else before they decided whether to do that. With each sentence, the rebels gathered closer, empty bowls hanging forgotten from their fingers, the air growing smothering with the heat and the thick, musty scent of unwashed bodies. Tal struggled to breathe through it. Claustrophobia clamped itself around him. He wondered if this was what drowning felt like, and that thought led him back to the icy lake, to

Elodie's limp and half-frozen body in his arms, to the feel of her cold lips beneath his and the terrible relief he'd felt when she had begun to breathe once again. He had realized then that he'd wanted the Unforged God's promise to come true after all. He wanted to save Elodie, and wanted to save the empire through her.

"God's hammer," swore one of the rebels. "What are we to do?"

"The empress shouldn't even have rightfully survived the explosion," another protested. "She was right in the middle of it. What must we do to finally end her?"

He didn't tell them that Sarai would be dead soon anyway, as must happen if Elodie was going to be crowned. He would have to tell them soon. Not yet, though.

"We can't reach the base in time to warn them. Not with a caravan like this," Nyx cut in, her eyes flashing.

"We could send a single sled ahead. One musher, minimal cargo. They would make it in time to give the evacuation order."

Nyx ground her teeth. She ran her hand over her head, pressing the pads of her fingers into the short, dark stubble that had grown there. When she then grabbed her pack and rummaged through it to come up with her razor, Tal at first wondered why she would choose this moment to shave the stubble away. Then she lifted the blade and said, "We kill her now."

Tal's breath caught in his throat.

"We cannot risk the empress rescuing the Destroyer,"

Nyx continued, "and we will run out of laudanum sooner or later–we can't keep her a prisoner on the run indefinitely. And if the base is going to be attacked, she can't have a proper trial there either. We kill her now, then later we can say her death was in retribution for the raid of our headquarters. That way maybe we'll even get the bonus of making Sarai think twice before she messes with us again. It's the only way the rebellion has a chance at some sort of victory if the base gets wiped out." She turned to her girlfriend. "Hel, hold Tal back."

Tal and Helenia looked at each other. She gave him an unbearably gentle look that meant the time had come to tell Nyx the truth, and his stomach churned in a way that made him want to find the nearest bush and be sick behind it. But he owed his sister the truth, so before he could allow himself time to think of how to evade the question, he turned to face her squarely and said, "You do not need to hold me back."

Nyx had taken a step toward the far side of the fire where Elodie lay, but stopped now and turned. "What? Have you...have you found a way to fight the oath?" Her eyes lit with hope.

Too miserable to face her, too ashamed to face his own words, he closed his eyes. "No. I am rid of it. She died at the icy lake. She drowned. My oath is gone. And so is yours, or at least the part of it that requires the Destroyer's death." *At least there is that,* he thought desperately, grasping for something good. At least there was one less vow to bind his sister.

There was silence for a long moment. "But," Nyx said slowly, "She's not dead, not yet. She's right over there."

"Because I saved her after she drowned. I breathed for her," he admitted. "I brought her back."

The silence turned slow and thick and deadly, a poison sap that glued them all in place until it began to turn hard and brittle. All at once, it shattered.

Nyx was shouting. He couldn't make out words past the tremors of fury and confusion and grief that ravaged her voice, so he didn't respond, but he did open his eyes, because he at least owed it to her to witness her anger. Hel stood behind her now, whispering quiet calming things into her ear that seemed to have almost no effect, holding her arms back as she tried to lunge across the space to Tal.

"How could you?" Nyx managed at last, eyes alight with tears, face twisted in disbelief. The words were knives, daggers, arrows. The trees caught her cry, dulled it against their leaves, absorbed the weight of it until Tal could almost bear it.

He struggled to find a way to explain his reasoning but of course couldn't do such a thing when he didn't understand the logic of it himself, so instead, he told her—he told them all—of the other visions. Elodie, small and afraid. Nearly killed by her own parent. Poisoned without her knowledge. The moon arced higher in the sky as he talked, explaining each detail of his dreams until his voice ran hoarse. At some point, the soup nearly boiled over and Helenia rescued it, ladling stew into each of their bowls and insisting they eat; good plans weren't made on empty stomachs. Tal let her fill a bowl for him but couldn't take even the thought of eating.

Nyx watched lifelessly, all emotion drained from her expression. She wouldn't look at Tal. She also wouldn't let go of the razor.

"How could Albinus have kept the mercury in the Destroyer's system for so long?" Helenia asked when Tal had finished explaining his visions and the remnants of the stew had gone cold. "He wouldn't have been able to change her bone marrow—that's what creates new blood when the body needs it. So her blood would have slowly changed back to red over time, the mercury used up bit by bit as she used her powers, diluted by the new blood as it was generated."

"Her treatments," Tal realized. His voice cracked from overuse and he had to clear it before he could go on. "The treatments Albinus gives her—it's not medicine at all, but a transfusion of mercury. She was late for it on the train."

"Which must have meant the metal in her blood was running low," Helenia said. "*That's* why Nyx's poison did more than it was intended to; it was formulated to weaken the magic of a Smith, but the Destroyer's magic was artificially induced, and already destabilized as her natural blood began to dilute it. The poison destabilized it even further and caused her to expel all her remaining powers at once in the explosion and then afterwards, her magic didn't recharge, because it *can't*. She has reverted back to her true, original condition. The trauma of it must have been what temporarily muddled her memories."

"Now we know what gave her the ability to wipe out thousands of innocent people," Nyx said dully, her eyes gleaming in the light of the waning fire. "Well and good. Let's kill her before we go back to arguing about what to do next."

"We can't kill her!" Helenia protested. "She's innocent."

The group grew very quiet again. The betrayal and shock in Nyx's eyes seemed to echo through Tal's own soul.

"She is not," he said softly, "innocent."

Helenia bowed her head. "I am sorry," she said, her words sounding stilted with the weight of emotion. She reached out to Nyx and touched her gently on the shoulder, the motion looking oddly formal. "I haven't been through what you, and you too, Tal, were forced to endure. It's not as visceral for me—I have no right to call her innocent when I haven't had to bear witness directly to what she's done. Nyx, I would do *anything* to save you from what she did to you, my love."

Nyx closed her eyes. "I know."

Helenia relaxed slightly at the sign of her girlfriend's forgiveness, then hesitated. "But still...Elodie was an innocent six-year-old infused with poison after her own father tried to kill her. There is tragedy and ill-placed trust in her own life, and a great wrongdoing was enacted upon her—one which had power to shift the whole direction of her life forever afterward. Perhaps Elodie, the girl with the red blood and the brown eyes, the girl who gave her life to save Tal from a mooncat, might be different from the Destroyer. Isn't that something she could decide for herself? Isn't that something she ought to be able to choose?"

"No," Nyx said ruthlessly, lifting the razor once again. "The mercury didn't *make* her do anything, Hel. Maybe it did make her paranoid, maybe it did give her a tendency to violence. But it didn't hold a knife to her throat and force her to slaughter entire towns of locked houses, with the men and women and children closed up inside. You make it sound like she deserves a choice now. The fact is, she's *always* had a choice. Mercury or no mercury, evil sister or no evil sister. Everyone's got a choice." She looked at Tal as she said this, and he bowed his head in shame and acknowledgement. It was too much, and he was so tired; he wished he could lie down and dream normal dreams and forget all of this. The rust phage was even now burrowing deeper into his leg, making it ache, making him feel slightly feverish and even more exhausted.

Helenia gave a grim nod at the truth of Nyx's words. "But is there no room to be allowed for redemption?" she asked. "No room for the possibility of eventual forgiveness?"

"There is none," Nyx bit out.

"*The blade of vengeance has no hilt,*" Helenia said softly, quoting scripture. "*It cuts all who wield it.*"

"Then let it cut me, but first, let me cut *her*."

Helenia was quiet for a moment, considering. Around them, the rebels shifted and murmured, and a few of them yawned and looked as tired as Tal felt, but no one else spoke up. They left the weight of the decision to Helenia.

Helenia turned then to Tal. "It is not a choice for me to make," she said heavily. "I have no firsthand experience of the Destroyer. I haven't the right to judge her, or to determine whether there is a real chance she could change, and I also don't have the right to seek her potential redemption over justice for her victims. You and Nyx are the ones who have been nearest to her, who have been most strongly affected by her. The choice is for you to make. Nyx has cast her vote. What is yours?"

Tal closed his eyes. He thought again of the feel of Elodie's still lips under his, of her silent heart beneath his palms. He thought of the Unforged God's promise that he would save her. He thought of the little girl in the scorch tree woodlands, pursued by her own father, poisoned by her own sister. Tal thought of all the nightmares he had ever woken her from. *There was a man standing over me and my mouth was full of blood and I was screaming,* she had told him in the cave. A part of her was still that frightened little girl.

And then he thought of the last two years. He thought of being forced to kill assassin after Saint after would-be revolutionary, of protecting the Destroyer from his own people while she looked on, utterly unmoved. He thought of finding her in the train's prison car. He thought of Nyx, hair burned short, beads melted to her clothing, body spasming.

He thought of her past victims, and all of the future victims she could make if she were to be crowned as his vision showed. Did her life, the life of one girl who might have been different if she'd grown up knowing the truth, really outweigh all of those other lives? Did it outweigh the life of his sister?

It didn't. He could not let it.

"We have to kill her," he said. He went to Nyx, stood before her, and held out his hand. This was how he would begin to ask his sister's forgiveness. This was how he would try to make up for his actions, for his lie. Elodie, with her red blood and brown eyes and sharp wit and innocent ferocity, might have been a person he could care for–God help him– but Nyx was the only precious thing in his life, and this was something he needed to do for her. After a moment, Nyx slowly lifted the razor and set it in his hand.

"I will kill her myself," he told them all, and wrapped his fingers around the weapon's handle.

CHAPTER SEVENTEEN

Elodie lay very still and listened to the Saints debate her death.

The sun had been setting, staining the temple with shades of rose and plum, when whatever they had dosed her with had first begun to wear off. The heat of the fire on her face had woken her. At first, the only thing she could do was try to turn her head away, unable to even summon the strength to open her eyes. And then familiar footsteps–the steady drumbeat that had underscored the terrible symphony of her last two years–moved past her, and someone said, "Tal has had a vision."

The words took a moment to penetrate the fuzz that filled her mind, and then she remembered...silver Smith. Tal was a silver Smith. She must not tell anyone. No–she shook her head, trying to jar herself into clear thinking. If they were saying Tal had a vision then they must already know what he was. It was no use worrying about him.

And then she heard what his vision was, and heard the stony anger in Nyx's voice when she said *we kill her now*, and she abruptly realized Tal was not at all the one she should be worrying about.

Her breathing quickened as she lay there. She felt the warmth of fire on her face but none at all sparking in her veins. She could not stand. Could not even make a pitiful physical attempt to save her own life—not that her strength would have been a match for any of theirs, even if she hadn't been drugged. She wondered how much it would hurt when Nyx killed her. She supposed that would depend on how much Nyx wanted it to hurt, and the answer to that was, of course, probably a lot.

Tal. Tal would save her. Tal was the only person she could ever trust to be on her side, if only because he had no choice. They would almost certainly think to restrain him, but he had fought off Elodie's attackers in worse conditions before—her breath caught as she remembered the incidents, one bloody, fiery scene after another, too much to hold in her mind at once—and surely he could do it again.

And then he said, "You do not need to hold me back," and Elodie's entire world inverted.

Numbly, distantly, still unable to do as much as open her eyes, she listened to him explain. *She was dead,* he said, and she recalled the burning cold of the water, the blur of his shadow through the ice, how much heavier liquid felt in her lungs than air. His voice shook with shame when he spoke of saving her. When he said *I breathed for her,* she felt the ghost of his lips on hers.

She had died.

Which meant his oath was gone.

But—but he'd saved her. She scrambled for the logic of it, for the good news, for anything other than the panic that was now scrabbling madly through her mind. He had saved her of his own free will, because...because he wanted to? Because he cared for her?

He could not care for her. She was not a person people cared for. She was an unlovable creature; she had made herself such.

She remembered the warp and weft of his scars under her fingers. The way he'd snapped at her before that: *You are not a kind person. Stop* touching *me. All my nightmares are of her.*

And she knew then he was sorry he had saved her, and that now he would kill her.

Her panic intensified. She forced her eyes open and began to consider how she might save herself. The uncomfortable heat of the fire on her face resolved into snapping flames a few feet away: a bland yellow-and-orange color, nowhere near as vibrant and alive as her own magic. But it still burned. It was here, and her magic was not. Maybe she could use it.

She didn't want to use it. She didn't want to wield fire, not against Tal. Never against Tal. And it wasn't as if she could just stick her bare arms into the flames and toss the burning wood at the Saints without injuring herself, too.

There was a pot suspended over the fire. It had to be full of some kind of hot liquid. She could...what? Pick it up and toss the scalding coffee or soup or bone stock over the Saints with all the strength she didn't have, and then flee into the forest to find her way home using all of the survival skills she also didn't have?

And even if she did make it home, the Alloyed Palace would be less of a refuge for her now than it had ever been. So many had tried to assassinate her when she was whole, when she was protected by both mercury and Tal. How long before someone succeeded now that she had neither? Returning there would be like walking into an adders' nest. Despair filtered through her panic, making it all the more potent as she imagined striding through those cold metal-plated corridors with an empty space at her side. It wasn't only that she would be unprotected. She would be *alone*. There was Sarai, of course, but she was as much the Iron Empress as she was Elodie's sister, and no matter how much love was between them, her loyalties could never belong wholly to Elodie. Not the way Tal's had.

Albinus could fix her. Then she could protect herself again. But...fixing her would mean giving her back her fire. Her silver eyes, her mercurial blood. It would mean becoming the Destroyer again. And she realized, with a sudden and violent certainty, that she did not want that. And even if she did, even if she became who she had once been—she would still be alone. She would still be afraid.

She knew she was feeling an emotion, one that ran much deeper than her current skittering panic and fear. It was something powerful and unwieldy, something that would fill her and bury her all at once like a valley beneath a landslide, but it was far off yet, still fuzzy and amorphous beneath the influence of whatever they had drugged her with. She had to make it out of here before it overcame her or she would be utterly useless.

She managed to turn her head, just a twitch, but it was enough to make out the brown bottle that was leaning against a log at her side. It was unstoppered and smelled faintly of bitter black poppy. Ah; so laudanum was what they had dosed her with. And, apparently, had been about to dose her with once again before something distracted them, allowing her to finally surface from her drug-thickened nightmares.

She could use this against them. Laudanum was a weapon she would be happy to wield, one that required no strength beyond the ability to lift her hand. Admittedly, even that was a strength she did not yet quite possess, but if the Saints could just stay distracted for a few minutes more she was certain she could make it work. All she had to do was dump the laudanum in the soup.

And hope they ate it before they killed her.

Fixing the laudanum bottle with her coldest glare, she ordered her fingers to twitch. They did. She ordered them to reach for the bottle. They merely twitched with slightly more vigor. Damn. The Saints were still distracted, at least, huddled up around Tal as he explained—

Her fingers stopped twitching. Her glare faded. A tremor went through her whole body as she registered what, exactly, Tal was explaining. As far away as she was from their huddle, she could only catch a few of his words as they floated over the campfire:

Sarai. Albinus. Emperor.

Misfire.

Misfire. The word echoed strangely in her mind, a key in search of its lock. Something dark and dangerous and long-forgotten blinked its eyes open behind the surface of her thoughts, and suddenly her old nightmare yawned like a crevasse below her. Frightened, she tried to pull herself back from it. She was not a scared little girl with a mouth full of blood. She was here, she was now, she was awake. But Tal was still speaking:

Moss

Arrow

Red

And the words were all keys and her mind the lock rusted shut, finally creaking open.

Her nightmare pulled her in.

She was a little girl in bed, the emperor's shadow suffocating her. *It is a father's duty*, he said, more resigned than regretful, and then he asked his nephew to join him for a drink before he killed his youngest daughter.

No. No. That wasn't right. That wasn't her nightmare. Her father had been a hard man, impatient for Elodie's blood to quicken, but he had never planned to murder her. She would have remembered such a thing.

Her mind and Tal's words pulled her inexorably onward. Sarai launched herself out the window, Elodie crept after. And then it was her old nightmare, but in new and vivid detail: scorch moss dripping crimson around them, a man's shadow—*her father's shadow*—pinning her down as her mouth filled with blood. For the first time, when she spat it onto the dead leaves, she could make out its color.

Red. *Red.*

Her sister saved her. Her father died. His blood flowed thick, molten iron gilding the moss and leaves just as it should, not lying in a puddle red and thin and weak like hers.

Six-year-old Elodie passed out. Her nightmare ended. But Tal wasn't done talking.

He spoke of Sarai carrying her to Albinus's chambers, of her demanding his fealty. He gave in to Sarai, because of course, no one could ever do otherwise with her sister. Albinus had healed Elodie. But then...

"Sarai told him to infuse her with mercury," Tal was saying, his voice rusty and dry now. "To give her magic even if it poisoned her in the process."

The Saints went still with shock and then, like a covey of startled hens, exploded into a flutter of denial and questions all at once.

Elodie's breath quickened, went jagged and rasping. This was not true. She would make Tal take it back. He was lying and she didn't know why, except that he must want to hurt her. *But he doesn't know you're awake,* whispered a small voice in her mind, and she crushed it without mercy.

Laudanum. She needed to put the laudanum in the soup. She ordered her hand to move and this time it did. She closed her numb fingers clumsily around the bottle and then considered the pot of soup. To reach it, she would have to stand. She wasn't sure her legs would hold her yet, and anyway, standing would certainly draw the attention of the Saints. Tossing the whole bottle in was the only option. She winced at the thought; she didn't have the best aim even when she wasn't drugged, and she could already hear how the glass would shatter on the edge of the pot, alerting the rebels and ruining her entire plan. But what choice did she have?

She had to make Tal stop talking. She had to get away from here, even if she didn't know yet where she would go.

She pulled her arm back and gently, carefully, tossed the open bottle toward the soup. It bounced off the inside lip of the pot. The thick glass didn't break, but it did make a sharp clanking noise. At that very moment, though, the fire leapt a little higher as a burnt log collapsed, sending sparks wheeling into the stars and making the other logs crackle and shift. The sound covered the clanking of the bottle, and it sank slowly into the soup, bleeding a trail of brown medicine that quickly diluted and became invisible in the broth.

Elodie closed her eyes in relief. Fire had, once again, protected her.

Someone was shuffling toward the campfire. Elodie quickly went limp, closing her eyes to slits, peering out through her lashes as a figure–the girl called Helenia, who had fed her the drugged bread—bent to pick up a ladle from the ground. She washed it off with a dribble of water from a canteen and then set about filling the bowl in her other hand with soup from the pot. Tal continued talking, his voice cracking from overuse and emotion, as the moon crept higher in the sky and Helenia handed out bowls of soup. Tal took his but set it down on a rock next to him so he could keep talking. Everyone else shoveled spoonfuls in their mouths, obviously hungry from their long journey even as their attention remained fixed on Tal.

They finished eating. A few of the Saints yawned. Elodie wondered how long it would be before the drug took effect. She had no idea how much laudanum it even took to put people to sleep; perhaps it had been too diluted, and would only make them a little sleepy. Or maybe, she thought wildly, it had been too much, and they would not fall asleep but perish. Would she be sorry? The Destroyer wouldn't be.

But even the Destroyer would mourn if Tal died.

Her eyes flicked open at the thought. Her gaze leapt between the empty bowls lying on the ground and the Saints they belonged to, until she found the still-full bowl that had been Tal's. He had not eaten. She released a slow breath that shuddered with a relief she refused to examine.

A motion caught her eye. Tal was standing before Nyx, holding out his hand. His fingers closed around the straight razor that his sister laid in his palm. "I will kill her myself," he said, and began to turn toward the campfire.

Elodie's breathing stalled. She closed her eyes before he

had turned all the way around. Her head was lying on the ground and she could hear the familiar rhythm of his footsteps as he approached her. They should be set to music, she had once thought, and now the trill of her own heartbeat in her ears provided it.

She inhaled. It smelled like dead leaves: rot and mulch and earth, pulling her into itself. She felt the cool of his shadow fall over her as he stepped between her and the flames. He knelt. Something thin and cold set itself against the side of her throat, resting on the soft skin just under her ear, where her pulse beat a frantic rhythm. Tal laid a hand on her forehead to hold her still. His fingers slipped through the strands of her hair as he settled his grip.

Even as the razor began to bite toward her vein, a part of her refused to believe it was happening. *I swear to protect you*, whispered his voice in her memory.

The blade slipped through the top layer of her skin. Her breath caught; she couldn't stop herself. She wanted to open her eyes. She wanted to plead with him. She wanted to know why he had saved her before, if he was only going to kill her now. She wanted to deny the pain of the razor, the thin trickle of blood already curving down her neck, the way it confirmed the inescapable truth that he was no longer bound to his oath.

And to not allow harm to come to you, whispered the voice of memory. She remembered the mist of that day, the way it drifted softly through the starlight, the way it caught in his hair like beads of glass. She remembered the cold and desperate trail of her own thoughts. The glorious hope when his oath had forced him to defend her for the first time. She had an ally, she had thought then. A refuge. Someone that none of her enemies could use to hurt her.

And to never harm you myself.

Anger rose then. It was hot and desperate and pure. Would she lie here and allow herself to be killed by a boy as she whimpered beneath his blade, unable to accept the truth of his betrayal? The fact was, they had both betrayed each other, and his god had betrayed him, and he had betrayed his sister. They were all wrapped up in it like flies in a spider's web, unable to find a way free of their pasts and their failures and the things they owed to each other. She knew, all at once, that Tal didn't want to kill her. If he had he would have thrust the blade into her throat in one swift, inevitable movement. Instead he was hesitating, his hand almost gentle on her forehead, holding the blade still at the mere nick he had made in her skin. He didn't want to kill her, but he would eventually do it anyway, because he thought he *should* want to. And suddenly, Elodie was sick beyond belief of people doing what they thought they should be doing.

She opened her eyes, grabbed the razor, and thrust it away from her, at the same time pushing her other hand against the ground to shove herself to standing. In her mind, the movements were quick and graceful, as all her movements usually were, but in real life she was still drug-addled and unused to relying on her hands rather than her fire for defense. As she thrust the razor away, it sliced deep across her palm, right along the scabbed-over spot where her hand had already been injured. She hissed and yelped as she scrambled to her feet, instinctively shaking her hand as if she had dunked it in hot water. The movement flung drops of blood all over her clothing and face—and all over Tal, who had stood up much more gracefully and was even now moving toward her with deadly intent. His hands were still bound with manacles, but as she had thought earlier, she had seen him do deadly damage under far worse conditions.

Frantic and still furious, she stumbled backwards and scanned the clearing. One of the sleds was nearby, the dogs unharnessed and dozing near it. A bundle was packed onto the sled and half-covered with a canvas. At the edge of the bundle, the hilt of one of Tal's swords peeked out. A weapon! She had never trained with swords, but it was better than nothing, so she launched herself at the pack, scrabbled to grasp the hilt with her blood-slick hands, and drew out the short sword. She swung it around and pointed it at Tal, who had stopped moving toward her but was still watching her with those steady, impassive eyes that he probably thought showed no emotion. But oh, she could see the tumult behind them, the guilt, the pain, the anger—and relief was there, too, when his eyes flicked to the thin line of blood trickling down her neck. He quickly shuttered that emotion away, though, and began to stalk toward her with the razor held ready. He had decided on his course and he meant to see it through.

She shook the sword at him in what she hoped was a threatening manner. "Stop!" she ordered. She tried to make her voice cold and commanding as it used to be but failed miserably. "I'll–I'll stab you, I swear I will."

Tal, predictably, did not obey her. "How will you do that?" he asked, voice flat. "You're holding that like it's a steak knife."

She swallowed, taking a step back as he approached. "Steak knives can stab."

His eyes narrowed. He shifted his weight. She saw the way the muscles in his shoulders bunched, saw how the razor moved and caught the light. He was about to end this. Instinctively, she dropped the sword and threw her hands up–a motion that would have been swiftly followed by a protective cascade of fire, if she still had magic.

Tal, too, had an instinctive reaction. He flinched away from her and flung up an arm even as he turned, shouting a warning. No, not a warning–a word.

"Nyx!"

All the breath went out of Elodie. She dropped her hands, fearing for a terrible moment that she somehow had sparked her powers after all, had used her fire against Tal, had burned him or, worse and more unforgiveable in his eyes, hurt his sister. She scrambled backwards, not picking a direction beyond *away*. She tripped over something warm and furry. Maluk. The gray dog blinked his eyes open in annoyance, grunted at her, gave her a half-hearted lick on the shin and then curled back up and went to sleep, utterly unconcerned by what was happening around him. Maybe he was still recovering from his own dose of laudanum.

Oh–oh, no. The *laudanum*.

Elodie's head snapped up. She spotted Tal, who was already on the far side of the campfire again and leaping over a downed log, rushing toward a group of figures that were splayed across the ground. That was why he had shouted Nyx's name. When he had turned his head away, he had seen her and the others collapsed. He skidded to a stop at Nyx's side now, dropping to his knees, horribly silent.

Elodie stared. She should run while Tal was distracted. But instead she found herself stepping forward, closer, trying to see through the shadows and the sparks to where Nyx lay as still as death. The look on Tal's face was, for once, utterly unknowable even to her, terrible and flat.

If Nyx was dead, he would never forgive her. He would almost certainly never forgive her anyway, but, she realized with an odd, distant sort of surprise, she wanted him to.

"Is she alive?" she asked, edging closer, trying to make out whether Nyx's chest was moving with her breaths.

Slowly, Tal lifted his head. When his gaze fell on her, she stopped moving, caught like a mouse before a wolf. "What," he said slowly, rising like a thunderhead to his feet, "did you do?"

"Laudanum," she said, trying to explain quickly, before he made a decision that she could only hope he would later regret. "I threw the laudanum bottle into the soup."

"A laudanum overdose can kill," he said, advancing toward her. She swallowed and held her ground. If he decided to slay her, he would, and no stolen sword or nonexistent mercurial magic would save her. All she could do was die on her feet, looking him in the eye when he did it.

"And have I killed them?" she dared to ask.

He stopped. His jaw worked. He was still holding the razor, and in one quick movement, he flung it toward her. She steeled herself and didn't dodge, but it only drove with a *thud* into the dirt at her feet. "You could have killed them all," he said, his voice getting louder with each word until he was shouting. "Just because you were lucky enough not to does not make it justifiable. You could have killed Nyx. You could have killed Helenia. She thought you were *innocent, redeemable.*"

"I cannot be held responsible for what other people think," Elodie answered angrily, wrapping her arms around her chest like a child in the cold.

He advanced on her. He was shaking now. His voice, when it came again, had dropped to something low and venomous. "What about your actions? Will you be held responsible for those, my lady?"

She flinched, the air going out of her all at once. "Don't," she said, weak suddenly with the memories of all the other times he had called her *my lady*, his voice by turns flat, furious, ravaged, broken. "Don't call me that."

He stopped right in front of her. "Destroyer."

She set her jaw. "Don't call me that, either."

"It is what you are."

She couldn't deny that, so she only turned her head away. Tal was silent for the space of a few breaths, then he asked, "Do you truly remember, then?"

She remembered too much. She could not recover from it. His words were a weapon, and she hated being helpless before them. "I remember you swearing to me on the palace docks. I remember you saying your god wanted you to defend me," she said, because she knew it was her own sort of weapon. "I remember your hand on mine when you saved Nyx from my fire. I remember where you got every one of your scars."

He was close to her now, too close. He leaned in. Her breath hitched in fear and something flickered in his eyes in response: pleasure. He was glad for her to be afraid of him. "Do you think I need that razor to kill you?" he asked softly.

"The only thing you need," she said, leaning in a little herself, hating the fear that flashed briefly in his own eyes but glad, so glad, for the scrap of power it returned to her, "is the will to do it. But you don't have that. Do you?"

"I could bind you," he said. "I could wait for Nyx to wake, and give her razor back. She would do it."

"Would you let her?" Elodie didn't mean for her voice to waver. She cursed the fact that she seemed to have less control of herself now. She was less certain, less powerful in every way. Had it only ever been the mercury in her veins that had made her everything she was? What was she now, without it?

Tal held her gaze for a long, dangerous moment. She sensed the way the air prickled around him, the way the night seemed to fade as his attention on her grew sharper. Then, all at once, he stepped back. "You are impossible," he said, and all of the hate and anger had drained out of him, leaving him ragged. He tipped his head back and closed his eyes. "*This* is impossible."

In such a position, with his eyes closed and his head stretched back, his neck was exposed. He held no weapon. He was allowing himself to be vulnerable before her, the person who had been his greatest enemy. How could he bear it? She couldn't fathom it, nor could she understand her own envy of such a thing.

The danger had gone out of the night, and with it had gone the energy of the panic that had been keeping her going. She sat down heavily on a nearby fallen log. Her hands felt empty and useless. She busied them with wiping the specks of blood from her face, a job at which she was as unskilled as anything else, and only succeeded in smearing half-dried blood over herself. "I couldn't agree more," she said, her voice shaking with the aftereffects of it all.

He opened his eyes and looked at her. "How long have you been able to remember? Did you know who you were this whole time? Were you only pretending to be Elodie?"

She held up her hand, which was still oozing red blood. "Why would I pretend to be *this*?"

He hesitated. "You helped me," he said at last, the words sounding as if they were being dragged from him. "After the explosion. You got me to the cave before the blizzard struck. And then with the mooncat, you..."

"Died saving you?" she snapped, unwilling to linger on that awful memory: the cold, the dark, the blur of him through the ice. "Yes. You're welcome, I suppose."

His eyes narrowed and his voice went taut. "Do you think I owe you something now? Do you know how many lives I have taken for your sake? Giving your own life is nowhere near enough to tip the balance. Nothing could be."

"I am aware," she said, angry again—mostly at herself this time—but refusing to be baited into another standoff. She gave up on her attempts to wipe the blood away. "The question we should be discussing is: what do we do now?"

"There is no *we*."

She stilled. Of course. She kept forgetting he was no longer bound to her. The thought was a thing with spikes and barbs that burrowed into her every time she recalled it, but she refused to allow her dismay and grief to show. She had bigger things to consider. She needed to think of some way to persuade him to help her evade the people who were currently set on killing her, and to help her get somewhere safe. If there was any such place for her now.

"What—what do you want?" she asked clumsily. If she could ferret out some need of his, perhaps she could find a way to use it to bargain with him.

He laughed, a sharp, humorless bark. "If I had any idea what I wanted, Elodie, I wouldn't be standing here."

Elodie. He'd called her Elodie. He'd said it like it was some sort of curse, but it was still many measures better than *my lady.* "Do you want money?" she went on, fumbling to think of what he might desire now that he had his freedom. "Clemency for your sister? A...a job?"

He stared at her, incredulous. "A job? What would you do, give me a reference? Would I note my experience with murdering in the application?"

"You weren't murdering, you were protecting," she protested, hating that he would see himself in such a negative light. She was only now beginning to realize that he had come to hate himself nearly as much as he hated her. He shouldn't do that. He was the only good person she had ever known.

He shook his head. "Stop it. Just...stop. I don't want you to defend me."

"Then what *do* you want? Tell me what it is, anything, and I'll give it to you in exchange for..." She groped for what exactly it was she wanted to bargain with him for. Her safety, yes, but in what way? What was it that she imagined for herself? Not returning to the palace. Not now that she knew what had been done to her there. She wanted to deny it again as she had when she'd first heard it, wanted to believe that Sarai would never command Albinus to do such a thing to her own sister, but it sounded too much like Sarai's unique brand of love. In the empress's mind, she had given Elodie a way to protect herself, given her a tonic to make her forget the worst night of her life, and created a new weapon to safeguard her own rule all in one neat stroke. Elodie felt sick just thinking of it. No, she could not go back to her sister, no matter how tenuous the safety she might find elsewhere. "In exchange for my safety," she finished, deciding she could clarify her side of the bargain later, after she'd had time to think on it properly.

"I've spent the last two years ensuring your safety, and I believe I have had quite enough of it," Tal said, and turned to stride back to where the Saints were lying on the ground.

The panic from a few moments ago began to flutter beneath her breastbone again. "You said you wouldn't let Nyx kill me," she said, standing up to hurry after him.

"It was *you* who said that." He slid his arms gently under his sister's back and legs and carried her closer to the fire, where she would be warm. When he set her down, her limp hand brushed over his leg—the spot where he'd been injured in the explosion—and he hissed a breath through his teeth as if he were in pain.

Elodie's eyes narrowed and she paused. The Saints had healed Tal, or at least, she had assumed they had when she'd seen him walking around rather than bleeding to death from the many injuries he'd sustained in the past few days. But perhaps she had been wrong. "Are you still hurt?" she demanded.

"It is none of your concern." He didn't look at her, busy scooping up Helenia to move her to the other side of the log near Nyx. When he stepped past the fire's light, this time she paid closer attention, and saw the faint trace of a glassy sheen in his eyes and the way he was sweating a little even though the night was cool.

"You're still feverish," she realized. "Did you get wound fever?"

But wound fever should have been cured by a basic healing potion, if they'd given him a large enough dose—and if the Saints had been able to cure the rest of his significant injuries, the dose surely would have been substantial enough to flush out a wound fever as well. But if it wasn't a wound fever, then what else...

Her breath caught as a possibility she wouldn't have considered before arose in her mind, throwing its long and terrible shadow over all the facts she had previously failed to connect. Tal's blood was silver. He had visions. He was a Smith. He'd been injured badly in the explosion, and he'd been sweating in the middle of a snowstorm afterwards, and he was still lightly feverish now even after a heavy dose of healing tincture.

"You have rust phage," she whispered.

His jaw tightened but he didn't respond, only continued carrying the Saints closer to the fire and making certain they were laid in comfortable positions.

"How long?" she demanded, her mind working busily to try to determine how he could be cured, how much more tincture they needed. Her fingers twitched, and it was only through great effort that she kept herself from marching across the small clearing and yanking up his trouser leg so she could see the phage spot for herself. "How long was I unconscious? How long have you been sick?"

"A few days," he said tightly.

She did the math. They had spent the night after the explosion in the cave. The day after that had been the moon-cat attack. Then the Saints had found them and drugged her. It was evening now, which meant it had been three days total at the very least, and likely a day or two longer than that. That was right on the border of how long a person could go without the right treatment before they passed the point of no return. "There must be more healing tincture," she said, though she knew if there was, Nyx would have already used it on him. She thought quickly; she had no idea where they were but surely there was a town nearby, somewhere with a priest, a physician. "We can get some—"

"Regular potions, or at least the kind non-Smith townships can get, are not enough," he cut in. He picked up the bowls of soup and began rinsing them out over the fire, probably so that the food remnants wouldn't attract predators while the Saints were helpless.

She wanted to shake him. Why was he just ignoring the fact of his own looming demise, as if it meant nothing? "The Saints headquarters. They have to have a stronger potion." Her voice was getting louder now but she couldn't seem to control it.

"They don't. Even if the base wasn't about to be attacked, there are no copper Smiths powerful enough to make concentrated tinctures outside of the palace."

A realization struck her like lightning then, scorching and illuminating all at once. "Then we must go to the palace," she said, hearing the tremor in her voice but unable to do anything about it.

Finally, finally, Tal stopped what he was doing and looked at her. "There is nothing," he said, enunciating each word clearly, "*nothing,* that would make me take you back there."

She matched him glare for glare. "I know a few things that could make you."

He dropped the bowl he'd been cleaning to free up his hands and turn fully to face her. "Are you threatening me?"

She lifted her chin. "If it will save your life, yes, I am absolutely threatening you."

"You have no fire. You can barely grasp a sword."

"But I know you, I know who you love and what you care about and how stupidly noble you always are, and that's more than enough to know how I can make you go back to the palace with me." She was bluffing—she had absolutely no power over him now, and she doubted she could bring herself to hurt Nyx again even if Tal wouldn't knock her flat on her back before she could so much as touch the other girl—but with any luck, he would take her seriously.

His gaze raked her up and down, taking her measure, and then he picked the bowl back up and turned away again: a clear dismissal. "If you think I'm going to let you use me to get you home, just so you can have me executed for being a Smith the second I walk through the gates of—"

"I won't let anyone touch you," she snarled, and for a moment, she felt truly like her old self: invincible in the clear, cold certainty of her mission.

"No," he said, not even bothering to look at her this time.

Her certainty faded to desperation. "But you'll die if you don't go back!"

"I'll die if I do!" he shouted back, hands clenching on the bowl. He took a deep breath and spoke again, in a lower tone this time. "How exactly do you expect me to be cured without anyone realizing *why* I have rust phage? Sarai made my blood illegal, remember? Her execution order is what killed my parents after they were caught during the Silver Coup.

Do you think I would forget such a detail? Why else would I have taken such pains to hide what I am for the last two years?" He exhaled. "I will not go back to my old life at the palace, not in any measure or for any reason. I will die out here, free, in the company of what family I have left."

Elodie shook her head, frustrated, but couldn't think of the right argument to gainsay him. In a way he had a point; she suspected this wouldn't be a simple matter of slipping into the physicians' offices and finding the right medicine for him to swallow. By the time they could get to the palace, Tal would likely need an intensive treatment that only Albinus could provide if he was going to have a chance at survival. And Albinus, as Tal's vision had shown, would not risk disloyalty to Sarai. There was no way for Tal to be treated without the empress finding out what he was.

Maybe she could talk Sarai into letting him live. After all, Elodie had basically been doing that for the last two years. Her sister never had been fond of Tal. Elodie flinched away from the very thought of speaking to her sister again, knowing what she now knew, but if it was necessary to save Tal she'd have to consider it. In any case, what happened *after* they saved his life was a matter to worry about later. Right now she needed only to convince him not to die nobly out in the wilderness like an idiot.

All at once, it hit her. "The Saints base," she said.

Tal set the last of the now-clean bowls in a stack next to the fire. "What?"

"In your vision. You said Sarai was going to attack the

Saints base to rescue me, because she thinks that's where I am. They'll have no warning, and even if they did they wouldn't have enough time to evacuate. Sarai will utterly crush the rebellion for my sake. There will be no one left, except those few stationed at outposts."

"I am aware of that," Tal bit out.

"The rebellion will be ended forever as of tomorrow night. Unless," Elodie said, dreading the words even as she spoke them, "you return me to her first."

Tal turned. He watched her through the veil of smoke and sparks drifting up from the campfire between them. "You're saying if I take you back to the palace," he said slowly, "you'll prevent the attack on the base?"

"I doubt I'll be able to prevent it entirely," Elodie warned. "If she's gotten the intelligence on its location, there's no way she will let it go for long before she strikes. But my return could buy them an extra day or two to evacuate while Sarai debriefs me." She nodded at the limp form of Nyx. "Once they wake up, they could send a warning to the base and get everyone, or at least almost everyone, out before Sarai attacks. And," she added, the idea coming to her as she spoke, "maybe this way Sarai would let you live, too—we could tell her that you fought off my kidnappers, brought me through the wilderness on your own, were brave and heroic and so on, and that you deserve healing and a pardon in recognition for delivering me. She'll think you're still under your oath, so perhaps she wouldn't consider you a threat to me even if you do have silver blood."

Tal shifted his weight to his uninjured leg, an unconscious movement as he considered her proposal. "And after that?" he asked at last. "Once the rebellion is saved and I'm healed? Do you expect me to go back to being your bodyguard?"

She didn't know what she expected, but she wasn't naïve enough to hope for that. She swallowed. "No. You can—you can leave then. If you want. I will not stop you."

The future yawned open before her, a crevasse as unyielding as her nightmare.

Tal sighed, sounding defeated. "I told you, I don't know what I want. But very well. I don't suppose there are any better options, and if I have to return you to your sister to save the rebellion, then it's the least I owe them." He gave her a hard look. "But know that—"

She cut him off, hope and impatience leaping within her. "Yes, yes, if this ends up being a trick I'm sure you'll kill me with your very impressive sword work, or perhaps you will just stand and glare at me stoically until I wither up and die. Now can we get moving? We are in a bit of a rush, as I'm sure you must understand."

He made a soft sound that she realized after a moment was a laugh. He sighed afterwards and tried to run a hand through his hair, but stopped short when his manacles clanked, reminding him of their presence. He ducked down to rummage through his sister's pocket and extracted a key. "I wish you weren't so different now," he muttered as he unlocked the manacles from his wrists.

She raised an eyebrow. "Oh? Why is that?"

"Because it shouldn't be this hard to hate you," he said, and without another word, he pushed past her to begin harnessing the dogs.

Chapter Eighteen

Nyx jerked awake all at once, and had counted six nearby blunt objects with which to bludgeon her brother—or whoever was currently threatening her brother—before she registered where she was.

Cool grass and leaves beneath her. Her torso and head propped up on a log, its stiff bark digging into her bare scalp. Tall mote trees edging her view of the silver-blue sky, their falling seeds more leaden now, coated with a lacy dew that labored their usual drifting movements.

Feeling drunken and half-paralyzed still, Nyx turned her head and squinted. The sun was rising, hovering just over the roof of the temple. It was then that she remembered *why* she wanted to bludgeon her brother, and why she feared he was being threatened.

She filled her lungs as deeply as she could and then

bellowed a string of inventively foul curses into the sky. She could also have yelled something like *help, what happened,* or *somebody had better produce my little brother unharmed immediately before I enact violence that everyone involved—except probably me—will regret,* but curses worked just as well, and if Helenia were nearby she'd be able to translate what Nyx really meant in any case.

Nobody answered. Nyx's heart rate kicked up a notch, and she gathered her strength to roll onto her side and lift her head.

She was surrounded by bodies.

Before she had even finished processing the fact, she was stumbling to her feet, gaze scanning the bodies wildly for the lean shape of Tal, the familiar curves of Helenia. Her heart pounded a frantic drumbeat: *no, no, no.*

It wasn't until she tripped and fell onto the body of one of the mushers, wringing a sleepy groan from him, that she realized the bodies weren't dead at all but only sleeping.

She felt dizzy with relief. Her body was shaking. Without bothering to check if her fall had done any damage to the musher, she pushed off him—eliciting another groan—and continued her search for her brother and girlfriend, only slightly calmer now that she had more reason to believe they were still alive. She made an entire circuit of the campfire area, accidentally stepping on two dozing dogs in the process, before she finally found Helenia sleeping peacefully on the other side of the log where Nyx had woken up. Nyx sagged down to sit next to her, not bothering to check that she was still breathing; she could hear Hel's snores from here. A bit of drool spotted her cheek and Nyx reached out to wipe it off with her sleeve, laughing shakily when she thought of how horrified Helenia would be to see the state she was in.

She had found her girlfriend. She could breathe now, and her heart was a bit calmer. But where, *where,* was her brother?

She was angry at him—no, she was downright *furious*— but she couldn't quite remember all the details of why. She dug through her hazy memories until she managed to recall him explaining his visions and then saying, *you do not need to hold me back.*

Son of a bitch. Son of a *bitch.* He was free of his oath, had been for days now, and he hadn't so much as hinted at it to her. Worse than that, he'd brought his own enemy back to life. When she thought of him saying *I breathed for her,* thought of the Destroyer's lips touching his in a mockery of intimacy, she wanted to be sick and she wanted to pummel them both until her fists bled. Why would he do such a thing? What could possibly compel him? Had his time with the Destroyer truly been enough to change him so? She'd heard of captives falling in love with their captors, and love or some twisted version of it seemed like the only thing that could even begin to explain his actions. She remembered seeing his new scars and thinking that his soul had always been so much more fragile than his body. Could the Destroyer have broken it entirely, warped it into something that could feel sympathy for a murderess?

Nyx hadn't found the Destroyer's body when she had done her circuit of camp. There were also, she saw now, a sled and five dogs—including Maluk—missing. She pressed a kiss to Helenia's forehead and then stood up to investigate further.

There were footprints all over camp, and it was impossible to tell which had belonged to whom, but there were also droplets of dried red-brown blood splattered near where the missing sled had been. Nyx's razor was nearby too, driven blade first into the earth. She yanked it out to examine it; its edge was crusted with red blood. So at least her brother had tried to carry through on his promise to kill the Destroyer himself...but then what? Something had gone wrong, obviously, something that had managed to put everyone except Tal and the Destroyer to sleep. Gold magic could do that. Had a gold Smith come upon them and used their powers to rescue the Destroyer? But if that was the case, why not slit the throats of all the Saints while they were sleeping, or take them prisoner?

And then she realized there was something else that could put a group of people to sleep, and took two steps sideways to peer into the soup pot. There was a stack of cleaned bowls next to it but the pot itself was crusted with the burnt remnants of stew. She rooted around until she found a stick and then used it to poke at the bottom of the pot—and immediately the stick clanked against something laying below the surface of the stew. With a snarl, she drew back the stick and drove it down hard, and the sound of shattering glass echoed through the clearing.

The bottle of laudanum. While they'd all been yelling at each other and listening to Tal explain his visions, the Destroyer had been awake, and had managed to dose their soup with the drug they'd been using to keep her unconscious. The Destroyer hadn't had any to eat, of course, which was why she wasn't among the sleeping bodies now...and Tal hadn't eaten any, either. At the time she had thought he was too upset to eat—she had been, too, but her mother-hen girlfriend had forced her to eat anyway—but now, there was a small, dark part of her that couldn't help but wonder if he and the Destroyer had planned this somehow.

She broke her stick over her knee and hurled the pieces in opposite directions as hard as she could. Then she turned and started toward a sled, meaning to harness the dogs while she waited for the others to wake—but then she spotted a page of paper pinned beneath the stack of washed bowls. Her name was printed at the top in familiar neat lettering. She snatched it up, tearing a corner off in the process, and read.

Nyx,
Go warn the base. I'll try to buy you a day or two.
Forgive me.

She read her brother's note three times before she could process what it meant. The only way he could hope to "buy her a day or two" to warn the Saints was by somehow keeping Sarai from attacking the base for that long. And the only way the empress would wait to rescue her sister was if she no longer needed to rescue her sister. Tal was helping the Destroyer get back to the palace.

Nyx dropped the note. It fluttered to the ground, where the dew-laden grass slowly soaked it, wet spots bleeding over the page like inkblots.

Tal had left her behind, again. Tal had chosen the Destroyer over her *again.*

She scrubbed a hand over her eyes, furious to find wet tracks on her cheeks. She was not going to *cry.* She was not going to stand here and whimper that her brother's spirit had been broken by a monster. She was going to track him down, and she was going to stop him, and then she was going to end the Destroyer if it was the last thing she ever did.

She went back to Helenia, her steps steadier now that she'd had a few minutes to begin recovering from her drugged sleep. She knelt down and reached out a hand, but then stopped, her fingers hovering over Helenia's shoulder. Her mind played out the scene that was about to happen: Hel would wake, Nyx would tell her what happened and what she was going to do, and then...Helenia would stop her.

Her girlfriend had always been soft-hearted. It was one of the reasons Nyx had fallen so hard for her; sometimes, many times, Hel was the only softness present in any part of Nyx's life. She smoothed Nyx's hard edges, provided calm in Nyx's many storms, and had guided her through some of the worst weeks of her life after Tal had first left. But Helenia's kindness, her tendency to think the best of others, sometimes extended to people it shouldn't—as last night's conversation had shown.

Helenia had recognized Tal's and Nyx's right to decide the Destroyer's fate then, but she had argued stridently against execution, and if she were awake now she would do it again. She would tell her to trust her brother. To trust the god who had given him his visions. To have hope that this twist of fate might mean "Elodie" was indeed meant to be redeemed. And even if Nyx managed to talk her around, the time it would take would allow Tal and the Destroyer to get so far ahead that Nyx would never catch them.

Slowly, Nyx withdrew her hand.

The other sleds were all where they had been last night, and the dogs Tal hadn't taken lifted their heads and watched as Nyx chose one and began hooking up the harnesses.

The rest of the Saints, including Helenia, would be fine. They would wake up soon and figure out for themselves what had happened. They would take care of warning the base.

And by the time they were done, the Destroyer would be dead.

CHAPTER NINETEEN

During their two-day journey south, Elodie did everything she could to endear herself to Tal. She was, predictably, not very good at it.

Throughout the first day, she noticed that he and Maluk seemed to have an affinity for each other. During their infrequent and brisk rest breaks, Tal checked the old dog over carefully, looking at each paw for any thorns or pebbles that might've gotten stuck, spending more time with him than any of the other four haulers. Maluk, for his part, leaned into Tal during these sessions and closed his eyes, the picture of canine contentment. So the first evening, when Tal went to hunt for the dogs' dinner, Elodie dug through the packs until she found a brush and then used it to clean Maluk's fur until he shone. The hauler leaned into her just as he did with Tal and she felt an unexpected fizz of happiness at the sign of his

trust. The dog, at least, seemed to like her—which was fortunate, because the gesture won her no goodwill at all from Tal.
He barely glanced at her when he returned, dragging a dead
hind behind him.

Then she and Tal took turns sleeping atop the packs
that night as the other stood on the rails and mushed. Elodie
didn't wake him when her shift was over, instead letting him
doze on as the fat, nearly-full moon rose. The stars flushed
and faded in its presence, entirely outshone. They had the
grace to know when they were beaten. Or perhaps they simply lacked the will for the fight.

The sled continued its southerly course, the foothills flattening around them, the Skyteeth receding into the distance,
the scorch tree woodlands growing into a blur of crimson on
the horizon as the sun dawned. The sled's retrofitted wheels
meant their journey was an uncomfortable, bone-rattling
one. She didn't know how Tal could sleep through it. When
he woke, his eyes glassy with fever, she got her answer. He
was limping visibly as he walked around to take her spot.
Something lurched painfully in her chest at the proof of his
growing weakness.

"I can keep going," she said, clinging to the handle even
though she was dazed with tiredness and starch-stiff from
balancing on the jouncing rails most of the night.

"No," Tal said shortly, and it turned out her will was as
weak as the stars', because she lay down on the packs without
further argument and slept through the entire day. She felt
perversely safe with him watching over her, as she always

had, even though he had held a razor to her throat less than twenty-four hours ago.

They were both silent the next day as they traveled through the dripping crimson moss of the scorch woodlands, though she was sure they had different reasons for their reticence. The closer they came to the palace, the more ghosts rose up to pursue her, and she had little endurance left to out-maneuver them. As for Tal, she was beginning to suspect that he was keeping something from her. She could see it in the way he avoided looking at her, in the tightness of his expression when he did and how quickly he looked away again. So when they came to the bank of the Entengre river and the plated-metal palace rose up before them at last, Elodie looked not at it, but at Tal.

He said nothing, same as the last two days, but now it wasn't just his silence that worried her. It was the quality of that silence. Always before it had been a tensely-held thing, not a lack of speech between them but rather the presence of something weightier and more terrible, something that could allow no words through the gaps in its defense. Now, though, Tal's silence was empty. As if everything that could be said had already been said, and there was nothing left at all to fill the blank space that stretched between them.

And now, the way he was looking at the palace: not with the resignation and hatred that he'd always had, but rather as if he'd never seen it before, as if it were a thing he'd only ever heard of in stories, and now he was trying to match those stories to the sight before him. She saw her home through his eyes: every wall a curse, every spire a blade. Every room filled with monsters.

She watched him look at the Alloyed Palace, and she knew that he would leave her.

She broke the silence at last, because she realized now that he never would. "You're not coming back with me."

The river's mist rose around them, a delicate sheen under the dying evening light. His eyes, which were already bright with fever, looked luminous in the haze. "I told you," he said quietly, "that there was nothing that could make me go back."

Her mind seemed to hang somewhere outside her body, suspended in the fog like a beetle in amber. Though she had spent the last two days trying to find some way to convince him to stay with her, the realization that he was refusing now to go back for even as long as it took to save his own life left her utterly without reply.

She could beg his forgiveness for her sins. She could promise his safety. But she could not lower herself to grovel for something he could never give and she couldn't rightfully promise him her protection either. If she had no magic, she could do nothing to stop any distant cousin or half-royal acquaintance from hurting him to get to her. And if she *did* have magic, then she would be the one to hurt him, one way or another.

"Tal," she said at last. "Don't do this."

"It is not something I'm doing, but something I am refusing to do," he said, so calmly that she thought she might throttle him. How could he so easily accept his own demise when the thought of it made her half-mad with desperation?

"Let me save you. Let me make reparations to you," she tried next. "I don't expect you to stay with me. But at least don't let yourself die just to spite me."

He exhaled, something that was almost a laugh, and turned at last to face her. "If I wanted to spite you, we wouldn't be standing here." He nodded at the palace. "It's nearly evening. Your sister will be preparing the zeppelin any moment now. You must go to her before she takes off."

Elodie glanced at the bridge that stretched across the river. Few people were on it at this time of day. She would be able to get across it and to the palace in the space of perhaps ten minutes. Judging by the timing of the base attack–or at least, what Tal's vision had revealed about the base attack– she still had a bit of leeway before the balloon would take off.

She turned back to Tal, squaring her body to his as if they were fighters in a ring, and lifted her chin. "No."

"What?"

"You heard me. No. I won't go back without you. I won't save the Saints from my sister unless you let me save you, too." It was a gamble, but one she was more than willing to follow through on, if that was what it took. She had never met anyone from his mountain base and the few Saints she *had* met had unanimously wanted her dead. She owed them nothing. She didn't particularly care if her sister killed them or not. But Tal cared. She would use whatever leverage she could to keep him alive, and she refused to feel even the slightest bit guilty about it. He had a claim on her soul and she was done denying it; he would live, even if it damned her. Not, she supposed, that she could be any more damned than she already was.

He closed his eyes. He didn't look angered by her blackmail like she would have expected, though. When he spoke again, she realized why. "Your sister will die in the attack on the base."

She stared at him. Slowly, the words sank through her until she could pick them apart and decipher the truth beneath them. "Your vision," she guessed finally. "You didn't tell the Saints all of it." Her hands began to shake and she curled them into fists, digging her nails into her palms to punish her traitorous body.

"Yes. I saw your coronation. That could only happen if Sarai dies." His answer was without a trace of guilt, so unlike him that for one wild moment she wanted to laugh. He sounded like *her*.

She exhaled. The mist swirled around her, and when she inhaled again, the taste of copper slipped under her tongue and coated her teeth. It was because of the mines upriver, she thought, but couldn't rid herself of the idea that it was blood and not metal at all that she was tasting. "You are saying that Sarai will die if I don't stop her from leaving now."

She had thought before that Tal had a claim on her soul. It was true, but her sister had a claim on it too. Sarai had done terrible things to her but she had done them in the name of a sister's love, and it was that same love that drove Elodie to take a step away from Tal and toward the bridge now. "You're lying."

"I am not."

She twisted quickly to look at the palace. The sun had begun to set. Hues of orange and pink laved the buildings on the other side of the river, gilding the roof tiles and glazing even the gutters in bright, hopeful stains, but none of it could touch Elodie through the mist. She could just make out the palace crouched like a dragon above the river, and the rust-and-cobalt shape that was slowly rising above its crenellations. The zeppelin was floating up to the level of the docking tower, where the empress and her soldiers would board.

If Sarai was dead and Tal was gone, what would be left for Elodie? She would be the magicless ruler of a palace full of her enemies, and the only two people in the world who she loved would be dead.

Love, she thought again. The realization was a fire. It burned through the shed skin of her past self, burned through her confusion, her anger, her fear, her helplessness. She loved Tal. Not merely cared about him. Not simply felt safe near him. *This* was the claim he had on her soul, and now that she finally recognized it, she wasn't shocked at its presence, but was instead shocked at just how deeply its roots had had to wind into her heart before she registered its presence. What a fool she had been, to miss it before. And what a fool she was now, to think it made any difference.

She could not save Tal. He did not wish to be saved. Even now he was already half-faded from the world: skin pale, sweat and mist mingled on his brow, eyes like glass marbles–fragile and unnatural in the way they caught too much of the light. He had brought her back to life when he had no reason to. Had she any right to ask this from him, too? To care for a person he should rightfully despise, just because she had finally realized she loved him? To save himself for her sake, when all of the despicable acts he'd committed over the last two years had been for her sake?

He wanted freedom. And even if it meant the ruination of them both, she wasn't sure she could deny him that any longer.

"Please," she said softly, trying one last time, even though she had resolved earlier that she wouldn't lower herself to beg. "Please don't leave me."

He reached into the pack he'd slung over his shoulders and withdrew something that shone blackly, catching all the shades of the sunset as the mist beaded on it: her crown. It was a delicate, twisted thing, its sharp angles too brittle to last, and yet somehow it had survived the arduous journey intact.

Tal held it out to her. "Goodbye, Elodie," he said, but the sound of her name was not enough to soften the sight of him holding her crown. She reached for it, and when she had gripped it, a memory surged through the metal like a spark of static electricity: the two of them standing at the palace docks not far from this spot, his hands on her crown as he swore to protect her. The metal was inert now, empty of any such promise.

She accepted the crown. He released it. Her hands dropped heavily to her sides. The roots he'd wrapped around her heart stretched and broke away, one by one.

The zeppelin was rising higher. She would have to run if she wanted to reach someone who could stop it in time. She looked back to Tal and lifted her free hand toward him in a helpless gesture, trying to think of what else she could possibly say that might change his mind—but he flinched away and his own hand raised slightly as if to shield himself. An old habit, one that he would never be rid of no matter how long she was magicless.

She let her hand drop. She took a long step backwards, river reeds brushing against her calves. She raised the crown and set it on her brow. "Goodbye, Tal," she answered at last, and then she turned and ran.

CHAPTER TWENTY

Tal stood in the reeds, the sky bleeding sunset across the horizon, river mist hanging over the shore like a funeral shroud, and counted to one hundred. Beyond the bridge, a line of sailboats and small merchant steamships bobbed at the royal docks. By the time he reached a count of twenty Elodie had disappeared behind them. At the count of fifty, the sound of shouts and distant running feet drifted over the water. She had been spotted. He finished his count. When he reached one hundred—when he was certain that all the patrolling soldiers within earshot had run to her, eager to assist the unexpectedly returned Lady of Mercury—he drew his twin swords and started over the bridge.

He had lied to Elodie. There was something that could make him return to the palace. Not a way to live, but a way to spend the coin of his death on something that might begin to make up for his choices.

He avoided the route Elodie had taken. He didn't want her to see him. He didn't want her to try to stop him. There was too high a possibility that, given one more chance, she might succeed. He had seen the bloom of realization in her eyes—a bloom not like a flower, but like the plume of smoke that rises up from a catastrophe—and had felt the pull of it in his own soul. He knew what she had realized, but he also could not afford to know it, so as he walked, he let himself drift away from his own mind. Free of worry and choice, he watched himself walk over the bridge. The cobbled roads here twinkled and blinked with bronze flecks like a carpet of stars unrolled beneath his feet. To his left were the palace docks: long lines of jetties and wharfs where ships flew under the Alloyed Empire flag as well as the colorful pennants of several neighboring countries. Ambassadors and courtiers, flocking to the scent of weakness. They would flee soon. Likely the moment the Destroyer got her magic back.

Silver eyes beneath an iron crown. Such a simple vision to have such an effect on him. He had known all along that the Destroyer would eventually return to herself, would swallow up the strange girl he'd met in the Skyteeth. Elodie had been a mirage. A deception, even if it was one that had briefly fooled her as well as him. And now the deception was over. He should not grieve what was not a true loss.

He turned left. The starry flecks in the road vanished. No one who walked this lane needed the travel-smoothing enchantment that was Smithed into the cobblestones of the main streets. To his left, a smaller branch of the Entengre vanished into the dark maw of a tunnel, where it would be carried into the aquifers below the city. There it would sink through the silt and be filtered and cleansed before it flowed back into the main Entengre downstream. The reason it needed to be cleansed first was because this was the spot where the palace dumped its sewage, and also its dead bodies.

There was a door just in front of the tunnel. It was set into the side of the plated metal palace, although here the man-sized scales were all dull tin, Smithed sensibly for defense rather than beauty and intimidation. On the other side of this door were the dungeons. Thanks to the tin's enchantments, the cells beyond could not be breached by cannonballs or fire, nor by any enemy army. They could, however, be breached by a lone soldier, if he was foolish enough to set himself against an entire regiment of the Iron Empress's guards.

The two men stationed at the door stood up quickly when they spotted Tal. One of them kicked the dice they'd been playing with behind the steps, out of his line of vision, and then relaxed when Tal stepped out of the evening shadows and revealed himself to be no one important. Neither of them took any action to conceal the two dead women whose bodies slouched against the wall. One of the bodies had a blue and purple complexion from the blood that had pooled beneath her skin when her heart was no longer beating to circulate it. The arms of the other twisted across her body at a stiff angle. They had been dead for a while, carried to this door and then stacked like firewood to await the completion of the guards' dice game, when they would be carried to the river and disposed of.

Tal recognized one of the bodies. She had pale porcelain skin, even paler now in death, and red hair that she had always kept in a frizzy braid. She'd been a friend of Saasha's. She used to watch over Tal and Nyx when they were young, right after their father's execution, when Saasha was mired too deep in grief to see to the needs of her daughter and newly-acquired stepson.

Tal wondered which of the two dead women had given up the location of the Saints base to the empress, and how much torture they'd undergone before that. These two would have been among the number who'd volunteered themselves for Nyx's mission, had been imprisoned on the train with her, and before that had saved the lives of innocent townsfolk by taking their place in the mining town when the Destroyer came to make their reckoning. Nyx had told him, in an unbreaking voice that was all the more awful for its bravado, the names of the Saints who had been in the prison car with her. Nyx had managed to escape. They had not. Instead they had been teleported along with the rest of the train to the palace, where they had been taken prisoner and, judging by the marks on these two bodies, interrogated without mercy.

"Halt," one of the guards called, then squinted, recognizing Tal. "God's hammer," he swore, "you live? Does that mean the Destroyer does as well?"

Tal didn't answer. He kept coming.

The guard's gaze shifted to the swords held loosely at Tal's sides. His eyes narrowed and his hand went to the falchion sword strapped to his own waist. The other guard caught both the movement and his friend's wariness, and drew his falchion.

"He said, halt," the second guard repeated, his tone steelier than the other's. "Bodyguards are only to come through secondary entrances if accompanied by their charges. You'll have to go through the main gates."

Tal had no plans to enter through any gate other than this one. Neither slowing nor stopping, he continued his steady approach. One guard cursed and turned, twisting the knob of the door at his back, raising his voice to shout for reinforcements. By the time he got the first syllable of his shout out, Tal's sword was already a blur of silver arcing toward his chest, and the second syllable ended in a warbling gurgle.

The other guard lunged forward in defense of his partner. One of his hands thrust his falchion forward while the other reached for the parrying dagger sheathed at his waist. Tal withdrew the sword that had been planted in the first guard's chest—the man's sternum making a cracking sound in the process—and spun sideways to avoid the dagger's blow. The second guard stumbled, off-balance, and Tal's left sword flashed downward after him. The man dropped both his falchion and his dagger, though the latter action was involuntary, as his left hand had been sheared off at the wrist. The inert limb landed at Tal's feet and he wasted no time in kicking the dagger into the river.

Rage and terror battled in the stiff lines of the second guard's body but he was too well-trained to give in to either, and stooped quickly to reach toward his falchion with his remaining arm. The weapon was out of his reach but it flew of its own accord toward the man's hand anyway. Tal brought both swords around and, in one clean movement, severed most of the man's head while he was bent over. White bone gleamed with bluish-silver blood—a zinc Smith, with telekinetic powers—as the man tumbled forward. Tal stepped aside to allow the body to stumble past him and then turned and kicked him square in the spine, propelling him the last few steps to the river. The body splashed loudly as it fell in and then was swept downstream to reunite with its dagger.

Tal turned back to the palace. He stepped over the body of the first guard, who was still gurgling weakly, and entered the dungeons.

The narrow hallway stank of defecation and death. The smell slipped into him like a thief in the darkness, and a forgotten memory rose up at his side. A sixteen-year-old girl whose graceful gait carried her through the door, boots snapping on the stained tile, each step a sharp announcement. The prisoners had wept and screamed to see her approach. *I do not care for the smell,* whispered the ghost of the Destroyer. *Then why don't you ask for incense, my lady?* Tal had replied caustically. He had still been new then, and outraged, and hopeful. Those emotions had brought all the sharp parts of him to the outside, where they could cut both himself and others.

Because it would be a lie, she'd replied. *I will give them pain. I will not give them false hope.*

Tal tried to force the memory away. It would not go. That was the power of this place: to resurrect all of the horrors he had somehow managed to dull over the last few days, to make him into the shade of who he used to be. This was why he had refused to let Elodie bring him back to the palace in search of a cure. Not because of what could happen after that, but because of what had already happened.

He would not have to withstand the ghosts and memories for long, though. Just for long enough to do what he needed to.

His god touched him then, a feather-light reassurance. He would be with Tal at the end. In the dreaming place. In the space between the end of life and the beginning of death. Tal wanted to be bitter, but discovered to his surprise that his old bitterness had changed—slowly but undeniably, the way copper turns green with time—to a tired sort of acceptance. If this was the end that the Unforged God had charted for him, then at least it was the same end Tal had charted for himself, too. He could allow himself to take comfort in that.

The hall opened into a wider area with a drain set into the floor and a desk at the far end. A burly, middle-aged woman was standing behind it, one hand lifted to yank on a thick cord dangling from the ceiling. The cord would trigger an alarm that would bring reinforcements from the nearby courtyard and mess halls.

Tal threw his right sword. It thudded into the wall behind the woman, pinning her forearm to the wood in the process.

She didn't scream, only whirled around and put her hand to the hilt to yank it out, but Tal let her get no further than that before he took three long steps forward and drove his left sword into her chest. She spat blood at him and it splattered on his shirt and over her own cobalt uniform before she slid down the wall, dead, her impaled arm still held above her.

Tal tugged his swords free. The dead woman slumped the rest of the way to the ground. He bent down and retrieved a ring of keys from her waist.

Why keys? Tal had asked during his second trip to the dungeons, when he was angry with no good outlet and not enough sense yet to hide his emotions. *Why not Smith the cells to open at your touch, as they do on the train? It would save time.*

The Destroyer had raised an eyebrow, then lifted the key ring and shook it. It gave a sweet tinkling sound like perverse wind chimes. *The anticipation of torture is often as effective as the torture itself,* she deigned to tell him. *They will hear me coming, and they will have time to peruse all possible plans for escape, realize there are none that will succeed, and give me the information my sister needs before I even have to open the cell. Keys are quite practical as time-saving mechanisms.*

Running footsteps stomped down the hall at his back, pulling Tal from his memories. He clamped a hand around the bloodied key ring to stop their jingling and then dropped them into a pocket, freeing his hands for his weapons again.

"You there—" started one braying voice from the far corridor, but it cut off when Tal ducked sideways, and the kick that had been aimed at his knee hid the solid wooden desk instead. Converting the momentum of his movement into a roll, Tal dove beneath the oncoming guard's outstretched leg and swung a sword upward in the process, slicing deeply across the inside of his thigh and severing the vital artery there. Blood—tinted gold this time—sprayed across the floor and ran in rivulets toward the drain. Tal came out of the roll to drive his elbow into the jaw of the second guard who was behind him, and kneed a third hard in the stomach. These would be the guards who had already been stationed in the dungeons. If he was lucky, the guard at the desk hadn't had time to pull the cord, and further reinforcements would be far enough behind for him to achieve his objective.

Without warning, a heavy tiredness dropped over Tal like a net, and he stumbled. The gold-blooded guard was not yet dead, and was using his power over sleep and dreams to try to render Tal unconscious. Tal sheathed one of his swords, snatched a fallen dagger from the floor, and hurled it at the gold Smith. It lodged in the man's throat and the veil of exhaustion lifted instantly.

The ploy had given one of the guards enough time to recover from the knee Tal had planted in her gut, though, and she lashed out quickly with her falchion to catch Tal on the arm. Her weapon came back stained silver and speckled with tiny orange crystals. The sight of his forbidden blood tinted with rust phage caught her off-guard and she hesitated for half a second too long, giving Tal enough time to kick her hard in the knee. When she buckled and fell forward, he caught her in one arm and used the other to drive his blade through the slot of her ribs. She shuddered once and then went limp. He dropped her corpse and looked around.

There was still one guard left, the one Tal whose jaw Tal had broken. He was young, only a year or two older than Tal, probably a recent recruit on his first tour of duty in the dungeon. His eyes were wide, the skin around his cheekbones bloodless and taut with terror. He turned and ran.

Tal had had more than his fill of killing, but if he let this man go, he would alert the nearest soldiers and endanger Tal's mission. Coming to a quick compromise, Tal swept up a fallen falchion from one of the guards and sent it flying after the man, taking him across the ankle and likely severing his hamstring. The man howled and fell to the ground. He would live, but he wouldn't be moving quickly enough to summon any more guards than were already headed this way.

Tal turned to examine the cells before him. The prisoners who were under active interrogation were kept on the second level down. He strode past the stinking cells on the first level, brushing past their grasping hands, closing his ears to their shouted pleas, promising himself that if he lived long enough, he would return to free them after he had found the people he was here for.

The steps downward were slick and stained, and the smell of the dungeons soured with the scent of vomit. It was a common enough smell down here. On Tal's fifth trip to the dungeons, he had made it only a little further than this point before he himself had thrown up. That was the day Sarai had accompanied them. She'd made Tal hold the prisoner down.

He stopped and touched a hand to the wall, pausing for a moment to take a shallow breath. How many times had he been in this forsaken place, how many times had he begged his god to release him, to let him flee, to let him fight back? And now he'd returned voluntarily, and there was still such little difference he could make. He might as well still be oath-bound. The Alloyed Empire would go on, with a mercurial empress at its head. He had saved her—maybe, possibly, depending on how one viewed the situation—but he had certainly not saved the empire either through her or from her. Only half of the Unforged God's promise had been true. He wished now that none of it had been.

Something moved inside him, protesting the lie, but he shut it out ruthlessly.

He came to the landing. Another guard was there and Tal took him by surprise, sweeping his legs out from under him and then cleanly breaking his neck before he had a chance to draw his sword, or to feel pain. He let the body sag out of his hands and kept moving.

This level was bright. The floor was plated in platinum, Smithed by the magic of light to give off a harsh glow that threw bizarre shadows across the prisoners' faces and on the ceiling. The light was more merciless than darkness would be—it gave these people nowhere to hide their despair. Cell after cell was filled with men and women who stared hopelessly at him as he passed, shadows carved into their features, stretching the lines of misery around their mouths into a mockery.

At the end of the third row, he found the people he was looking for.

Dark brown hands wrapped around the bars ahead of him. Steely eyes watched him come, as if she had given him an order and he was late in following it. Her short halo of curls was matted and tangled but she still managed to make it look regal.

"Saasha," he greeted her.

"Tal." Her voice cracked—with pride, he thought, noticing how her eyes changed and shone. He wondered if her plan had extended this far. If, as she was concocting the poison for Nyx, she had imagined that she would end up here and he would rescue her. Or had she considered her own life as forfeit as her daughter's? *Saasha raised her on those gruesome texts of the ancient Saints' martyrdoms,* he remembered Helenia saying, and he realized then that Saasha had expected all of them to die.

He found he could not quite resent her for it. He had always been willing to sacrifice to save those who needed him, after all. He was not, however, prepared to sacrifice Nyx. For that, he *could* fault Saasha. He leveled a look at her and saw her recognize the censure in it. The shadows lining her face shifted, painting her expression in unfamiliar lines and ashen hues, and then she spotted his injury and the rust-colored crystals staining it and her expression turned into something complex and unnamable.

"Does she live?" Saasha asked then, quietly.

"Nyx is well," Tal said, taking pity on her.

"And the Destroyer?"

"Her too. And," he added, as if the words were being pulled out of him by her relentless gaze, "she will be crowned soon."

Saasha's lips thinned, and behind her, one of the other Saint prisoners let out a half-muffled wail. "Then we've failed."

A tumult of footsteps sounded overhead. Distant shouts and cries filtered down as the carnage he'd left behind was discovered.

Tal lifted the key ring so Saasha could see it. They chimed sweetly, silver against bronze against copper. "Which one?" he asked.

"Tell me first: where is Nyx? And when will the Destroyer be crowned?"

Footsteps clattered on the stairs. "It's not the time for planning more assassinations, Saasha," he replied, his voice taut.

"The tin one with the crooked teeth," she said, nodding at the keys. He set it into the lock and opened the door. The Saints gathered themselves up and hurried into the hall.

"Go out the south entrance, down this hall and then to the right," he told them. "The guards there will be distracted right now by...some things happening on the zeppelin landing towers. I'll distract the guards here long enough for you to get across the southern bridge over the Entengre; there's a sled and dogs ready to go at the edge of the scorch woodlands there."

Saasha was still in the cell. She let go of the bars and backed away, shaking her head, her arms wrapping around herself in a way that made her look uncharacteristically uncertain. "Tell me where my daughter is."

The guards' footsteps were growing closer. He stepped into the cell, hissing a breath out through his teeth, and grabbed her by the shoulder to pull her bodily into the hall. She resisted. "Nyx is probably on her way to the palace right now," he said, since it was apparently the quickest way to get his stepmother free. "Perhaps half a day behind me if I had to guess, and she will likely come here even though she is supposed to be warning the mountain base of impending attack. As for the Destroyer, I don't know when her coronation will be, but it'll be soon. Find Nyx and get out of the city before it happens. Your freedom is my parting gift to her."

Saasha bowed her head. "What will you do?"

"I will get you away from here or die in the attempt. After that…" He hesitated, glanced at the stairs where the first few soldiers were hurrying into the corridor. He hadn't thought much about what he would do if he lived through this plan. "I will try to find Nyx myself. I want to be with her at the end, if I can."

Saasha reached out her arms and folded Tal into a hug. Then, suddenly, she spun around and shoved Tal backwards. Caught off guard, he stumbled. By the time he righted himself she was on the other side of the bars. The cell door shut with a thud and the lock slid closed. She tossed the keys down the hall. They skittered and clinked against the glowing floor plates.

He stared at her, wordless. She stepped back. "I'm sorry, Tal," she said, her voice full of the fierce certainty she had always worn, "but the scriptures are clear. Great victory never comes without great sacrifice, and if Nyx is not an exception, you are not either."

She turned her back, leaving him locked in the empress's dungeons with only his ghosts and his god.

CHAPTER TWENTY-ONE

THERE WAS A HOLLOW SPACE AT ELODIE'S BACK. IT RESO-
nated with the melody of missing footsteps, with the way
the air moved differently around her now that no one was
in that spot, two feet back and a little to the side, where
Tal had always walked. When the guard captain who was
escorting her stepped through the space, Elodie turned her
head and gave him a look that made him freeze in his tracks
without regard to the fact that her eyes were brown and her
blood magicless. It didn't lessen the ache that was creeping
through her like frost slipping under a windowsill, but it did
give her a momentary satisfaction when the man dropped
his eyes and moved up to walk in front of her instead.

She could send a soldier out to retrieve Tal from the
bridge. She had thought about it. He couldn't have gone
far in such a short time, and the palace had many excellent

trackers. She could have him hauled bodily to the palace and dragged before Albinus to be cured. But she knew that it would only be one more betrayal to him, and he'd had far more than his share of that already.

It infuriated her that she had to let him die in order to honor him. It infuriated her that she *wanted* to honor him, that she wanted to give him a choice and that she cared which choice he would make. He was a weakness. He had always been such, and it had only been sheer luck that none of her enemies had noticed before.

A whisper broke through her thoughts and she lifted her head. A woman was standing in the arch of a nearby hallway. She was dressed in garishly bright silks that draped all wrong on her bony frame, and paired with a short bald man who draped over her all wrong as well. The woman's eyes were lit up with malicious glee as she watched Elodie sweep down the corridor. Her name was Countess Ysayle. She was Elodie's great aunt and utterly unworthy of the moniker, having twice attempted assassination against the Destroyer. Elodie wasn't sure which made her think less of Ysayle: the fact that she had tried to have her own niece killed, or the fact that she'd failed so embarrassingly to achieve her goal. Ysayle was currently whispering to the man at her side, both of their gazes glued to Elodie's face—to her brown eyes, she was certain, until she registered that her cheeks were wet.

Elodie raised a hand to touch the soft skin below her eyes. She was crying. This place had already wrung tears out of her, and she was only a few hundred steps into it. The tears were as good as blood in the water to the countess, whose smirk widened as she watched the once fearsome Destroyer weep in the halls of her own home.

Elodie swept the tears off her face with a fingertip and flung them to the plush carpet. "Ysayle," she called, her voice cold and steady as she intentionally dropped her aunt's title, "please keep your toys stashed in your rooms and out of sight. It's unseemly to parade them out in the hall."

Ysayle looked confused for a moment until Elodie raised an eyebrow at the man who was draped over her, and then Ysayle's smirk turned ugly—or uglier, anyway—and angry. Elodie counted one point scored for herself. She couldn't care less about the string of lovers her great aunt took—it was no one's business, really, and if she were a man no one would give it a second thought in any case—but it was a quick way to make the point that silver eyes or no, Elodie was not to be mocked. Of course, it was also a quick way to make Ysayle even more of an enemy than she already was, but that was a matter for future Elodie to worry about.

Future Elodie. She snorted lightly. As if she would somehow know how to successfully navigate the ballrooms and dining halls and audience chambers full of her many enemies if she merely gave herself an extra day or two to figure it out.

"I am glad you find some amusement in your predicament, sister," came a voice so charged with emotion it nearly crackled, "because I surely haven't been able to."

Elodie jerked her head up. The empress Sarai strode down the hall, clad in shining armor, glorious golden hair hanging wild over her shoulders, sharp eyes sheened bright with ferocity and joy and, Elodie thought, perhaps grief as she met the now-brown eyes of her little sister.

Sarai didn't pause even for a moment. She closed the distance between the two of them and wrapped her whole self around Elodie: a shield against the world, formed by the impenetrable love of a sister. Elodie turned her face against the cold plate metal covering Sarai's chest and, hidden there from her enemies, allowed her breath to come in the gasping shudder of a girl who wanted very badly to sob.

At least she had this: her sister, alive. One single person left in this awful place who would never, ever leave her.

Sarai's arms tightened around her. She snapped out orders to the soldiers and the handful of nobles surrounding them and then moved so that one arm was still wrapped around Elodie, guiding her further down the hall. The tapestries and sculptures and metallic-paint murals to either side were a blur as they turned east, toward the physicians' offices. Elodie was so focused on trying to regain her composure that it took her a moment to realize Sarai was moving more stiffly than usual. She glanced over at her sister, having to crane her neck inelegantly to do so at such a close distance, and saw that a woman was walking on her other side with one hand laid on Sarai's shoulder. It was Tirine, head of the House of Lead, wielder of illusory magics. Elodie's gaze flicked back to her sister, but Sarai only gave her a cool smile that clearly meant they weren't going to discuss anything until they were safely ensconced in Albinus's healing chambers, far from listening ears.

Sarai stopped at the massive green copper doors of the physicians' wing, which were currently standing open. "You may leave us here," the empress said. The soldiers bowed and stepped away. Tirine started to as well, but Sarai laid her fingers atop the hand that was still resting on her shoulder, and Tirine stilled. "May I have the charm before you go, Tirine?"

Tirine bowed, and with her free hand pulled a palm-sized mirror from her pocket and handed it to the empress. Sarai accepted it and then waved her away.

The two sisters stepped into the physicians' wing. This area was bright, full of wide windows and exotic potted plants that filled the air with the heady scent of blossoms, though they weren't quite strong enough to block out the acrid smell of chemicals and vinegary cleaning solutions. Albinus was bent over next to a succulent plant nearly as tall as he was, carefully clipping off one of its spiny red protrusions with a tiny pair of shears. He straightened when he saw Sarai and set the plant clipping on a wheeled table at his side along with other leaves and bits of flowers, which he must be studying for medicinal uses.

"Cousins!" he said, his delighted tone at odds with the nervous way his eyes flickered from Sarai's face to Elodie's.

Sarai tilted her head. "I believe you mean, 'Your Highnesses,' don't you, Albinus?"

He flinched. Elodie didn't react to this outwardly, but her attention focused more sharply on Albinus, noting the way his fingers twitched and the way he was still holding tightly to the small shears even though he had already set the succulent cutting aside.

"Of course," he said smoothly with a bow, one just deep enough to be respectful. His white-blond hair flopped over his forehead and he pushed it away. "Your Highnesses, I am cheered at your presence. Destroyer, I see that the assassin's foul poison has damaged your eyes and, I assume, your magic. But not to worry, I have already prepared your treatment, and I am pleased to administer—"

"*I* shall administer her treatment," Sarai said, cutting him off.

Elodie considered whether to say yet that she knew exactly what her "treatment" entailed and wished to refuse it, but reluctance glued the words in place until they could not escape. Once Elodie declared her knowledge and intentions, it would change everything between her and Sarai, and she wasn't quite ready to do that just yet.

Albinus swallowed. "But…I may need to infuse it with extra strength, to account for any side effects the poisoning might—"

Sarai cut him off yet again. "You are dismissed, Albinus."

It was a calculated move, to dismiss the royal physician from his own wing of the palace. Elodie expected him to take offense, but he seemed relieved instead, finally setting the shears down and leaving through the copper doors. He tapped a finger against them as he left and they shut silently behind him.

Elodie turned to her sister. "He seemed tense."

Sarai stepped toward a nearby door that led to a smaller side room. "Fearing for one's life often does that."

"Why would he fear for his life?"

"Because I am considering ending it," Sarai said, opening the door and waving Elodie in.

"A good reason for tension," Elodie allowed. "And as I have never been overly fond of our cousin, I won't try to dissuade you." The casual words didn't come close to expressing the anger she felt when she recalled Tal's vision and her own matching dream-memories of Albinus standing at her father's side, offering to fetch a poison to end her life. "But why, exactly, are you thinking of having him assassinated?"

Sarai stopped walking then and turned back to her sister. Her features were suddenly tight with fury. "I am not thinking of having him assassinated," she said in a fearsome tone Elodie had heard only a few times before from her. "I am thinking of having him publicly gutted, drawn, quartered, and executed in the central palace courtyard."

Elodie shied back a step before she caught herself. Before her stood not her beloved, if intimidating, older sister, but the merciless Iron Empress. Albinus must have done something very terrible indeed to cause a reaction like this, and to make Sarai consider taking such open action against him when he had several powerful allies in the palace. In fact, Elodie could only thing of one thing terrible enough to spur such fury.

There was a wide cot in the middle of the room. Elodie sat on its edge, making sure she was steady before she said,

"He formulated the poison that the Saints used against me, didn't he?"

Sarai let out a breath and the fury drained from her expression, coiling back into place deep within her. "My interrogations have uncovered information that confirms he has been supplying a Saints outpost with the poison for the last two years in anticipation of an attack like the one that was enacted on the train."

"So he is a Saint?" Elodie found that very hard to believe. Albinus didn't believe in anything except himself.

"No. He is an opportunist, and he wants the throne, and only you and I stand between him and it."

Elodie considered this, then took a deep breath and let it out. "That bastard," she said at last, with great feeling. She wasn't quite sure what the feeling was, though. Anger, certainly. But fear was there too, a great and dark fear, because this was how she would spend the rest of her life once she refused to allow her sister to carry out the "treatment" that would have turned her back into the Destroyer. How many others would follow in Albinus's footsteps once they knew she was a powerless misfire?

"I am sure he is even now scurrying off to meet with some rebel or other in hopes of finishing the job," Sarai said dryly, "now that you are unprotected. But we shall soon fix that. Come, I'll get the treatment set up." Sarai turned to a shelf in the corner that held syringes, other medical equipment, and glass jars full of silvery liquid.

So they had finally come to it. Elodie pushed the words

out before she could reconsider: "You mean, the treatment that will infuse my blood with mercury once again, as it did on the eve of my seventh birthday?"

Sarai paused, her hand hovering over the glass jar. She turned. "Ah. You remember the truth at last, then." Her voice was resigned, sad, but unrepentant.

"Are you going to force a memory tonic on me again?" Elodie half-wished she would; then she might forget Tal, and know she had no hand in the forgetting herself, and therefore be free of both her love of him and the guilt of choosing to forget him. But of course, if Sarai gave her the tonic, she would also forget herself—forget Elodie, the person she could be—and become wholly the Destroyer again. She had been changed by her journey of the last few days and she couldn't bear for that to dissipate like so much steam in the sunlight. She couldn't go back to her old cruelty, her old coldness, no matter what other comforts and protections that identity might offer. She wasn't sure who she was now, but it was someone new—someone she would have to discover for herself.

"No," Sarai said. "I will not give you a memory tonic. You were a child then. You are nearly a woman now, and old enough to choose for yourself what you wish to do. But before you do choose, you should have all the pertinent information." She pulled something out from a pocket between the plates of her armor. It was a little mirror, the Smithed charm that Tirine had handed to her a few moments ago. Sarai gave Elodie a last, unreadable look—something like regret—before she dropped it to the floor and broke it with the heel of her boot.

When the glass of the mirror shattered, so did Sarai. Her features came apart along thin fault lines, cracking like she was a porcelain doll dropped from a great height. And then the pieces of her–the illusion of her–flaked away completely, and what was left beneath was the reality of her sister.

Her beautiful golden hair was gone. In its place was a burnt, patchy stubble. One of her eyes was swollen shut and the other was full of dark gray blood where it should be white. Her face was a patchwork of twisted red and white scar tissue. One of her hands was missing, the stump inelegantly sticking a few inches out of her armor's sleeve. The Iron Crown was the only unmarred part of her, grotesque in its pure and untouched normality.

"Our subjects wonder," Sarai said, her voice changed now to a wheezing deathbed rattle, "how I escaped the explosion unscathed. The truth is I did not."

Elodie was still staring at her. There was an alien expression on Sarai's face, something at once worried and sad, and the empress kept her gaze turned away. She didn't want to see the look on Elodie's face. Didn't want to see her reaction to her horrible injuries, to the difference between the way she looked a week ago and the way she looked now.

Something settled over Elodie, a soft certainty. She stepped forward and, as gently as she could, drew Sarai to her. It was her turn now to wrap her whole self around her sister, to be her shield against what anyone else–even Sarai herself–might think of her.

"Your injuries do not lessen you," Elodie said, with all the devoutness of anyone who has ever loved a sibling.

Sarai sagged in her arms and let out a laugh that was only a little bit choked. She hugged Elodie back for a moment and then stepped away, the worry wiped clean from her expression but the sadness remaining. "I'm afraid they are, however, killing me."

Elodie was still for three long heartbeats, trying to fathom her sister's words. "But you are...you are fine. You're here, days after the explosion. Albinus must have—"

Sarai waved a hand, cutting her off. "There is only so much that even a royal physician can do."

"But you said already that he wants us both dead! He must have put something in the healing tinctures he gave you, must have held back some treatment that could help. If we get a second opinion—"

"I have had second, and third, and fourth opinions. I have had Albinus carefully watched by my spies. All that can be done by magic and medicine has been done, and I am yet dying. I have perhaps a few hours left at this point. I was going to spend them raiding the Saints base, as there was word you might be imprisoned there, but as much as I wanted to die slaying the zealots who attacked you, I am happy now to leave the vengeance to you and spend what time I have left at your side."

Elodie was shaking her head. This could not be true. She had *saved* her sister's life by stopping the zeppelin, she had gotten here in time, Sarai could not die now. She could not die from the explosion that Elodie herself was ultimately responsible for. The thought entrenched itself in Elodie's soul, turning it to a desert: forsaken, unbearably empty, horizons stretching into desolation.

Sarai stepped forward and took Elodie's fingers in her one good hand, putting her stump of a wrist atop them. "My dear one," she said softly, "it is true. I would change it for you if I could. But I cannot, and there is a more important matter we need to see to before this is over."

Elodie realized that she had sat back down on the cot at some point. Her eyes were horribly, achingly dry. Why was it that she only cried when she didn't want to, and not when she truly needed to? "What could possibly be more important than your death?" she snapped.

"Yours," Sarai said bluntly.

Elodie looked up at her, brow crinkling. "I'm...I'm fine. I've lost my mercury, but I'm not dying."

"Not yet. But I'm sure you noticed on your way in just how many of our beloved family members hope to take advantage of your new lack of magic. If you choose to remain in your natural state, without any mercury in your veins, I will protect you. But I fear I won't be able to do it for very long."

Elodie pulled her hands away. "This isn't about me."

"But it is. I told you I have a few hours left, and that's true. There are, however, some treatments that could extend my life a bit longer—a week, perhaps two. I could be here to settle you. To crown you." She touched the Iron Crown on her brow, and something about the gesture looked oddly rueful.

It made Elodie remember that the crown had been in the explosion too, and that while the fire had been enough to injure her sister terribly, kill dozens of others, and explode several train cars, it had apparently not left even a single scratch on the Iron Crown. While Elodie's mind caught on this detail like a nail snagging a loose thread, Sarai continued: "But it would be immensely painful for me, and there's a good chance the treatments would kill me anyway. Still, I would do it for you, even though I know it would do little good—because the moment I die and leave you to take the throne, one or another of our enterprising cousins or aunts or uncles will have you murdered. And they'll be able to do it easily, because you are defenseless."

Each word was a hammer wielded against her. Elodie could not yet absorb the blows, and so turned her mind to a different question. "Why is the crown intact?"

One corner of Sarai's mouth tilted up, and that same ruefulness flickered across her features again. "I knew you would notice. I'm afraid it's because I used the vast majority of my powers to protect it during the explosion."

Once the words sank in, Elodie was on her feet, anger and shock humming in her bones. "You protected the *crown*? If you had enough magic to shield anything, you should have protected yourself!"

"The crown is more important that any one ruler. It's the source of our strength."

Like everyone else, Elodie knew that the Iron Crown was enchanted, but no one except the current ruler knew the actual nature of the enchantment. Sarai took the crown off now and set it in her lap, smoothing a finger over it.

"Our nine-times-great grandparents did the Smithing, assisted by their entire court," the empress said. "It took nearly their entire lifetimes. They enchanted the crown to channel the power of the land's magic and concentrate it in a tight vicinity around the crown itself. The actual enchantment is quite complicated, but basically, it pulls magic away from the peasant villages and mining towns and such, and concentrates it here in the palace. That is why all the great Smiths are born here, to noble houses, and any magical children that the peasants can manage to sire are too weak to do anything of use. A few slip by here and there, but without the crown's power, there would be as many strong Smiths among the Saints as in the palace." She tapped the crown gently. "The enchantment also protects the crown from destruction. I imagine your fire—if you were using *all* your fire—is probably the only power strong enough to break it. Which is why I had to use so much magic to protect it in this case. And what an irony that is; if it had been destroyed, it would have released all of its pent-up magic at once, magics from every metal, from every corner of the land. The copper magic would have been enough to instantly heal everyone on the train including myself if it were channeled properly."

"Then why didn't you let it burn?" Elodie demanded. Her hands bunched in the coarse fabric of her trousers. "We could have Smithed a new one. It is metal. *You* are irreplaceable." She hated the thread of desperation in her voice, of pleading. Her sister was already dying and the past could not be rewritten. Still, she couldn't let it go.

Sarai laid a hand over one of Elodie's. "It too is irreplaceable. The Smithing methods that created it have since been lost. Not to mention there was no copper Smith close enough who could have channeled the magic to heal me in any case."

Elodie stared at the crown. It seemed suddenly malevolent, this creation that had stolen life from her sister and Tal's people both. But just as strongly as she reviled it, she found herself longing for the safe weight of it on her brow, the security of wrapping herself in the power of the whole empire.

She turned away, disgusted with herself, and afraid that the disgust would overpower the desire. The parts of herself—the Destroyer, Elodie, all of their separate facets and edges—were at war within her. They scraped through her like broken glass, and she feared they would shred what was left of her soul to bits before it was over.

The cot creaked. Sarai had sat down on its other side, and reached across now with her good hand to set one of the glass jars full of the mercury concoction on the little table next to the bed. "You must choose," she said softly.

Elodie closed her eyes.

She had wanted to be Elodie. She had tried and *tried* to be her. But Elodie hadn't been good enough. She couldn't make Tal stay, couldn't make him love her back, couldn't win herself free of a past that she hadn't even been able to remember. She certainly couldn't defend herself against the tribulations that awaited her within the walls of her own home. Elodie would never, ever be safe, and she would never, ever be free. She was soft. She was vulnerable. She was broken.

But if she went back to being the Destroyer...she wouldn't be any of those things. She would no longer be the weapon of her sister, either, but would instead belong wholly to herself. No one would crack the defenses of her body or her heart ever again. She wouldn't feel everything so much. Her mind could be cold and clear again like ice, the way it used to be.

Before, she had wondered what future there could be for her. She understood now that this was the only future there had ever been.

Wordlessly, she held out her arm.

Sarai fetched the necessary contraption, a series of glass-and-copper tubes and tiny clever pumps. She slipped the needle at one end into Elodie's arm, and the tube at the other end into the jar. Then she laid down at her sister's side, her breathing labored, her crown on the bed between them, and held Elodie's hand.

The mercury hit Elodie's blood like a drug. A heavy sleepiness drew itself over her—a calming potion that had been mixed in to ease the transition from misfire to Lady of Mercury. She turned her head to look at her sister, wanting someone she loved to be the last thing that she saw.

And then she fell asleep, knowing that the Elodie she had been would never wake again.

CHAPTER TWENTY-TWO

MORE THAN TWENTY GUARDS HAD PASSED TAL'S CELL IN the last hour. None of them had spotted him, or at least, none of them had realized he was someone who wasn't supposed to be there. He'd tucked himself against the wall, hidden his swords behind the chamber pot, and relied on the fact that they were searching for people escaping the prison, not people trapped within it. If they did discover him–bleeding undeniably silver blood, with the multi-colored blood of the slain guards spattered atop that–he would be executed. Of course, things wouldn't be much better if they didn't discover him.

None of the Saints had been recaptured, at least. They might all have been killed in the pursuit, but Tal chose to hope that at least some of them would make it. He wondered if Saasha had. He hoped that whatever plans she might have that had led her to lock him in here, they didn't involve Nyx. Either way, though, there was absolutely nothing he could do about it now.

He leaned his head back, tired to his very marrow. When he closed his eyes, eerie spots swayed behind his eyelids, afterimages from the floor's glow. They coalesced into figures. Dipping and spinning, they danced across his vision until they became a memory.

A dance hall. The illusion of a glass-calm ocean as the ballroom floor. Men wearing suits in brash colors and exquisitely detailed patterns slipping in and out of the complicated group dance. Most of the women wore ball gowns in shades of red that flared like sunspots when they twirled. Tal had stood against the wall and watched it all and tried not to be sick.

Earlier that same day, he had sworn his oath to the Destroyer and then stabbed the soldier who had–on her own order–attacked her. *Take him to the physicians,* she'd said afterwards. *He may live.*

He hadn't lived. Tal had walked to the physicians' wing, getting lost several times in the endless corridors paved with extravagance before he stumbled upon the morgue. That wasn't where he'd meant to go, but it was where he found his answer. The soldier was laid out atop a ceremonial gold-gilded gurney. An attendant was clutching a pair of tongs that held a cup of steaming molten lead over the stab wound in the soldier's torso. Tal watched, frozen, as the woman poured the lead into the injury until it was filled, and then pried the dead man's mouth open and filled that, too. The stench of burning flesh and hot metal drifted down the hall. It was a ceremony of honor for a person who'd died in the course of duty, Tal learned later, but then it had only seemed obscene. He had thrown up right there in the hallway. The attendants had been amused and annoyed in equal measure.

It had been the first person he'd ever killed.

An hour after that, the Destroyer summoned him to attend her at the ball. He'd refused to dress in finery, keeping his practical, blood-flecked peasant clothing on as both a memorial and a protest. He had hoped the Destroyer would ask about his choice of evening wear and then he could confront her, perhaps shock her with the knowledge that she had effectively killed her own soldier, but she'd only raised an eyebrow when she saw him.

We make a matched pair, she'd said, glancing down at her own slender red dress. *Though the color of blood on your outfit is a bit more authentic.*

She hadn't danced. She had stood near him, a full glass of untouched wine dangling elegantly from one gloved hand, watching the ball with her usual untouchable, distant amusement.

Then, he had thought she seemed like a queen passionlessly surveying her subjects, or a well-fed lioness content to watch the antics of her prey. But now, in his cell with nothing left to lose and nowhere to hide from the truth, he remembered how lonely she had looked. How the amusement on her face turned brittle around the edges when a giggling group of her nieces had asked why she had no dance partner. He remembered how she'd raised an eyebrow and turned to him, giving him a moment to save her, to ask her to dance in front of the people who weren't even trying to hide their mockery. But that had been the beginning of the death of his idealism, because every time he looked at her now he saw a dead man's mouth filled with lead and felt the jarring impact of ribs breaking beneath his sword.

He would defend her if one of these chittering peacocks attacked her. He would have to. But he refused to dance with her.

Idly, he wondered now what would have happened if he had. Would that brittleness in her have cracked? Would he have caught a glimpse of what was underneath? If he had realized earlier, when he was still hopeful and idealistic, that she could be a person like Elodie—would he have been able to sway her?

He realized suddenly that he missed her. She had left him because he had given her no other option, and he found that he regretted it. He examined the feeling with distant curiosity, because what did it matter now either way? She had by now already returned to her sister. She might or might not be convinced to restore her magic, and the poison it brought with it. His realization that he loved her would make no difference to any of that, because he would die down here in the dungeons of the one place he would give anything to be away from, and she wouldn't even know until it was too late.

He buried his head in his hands. He loved her, he thought again. What a fool he was. Just when he thought he'd left behind that naïve boy of two years ago, he went and fell for the one person he should despise above all else. And he did despise her, but he loved her too—the brittle girl who had been afraid to ask aloud if he wanted to dance with her because she knew he'd refuse, the fiercely innocent girl who'd offered him a headless rabbit like it was a trophy, and the girl who'd wept because she didn't know how to start a fire. What he felt was impossible, but it was also true, and he could no longer maintain the mental distance it took to deny it.

He sighed. *Very well,* he said to his god with the resignation and relief of someone who has exhausted absolutely every possibility, including death, and must now finally be honest with himself. *What do you want me to do?*

It had been Saasha who had trapped him here—he didn't know why she would do such a thing, but somewhere in the space of the last few days, he had utterly lost the ability to be surprised—but he knew that his god had been behind it. She might have shut the door on him, but it was the Unforged God who had led him to this spot. Not because he was sadistic. Because, Tal thought now, he wanted to offer Tal a choice, and this was the only way Tal would listen to it. He had refused to be honest with himself about his feelings for Elodie until he'd been literally locked in a jail cell with no other option, and now a vision was hovering on the horizon of his mind, waiting for him to decide whether to open himself to it and whatever possibilities it might offer, or stay here in this cell and die. *Of sheer stubbornness,* Elodie would probably say if she were here. He smiled a little and then shook his head with another sigh.

Show me, he prayed.

The dreaming place pulled him in.

He spent only a moment in the dark space surrounded by a weighty presence before the vision opened around him. It was Elodie–no, it was the Destroyer, silver eyes bright with brittle cruelty. She sat on the empress's throne. It was a cold and unyielding thing, much more suited to her sister than to her, as was the Iron Crown on her brow. She opened her mouth. *"I pronounce the sentence of–"* she began, and then something slender and wooden flew toward her. Some sort of small crossbow bolt.

Tal saw himself in the vision then. He was on his knees before her, hands in manacles, his back to her as he looked out over a crowd. The crossbow bolt arced toward the Destroyer.

And then he stood up. He whirled around, face-to-face with those bright, and now surprised, silver eyes. The crossbow bolt burrowed into his own back. He watched his eyes close, his face twist. He dropped back to his knees, then, lifelessly, fell forward on his stomach.

The vision faded. His god remained. Tal was back in the cell and no longer in the dreaming place, but the weight and presence of the Unforged God still enfolded him. It was asking him a question. And, he realized suddenly, the visions had *always* been a question.

His god had never coerced him. He had never forced Tal to swear himself to the Destroyer. He had shown him a vision and asked him to have faith in its message, and Tal had always, unfailingly, answered with a yes. Most of his visions had led only to trouble and pain...but then, the Unforged God had never promised safety, had he? Nor a long life, nor even a happy ending. What he had promised—not in words, but in a deeply-planted and unshakeable knowledge buried somewhere inside Tal—was that if he said yes, he would save the Destroyer, and save the empire through her.

Tal had felt bitter for so long that the sudden absence of the feeling made him dizzy with its loss. He accepted at last that he had not been betrayed, or at least, he had not been betrayed by his god. He had perhaps been betrayed by his own certainty that being a believer meant a life without anguish. He thought now, though, that sometimes being a believer—that saying yes—meant inviting pain. The Unforged God himself had sacrificed when he built the world from the broken pieces of himself. How could Tal rightfully expect his own life to entail less sacrifice than his god's?

The promises he'd made Tal had not yet been fulfilled. Tal sensed a finality to this vision, though, a true ending. If he did this, if he trusted in it and followed it, he would at last save the Destroyer and the empire. He would also die. But hadn't he already accepted his own death? And wasn't it better to die honestly, in a final acceptance of what he had once believed, and turned away from, and finally—if reluctantly, and somewhat more cynically—might believe once again?

He had come to this place because he had wanted to spend the coin of his death on something that mattered. He did not think now that there was anything that could matter more than this: the salvation of the girl he loved, and the redemption of his own soul.

Tal bowed his head and, one last time, said yes to his god.

Then he stood up and called for the guards.

CHAPTER TWENTY-THREE

THE DESTROYER WOKE NEXT TO A CORPSE.

She regarded it with faint curiosity. Her vision was blurred and her recent memory even more so, and she was content to lie there on the comfortable cot for a while as both reasserted themselves. By the time her sight was clear enough to make out the scarred, still features of her sister, she was also recovered enough to recall that this corpse was one she herself was ultimately responsible for, and to distantly register the landslide of horror and grief spurred by that realization. The emotions would have been enough to suffocate Elodie. A good thing, then, that Elodie was no longer present.

Tears gathered in the corners of the Destroyer's eyes. She bent her head and lay a hand on her sister's brow. For a long time, she stayed that way, waiting for the grief to gather enough weight to make the tears fall. They never did. Her emotions felt as if they were at arm's length–easily observed, easily calculated, but not entirely experienced.

That, she supposed, would be the mercury's doing.

She called on her power. The hand that was on her sister's brow sparked with scarlet flames like phoenix feathers. Everything within her relaxed at the sight, and she let out a long exhalation to see herself finally made right. The Destroyer bent down and gently kissed Sarai's cold cheek, and then she channeled more fire through her hand and into her sister's body. There, on a cot in the middle of an insignificant side room in the physicians' wing of the Alloyed Palace, the Destroyer crafted a royal pyre. It wreathed the bed in beautiful dancing flames, and when it was done, nothing at all was left of the late Iron Empress.

The Destroyer pulled back her hand. The Iron Crown had fallen to the floor. She bent down and grazed its cold metal surface with a finger, both hating it and desperate for its weight to settle on her own head. At last, she removed her own twisted-briar crown and picked up the iron one.

There was a mirror across the room. Her gaze caught on it just as she lowered the empress's crown onto her brow. It looked impossibly heavy on her head, dull and cold above her shining quicksilver eyes. This, she thought, must have been the vision that Tal had seen.

The thought of him pierced the veil of her emotions like a dart, a quick but undeniable pinch of pain. It made her catch her breath. It made her feel, for just a moment, like the fragile girl she had been a few hours ago. But after a second the pain faded back into the distance with all her other emotions, and she took a grateful breath as she straightened and made her way to the door.

The bright, plant-filled space beyond was still empty of people, but she could hear the hum of voices past the closed copper doors. She strode toward them and touched the green metal. They didn't move, didn't recognize the magic in her veins or open at her touch. She narrowed her eyes, recalling then that Albinus had, in his pride, had the doors enchanted to respond only to the touch of a copper Smith. It was meant to be a petty show of power here in his own hall; everyone but himself and his minions would have to either expend quite a bit of physical energy—and portray a good deal of impropriety in the process—to heave them open, or else lower themselves to calling on guards or copper Smiths to open them.

The Destroyer did neither. She lifted a hand and set it against the copper, then pushed her power into it. Snakes of silver flame wound their way around the doorframe, thirstily drinking up the oxygen that flowed through the cracks and fueling themselves until they melted through the door itself. Rivulets of molten metal dripped and smoked but the silver snakes lapped that up too, writhing through the doors until there was nothing left of them at all.

She let the flames dissipate and stepped through the empty, charred doorway, a pleasant burn of satisfaction kindling in her chest at the destruction.

Albinus was in the hallway. So were perhaps two dozen soldiers. Their eyes were already so wide she could see white all the way around their irises as their gazes darted from her face to the crown to the remnants of the scorched door-frame. Their terror was a balm. A small smile curved across her face. She felt powerful again, at last. She felt unstoppable. It seemed at once both deeply right and also, somehow, not quite right at all. She did not feel like herself, but the emotion was a squiggly and unquantifiable thing, small enough to shut away until it stopped bothering her.

She raked her smile across the soldiers, who all quailed further at her attention, until she spotted the highest-ranking guard. "My sister is dead. Announce my ascendance," she ordered.

The guard bowed at once and left, his steps hastier than the situation merited. She reveled in the power she held over him. She turned then to the next highest-ranking guard and asked, "For what reason are you all gathered out here?"

Albinus cleared his throat and answered for the man. "There is a prisoner that requires the attention of the empress," he said, then cleared his throat again. "That is, I suppose, your attention." Something like glee loosened his features, dimming the pleasant fear. He had some sort of trick planned.

Her eyes narrowed. "You suppose correctly, cousin. I will let your improper address slide this one time but in the future, you will call me Highness, as you did my sister."

Albinus clenched his jaw and his glee diminished. She could see his mind working quickly, trying to calculate how he might come out ahead in this situation—how he might use his knowledge of her secrets to blackmail her or gain the leverage to dethrone her, probably. She stepped forward until she was right in front of him and then leaned forward even further. "You have not outed me in all these years because you were frightened of my sister," she murmured. When her breath brushed over his ear, he shuddered. "You should now be frightened of me."

She stepped back. Albinus swallowed, gritted his teeth, and then lowered himself to the floor. He performed a full obeisance to her as he once had to a young Sarai. The Destroyer let him stay there for a long count of five, and then said, "Good. You may rise, and tell me about this prisoner that requires my attention."

Albinus dipped his head—likely to try to hide the impotent rage that gripped his every feature now—and gestured at the hall behind the Destroyer. "He is there. Your Highness. Normally such prisoners would be executed on sight, but he has demanded his right to a trial. With your leave, I will assemble the representatives of the high courts to witness the event tomorrow morning." Then he raised his head to meet the Destroyer's eyes, and she saw that it was not rage, but a bright and devilish malice that shone from his expression. She had embarrassed him in front of her guards, and he did not care—because whatever was happening now, it could only be to his great favor.

A premonition feathered across her spine. Slowly, she turned.

The prisoner knelt on the opposite side of the hall. Dried blood of many colors spattered his clothing, his dark hair, his skin. Fresher blood stained the carpet beneath him silver and orange, leaking from a long, shallow cut that followed the line of his cheekbone. When he met her eyes–her newly mercurial eyes–he flinched.

His presence pulled her forward like a magnet tugging at the mercury in her blood. She knelt before him so that their gazes were level. The soldiers behind her were too well-trained to gasp or mutter amongst themselves, but she could hear the whisper of their feet against the carpet as they shifted their weight, uncertain of what was happening.

Tal didn't look away from her, but she could see the desire to do so playing across his features. She lifted a hand–slowly, so that he had time to brace himself and not flinch again– and brushed a knuckle over the cut in his cheek. He closed his eyes then, and though his mouth was still tight with fear, he leaned into her touch so slightly that she would not have felt it if she was not so keenly attuned to him.

"Who," she said, her voice as cold as the Skyteeth blizzard that they had survived together, "has cut him?"

One of the guards standing at his side cleared his throat. "I did, Your Highness. It is protocol to check the blood of an accused–"

She was on her feet. She was lifting a hand. She was calling up every scrap of power within her, more than she had used to burn her sister's pyre, more than she had brought to bear on the copper door, more than she had used to incinerate the entire mining town last week. He had hurt Tal. He had made him bleed, revealed his greatest weakness for the world to see. She would make him pay dearly for it.

Tal stood then. His hands were manacled behind his back and he was favoring one leg—the one weak from rust phage—but he still managed to put himself between her and the guard. "My lady," he said. "Please don't."

She stopped. The words arrested her, the sound of her old title falling from his lips like poison. *Don't call me that,* she recalled saying. The memory tore briefly through the veil of her emotions once again, and she gasped at the sudden loss of equilibrium.

Behind her, Albinus's voice rang out. "He begs for his own life!" he said, trying to sound scandalized but barely hiding his elation. "Will you allow such impertinence from a boy who has lied to Your Imperial Highness for years, flouted your wise sister's laws in the halls of your own home?"

Tal held the Destroyer's gaze. To everyone else assembled, it looked as if he were indeed pleading for her to spare him. The two of them were the only ones who knew the truth: that she was seconds away from killing every single one of these guards and Albinus too, that she was so close to violence she could already hear the way they would scream and writhe beneath her fire. That the only reason she stayed her hand was because Tal had asked her to. He was still holding her with his gaze now, refusing to release her, or perhaps it was her who was allowing him to steady her.

"I will allow whatever I see fit," she told Albinus at last.

Some of what she was thinking must have bled through to her voice, because when he answered again, his voice was slightly more subdued.

"His crimes are not limited to bearing silver blood, Your Highness. He was found in the dungeons. He freed over a dozen zealot prisoners and killed half that many dungeon guards."

Her eyes widened. He had come back? He had come back…to the *dungeons*, to free the prisoners who had tried to assassinate her, when he'd said there was nothing that could sway him to return to the palace?

Apparently, he had only meant that *she* wasn't enough to sway him.

She had thought that she would never feel broken again as the Destroyer, and now she had already been proven wrong barely a few minutes into her new life. He had stripped away her defenses. She loved him—or at least, Elodie had loved him, even if the Destroyer was incapable of such a thing. How could he have lied to her in such a way? Would he have sacrificed his own life to spite her, if he hadn't been caught by the guards? Some of what she felt must have shone through on her face, because Tal's mouth tightened as if he wanted to say something, but then his eyes went to the guards behind her and he stayed silent.

"Your Highness?" came Albinus's voice, even more nervous now as her silence stretched out. "Shall I order the court representatives to gather? If I may dare say, the public will be quite interested in such a trial too. It would be a great opportunity to quickly establish the strength of your rule."

Her jaw clenched. Albinus had boxed her in neatly. If she ordered Tal released—and presumably healed—then she would effectively confirm him as her weakness, and he would very quickly be used against her. It would deteriorate her sway over her subjects from the very start. He would make her vulnerable. But if she held a trial for him and found him guilty, he would surely be executed, and Albinus would have neatly removed her sole remaining ally.

Tal shifted, recapturing her attention, then bowed his head, finally breaking eye contact with her. "My lady, I request my right to a trial."

She stared at him. He *wanted* a trial? She had assumed he'd demanded a trial when he was caught simply to avoid being executed on sight.

Whatever the answer, she wasn't going to discover it out here, surrounded by her enemies. Ordering a trial would buy her time to decide what to do, at the very least. "Very well," she said, lifting her chin. "Have the seneschal assemble the required witnesses. We will hold the trial in the morning." She hesitated. "In the meantime, he will stay in my chambers and I will question him privately."

His shoulders moved slightly, hunching inward as if he were bracing himself for a blow that was soon to land. She ached at the sight. *I will never hurt you,* she wanted to tell him, but what right did she have to say such a thing when she had hurt him so much already? When tomorrow she might deliver a guilty verdict that would end his life? Her eyes burned and her throat thickened. She had to retreat, right now.

She turned her back to Tal and strode down the hall, her sharp steps muffled by the thick carpet. "And remove those manacles," she snapped over her shoulder. At least she could do that much. She didn't watch as her orders were followed, though, because she didn't think she could bear for Tal to meet her gaze again—to look into her eyes and see only the Destroyer where Elodie used to be.

Her chambers were on the other side of the palace, down the length of two long private hallways and up three sets of stairs. Before they had made it even halfway there, she could hear Tal's breath becoming labored, could feel the drumbeat of his footsteps lagging. She eagerly grasped at the excuse to ease his suffering at least a little.

"Albinus," she said sharply, because of course her cousin was escorting them all the way to her rooms and would likely stand guard outside afterwards to make sure there were no unfortunate escapes. "I will not have my guard too injured to make it to his own trial. Heal him. And heal the rust phage, too," she added like it was an afterthought. Her heart beat a little quicker in the rhythm of desperate hope.

Albinus sighed through his nose. "As Your Highness requests, I will heal what injuries I can, but from the looks of how far his phage has progressed I doubt there is any treatment that might save him from it at this point."

Some feeling churned just behind her breastbone. She considered it for a moment, trying to dissect it so that she might identify it, but it didn't last long enough. She should probably be glad she couldn't feel anything more strongly in this state. "Do as much as you can," she ordered her cousin. "And know that I will find out if you hold back."

There was quiet behind her for a moment as Albinus presumably channeled his magic through Tal; in addition to making tinctures and infusing medical treatments with magic, copper Smiths could also use their magic directly on a patient, though it was much more draining. "There," Albinus said after a moment, and to his credit he did sound a bit weaker than he had been a moment ago. "I have healed what I can, Highness, and alleviated some of the symptoms of the phage."

They had reached her chambers. A guard stepped forward to open the carved scorch-wood door for her. "Shall I light the—" the man started, but she cut him off.

"No," she snapped. "Leave it dark. Begone, all of you." She stalked into her rooms with Tal at her back. The door closed gently behind them. It was well-made and the carpet beneath it plush and thick, and no light at all seeped through any cracks. She knew well the geography of this room—an antechamber that held her carved writing desk and small library, along with a seldom-used reclining couch—but in such darkness, the space suddenly felt far smaller and more intimate than she remembered.

The Destroyer stood very still. She ached to demand an explanation, to fling either herself or her magic at Tal, and most of all to see his face so she could reassure herself that he truly was there, in the space just behind her and a bit to the side, where he had always been.

"Elodie," Tal said quietly.

She shuddered at the name. It wasn't hers. Not anymore. But it still seemed to hold some sort of sway over her–or maybe it was just him who had that, no matter what it was he was saying.

"Talk to me," he said.

"I do not take orders from you," she replied, keeping her back to him. She tried to make the words cool and detached but they came out flat instead. She took a breath, tried to focus. "Albinus will have his spies watching the exits, but you may be able to hide until it's safe to go."

"I don't want to hide," he said. A whisper of fabric rustled against her ears as he moved, those familiar footsteps slow but certain as he stepped toward her, circling around until he stood in front of her. "I don't want to go."

"You do. You *did.*"

"I came back."

"Whatever could possess you to do such a thing?"

He was not far, perhaps an arm's length away. She could feel the outline of him in the darkness. She wanted so badly to close the distance to him, to be able to see the way he was looking at her now, but she remembered why she had kept the room dark–because she couldn't bear to see him flinch again when he met her eyes. And even in that darkness, if she reached out to him she would only feel him recoil, because that was the instinctive reaction when one was faced with a predator.

It wasn't until Tal's fingers settled against her cheek that she realized she was crying.

The touch was so unexpected, and suddenly so completely and exactly what she needed, that she gasped aloud. She didn't dare to move, though, only stood quaking as his other hand lifted, slowly, carefully, to graze her other cheek.

"I came back," Tal said, his voice so low she could barely hear it even though it seemed to reverberate through every part of her, "because I could no longer pretend, even to myself, that I don't love you."

She raised her hands then, gripped his wrists, not because she needed to hold him in place but because he was her anchor and she was in the midst of a storm and she knew that if he backed away now, if he flinched, she would be torn apart by it.

He didn't flinch.

"Elodie is gone," she said. Her voice was not thick with her tears. She'd had too much practice acting as if she weren't crying. "It isn't me who you love."

"It is," he said steadily. "I love you, the girl I so foolishly swore a metal oath to two years ago, with the tired smile and the twisted crown. I love you, the girl I hated when I had to kill assassins and Saints for your sake. I love you, who has been used as a weapon by your own sister. And most of all I love you, the girl who saved me from a blizzard and a mooncat and from myself. You were right when I said I loved Elodie. But you were wrong when you said you weren't her. You have always been Elodie, and as hard as you might try to kill her, I am afraid she is quite a bit tougher than that."

She closed her eyes. Earlier, he had stripped away her defenses. Now, his words had replaced them with something new and far stronger, something insurmountable, impossible. Something unutterably beautiful.

She took one hand off his wrist and reached tentatively for him. She brushed his face. He turned into her touch as he had earlier, but this time the movement wasn't small. It was a leaning of his whole self into her; an acceptance, an offering. She stepped closer to him. His breath ghosted over her hair. She paused barely a few inches away, realizing what she had been about to do, the boundary she had been about to cross— and then Tal crossed it for her, leaning in and finding her lips with his own.

The kiss was whisper-soft. It was a knowing that passed between them, spinning out like a blown glass ornament, fragile and precious as it grew. She trembled beneath his touch and he trembled beneath hers. She was helpless, out of control, and drunken with the headiness of it. It reminded her of a sled ride down a steep hill, snow in her hair and a blizzard on the horizon, the world laid out before her as she whooped with joy.

He loved her. He trusted her enough to give himself to her in this way, even though she had quicksilver eyes and mercurial blood and enough fire to level a city, even though she had hurt him, and even though she knew there would always be a part of him that hurt to be with her.

As if his touch were a conduit that connected her to herself—to Elodie, to her own formerly distant emotions—the weight of what she had experienced in the last few hours crashed down on her all at once, and a sob rose up within her. She broke the kiss, wrapped her arms around Tal, and buried her head in his chest. The tears that had refused to fall when she'd found her sister's body flowed at last. She shook with the grief of it, with the anguish of losing the only family member who'd loved her, and with the agony of the knowledge that she would soon lose Tal too—either to the trial, or to the phage.

She could not endure it. She could not bear to lose him, too.

"Yes, you can," Tal said to her, which made her realize she had spoken her thoughts aloud.

She stepped back, suddenly furious. She knew that the flash of her changing emotions was mostly due to the mercury and tried to contain it, but only partly succeeded. "I love you too, you idiot," she hissed, "and *no,* I *cannot* bear to lose you."

She felt his chest shake beneath her hands and realized he was laughing. "If I were not already convinced you were still Elodie, that needlessly aggressive declaration of love would do the trick."

She let out a frustrated breath and barely kept herself from shoving him away. "How can you expect me to withstand your death?"

He sighed and leaned his forehead against hers, resting there as if she was an entirely safe spot for him to abide. "Because you are human," he said softly. "We were made to withstand such things." He hesitated a moment then, and said, "I am sorry for the pain you must feel at the loss of your sister. I truly did think you could save her."

It was both honest and kind, but not the whole truth. He was sorry only for her pain and not the actual loss, which he did not mourn at all, because he hated her sister and felt no trace of the love for her that softened his hatred of the Destroyer.

"I do not feel it as Elodie would," the Destroyer admitted. "Even now. And I am glad."

Tal was quiet, but she felt him tense against her. "You must promise me something," he said at last.

"I must do no such thing," she answered, wary with the knowledge that he could only be asking her to do something she very much did not want to do.

He plowed onward without regard to her reply. "Whatever happens at the trial, you must find a way to give up your mercury."

She pulled away from him at that. "I will not give up my power." Her heart turned over at the thought—the wretched emotions that she would once again wholly feel, the defenselessness against her enemies.

"It is not power," Tal argued. "It is poison. Perhaps you can withstand the mercury now, but the more time that goes by the more it will overtake you, until there is nothing at all left of the girl I loved."

She noted his use of past tense. Her hands curled into claws in his shirt. "Tal, you will not die. I will not allow it."

He said nothing. The quality of his silence changed in a way that felt somehow rueful and familiar, and she realized then what had to have happened to bring him back to this place. Her mouth filled with a sour taste. "You've had another vision, haven't you?"

"I have."

Her whole being filled with an incandescent rage, underlaid by a terrible sorrow that felt inevitable. She warred with it. "So you have come back not for me at last, but for *him*."

"I came back for you because he finally made me understand that I love you."

She gritted her teeth. The anger was so intense; she had forgotten how it blew through her like a windstorm, uprooting sense and logic, leaving only destruction in its wake. It turned out there were some emotions she could still feel strongly after all—but at least these emotions made her feel more powerful, not less. "If he allows you to die, I will raze all of his people to dust."

"Please don't say that."

"Why? Because it's blasphemy? He betrayed you! Remember—he led you to *me*, to two years of pain, to the embittering of your very soul because of it, and I will never forgive him that."

"But I think I might," Tal said softly, "someday."

"You cannot forgive him." The words were final, an order from an empress.

His fingers found her jawline. His thumb smoothed away a tear there. "I will forgive who I wish," he said, a trace of heavy humor in his tone now. "And you cannot command me otherwise."

He gently kissed the spot where his thumb had rested, and some of the raging fury within her subsided. Like a retreating tide it left behind the wreckage of its passing. "You cannot forgive me either," she said quietly.

His fingers paused on her face and then dropped away. She could almost hear him wrestling with his thoughts. "I love you," he said at last, "and I will forgive you someday, too."

"But not yet?"

He let out a breath. "Finding the end of a journey satisfactory does not erase the pain of the path that brought you there. It wouldn't be honest to love you, or to love my god, and not admit to myself that both of you have hurt me too. Someday the pain may be distant enough for me to forget it, to remember only the rightness of the ending. That's not today. But I have faith," he said, and she could feel that rueful smile of his in the darkness, "that it may be so eventually. Until then, I will just have to live with it all together: love, and hate, and grief and betrayal and joy."

At least he was speaking as if he would live past tomorrow now. "How will you bear it?" she asked. "How could anyone bear to have so much inside them?"

"We were made to withstand these things, too."

"Tal. Tell me your vision."

The suddenness of her request did not catch him off-guard as she had hoped. He only said steadily, "If I tell it to you, it may not happen."

"And you want it to happen?" Maybe it was something good that he'd seen, some way out of the corner that she and Albinus and Tal himself had backed her into.

"I've said yes to my god, and I will not go back on my

word," he replied, which wasn't an answer at all. She made a sound of frustration and disgust, and felt his chest shake with laughter again, just a little.

That was when she finally got the courage to say what she had wanted to say ever since she saw him kneeling in front of a contingent of soldiers outside the physicians' wing. "I *want* you to forgive me," she whispered as if it were a sinful thing to confess, which it certainly was. People like her shouldn't be forgiven.

He said nothing, only wrapped her in his arms and held her together. They stood like that for a long time as the moon lifted higher on the other side of her curtains, until eventually exhaustion overtook them both and they went to her bedroom to sleep. Tal tried to stop at his cot in the corner but she pulled him away from it so hard he nearly tripped. "Stay with me," she said, and although it was meant to be an order it came out shaky and unfamiliar—a request. One she knew he had every right to deny.

Without a word, he went to her bed and drew the covers back. Neither of them bothered to change, but only slipped beneath the blankets in their peasant's clothing, dirty from travel and in Tal's case stained with blood. He pulled her against him and she rested there, knowing she had no claim at all to such a thing, and together, they waited for the morning.

CHAPTER TWENTY-FOUR

By the time the midnight moon reached the zenith of its rise, Nyx had finished her third barfight and had just about decided on the location for her fourth.

Bars were, as any good reprobate knew, excellent places to search out news in the form of gossip. For instance, there was the rumor about the young bodyguard who had slain three dozen palace soldiers that evening only to hang himself before he could be caught. That had been the basis of her initial barfight. When the rude, drunken, middle-aged rumormonger had insisted that the bodyguard had indeed died to avoid the shame of facing his misdeeds, she had ended the argument by introducing the back of his head to a very heavy beer mug. Afterwards, the barkeep had unceremoniously introduced her face to the outside sidewalk, which she took as an invitation to try her luck at the tavern across the street. There, she started her second barfight after another rumormonger–a woman only a few years older than her this time, but equally as drunk as her predecessor–insisted that she had seen the bodyguard go up in a column of magical flames before he even set foot inside the palace. That barfight had been more invigorating, as the woman had fast reflexes and seemed as eager for a brawl as Nyx, and it had come to an end only when Nyx locked her arm around the woman's neck and choked her until the woman at last gave in and admitted that she had made up the rumor in hopes of earning a free beer in exchange for the news.

The third barfight had not been a result of any rumors at all, but rather because Nyx's desperation and anger had brought her to her breaking point, and she needed to hit something before she did something even stupider–like march up to the palace and demand to be taken to the Destroyer so that she might kill the bitch properly this time.

Nyx had reached the city not long after sunset, only a few hours behind Tal and the Destroyer. She knew it hadn't been longer than that because she had found their abandoned sled, and the mud caked to its retrofitted wheels was not yet quite dry. She had left her own sled beside it, letting her dogs loose along with Tal's so that they could drink from the river and rest, and then she'd marched into the city intent on finding and saving her younger brother even if she had to drag him out by the scruff of his neck. Even then, a frantic fear had swirled beneath her determination, because she knew how far the rust phage must have gone by now. She knew that he would only have allowed himself to be coerced into returning here—where he would almost certainly be executed as a silver Smith once captured—if he thought there was no other option. He had told her to warn the mountain base of the coming attack but if he understood her at all, he knew she would do no such thing until she had first ensured his safety.

The only problem with that was she had to find him first.

Hence her strategy of tracking down drunken gossip. She had learned some information that was likely accurate so far—all of the rumors confirmed that the Destroyer had returned, and several people had stated that her bodyguard had slain varying numbers of dungeon guards—but it was only enough to stoke Nyx's despair further. She still had no idea where her brother was or even if he was alive. She'd need much more detailed information if she was going to stage a rescue attempt that had any chance at all of success.

The next tavern—site of her impending fourth barfight—was a seedy place with cracks running through its bricks and mushroom-colored mortar breaking off in flakes. The door hung off a single rusty hinge, which wasn't even Smithed to detect when someone entered with a weapon as the door hinges of the other bars had been. She wished now that she hadn't left her dagger with the sled.

She grabbed a stool—an act she regretted immediately, as its surface was wet with some sticky brown substance—and slid a coin across the counter to the woman on the other side. "A glass of your most disgusting ale, and any information you might have on the return of the Destroyer and her guard," she said.

The woman paused in her ineffectual scrubbing at the bar's counter and peered at Nyx. "Ah," she said, slipping the coin off the counter and into her pocket, "I think the woman you want to talk to is in the back room." She made no move to fetch the requested ale, but Nyx didn't care, because this was the first time anyone had reacted so knowingly to Nyx's demands for information. That could only mean one of two things: either she actually had access to someone with relevant and accurate information, or else this was a trap.

Nyx turned toward the back room, which she assumed was through the dilapidated door beyond the end of the counter. She grabbed a beer mug—they made a decent weapon in a pinch, as she'd discovered earlier in the night—from an empty table and wove her way through the handful of patrons who were still drinking or gambling at this late hour. She nudged the door open with her foot, muscles tense and ready for anything...

Except, perhaps, for what she found.

Sitting at a table in the shadows, drinking herbed tea from a remarkably clean mug, was her mother.

Nyx stared as Saasha. She had bathed recently and even washed and oiled her hair, her short black pouf shining with it. Her skin was scrubbed clean of the dirt from her travels. Nyx could smell the faint hint of marigold and lavender that she used in her favorite perfumes. Even her clothes looked comfortable and clean, if not new, and she sat straight and stately in the rickety wooden chair as if it were a throne.

Nyx knew that she should be happy to see her mother alive and well and not a prisoner. But what she felt in that first instinctive moment, that split second of surprise when she had not yet had time to lie to herself, was anger.

During the mission that the two of them had concocted together, Nyx had poisoned herself, had prodded the Destroyer into torturing her nearly to death, had been dumped in a snowbank in the middle of nowhere, and had been dosed with laudanum while her brother was taken hostage yet again–and Saasha had come back from their mission literally smelling of flowers.

What kind of a mother? whispered Helenia in her memory again.

Saasha spotted her then. She set her mug down with a thunk heavy enough to slosh yellow-brown tea over its lip. Her eyes flew wide with her own instinctive emotion–shame, Nyx thought, but there wasn't enough time to register it fully before her mother was striding across the room and pulling her into a fierce hug. Nyx hugged her back weakly with one arm while she searched for somewhere to put the mug in her other hand down.

"What are you doing here?" Nyx managed at last.

Saasha pulled back with a frown. "What am I doing here? That's the greeting you give your mother?" She shook her head and waved a hand as if to brush the question away before Nyx could answer it. "Never mind. I'm just so happy to see you well. Praise the Unforged God in all his mercy, he's delivered you to me whole and well."

Nyx was neither whole nor well, but chose not to speak of such things because she wasn't sure yet what she would say about the matter. "Do you know where Tal is?" she asked instead.

Her mother bowed her head and, after a moment, motioned Nyx to sit down at the table. Slowly, Nyx complied. "You look beautiful with your head shaved," Saasha said with a sad smile as she reclaimed her own chair.

Fear fluttered in Nyx's chest. Her mother wouldn't be delaying her answer to Nyx's question unless it was bad. She dropped her mug on the table and spread her hands flat to brace herself. "Mother," she said, her voice tight. "Where. Is. Tal?"

Saasha sighed. "I will give you the answer, but you must promise not to leave this room until I've had time to tell you everything."

Nyx gritted her teeth and spat out her answer: "Fine. Be quick."

Saasha folded her hands in her lap and drew a deep breath. "After the explosion, the train's emergency magics teleported it to the railyard here. We prisoners were pulled out and placed in the dungeons. The empress—who must have used her ungodly powers to survive, at least temporarily—came to question us not long after. She went through us one by one, tearing us apart body and soul."

Us, Saasha said, as if she too had been torn apart even though there wasn't a mark on her.

Saasha's lips thinned as she seemed to pick up on the direction of Nyx's thoughts. "I was supposed to be interrogated next," she said. "But the woman before me gave up the location of the Saints' base, and said that the Destroyer would likely have been taken there if she'd survived and been captured. That is what the empress wanted: her pet weapon back."

"And now she has her," Nyx said bitterly. If only she had slit the Destroyer's throat when she had the chance instead of giving Tal the opportunity to do it himself.

"She has Tal, too."

Nyx's hands tensed on the tabletop and she half raised from her seat, until Saasha reached out her own hand and laid it atop Nyx's to keep her in place. "Where?" Nyx growled.

"I'm not done explaining everything yet," Saasha said sternly. With great effort, Nyx forced herself to sit back down. "Tal came for us," Saasha continued when she was resettled. "God sent him to free us, and he killed a good number of prison guards on his way there. But he was...captured in the process."

Nyx closed her eyes, pain lancing through her. If he'd been captured then there could be no good end to this story.

"I and six others managed to get away. The rest of them went to ground in safe houses scattered throughout the city until they can leave, while I came to this bar, which is owned by one of our agents."

"Why?" Nyx snapped, eager to get the story over with so she could plan her brother's rescue.

"To wait for you. Before Tal was captured, he said that you were likely only a little way behind him. I knew that once you arrived you would search for news of him. You wouldn't have been able to ask any officials or guards, because of course you'd know there is a good chance the Destroyer would have put a warrant out for you as soon as she returned. So what else would you do at this time of night but go to bars and listen for rumors?"

"I didn't find any actionable information," Nyx admitted.

Saasha's eyes suddenly went dark and fierce. "I will give you actionable information," she said, lowering her voice in volume but not intensity. "Tal is alive, for now. Our spy in the palace says he is to appear at a trial tomorrow morning for the illegal act of having silver blood. The Destroyer will personally preside over this mockery of justice, and will execute him immediately once he's found guilty."

Nyx's blood seemed to freeze, to crystallize, until her heart labored to beat at all. "There must be a way to stop her."

Saasha exhaled then and lowered one of her hands to the seat of the empty chair beside her. "There is," she said, and lifted up a small contraption that looked like a miniature crossbow. "With this."

Nyx leaned forward to examine it eagerly, but shook her head with a frown after she'd had a moment to take a closer look. It was small enough to sneak past guards and unfolded to shoot a bolt that was about the length of her forearm, but there was no way it could hold enough tension or fire a large enough bolt to be fatal. "What good will this do?" she demanded.

That was when Saasha lifted a vial of purple liquid to the table. "Our spy provided me with the ingredients to make this. If we can get someone—an assassin with a keen eye—into the trial in the morning, they can coat the arrowhead with this poison and use it to kill the Destroyer before she can kill Tal, or use her magic in retribution. The trial is the perfect opportunity; the spy was able to ensure it would be public, so the assassin should have no trouble getting in."

"I will do it," Nyx said instantly.

Saasha looked away. "I knew you would volunteer, my daughter," she said softly, and shame flickered across her face again, "and I am proud. But know that this...this will not be an easy mission. You see—the Saints' spy in the palace is Albinus. The royal physician."

Nyx was surprised, but only for a moment. "I don't care if he's the Unforged God himself, as long as he can get me near enough to end the Destroyer."

"The thing is, it turns out the Iron Empress sustained wounds from the explosion that turned out to be fatal after all. She died a few hours ago. The Destroyer is the empress now, but if she were to be killed, then the Iron Crown would pass to Albinus." Saasha leaned forward, an almost fanatically eager light illuminating her features from within. "He would be on our side, Nyx. He was the one who provided the poison you drank for the last two years, the poison that should rightfully have ended the Destroyer."

Anger flashed briefly through Nyx again at the mention of the poison, but she shoved it away. There was no time for such emotions right now. This was the time for logic, for planning. There would be time to figure out the way she felt about her mother later. "Have the other Saints agreed to this plan?" she asked.

"We have no ranks. There is no need for anyone else's approval," Saasha scoffed. "God himself gives our commands, and whoever is meant to lead any given mission is entitled to do so."

Nyx rolled her eyes. Saasha made it sound like their system worked flawlessly, when she knew for a fact it more often lent itself to chaos.

"If Albinus were crowned," Saasha went on, "he would make a treaty with the Saints. He's promised to do so. Peasants would have more protections, and silver Smiths would be legal again. He even said he would try to talk the high courts into making worship of the Unforged God compulsory and demolishing the heathen temples in the outlander settlements."

Nyx raised her brow. "You would destroy the temples of other religions? That can't be wise."

"It is righteous," Saasha insisted, and quoted one of the scriptures she'd raised Nyx on: "*When God's people are crushed, he will send his saints to avenge them. Great will be his fury; at his order, his saints will neither cease nor be merciful until all who are left worship him alone.*"

It used to be one of Nyx's favorite passages. Saasha had brought her up to embrace a philosophy of martyrdom and vengeance, and Nyx had been a child who appreciated violence, so she had accepted her mother's interpretation of God's character without much thought. Now, though, a different voice rose in her mind–that of Helenia, quoting her own favorite scripture.

For he is the great Smith and we are the tools of his forge, and the purpose to which he bends us is to mend that which is broken. He repairs all, forgives all, is all-loving and ever-merciful.

It portrayed a god who was the exact opposite of the god from Saasha's scripture, and yet the two verses were found only a few pages apart.

Nyx looked away, her lips tightening to a thin line as she grappled with the growing discomfort within her. She had listened to her brother and girlfriend and mother enough to know that the holy texts could be wielded as weapons on any side of any argument, because they were full of contradictions. Every scripture could be answered by another, and theological interpretations both wild and wise could find a myriad of supporting verses. Nyx wondered now if the way a person interpreted the holy texts might reflect more about who they themselves were than who God was; Helenia had found a deity of love and mercy and redemption, and Saasha held fast to one of retribution and violence.

"I'm not sure I can support that anymore," Nyx said slowly to her mother.

Saasha's eyes lit even more brightly with righteous zeal. She leaned across the table as if she could hypnotize her daughter with it. "Nyx, this is the chance we've fought so hard for. We can return our nation to God together."

Together, she said. Again, as if she were planning on taking any risk upon herself, instead of asking Nyx to play the assassin and Albinus to make the law and mete out any of its potential punishments.

Nyx tried to shake off her growing unease. "It doesn't matter," she said. "One way or another, I'm killing the Destroyer. We can argue about the aftermath later."

Saasha looked as if Nyx had struck her. Then, slowly, she reached across the table and put both her hands on Nyx's. "That's the thing, my daughter," she said, her voice shaking just a little. "That is what I was trying to tell you. If you do this, there will be no later. Not for you."

"What?"

"If a known Saint assassin is caught killing the new empress, Albinus will not be able to make any treaties with us at all. The high courts will blame the Saints as an organization for her death. They'll demand reparations that we cannot give at the very least, and wipe us out completely at the worst."

Nyx tried to follow her mother's logic. "But if that's true, then I can't be the one to kill her, because I'm a known Saint."

Saasha shook her head. "You are not. The Destroyer has been so caught up with her sister's death and the preparations for Tal's trial that she's not released any details at all about her capturers. No one knows who you are. The only thing they will know is that you are Tal's sister...and willing to give up your life to save him."

The logic of it all slid into Nyx like a well-oiled blade. She held herself very still. Of course. Of course, this was how it would have to be.

Saasha kept talking. Her voice took on a pleading note, though Nyx wasn't sure if she was asking Nyx to go through with the assassination, or to not think badly of Saasha for engineering it. "It can't be allowed to get out that the Saints have anything to do with the Destroyer's death. It's the only way for the empire to move forward."

Nyx licked her dry lips. "What about you?" she asked, her voice barely audible. "Will you move forward?"

Saasha cringed. "It will be quick. That much I have made Albinus swear. There is no way the royal guards will let any assassin escape but he can ensure that you don't suffer."

"Mother."

Tears gathered in Saasha's eyes. She squeezed Nyx's hands. "I will be so proud," she said, her voice breaking a bit. "So very proud of you and what you have achieved for us all. I will think of you every day. You will be our most honored martyr."

"That is not a good balm for being dead."

"But how else will Tal survive?" Saasha asked, and there it was: the crux of the matter. "As long as the Destroyer lives, she will honor her sister's laws. All silver Smiths must be executed. But if you were to kill her before she can render judgment, Albinus will take the throne, and he will forge a new path for the empire. Tal will be pardoned. And Albinus has sworn that he can save him from the rust phage, too."

Nyx squeezed her eyes shut. Tal would be saved…and she would be dead. He would despise her for it. It would break his heart, and it would certainly break Helenia's.

Nyx had imagined that, when all of this was over and both she and Tal were free, she would ask Helenia to marry her. She had dreamed of a winter garden blooming with whimsical snow vines and hardy white roses, all thorns and beauty. Perfect for the match between Nyx and Helenia. Tal would have been there too, dressed in his finery with no swords in sight, smiling for once as he escorted Nyx to her beloved. But there was no way now that such a vision would ever come true. It was only for her to decide which way she would wreck it, and who would be missing from the scene. Herself...or her little brother.

She tried to think it through logically. Tal was free of his oath, and she was not, or at least not entirely. She had yet to see the empire fall and the Destroyer's rule ended. Even now, the vow itched beneath her skin. If she chose to do nothing and leave Tal's fate to the girl who had already ruined his life, Nyx would still end up back here one day with an assassin's weapon in her hand—but Tal would no longer be there to be rescued.

She knew that there was every chance Albinus was lying, that he was using the Saints to gain the throne for himself. But what if he did follow through on his promises, or at least his promise to free and heal Tal?

Nyx was going to have to end the Destroyer's reign one way or another. Wasn't it better to do it when there was still a chance of saving Tal in the bargain?

She reached across the table and picked up the miniature crossbow and the vial of poison. Her hand looked like it belonged to someone else; it shook, when her hands never shook. But it was her making this choice. Her deciding her own destiny. Her deciding what—and who—was worth dying for.

"Very well, Mother," she heard herself say. "I will do it."

CHAPTER TWENTY-FIVE

ONCE, THERE WAS A BOY WHO BELIEVED.

His belief was no longer an easy thing. It used to feel infallible; it used to feel as certain as the sun. And then, when it dimmed and vanished, he'd thought his faith had been more like a desert—something created with the sole purpose of evaporating and demolishing any trace of life. It was only lately that he'd come to realize it was nothing so vast or grand as either the sun or a desert. It was more like a weed: small, and vain, and much harder to extract than he'd anticipated.

He was glad of it. At least weeds were honest. And valiant, in a way: to be pulled up and burnt down and kicked through, and grow back again without regard. If he was going to die today, at least he would do it honestly. And at least he wouldn't be alone.

He'd roused in the morning in the midst of a fevered

nightmare only to find Elodie mired deep in her own. He woke her, as he always did. They stared at each other wordlessly, his arm still bracing her chest, one of her feet wedged between his, as their separate dreams seemed to crackle and spark in such close vicinity.

She shut her silver eyes, knowing that hers was the face that had haunted his nightmare. Unable to deny it, but equally unable to see her looking as tormented as she did at this moment, he gently kissed her.

And then Albinus knocked on the door to summon him to his trial.

Once, there was a girl who believed only in her brother. Her belief didn't grow up within her like a green thing, as Tal's did, but instead coated her in the same way the violet poison in her pocket would soon coat an arrowhead. She had spent the night hardening her belief until it cleared into an invisible, shatterproof cocoon around her. It did not let fear through. It did not let anything through at all.

The soldiers gave her a cursory weapons check when she arrived at the gate to the great garden courtyard where public trials were held. They found the poison, but she had put it in a flask and then sprinkled sour beer all over the container, so their only reaction was to wrinkle their noses, assume she was a drunk—which was only helped by the fact that her whole self smelled of sour beer after last night—and keep searching her. The miniature crossbow was harder to hide, so she didn't try. It folded up cleverly to look like some sort of mechanical toy and she let them assume that was what it was.

The arrowhead was hidden in a hollow she'd carved out of the rubber sole of her boot. The arrow was nothing but a small stick, too innocent for the guards to bother with. And then they finished with her and just like that, she was let through, and had the next twenty minutes to scout out the perfect position from which to assassinate the Destroyer.

Once, there was a girl who was afraid.

She was afraid now. She had always been afraid. Her fear and her rage were twin hearts beating within her. Her power was a beast on a chain lunging to get free. She felt small and fragile, and so she made herself terrible and powerful, her skin lustrous with a wreath of white flames as she entered the garden. Her face was set in lines of carelessness, of cruelty. The Iron Crown shone on her brow. The willow trees and river birches seemed to shiver at her passing.

No one would sense her fear. No one could see her weakness.

But Tal did. She could feel his attention on her even as the guards marched him to the high stone stage. They stopped in the spot where the rock was blistered and scored, charred from the many death sentences the Destroyer had carried out here before. When they locked manacles around his wrists and turned him away from her and kicked his knees out from under him, she felt him wince as if his pain resounded through her own body.

Her fury rose. She twitched a finger and a noose of fire curled around the neck of the soldier who'd kicked Tal. She ought to end his life.

No. She ought to end this whole travesty of a trial.

But then what would she do? She let her eyes lift to the audience. Cobalt-and-rust pendants fluttered in the breeze and metallic bunting hung between the towering trees like moss. The whole garden turned on a strange air, something between celebratory and hungry. A large portion of the city had turned out for the event, perhaps nearly a thousand people who were shaken by the empress's death, eager to evaluate their new ruler, and of course morbidly eager for the spilled blood of the accused as they always were.

The Destroyer was the sole judge in these proceedings. She could ensure that Tal's blood didn't spill. She could proclaim him innocent, or upend the law regarding silver Smiths. But making such a move to protect her bodyguard on the very first day of her reign would mean giving her enemies an immeasurable amount of leverage...and then Tal would die anyway.

She remembered how he'd looked when he'd woken her this morning: tousled hair, unnaturally bright eyes, cheeks flushed with fever. He had perhaps a few days left to live, each more painful than the last as his heart struggled to circulate blood clotted with tiny crystals, as the phage shredded his veins and vital organs. She wasn't sure she could bear watching him go through that.

We were made to withstand such things, he'd said last night. But she wasn't built the same as him. She could withstand so much less than he could. Her whole self was so much less than he was, and that frightened her as much as anything ever had.

A strangled whimper pulled her thoughts back to the soldier before her. The noose was burning through the skin on his neck, making a horrible sizzling sound. Tal was looking at her over his shoulder. His eyes were grave. In her mind she heard again what he'd said last night: *the more time that goes by the more it will overtake you.*

She set her jaw. It would not overtake her. She released the rope of fire and it fizzed out. She itched to call it back the moment it dissipated, to let it curl reassuringly in her hands, the way a guard might grip a sword hilt to settle himself before a fight.

The soldier gasped gratefully, hands over his neck, a thin black line burnt into his skin. He stumbled to his post at the edge of the stage. The light breeze of the day strengthened and became brisk, and the trees shivered harder than ever, flinging their leaves across the stage like offerings.

The Destroyer gazed down at the audience again. They were silent, their eyes wide at the display of her power. Pleasure flared within her. She turned and paced slowly to her small throne a few steps away and sat.

"Let us begin," she called out.

Nyx thought nothing could shatter her self-made cocoon of determination. She'd been wrong; Tal could.

The sight of her brother stole every thought in her mind. Her seat was close to the front—she'd made menacing gestures at the man who had claimed the spot until he gave it over—and she could easily see from here just how ill Tal looked. He was afraid, too, though he tried to hide it as he always did. *Hang on, little brother,* she told him mentally. As if he could hear her, his gaze lifted to scan the audience but didn't find her.

A man strode to the front. Pale skin, watery eyes, floppy hair: Albinus, the royal physician and would-be emperor. He spoke. "As this boy served in the palace at the side of the new empress, long may she live, and her late sister, I thought his case merited someone in a high position to bring the accusations against him," he said smoothly. The garden tried to swallow up his words, the unnaturally neat rows of bushes and flower plots absorbing much of his volume. The audience rustled as the people further back asked those in front of them what had been said.

Time to move. While those around her were distracted, Nyx bent down as if to scratch an itch and pulled the arrowhead out of her shoe. She twirled the stick in her hand and attached one to the other. Everyone was watching the Destroyer. Everyone was shifting uneasily, wondering if it had truly been wise for them to come here to see the volatile new Mercurial Empress on the first day of her reign. Whatever she did today would set a precedent, would set the tone for the length of her rule. They worried she would be cruel.

They wouldn't have to worry much longer.

Nyx dropped the arrow on the ground and reached for her flask. She lifted it as if to drink, then fumbled it, splashing its purple contents at her feet. She grumbled for the benefit of anyone who was paying any attention to her and put the flask away again. On the ground beneath her, the metal tip of the arrow shone violet with poison.

The Destroyer smiled at Albinus, making an effort to look sincere when he turned around to beam that smug expression of his in her direction. He saw her face and looked for a moment like a cat who'd been unexpectedly dunked in a bath: startled, affronted, and not quite sure what was happening.

Taking advantage of his disorientation, the Destroyer rose from her throne. "Thank you, dear cousin," she said, every word a threat. "I will hear the accusations now."

Albinus skulked across the stage to stand in the traditional spot of the accuser. Power thrilled in the Destroyer's veins at her minor victory in putting him off-balance. Perhaps she could still find a way to pull this off after all. She could not bear to watch Tal die slowly of the rust phage, but neither would she allow him to be humiliated and slandered before her subjects. And never, never, would she end him with her own fire.

Which meant she had to find some believable reason to proclaim him innocent.

"The accusations are thus," Albinus said, raising his voice as the breeze strengthened again. "The boy is a silver Smith."

Gasps rippled through the audience. They had known who was on trial today, but the charges had not been made public. There had not been a silver Smith found for years now. Tal was a novelty in their eyes—a dangerous one, whose kind were known to be treasonous dissidents.

The Destroyer kept a pleasant expression on her face as her mind raced through the possibilities. She had been up all night thinking of them, and attempting to discuss them with Tal, who seemed infuriatingly uninvested in his own survival. The best option, she thought now, would be to claim that Tal would be useful to her regime. That he was indeed a silver Smith, but a loyal one who was sworn to defend her—an oath which, she could postulate, would now extend to the entirety of her empire. He was useful. A seer on a leash. She could make them see that.

Even if the idea of anyone trying to "leash" Tal made her want to call on her fire noose again.

"And not only that," Albinus was continuing, "but he has committed the crime of treason by hiding this knowledge from the late Iron Empress and the newly-crowned Mercurial Empress, pretending loyalty while using his visions to undermine their rule."

Tal finally spoke. "I have done no such thing," he said in a low tone that nonetheless carried through the audience. They murmured and rustled again in response.

Albinus narrowed his eyes. "The accused will be silent, or the accused will be made to be silent."

"Touch him and you will be the one on your knees," the Destroyer snarled.

The audience shifted, their wide eyes darting between her and Albinus and Tal. Internally, she cursed herself. She couldn't let them know how desperate she was to save him. She had to retake control. "The accused has served me loyally for years, and his 'treason' has not yet been proven. I will not have any faithful subject harmed without the requisite evidence." There. The audience would surely be glad that she appreciated loyalty and was not quick to jump to deadly conclusions.

But Albinus strode across the stage, grabbed Tal's arm, and cut a shallow slice across his bicep with a small copper blade he must've hidden in a pocket. The audience cried out, but not on Tal's behalf; in the morning sunlight, the silver trickle of blood running down his arm shone brightly.

Albinus held up the blade that was now dripping silver. "The requisite evidence, Your Highness," he said, one eyebrow raised in triumph.

Nyx had stolen a cloak this morning. She pulled it closer over her shoulders now as if she were cold, in actuality using it to cover the crossbow as she unfolded it.

She wanted to growl when she heard the Destroyer defend Tal. The bitch didn't care about Tal for his own sake; she was possessive of him like a spoiled child with a favorite toy, not liking anyone else to break it. But even as Nyx thought it, she heard the waver in the Destroyer's voice, saw the way her magic flared around her and made the air sizzle with violence, and she was pierced with a needle of doubt. The Destroyer didn't sound petulant. She sounded worried, and furious.

The people around her caught on her tone too, whispering and staring, wondering if the new empress was either even more unstable than they had thought, or perhaps—somehow, unimaginably—cared for her bodyguard as she had displayed care for no one else before.

Nyx hesitated as she unfolded the last wing of the crossbow. She watched Albinus, and she watched the Destroyer, and she wondered which one looked like a petulant child and which truly cared about Tal's life.

She steeled herself then, pulled the shattered bits of her cocoon back around herself, glued them in place with will and determination. She made herself remember how she had felt in the prison car, with the smell of burnt hair singing her nostrils, her hands spasming on the floor like dying creatures as the Destroyer loomed mercilessly above.

She finished unfolding the crossbow. She loaded the arrow.

Tal barely listened as Albinus continued the list of accusations, comparing him to past traitors and revealing that he had dug up the records of Tal's parents, who had been among those ill-fated silver Smiths who had attempted to lead a coup on the eve of Elodie's seventh birthday. As the audience shifted their wide-eyed attention from him to Elodie, Tal scanned the audience, searching for the assassin who would end his life.

He recalled his vision, trying to judge from the angle of the small crossbow bolt where it would originate. If Tal himself had come here to kill someone on the stage, he would hide in one of the taller trees where the foliage would shelter him. There was a strong wind today, though, which was likely to impact the aim of even the most experienced archer from so high up. Plus the guards had certainly done a security sweep of the entire garden before they had let anyone in. That left lying in wait amongst the audience as the best option for an assassin. They would need to be close to the front for the wind to not affect their aim. He narrowed his search to the first five or ten rows.

At his back, Albinus finished speaking. Elodie spoke next, each word carefully weighed and delivered as she spoke of Tal's service to the crown, naming the assassins and Saints he had killed in defense of her, the plots he had unmasked within the high courts themselves. He steeled himself against the memories each name jarred loose. Perhaps the arrow that would end him today belonged to a family member of someone he had killed. He hoped so. That way, maybe his death might begin to pay the blood debt against him, and bring some form of justice. That wasn't promised to him, though, and most of all he wanted what *had* been promised. If the price he had to pay for that great goal was his death, so be it.

But he couldn't deny, even to himself, that he was afraid.

Nyx watched the Destroyer rise from her throne. She paced to the traditional spot of the defender, standing just behind Tal. She spoke of his virtues. In a clear, even voice, she spoke of his oath as if it were still intact. She wondered aloud if his silver blood might be of benefit to the empire, if perhaps it would be hasty to end the life of someone so loyal to the crown, someone sworn on metal to defend it, someone who could give the country and its ruler a remarkable advantage against their enemies. Skillfully, with subtle turns of phrase and thoughtful questions, she led the audience to wonder what made Albinus so eager to kill a loyal subject who could give all of them such benefits.

Nyx listened as the crowd rustled, pondering their empress's words, peering now at Albinus with narrowed eyes, wondering where his loyalties lie–and where they wanted their own loyalties to lie. It was a dangerous game the Destroyer was playing now. She was leading her subjects to question Albinus's motivations, but in so doing, she was giving them the chance to potentially ally themselves with him—with a would-be ruler who had healing magic instead of the unstable and destructive magic of mercury, who was older and therefore more experienced.

Nyx hesitated, the loaded crossbow on her lap hidden by her cloak. She could think of no reason why the Destroyer would risk such a thing for Tal's sake...unless her feelings for him could possibly echo the same care that Tal seemed to feel for her. Nyx had not been willing to believe such a thing of her enemy before, but now, with an assassin's weapon in her lap and the end of her own life fast approaching, she wondered if there might be another way. If she might have missed something, or been unwilling to see it.

What would Helenia say if she were here? Probably something annoying like *violence is never a good answer,* or some proverb or scripture that would gently but firmly condemn Nyx's plan. Except it wasn't really even Nyx's plan, was it? It was Saasha's. Nyx had left her mother last night not long after their conversation, certain of what she had to do to save her brother, but now that the moment was at hand she found that certainty draining away. Saasha had said that killing the Destroyer was the only way to save Tal but now it seemed that the Destroyer herself might want to save Tal.

And then the Destroyer raised her chin and took a breath, ready to end her line of argument. "Tal is a seer, but I believe he is one who can be leashed for the good of the empire."

And just like that, Nyx's certainty flooded back in, surging on a tide of fury. So *this* was why she had wanted to save

Tal. Not because she cared for him, but because she wanted to use him. Tal had served her at the cost of his soul for two years and now she wanted to corrupt his magic as well. Even if the Destroyer forced Albinus to heal his rust phage, it would only be for the purposes of wielding him like a weapon against those who opposed her. The fact that he was no longer truly under oath to her didn't matter; she had plenty of ways to enforce her will against him.

Nyx waited for the Destroyer to glance away, at Albinus, before she raised the crossbow.

Tal's breathing had accelerated. The arguments had reached their end. Elodie was about to pronounce his sentence. Even if it was to be a favorable one, even if she managed to find some way to pardon him without giving up her power or weakening her reign, this could still only end one way.

His god had shown him what had to happen for his promise to be fulfilled. He had asked one last thing of Tal. And Tal had said yes. He would not go back on his word now, no matter how frightened he was.

Something burgeoned around him, an invisible sense of weight, a presence. His god steadied him. *It will be well,* whispered a voice that wasn't a voice somewhere deep within.

The Destroyer returned to the empress's elevated iron throne. She sat down, prepared to render her ultimate judgment.

Tal scanned the audience one last time—and spotted the assassin.

Shaved head. Fierce brown eyes and sharp cheekbones and a face he would recognize anywhere: Nyx. She held a miniature crossbow whose bolt dripped with purple.

No. No. Not Nyx. If it was her who killed him, she would never forgive herself. She could never be happy. She would never be able to forget this moment, this choice, her finger on the trigger and her arrow lodging in her own brother's back.

But neither could he let the arrow strike Elodie.

He shifted his weight, desperate to catch her attention. Her gaze moved from the Destroyer to him. Their eyes locked.

Nyx's finger froze on the crossbow's trigger. Tal's eyes held her. He shook his head minutely, his jaw tight, his gaze pleading. He didn't want her to do it. Because he didn't want the Destroyer's death, or because he knew that Nyx herself would be killed afterwards?

She hesitated again. She looked at Albinus. His mouth was a straight line, his expression surly. The Destroyer, in contrast, looked triumphant. The white flames that had wreathed her had died down to sparks. She seemed…relieved.

Nyx's gaze returned to Tal's. Her hesitation stretched out into the space between heartbeats, filling her up and displacing her certainty once again.

She couldn't do it. She wasn't sure enough that it was the right thing.

The thought brought with it a heady rush of her own relief. She would trust Tal, and not her mother, who longed for a vengeance that would end the life of her own daughter. Nyx would trust the exasperating and beloved voice of her girlfriend, who was apparently able to wedge herself into Nyx's thoughts even though she must be miles away in reality.

With a shaky exhalation, Nyx began to lower the crossbow.

"I pronounce the sentence of…" the Destroyer began, and then Nyx's neighbor shifted in his seat and jostled her arm.

Nyx's finger jerked on the trigger. The crossbow fired.

Tal saw his sister make her decision. He saw her lower her weapon. A stunned sense of impossibility swept over him then—his sister trusted him, even over her own hatred. She would not go through with the assassination. He started to smile at her.

And then his gaze fell to the man next to her. He was wearing peasant clothing, but his bearing was much straighter and his gaze sharper than most of the audience. He looked like an off-duty guard or perhaps a mercenary. Tal followed his line of sight.

He was looking at Albinus. And Albinus was looking at him.

Tal inhaled sharply, his instincts screaming a warning, but before he could say anything the man reacted to some signal from the Lord of Copper and elbowed Nyx.

Her finger hit the trigger. The bolt flew from the crossbow.

And here it came: Tal's decision.

The weight of his god lifted, hovered. Warmth enveloped him. The choice, even now, was his to make.

He made it.

CHAPTER TWENTY-SIX

THE DESTROYER BURNED WITH A FERAL SATISFACTION AS she began to pronounce her judgment. She was certain that she had guided the trial well, that her subjects were likely to see Tal's potential as an ally now and not think him to be her weakness. The rust phage was still an obstacle, of course, but she was the Mercurial Empress. She would find a way to cure him. She could offer a coffer of gold to whoever could fix Tal, or maybe just hurt Albinus until he did the trick. Surely the royal physician—the man who had infused a misfire with mercury magic—had some experimental procedure, some secret cure, that could ensure Tal lived.

But in the middle of her pronouncement, Tal stood up suddenly and spun to face her. His gaze locked with hers and then, without warning, he staggered forward a step as if someone had struck him from behind.

She cut off her pronouncement, startled. She raised a hesitant hand. "Tal?" she asked, her voice too high, too questioning, potentially ruining all her hard work at appearing dispassionate and reasonable. But there was something sad and final in his eyes that frightened her beyond caring.

The audience started screaming. People leapt over each other, running for the exits. Guards and soldiers were shoving through them to get either away or to the stage. Someone, another soldier perhaps, grabbed her arm and tried to pull her backwards. She put her palm out and blasted a hole through his chest. No one else laid hands on her after that.

"Tal?" she asked again, her voice loud and panicked in her own ears. She didn't move. She couldn't make herself move. She had so much practice in reading Tal even when he tried to hide his emotions from her, but now they were playing across his face like shadows from the windblown trees, flitting too quickly to make out fully.

All at once, the emotions vanished, leaving his eyes dark and lifeless.

He exhaled. He dropped to his knees. He fell forward, revealing the arrow lodged in his back.

And the Destroyer exploded.

All around Nyx, the crowd was screaming, lunging, knocking over benches and each other to get away. The Destroyer's wreath of fire had expanded explosively outward, encompassing most of the stage, burning at least three lords of the high courts to ash instantly and landing several others with fatal wounds. Nyx heard an unearthly wail, one that was underlaid with the roar of a forest fire. The Destroyer was walking to Tal, who was the only person on the stage untouched by the fire. She was kneeling at his side. She was weeping.

Nyx dropped the crossbow. She stared at her brother's body. She tried to understand what had happened. She tried to understand what she had done.

She could not.

A movement at the edge of the stage caught her attention. Albinus was backing away, face tight in a rictus of fury. He was turning to the soldiers beside him, snapping orders. One of them began to hand him a weapon.

Albinus. He had engineered this. He was going to try to kill the Destroyer now, while she wept over Tal's body.

A sudden clarity descended on Nyx. She welcomed it, even though she knew it was powered by adrenaline and not necessarily by logic. She leapt onto the toppled bench in front of her. She kicked a woman out of the way. She launched herself at the stage. Heat blistered her as she sprinted past the edge of the veil of flames, catching a dozen tiny fires on her clothing, but she didn't even feel the spots of pain. There would be a much greater pain waiting for her later.

Albinus spotted her too late. She threw herself through the air and tackled him to the ground. She snatched his weapon—a throwing dagger, which he likely couldn't wield with any degree of skill anyway. He must have been desperate to bend this swiftly-dissolving situation to his advantage. She would not let him do it. It was her fault that her brother was lying dead twenty feet away, but it was his, too. She would not let him walk away from that.

The Destroyer pulled the arrow from Tal's back. It wasn't lodged deeply enough to do much more than superficial damage, but some sort of violet substance–undeniably a deadly toxin of some sort–dripped from its head. She tightened her hand around the shaft. It disintegrated into smoke instantly and the poisoned arrowhead clinked to the ground.

She turned Tal over. She pulled him into her lap. Fire raged everywhere, without and within.

His eyes were closed. His heartbeat had gone still. He was not breathing.

She remembered how he had breathed for her after she had drowned in the icy lake. She bowed over him, bent her head to his, and gave him all of the breath in her body.

She would give him anything. *Anything*. Her life. Her empire. Her crown.

...her *crown*.

The memory of her sister whispered: *The copper magic would have been enough to instantly heal everyone on the train.*

Your fire–if you were using all *your fire–is probably the only power strong enough to break it.*

She laughed wildly, and it came out a sob. Of course, this

would be it. Of course she was finally going to have to make this choice. She could keep her crown and the power in her veins—or she could use up all of her magic to destroy the crown for good, and in so doing perhaps save the life of the boy she loved.

Earlier, she had thought she might be torn apart by the pieces of herself that scraped through her like broken glass. Now that feeling intensified. Her magic surged protectively, hardening the shield of fire around her as she struggled with herself. If she gave her magic up, she would be vulnerable. Helpless. Weak. Tal had said she was made to withstand such things. But how could he know that? She didn't know it, not at all.

If she did this, maybe she could force Albinus to replace the mercury in her blood again afterward. But she didn't know the formula for her treatments as Sarai had, and Albinus could just as easily poison her as re-infuse her. But then, he wouldn't need to poison her, would he? The mercury *was* the poison.

The pieces of herself grew sharper. The Destroyer clung to her power. Elodie fought fiercely to save Tal's life. The battle held her immobile, and with every second that passed, Tal's body grew colder.

How long had she been drowned before he'd saved her? How long could a body be dead before death was irrevocable? She could not keep fighting with herself. Some part of her must win: the Destroyer, or the girl from the Skyteeth who'd lost her memories but found her own soul.

Tal's words came to her then: *You were right when I said I loved Elodie. But you were wrong when you said you weren't her.*

The fire around her, which had been raging as if driven by gales, went still. So did the fire within her. There was no duality in her, no distinctly different personalities harbored in her being. There was only a girl. She was small, and scared, and lashed out with whatever weapon she had at hand—her words, her magic, her anger—when she felt threatened. The poison within her had only amplified those natural instincts.

It was not power and Tal that she had to choose between. It was not the Destroyer and Elodie. It wasn't even strength and vulnerability.

It was fear, and love.

Nyx had one arm locked around Albinus's neck and the other drawn back, about to plunge the thin throwing dagger deep into his chest, when a hand wrapped around her wrist to stop her. She looked up. The Destroyer stood before her. The tracks of tears still shone on her cheeks, but only resolution showed in her eyes.

"I can save him," the Destroyer said.

Nyx stared at her. Her mind worked through the possibilities: this was a trap, the opening salvo to the Destroyer's revenge for the death of her favorite toy, or an attempt to capture Nyx alive for interrogation. But none of that mattered, because the Destroyer had just said the single phrase that could make Nyx do whatever she wanted no matter how impossible it seemed.

She dropped the dagger. "What do you need?"

"I need Albinus," the Destroyer said steadily. "I need a copper Smith to channel magic from my crown."

Albinus gave an ugly laugh, the effect of which was dampened by the fact that he was currently choking to death. "I will do no such thing," he gurgled, or at least that was what Nyx was pretty sure he was probably saying.

Nyx picked the dagger back up and gave him a shallow slice across the ear, knowing a cut in such a sensitive spot would sting like hell. He howled and snarled and she bared her teeth in a smile. "Go ahead, Al," she said, drawing the dagger back. "Turn her down again and let me mar your face further. It's not that pretty to start with—you should probably be more interested in conserving what traces of palatability it still has."

Albinus gritted his teeth, glared at her, and then reluctantly nodded.

Sorry, Helenia, Nyx said mentally. *Apparently violence is* sometimes *a good answer.*

She dragged him to the spot where Tal was lying. When she saw her brother's lifeless body, a shudder of grief and denial wrenched through her so powerfully that she nearly lost her hold on Albinus, who immediately tensed to make a run for it. Nyx got control of herself—*she said she could save him, it might be true,* she told herself fiercely even though she knew she shouldn't believe it—and firmed her grasp on the Lord of Copper.

The Destroyer took off her crown. Her hair was braided around it and strands of it tore as she yanked the crown away, but she paid no mind. She held it out above Tal's body. Her jaw was clenched—with the effort it was taking to hold her power back, or perhaps with the same grief and fear that was raging through Nyx.

"I am going to burn this," the Destroyer told Albinus.

He went still and then jerked. He gurgled something. Nyx eased her grip a bit so he could speak. He sucked down great lungfuls of air and then managed, "You can't! The high courts will lose our advantage, the crown holds the power of the whole empire—"

"Then it will be a good trade for Tal's life," the Destroyer said icily. "When I destroy it, you will channel the copper magic from it into Tal. You will use it to restore him. *Fully.* No poison, no rust phage."

Nyx's heart sped with hope. It was like a drug, loosening her muscles, making her feel almost delirious with it.

Albinus licked his lips, his gaze flitting from Tal's body to the Destroyer's face. "I'm...I'm not sure I'd be able to restore him fully, even with as much magic as the crown is rumored to hold."

The Destroyer lifted her eyes to Nyx, her features dark with the promise of violence—a violence that, for once, Nyx understood and was fully on board with.

Nyx twirled the dagger in front of Albinus's face. His eyes followed it as if hypnotized. She stopped its spinning and touched it to his cheek, making him shiver. Then she motioned at the Destroyer and the walls of fire around them. "If my brother dies, so do you," she told him, conviction clear as daylight in her tone. "By knife or by fire or by my own bare hands."

"Or *my* own bare hands," the Destroyer added. The curtains of fire around them leapt higher and crackled with her barely-restrained fury.

Albinus hesitated a moment longer and then gave in. "Very well. We—we must hurry, though, his heart will have been stopped for too long to restart it soon." His eyes darted around as if he were looking for backup. The few guards who were still in the courtyard were a sensible distance away, though, and didn't look like they were about to charge through the flames to rescue the royal physician from their empress.

The Destroyer lifted her chin, bracing herself. "I will have to focus," she warned Nyx. "Keep an eye on Albinus. If I lose concentration, the release of so much magic of so many different kinds could blow up half the palace."

"I'm okay with that," Nyx assured her.

The Destroyer turned her focus to the crown and the boy beneath it. The walls of fire began to contract around them. "Nyx," she said then, with her gaze turned away and her voice dangerously even, "am I right in assuming it was you who did this?"

Nyx debated, but ultimately—"Yes."

"You could not have thought you would leave here alive."

Nyx wasn't sure if it was a threat or an observation. "Revive my brother," she said at last. "We can debate who's going to kill who later."

The curtains of fire answered Elodie's call. They spun ash from the ground and fed it into the wind that had been churned up by so much heat, and soon the flames spinning around her were soot black. They eclipsed the sun. They shaded the mountains on the horizon. They blocked out what was left of the fleeing peasants and the shouting soldiers, the bowing trees, the scorched irises and charred oleander. Only a few moments ago, the garden had been a riot of color and life. Now it was ruined, because her fire was capable of nothing else.

The Destroyer. That was the name her sister's subjects had given her when she performed her first public execution at eight years old. They had looked at her with awe in their eyes, and fear, and she'd found that nothing had ever pleased her more—except perhaps the warm and proud weight of Sarai's hand on her shoulder. She would never feel that weight again, now. Neither would she sustain the mercury and magic that had been her sister's first—and then final—gift. There would be nothing left within her except herself.

She wasn't sure if she could bear it.

She pulled power from the fires around her, and from the magic that was blazing through her veins. She fed it into the crown. It began to warm beneath her hands.

Once, she was afraid. Still, she was afraid. But: *we were made to withstand such things,* whispered the voice of the boy she loved. He was a boy of ill-placed faith, a boy whose belief in both her and his god was relentless, without mercy. He wanted nothing from her except the impossible. Somehow, he had made her want it too.

The crown grew hotter and began to glow. The flames surged into it and through it. They too were relentless, and she would make herself so as well.

At her side, Albinus tensed and then reached out a hand to Tal's body. The magic within the crown was nearly to the breaking point and he was preparing to channel it.

The fire was tearing through her, each fingertip a jet of flame, each artery and vein and capillary a raging torrent of sparks. She had lost control. Her power was following only itself, like a waterfall crashing down inevitably from the heights. She began to grow faint. She heard screaming, something feral and furious, and realized that it was both her and the fire.

The crown melted.

Nyx shouted. Albinus cried out in pain as he drew magic into himself, his veins glowing a bright copper that shone even through his skin. His hand on Tal's shoulder spasmed into a claw. Tal's body seized, his spine arching.

The waterfall of Elodie's power stopped all at once. There was a sharp pain in her eyes. Something wet curved down her cheek and spattered onto Tal's shirt: a single bead of red blood.

The flames that had been wailing in a cyclone around them stopped suddenly. They hung in the air, fire and sparks and suspended ash, and then, like an imploding star, they rushed inward.

The last of the crown dissipated into steam, releasing a torrent of raw magic just as the curtains of fire collapsed around it. The two forces roared into each other with a thunderous crack that spider-webbed the stone stage with fault lines. A mighty wind rushed out from the spot where the crown had been and sent all of them flying, tearing branches from the trees and flattening bushes on its way.

After that came a great silence.

The garden slowly settled. The trees stopped thrashing. The multitude of small fires that had caught in the grass sputtered out, unable to chew through the green and well-watered plants without the fuel of magic. Four figures splayed across the stage like points on a compass: Tal, Elodie, Nyx, and Albinus, who was slowly sitting up.

Copper burned through his veins still, more power than he had ever felt before. He flexed his fingers and watched the fascinating glow of it through his skin. His spies had found out the truth of the Iron Crown's enchantment years ago, but he had never guessed the sheer magnitude of magic within it. He had planned to wear it, but wielding it would do just as well.

Blinking, he surveyed the damage around him. The soldiers and the few peasants who hadn't fled were now either unconscious or dead. He didn't trouble himself to check. He didn't need them for what he knew he had to do next.

He had always been clever, a quick planner, excelling at both spinning and revising schemes. His old plan to have the Destroyer assassinated wouldn't work now but there was still a way to salvage the situation nicely. He just had to do it before any of his enemies woke up.

The young would-be assassin—Nyx had been her name, he recalled—lay prone on the eastern end of the stage, her chest moving steadily up and down with her breaths. He staggered over to her and then knelt, searching for the throwing dagger she'd taken from him. He would need to kill her first, since she'd seemed to have both the greatest desire to see him dead and the actual ability to do the deed. After that he'd move on to Tal—his would be the most truncated resurrection in history, if Albinus had in fact succeeded in reviving him—and last of all, the newly powerless Destroyer, who was now as helpless as any babe without her fearsome magic.

He found the dagger wedged under Nyx's shoulder. He tugged it free and then pondered for a moment. He wasn't nearly as self-assured in violence as this young woman had been, but being a man of medicine, he did know the best places to strike to ensure she never rose again. He moved the blade up to hover above her neck and then drew it back for the killing blow.

Something gray and white and ferocious barreled into him, snarling, and latched its jaws on the hand that was holding the dagger. Albinus yelled in shock as much as in pain.

The dagger fell, its hilt glancing off Nyx's shoulder as the creature–a dog?–bore Albinus to the ground. He beat at the beast, mostly ineffectually, with his other hand. He scrambled for the dagger. The dog's teeth were ripping through the tendons in his wrist now, grinding against bone. Some other sharp thing was scraping against his leg.

He spotted the dagger lying on the ground a few inches from his face. He grabbed for it.

A hand closed around his arm and bore it to the ground, where it was then pinned by a knee. The dagger was plucked neatly from his grip. "Back, Maluk," said a calm female voice.

The jaws around Albinus's wrist released. He turned his head to see a girl leaning over him. She was hefty and curvy, with brown skin and long, curly black hair and a face made for smiling. She wasn't smiling now, though. In fact, she looked very angry indeed.

He licked his lips. He could talk his way out of this. After all, judging from her clothes she seemed to be a mere peasant, and what peasant would dare kill the Lord of Copper? "My dear girl–" he started, but felt suddenly faint and oddly queasy.

"I imagine that would be the poison taking effect," the girl said conversationally, and nodded to the ground next to Albinus's shin, where a purple-stained arrowhead lay dripping with blood both silver and copper.

Dread hardened in Albinus's gut. The thing that had poked him in the leg earlier–that was what it had been. "You...you could save me if..." he started, trying frantically to remember if this particular poison had an antidote, but the girl merely looked at him.

"You have just held a dagger above my girlfriend with the intent to murder her. Before that, you helped formulate the poison that sickened her every day for two years. I would let Maluk rip your throat out if you weren't already dying. I'm sure I'll feel terrible later for not saving your life, but I'll have to settle for saying a prayer for your soul in penitence."

His vision wavered. He tried to call up his magic to save himself, but his concentration was too erratic to direct it. His head drifted toward the ground. The world went silent and the Lord of Copper closed his eyes, never to open them again.

"Good riddance," Helenia said softly to Albinus's corpse. Maluk growled softly in apparent agreement.

"I'm not sure if I'm impressed or intimidated," said a weak voice from beside her. Helenia twisted around quickly to see Nyx pushing herself up to sitting. Helenia checked her over—not bleeding, breathing seemed normal, a little shaky but none the worse for wear.

"Be intimidated," she answered sharply when she was sure Nyx was okay. "Then perhaps you'll give it a bit more thought next time you consider leaving me drugged in the woods while you run off alone to face the Destroyer."

A change came over Nyx then, her face going grim. She picked up the dagger and turned her head until she spotted the Destroyer—who was still unconscious, but twitching slightly as if she would wake at any moment—on the opposite end of the stage. Nyx started trying to stand.

"Stop being stupid," Helenia snapped.

"I am obligated to do no such thing."

"Sit down this second or I swear, I'll turn down your proposal."

Nyx stopped. She looked at Helenia. "What proposal?"

"The proposal where you get down on your knees and beg me to marry you even though—I repeat—you left me *drugged* in the *woods* while you ran off to face the Destroyer."

Nyx blinked a few times, then sat back down. After a moment she managed to reply, "Is this the same proposal where you break down crying with happiness and kiss me senseless right after you agree to be my wife?"

Helenia's lips twitched. "It might be," she allowed, "if you can manage to keep yourself from murdering anyone for the next twenty minutes while I get this mess straightened out."

Nyx considered this. "Ten minutes," she negotiated.

Helenia let out a noise that was part laugh and part exasperated huff, and then leaned across the space between them and kissed her foolish, feral, beautiful fiancé senseless.

Nyx broke away after a moment, her eyes widening. "Tal," she gasped, and scrambled to her feet again, searching for her brother.

Helenia put out a hand to keep Nyx from falling back down, as she was still disoriented from whatever had caused the magical blast a few minutes ago. "He's okay," she said quickly. "I saw him as I was coming to stop Albinus from kill-ing you. He's breathing. He'll likely wake up any moment."

"It worked?" Nyx rubbed a hand across her head and then collapsed back to sitting. "How did you get here? What did you…" Nyx trailed off, probably because she'd finally regained enough of her senses to look around and see the flood of Saints who were currently flowing around them, securing the exits to the garden and marching toward the palace gates.

When Helenia had woken up back in the temple clear-ing, she'd quickly put the clues together to realize what had happened and the danger that Nyx was almost certainly going to throw herself into. She'd travelled past the city and straight onward to the Saints' mountain base, but rather than merely evacuating them, she'd gathered them into a makeshift army, promising that there was going to be a prime opportunity to strike the palace soon based on Tal's vision. They'd met up outside the city with the former pris-oners who Tal had released from the dungeons, and had thus been updated with more recent events.

After that, Helenia had gone ahead into the city and vis-ited safehouse after safehouse until she tracked down Saasha and made the woman tell her what was happening. A part of Saasha must have wanted Helenia to save her daughter, because the woman held nothing back, telling Helenia every detail of the plan she'd manipulated Nyx into carrying out.

Helenia had wasted no time returning to the waiting army of Saints and using the chaos of the impending trial to get them into the city. They had arrived in the garden too late to have any effect on the planned assassination—but not too late, it turned out, to use the destabilization of the empress and the deaths of half of the high court leaders as an opportunity to invade the palace.

She told Nyx all of this.

"You are brilliant," Nyx informed her.

"I know," Helenia said primly, and kissed her again.

When Elodie woke twenty minutes later, she was predictably disgruntled about the invasion of her palace. The two dozen Saint guards surrounding her provided reason to keep her peace, but unfortunately, Elodie had never been good at keeping peace. She was far better at making threats.

"Jostle him one more time and I'll break your fingers off," she said to the young copper Smith who had been captured and then swiftly put to work by Helenia. He was currently checking Tal over to see why he was still unconscious. Maluk growled to back up her threat, one of his paws placed protectively on Tal's chest.

"My—My lady," the copper Smith stuttered, eyes wide. "I—"

"Don't call me that."

Helenia interceded. "I doubt threats will inspire the boy to work harder."

Elodie shot her a glance. "In my experience, threats very often prove inspirational."

"Ugh," Nyx said from her spot a few feet away, where she was ostentatiously sharpening her confiscated dagger on one of the rocks that had cracked off from the stage. It seemed to be some sort of stress-relief measure for her. "I forbid you to banter with her, Hel." Her voice lacked some of the spite that it used to have whenever she spoke to or about Elodie, though.

Helenia snorted. "I banter only with you, my darling." She turned back to the Saint she'd been speaking with regarding the palace's invasion. Apparently two wings had been taken mostly bloodlessly during the chaos. The remaining lords and ladies of the high courts had barricaded themselves in the last three wings and the fighting was now proceeding room to room.

Elodie found that she didn't much care who won. She had already burned her crown and given up her magic. She supposed she might as well give up her empire with it. All she cared about was that Tal would wake up, and be well.

Although, she thought ruefully now, *he* would probably care who won the battle, and how many innocents and Saints would die in the process.

"Fine," she said abruptly, looking back at Helenia.

Helenia sent the Saint she'd been speaking to away with new orders and then turned back to Elodie. "Fine, what?"

Elodie waved a hand at the far edge of the stage, where the bodies of several leaders of the high courts were slowly growing cold. "Pick a crown. I think gold would suit you best, personally, but you can choose for yourself."

Helenia tilted her head. "What exactly are you offering?"

"A truce. A compromise. Pick your crown, and tonight, I'll put it on your head myself and name you co-empress. I know the courts; they're full of people just like Albinus, all of them scheming how to stab each other in the back—sometimes literally—to gain power for themselves. You'd have to drag them kicking and screaming before they pledge loyalty to any outsider you might try to install if you get rid of me. Co-ruling is the only relatively peaceable solution. We can end the fighting before it escalates."

Helenia's eyes slowly narrowed. "Co-empress. I am...not sure about that."

"Well, get sure quickly, because it's the best offer you're going to get," Elodie snapped, her gaze returning once again to Tal's face. She thought she had seen him twitch. "I know how the empire runs and how it will respond to the sort of change you want to initiate. I can help you save lives and livelihoods during the transition."

"The transition to what, pray tell?"

She waved a hand. "What is it they do in the east now? A democracy, or something like that. I'm assuming that's what you were hoping to achieve." A democracy would mean her moving out of the palace—away from the den of vipers where she had never, ever felt safe—and finding someplace to settle down and finally learn about herself. And maybe, if she was very, very lucky, she could also learn what she and Tal were together.

If he would only wake up.

From the corner of her eye, she saw Helenia and Nyx

exchange a shocked glance. A democracy was indeed all the Saints could have hoped to achieve in their wildest dreams.

"You will pardon the Saints involved in today's incursion?" Helenia asked—the tentative beginnings of a negotiation that Elodie knew was certain to go on for quite a while. "You will formally forgive Nyx for her attempt on your life? For *all* of her attempts on your life, that is."

Nyx paused in her dagger-sharpening, her wary gaze settling on the two of them.

"Yes, very well," Elodie said impatiently. It wasn't as if Tal was going to tolerate her trying to exact vengeance against his sister anyway. And if she was honest, there was a good-sized part of her that had come to grudgingly admire Nyx; she was stubborn, courageous, and charmingly violent.

Nyx scoffed. "As if we would believe you. As if you would forgive the crimes of a Saints assassin."

The young copper Smith interrupted, probably eager to be away from the group. "I see no signs of rust phage or the poison. He is merely recovering, and will wake when he's ready, my lady."

Tension drained from Elodie all at once, leaving her trembling with relief as the Smith waited for her reply. She looked down at Tal. She remembered that he had looked this same way when she had found him after the train's explosion, too. She'd thought then that he looked beautiful. He still was. The drumbeat of his footsteps, the green eyes that showed her everything he was feeling, the strength of his character—he was beautiful in all that he was.

She reached out and brushed a strand of hair off of his face. He leaned into her touch, and she smiled.

"My name is Elodie," she said to them all. "And I will forgive who I wish."

Tal dreamed.

He dreamed of a boy from the mountain ward whose belief had changed his destiny. He dreamed of his sister, happy. He dreamed of an empire forged anew with effort and compromise and hard-won trust.

He dreamed of a god who was proud of him. A god who authenticated the pain he still felt, and would always feel to some measure. A god he would love and question and wrestle with and fight for every day of his life—a life that he would now, quite unexpectedly, get to live.

Last of all, he dreamed of Elodie.

In his dream, her indomitable spirit shone through her brown eyes like sunlight through stained glass. Bloodred tear tracks were drying on her cheeks. Her hands were burned and blistered, a match for his own scars. She was injured, as he was, but she had also finally made room for her own happiness.

She leaned over him. She kissed him. And then he opened his eyes, and realized he was not dreaming at all.

BONUS SHORT STORY:
THE ROSE WITCH

Everyone knew a witch lived at the base of the mountain. The seasons there were strange, where the steam of the Entengre met the heartless frost of the Skyteeth, where the mote trees splayed their drifting seeds across the frozen mud and blooming snow roses alike. The witch, too, was a strange and fearsome contradiction. Wild, irreverent, lovely, ferocious—every person who visited her cottage described her differently. The only thing that was the same was the way their voices shook when they returned to tell the tale.

All of this, Theon had learned in his first week in the village there at the base of the mountain. He was a weak boy, he knew, small for his age and easily frightened, but at least in this matter everyone else seemed to be frightened too.

"*I'm* not frightened," his sister insisted one dark evening as they returned from the schoolyard, their empty lunch baskets swinging, a neighbor's cat yowling at them from a nearby porch.

The boy longed to impress his sister. Twelve years old and already she was the most painful sort of idol: the kind who had no idea that anyone at all worshipped them. "I am not frightened either," he told her.

Her teeth gleamed in the red light of sunset. "Prove it."

His heart stuttered, but he mustered himself and lifted his chin. "How shall I prove it?"

"Bring me one of the cursed flowers that grows under her window."

And that was how Theon found himself creeping through a witch's garden.

It was a wild and overgrown garden, the sort that could swallow a monster whole, much less one small boy. There were enormous hellebore blooms with bold yellow pistils, fragrant night-blooming jasmine, pops here and there of coppery witch-hazel, and everywhere, everywhere there were roses. Their thorns seemed to reach for him, whispering as they scraped gently over his sleeves and curled at his ankles. He crept through it all carefully and tried to comfort himself with the thought that the garden could not *truly* be as wild and dangerous as it seemed. Everywhere there were small signs that this plot of land was both beloved and mercilessly tended to. Smooth paving stones were set into the many wandering paths, and there were no brown petals to be seen on the beautiful ice-white roses he slipped past now. Not a single weed dared show its sprouts anywhere.

But tame or not, the garden was still an easy place to get lost in, and the boy had to follow the trail of smoke from the cottage's chimney to find the witch's place.

The closer he grew to the hulking shadow of a house, the quicker his heart beat. It wished to gallop out of his chest and go hide under his bed, he thought. A large part of him was terrified that he would be found out by the witch. She would do something terrible to him. Eat his liver on toast, perhaps. His mother had pursed her lips and shook her head when he'd expressed that worry to her just yesterday.

She isn't dangerous, she'd said, then paused and let her eyes slide sideways as if she was reconsidering her words. *Well. She isn't a witch, in any case. She was once powerful and then gave up her power, and now she gardens. Don't bother her and hopefully she won't bother you.*

Theon hadn't believed her. He'd heard enough scary stories to know when an adult was censoring out the frightening bits.

Now, though, as he tiptoed closer to the window of the cottage, he repeated the words over and over in his mind like a prayer. *Don't bother her and she won't bother you.* He would not be seen. He would not be caught. He would take a flower—a small flower, or maybe just a petal or a leaf or a pebble, something too small to be discovered missing—and then he would go. No one but his sister would ever know he had been here at all.

The cottage was near enough now that he could make out its details in the thin moonlight. Earlier he had thought of it as a hulking monstrosity, something with eyes and teeth that lurked in the dark, but now he could see that it was actually quite small and jarringly pretty. It was as neat as the garden was wild: whitewashed bricks, a sensible red-tile roof, and painted window boxes for flowers—though the plants spilled out of their containers in every which direction, as if in protest against all the orderliness.

His eyes lingered on the nearest window box. *One of the cursed flowers that grow under her window,* his sister had specified, and although he couldn't tell if these particular blooms were cursed or not, they were definitely under a window. He tried to measure the distance between himself and the box. He would have to leave the shadowy garden and slip across open ground to get there, and he was trying to decide which method would be best: quick, or quiet.

He was not quick enough to escape the witch if she spotted him. He decided on quiet, and crept out of the rosebushes.

The window before him glowed with honeyed light. He could make out the interior of the room beyond the rippled glass. There was a table, and a crackling hearth, and a floor swept clean except for the three immense hauler dogs who were splayed across it. At the table sat a man. He looked about the age of Theon's father. But unlike Theon's father he was tall and lean, with a soldier's corded muscles visible on his forearms as he lifted a writing quill to tuck it behind one ear. His hair was longish and dark and rumpled and he wore round, silver-rimmed spectacles. He was saying something to a little green-eyed girl who was nested in his lap, and the devotion in his gaze said she was his daughter. As

Theon watched, the girl reached up and plucked the quill out from behind his ear with a triumphant giggle, then scribbled down something on a sheet of parchment before them. Theon twisted his neck to try to read it: *Alaya*. Her name, he guessed. Her father laughed gently and made a half-hearted grab for the quill, but Alaya squealed and curled herself into a ball around it, nearly knocking them both to the floor.

Theon edged closer, craning his neck, breathing shallow breaths as he searched for any sign of the witch in this eerily domestic scene. As he neared the window, he spotted another girl crouched on the floor nearby. She was a mirror image to the first, with a pile of wavy, tangled hair as wild as the gardens, but her expression was much sterner and her eyes were gray rather than green. She seemed to be carving a design of some sort into the wooden floor with a butter knife as one of the hauler dogs at her side looked benevolently on. The man at the table glanced up at her and said something, and the fond exasperation in his voice meant she was his daughter, too. The girl waved him off impatiently and continued in her carving.

Nowhere was there any sign of the witch.

A cautious hope welled up in Theon. Maybe he had gotten lucky. Maybe the witch was out. He had heard rumors that her husband could be dangerous in his own right, though—the man was a metal-worker now, spending his days restoring old temples, but according to the rumors he was still a formidable bodyguard employed by the Council of Delegates when they traveled beyond the borders of the empire for their democracy-building work. Theon searched for the man's weapons, a pair of twin short swords. They were leaned up against the wall next to a stack of firewood and a woodsman's axe, as if they had been dropped there weeks ago and then forgotten.

Theon took another step closer, and his shoe scuffed against a paving stone with a sound softer than a whisper—and when Theon froze and looked up, the man's head was lifted and his bright green eyes were locked on him.

Theon quivered, right down to his bones. His heart tried again to leap out of his chest. His knees went shaky, and he could already picture his mad dash back to the village—but he needed a flower. He would not leave without a flower.

His gaze dropped to the window box to judge the distance between him and it again. It would take him perhaps three seconds to reach it, snatch a flower, and run, but he had lost any hope now of escaping undetected. The best he could wish for was to go unrecognized, and to get away without being caught. He looked back up to see if the man was going to the swords or straight to the door, but to his surprise saw instead that the man's head was once again bowed, and he was now tickling the girl in his lap as he tried to retrieve the quill, as if he had never even seen Theon at all.

Was it a reprieve, or a trick? It didn't matter. Theon's already-small reserves of courage were nearly drained in either case. He took two long strides to the window box and reached for a dainty blue flower, intending to run the second he laid hands on it.

Something sharp poked him in the chest. "If you've come to throw rocks at our window, you had better think again," said a young but very imperious voice.

The boy froze. The tip of a sword—one of the short swords that had a moment ago been leaning against the wall inside—rested now against his breastbone. On its other end was the girl with the wild hair and the gray eyes who'd been carving into the floor. She glared at him as if she were deciding whether or not to run him through here and now.

She was the witch's daughter. Perhaps she was a witch herself. Perhaps Theon would never emerge from this garden, and no one but his sister would ever guess his fate.

Theon tried to say something. His mouth wouldn't work. His legs wouldn't, either. His knees had already been weak and at this new threat, they seemed to liquefy entirely, and made him stumble forward into the sword's point. Its razor-sharp edge bit a stinging line across his chest.

All thoughts of flowers vanished. He threw himself backwards and fled.

At his back, a door slammed. "Mama!" called the imperious girl. "There's an *intruder* in the garden!"

"It was just a boy. I saw him a moment ago," said the man's voice mildly. Then, a second later: "Why do you have my sword?"

As Theon dove into the rosebushes, he heard sharp footsteps and then a woman's voice. "Nettle Sarai Melaine-Ironheart," said the witch in a foreboding tone, "have you stabbed *another* boy with that?"

"He fell into it," said the girl, unrepentant.

A door slammed again. The witch was coming after him.

Heedless of the path, Theon threw himself straight through the rosebushes in the direction that he hoped led homeward. He barely felt the sharp thorns scrape over his skin, barely noticed the beads of blood that welled up in their wake. He was foolish. He was weak. He was terrified.

And, he realized a minute or two later, he was lost, as well. He stumbled through a hedge and onto a path and spun around there, searching for signs of anything that looked familiar, but all he could see was the night sky with its dazzling stars and the smoke from the cottage winding through them. There were wandering paths all around but he could see from here that many of them led to dead ends, to carved-out clearings with ponds and benches and wrought-iron arches draped in wisteria.

Impatient footsteps snapped against the paving stones not far away. He turned himself in a direction that was opposite from the smoke and the footsteps both and plunged through another rosebush. This one, though, was not as permissive as the bushes he'd shoved through earlier. It was full of heavy yellow-orange blooms like flames, and like flames, they seemed to want to consume him. The thorns were nearly as long as his fingers. The branches were thin and creeping and hungry; they embraced him, and he could not escape. He tried to back out of the bush in the way he'd come but every movement sent thorns burrowing deeper into his skin. He was caught, a fox in a snare. Drops of his blood spattered against the roses. Dizzy with fear, he cried out.

A shadow fell over the brambles. Something bladed and metallic glinted in the moonlight. The hunter had come to retrieve her prey. Another cry caught in his throat, but with all his might, he held it down. A small bit of courage had found him at last.

The bladed thing slashed downward, and then slashed again, and again after that. None of the swipes touched him. Instead, the thorned branches began falling away until he stood in the midst of a felled rosebush, blooms and chopped-off twigs scattered across the ground all around.

The witch stood before him.

Her dark hair was as wild as her daughters'. Her eyes were brown and carried an expression that looked both annoyed and faintly curious. A carnage of petals clung to her curls and her shoulders, falling like sparks when she took a step toward him. The bladed thing caught the moonlight again: a pair of long, sharp gardening shears.

She extended her free hand toward him. "Come out, little rabbit."

"Are you going to eat my liver on toast?" he demanded, unwilling to move until he had at least some assurance that it was safer out there than in here amidst the demolished roses.

Her brow arched gracefully. Her eyes flickered with some emotion that was no longer annoyance or curiosity, but instead something like sadness, or perhaps regret. She shuttered it away quickly. "The night is yet young," she mused, as if she were indeed considering eating his liver on toast, but perhaps only when it was closer to midnight.

Her answer made him feel oddly comforted. If she were planning to do awful things to him, she seemed like the sort of person who would simply do them, not make threats that sounded like jokes in that cool, amused voice of hers. He stepped out of the rosebush.

Several branches were still stuck to him, their thorns buried too deep in his clothing or skin to fall away when they'd been cut. She saw them and frowned. She reached out and, heedless of the thorns as they dug into her own skin, pulled the branches away. Her hands were strangely gentle. "Why are you in my garden, rabbit?"

"My name is not rabbit," he dared.

"A brave rabbit you are," she remarked. "What's your name, then?"

"Theon."

She waited, pulling another branch away from him. A drop of her blood smeared on his sleeve.

"I was here to take a flower," he admitted at last. "For my sister. To prove I am not a coward." He braced for punishment.

She only responded mildly, "You don't seem at all cowardly to me."

"You called me a rabbit," he pointed out reasonably.

She pulled another branch full of thorns away from his leg. He winced in pain. She answered him, "Rabbits are not cowards. They are simply very frequently afraid. There is a difference."

He could not believe he was having a conversation with the witch. The whole scene had taken on a sort of sideways, otherworldly quality, and it made him less cautious than he would normally be. "What's the difference?" he asked.

She pulled the last branch off him, dusted an errant petal from his shoulder, and stood back. "How one chooses to respond to the fear," she said, and then glanced over to where the cottage's smoke trailed into the sky. "You had best go in and be seen to. No sense sending you home like this." She turned and pointed at a path that looked, to Theon, exactly like all the other paths. "Follow that one until you reach the cottage. Tal will take care of you. Tell him I'll be in in a moment."

Theon hesitated but finally followed her orders, creeping down the path she'd motioned at. He was still lost, after all, and at least this way he would gain some distance from her.

The girl who'd stabbed him—Nettle, the witch had called her, which seemed a very fitting name—was waiting at the door. She had her arms crossed and her legs braced wide and her chin defiantly lifted, clearly barring the entrance. "Go," she told him coldly, "away."

Theon lingered at the end of the path, examining her carefully for any signs of weaponry. When he found none, he dared to edge a little closer. The witch had ordered him here and Nettle was ordering him away, and he found himself less willing to disobey the mother than the daughter. "I did not come to throw rocks." He hesitated. "Do...people throw rocks at you often?"

"They do, because Mama used to be the Destroyer and she burned up an awful lot of people. Now that she doesn't have fire and she hasn't murdered anyone in a long time, some folks think that makes her an easy target. It doesn't. Because she's got *us* to look after her." Nettle continued barring the doorway, staring at Theon through narrowed eyes as she waited for him to digest this undigestible statement.

The Destroyer. Theon's world at once inverted and imploded, shrinking to something so small that this moment of time touched another from his past, and then another, and another: when the bullies at his old village had taunted that the Destroyer would burn him up, when his father told him that the Destroyer came for bad little boys who wouldn't go to bed on time, when his teacher made him read a history of the old empire. *A mercury Smith with a long record of war crimes, the Destroyer was crowned Empress for a single day, and in that day, she felled the empire.* She was the villain of every scary story he'd ever been told.

And she had just freed him from a rosebush.

He tested the thought. It held his weight. Slowly, slowly, his world began to stretch out again. Tentatively, he prodded at its borders. She had freed him from a rosebush. She had felled the old empire and helped replace it with the new democracy. He recalled his mother's words: *she gave up her magic, and now she gardens.*

Theon attempted to wrap his mind around this. Nettle watched him do it. There was a challenge in her gray eyes, but also something a sliver of something murkier and sadder and *wanting*. Theon wasn't sure what it was she wanted, though. With the warm light of the cottage behind her and the silvery moonlight gilding her features, she looked at once terrible and unknowable, a creature of impossible duality, a twin to her mother. And then she turned her face slightly to listen to something someone behind her was saying, and her actual twin took the opportunity to slither through the doorway between Nettle's legs.

Nettle stumbled, thrown off balance, and grasped for her sister's arm. "Alaya!" she said, alarmed and suddenly much more normal-seeming, her earlier coldness shucked off like an old snakeskin.

Alaya squirmed neatly away and flounced forward, seizing Theon's arm before he could move. "Hi!" she chirped, smiling brilliantly. "Don't mind my sister, she is 'incorrigible' and 'overly protective,' Mama and Da say it all the time."

"Also 'excellent at biting people,' don't forget that bit," Nettle called threateningly from the doorway, baring her teeth to demonstrate.

Alaya leaned forward and whispered conspiratorially, "They don't actually say that."

"Girls," came the man's voice, disorienting because it emanated from the shadows at the outside corner of the house rather than inside the cottage where Theon had assumed the man would still be, "perhaps we should stop frightening our visitor, and tend to his injuries instead."

The girls' father—Tal, the Destroyer had called him—stepped out of the pooled darkness as if he'd been a part of it just a moment before. He wasn't wearing any weapons as far as Theon could tell, but something about the set of his shoulders said he didn't need one. Still, his face was kind.

Tal stopped a few feet before Theon and crouched down, running his gaze quickly and expertly over Theon as if he were tallying up all the parts of him and seeing what they added up to. "Where is Elodie?" he asked when he was done, and Theon suddenly realized that this must be the Destroyer's name, and he had a moment of dizzying uncertainty at the sudden knowledge that the witch, who was also the Destroyer, was also an actual person.

Tal was waiting for an answer. Theon thought it was probably a bad idea to keep him waiting. "She chopped up a rosebush to get me out of it and then said that I should go to your cottage and have my wounds tended and that she would be along in a moment," Theon said quickly.

"Ah," said Tal, and his expression eased, a small smile wrinkling the corners of his green eyes. "I suspect she is doing something sentimental, then."

This statement struck Theon as bizarre since Elodie seemed like the type of person who would strangle sentimentality with its own necktie, but it would be impolite to naysay a man when you were an uninvited guest in his garden, so he didn't say so.

Alaya moved her grip from his arm to his hand, ignoring the smears of blood on it. His fingers twitched in hers like a trapped spider but she paid no mind. She dragged him merrily toward the door, where her twin was still trying to skewer him with the force of her glare.

"Scoot, my thorny girl," said Tal with that note of fondness from earlier, and Nettle unwillingly moved away into the house to let the three of them enter. Tal dropped a hand on her head and smoothed down her wild hair as he passed, and a bit more of her coldness thawed. Her quicksilver eyes flashed to adoration as she gazed up at him, and then she saw Theon looking and pulled her features back into a stony glare.

"You better not have hurt Mama," she hissed in a low tone as Theon moved past her, "because if you have, I know where Da hid his swords just now."

Theon stared back at Nettle, utterly bewildered at the implication that he was capable of hurting the Destroyer, but made no answer because he had just spotted the three hauler dogs who were still lying across the floor in various poses of laziness. They did not seem aggressive, but they were enormous and looked a bit like wolves. One of them flicked an eye open, assessed Theon, and then went back to sleep. Theon took that as a relatively positive sign and moved cautiously forward, doing his best to avoid stepping on tails or toes.

As Tal moved into the kitchen and opened a cupboard, Alaya, who still had ahold of Theon's hand, used it now to tow him toward the table. A full bowl of stew sat at its end, steaming. "I dreamt about you last night," she confided to him, "so I made sure Mama made enough stew for a visitor. She's a terrible cook but I snuck in some carrots and extra bone broth when she wasn't looking so it should taste okay."

Theon gave up entirely on trying to process or respond to anything the twins said, and sat down as he was directed.

Tal had found whatever he was searching for in the cupboard and moved toward the table, carrying a vial of pearlescent liquid that gleamed with coppery flecks. Theon recognized it as a copper-Smithed healing potion. His parents kept some in their own cupboard, but it was only for emergencies—it wasn't as rare and expensive as it once had been, they'd told him, but it still cost enough to merit use only when absolutely necessary.

Tal poured half the bottle into the bowl of stew, then dropped a spoon in it and pushed it toward Theon. "Eat up," he said. When he saw Theon staring at him, he explained, "You have too many small injuries to try to treat them all topically. This way, it'll treat the pain of all of them right away, and help them heal more quickly than they would naturally—overnight, probably. In the morning you should be good as new. Eat up," he repeated.

Theon mechanically lifted the spoon to his mouth as ordered. The stew was, as Alaya had predicted, okay. He ate it all. When he was scraping up the last spoonful, Elodie returned.

The woman who had formerly been the Destroyer strode through the door with no particular sense of ceremony and dropped what she was carrying onto the table before Theon: a beautiful bouquet of the yellow-orange roses from the bush she'd shredded to free him, tied together neatly with a white silk ribbon. The bouquet caught the corner of his stew bowl, which skidded across the table and sent the spoon flying.

"For your sister," said Elodie, and somehow the words sounded like a dare.

No one moved to pick up the spoon. Everyone stood, silent, and watched Theon–except Elodie. She had already turned and was striding towards the door to the next room, shoulders thrown back carelessly, every movement elegant and commanding.

Theon was reminded, suddenly, of Nettle; of the way she'd stood in the door and braced herself and glared at him, trying to hide that sad *wanting* in her eyes. He thought he knew now what it was she wanted, even though it wasn't anything he could put into words yet. And in the same way, he thought he understood why everyone was watching him so carefully, and why Elodie had dropped the bouquet as if it didn't matter at all to her, even though he could tell from the blood on her hands and the way she must've had to take great care not to get any of that blood on the white silk wrappings that it did, indeed, matter. It was an offering. She was offering something to Theon. Not just the bouquet, but the knowledge that she was the type of person who would give a bouquet of prized roses to a boy so he could prove to his sister that he was not a coward. It was a glimpse of some small, secret part of herself, he thought–and she would be hurt if he did not accept it, so she was trying to pretend she didn't care whether he did or not. Her family knew this, and that was why they watched him so carefully, as if he was holding something precious.

Theon looked at the bouquet. He looked at the Destroyer's retreating back, and saw how the set of her shoulders was not careless but fragile. Theon had not been raised to destroy fragile things, so he picked up the bouquet.

Everyone seemed to exhale at once.

Nettle, who was still standing next to the door, eyed him. Then she left her post and sat down in the chair next to him with an ungracious plop. Alaya smiled beatifically from her spot at his other side. All the tense lines of Tal's posture relaxed at once, and he rewarded Theon with another small smile. Then he reached out and touched Elodie's shoulder as she was passing him. She stopped immediately but didn't turn. The tilt of her head, the lift of her chin, the curve of her spine: all intimidating elegance. Theon was no longer certain if she was wholly the villain the rumors and stories had made her out to be, but there was a part of him that still couldn't quite bear to look at her, the same way he couldn't bear to look too long at the sun.

Tal didn't seem intimidated, though. He lifted one of his hands and let it hover between them, a silent question. Again unhesitating, she put both of her thorn-pricked hands in his, turned upward with her slender fingers slightly curled over her palms. Tal lifted his free hand, which was again holding the healing potion, and gently emptied all that was left of it over her injuries.

She finally lifted her head to look at him. An echo seemed to pass between them, another moment nested within this one—something old and private that Theon could not guess at.

Tal set the potion down. Elodie lifted up onto her toes, took Tal's face in her hands, and kissed him. Coppery flecks from the potion dusted across Tal's cheekbones where she splayed her fingers. Her grasp knocked his glasses askew but neither of them noticed.

Theon's ears heated. He looked away.

When the kiss was over, Elodie turned, her brown eyes newly bright with emotion. Her glance took in the bouquet, which was cradled in Theon's lap, and Nettle, who was slouched in a chair at Theon's side. Elodie smiled. It was a small but dazzling thing.

"Shall we get you home, brave little Theon rabbit?" she asked.

Theon hesitated. He looked at Alaya, who was watching him with her hopeful eyes. He looked at Nettle, who had appropriated his spoon and was using it to pick at the dirt under her nails while she very studiously did *not* watch him. The wanting was in her eyes again, he thought. It reminded him of loneliness.

But: the Destroyer. But: mercury Smith, war crimes. *The Destroyer burns up bad little boys who don't go to bed on time.*

But also: gardening shears flashing in the moonlight. A bouquet of flamelike flowers wrapped up in white silk. *She's got us to look after her.*

He swallowed, mustered himself, and made his choice. "I would like it, ma'am," he said, "if I could come back sometimes? Maybe...maybe help you with the garden, to make up for the bush you had to ruin. And I...I could bring my sister too. I think you might like her. And I think she might like you all."

Alaya's hopefulness intensified. Nettle's grip on the spoon tightened. Tal and Elodie looked at each other, some unspoken instant conversation passing between them in the manner of two people who knew each other as well as anyone could know another person. Elodie looked hesitant and uncertain for a fleeting moment; Tal brushed the backs of his knuckles across her cheek in reassurance. Her expression eased. She took a breath.

"We would like that, Theon," said Elodie with an odd formality. "It would be very nice to have visitors."

Nettle muttered, "Who don't throw rocks at our windows," but the words were venomless and her voice wobbled a little, robbing her tone of its usual biting effect.

"I will bring you a new carving knife instead," Theon told her, and earned a quick glance and a half-hidden grin that made him feel like he had won a prize.

Alaya leaned toward him. "Come early next week," she whispered. "I had a vision of it raining; Ma can't make us plant new rosebushes then."

He promised he would do so. He handed his spoon and bowl to Tal, who set them in the sink and started washing dishes. Theon politely bade farewell to Alaya and Nettle; the former politely farewelled him back, and the latter grunted in a not-unfriendly way, which for her seemed to be the same thing.

He stepped out onto the porch. He felt Elodie step out beside him, just far enough away that she might be admiring her garden or she might be waiting to walk him home.

He turned his head and looked at the little blooms that spiraled crazily out of the window boxes, the ones his sister had dared him to steal. He felt like a different boy entirely from the one who had crept in here to prove himself. He considered the flowers, and he considered himself, and he considered the nature of courage. He drew a conclusion. It was not bravery to pilfer a flower from a witch's garden. This, he thought, was bravery: a family knit together against the darkness of their own past, and a woman who chose roses over flames.

He took Elodie's hand and let her lead him home.

Acknowledgements

At the heart of this book, buried deep beneath my own inspiration for the characters and plot and world, is a woman named Rachel Held Evans—a woman I consider a mentor even though I never got to meet her before her passing in 2019. Her books brought light and joy during an otherwise dark time when I was renavigating my own faith, and I honor her for that. Without the hope and wisdom in her writings, I don't know that I would have had the courage to so deeply explore the themes of belief that are now present in this story.

Thanks also to the other authors and speakers who helped me find my path: Sarah Bessey, Jen Hatmaker, Dr. Frances Collins, Jacqueline Bussey, Rev. Dr. Martin Luther King Jr., and all of the brave and gentle and generally wonderful people from the Evolving Faith podcast discussion group.

I also want to thank the amazing fiction authors whose novels have inspired me: Megan Whalen Turner (if you haven't read her *Queen's Thief* series yet, go do it right now. Seriously.), Holly Black (I would DIE for Jude and Cardan), and Marie Rutkoski (let me just swoon for a minute over her gorgeous *Winner's Kiss* series). Thank you all for being amazing, and for writing books that not only gave me master classes in characterization, world-building, and plotting, but also just entertained the heck out of me when I needed a break from the world.

Mercurial is my very first self-published book, and it was a whole different experience from the traditional publishing process I'm used to. I'm eternally grateful to the people who helped me bring this story into the world: my agent Naomi Davis, editor Alison Weiss, amazing cover designer Amelia (also known as @sakuraartist on Instagram), and interior formatter Lorie DeWorken.

And Britton. My very best friend in the entire world. There aren't enough words to express the impact you've had on my journey and how much your encouragement and belief has meant to me. Without you, I would be a lesser author and a lesser person.

Thanks to my brilliant, kind, and supportive husband Caleb. You are one of the very few people who truly get me, and without that I honestly don't know who I would be. Thank you for covering for me when I needed time to work, and for dragging me away from my computer to get hot cocoa when I needed time to rest.

Lastly, thanks to my daughter—my little girl, full of fire. Your zeal and your absolutely ferocious love have changed my life in ways that are beyond my own comprehension. When you read this story someday (when you are *much* older), I hope that you see my heart in it, and I hope it speaks to you the way it spoke to me.